To Stephan, Kaitlyn, and...

Enjoy !!

A Dragon's Whisperer

Cecilia Lietz

A Dragon's Whisperer

CECILIA LIETZ

iUniverse, Inc.
Bloomington

A DRAGON'S WHISPERER

iUniverse books may be ordered through booksellers or by contacting:

iUniverse
1663 Liberty Drive
Bloomington, IN 47403
www.iuniverse.com
1-800-Authors (1-800-288-4677)

ISBN: 978-1-4620-6928-6 (sc)
ISBN: 978-1-4620-6929-3 (ebk)

Printed in the United States of America

iUniverse rev. date: 09/13/2012

DEDICATIONS

A special thanks to Corinne. O, Amanda. B and Rachel. S for helping me out on my book through the past few months.

I want to thank my family for their encouragement and my fellow classmates for the inspiration to help me write this book.

PART 1

CHAPTER 1

The End of Summer

You know, when a girl first enters high school she has high hopes that she'll have the best boyfriend, everyone will like her and she will achieve the best grades. Well, I kind of had the same expectations, and unfortunately, instead of being a regular fifteen year old school girl, I ended up as a whisperer.

My name is Connie Helen Whitsburg and this is the story of how I became a dragon's whisperer.

My family and I lived in a small town named Small Valley; it is located at the bottom of a majestic ravine. The ravine is massive. It seems endless unless you can figure out the twists and turns. There are only two ways out of the ravine and those are hours upon hours of driving east or west. Otherwise you would have to scale the rocky, tree bedded wall or fly out. I didn't mind living there; it wasn't that bad of a place to live. The town is average size; the farming population isn't big, but the people that do live and work in the ravine enjoy every second of it. I had been told many stories about the ravine. It's oddly shaped because someone or something shaped it like that or how our town came to be and why it was placed at the bottom of the ravine, because the town was supposed to protect and guard something valuable. There was one specific story that always seemed to capture my curiosity, and that was where Small Valley had been placed. In any other area of the ravine it hardly receives any sunlight, the trees don't grow very much and animals of forests refuse to live down in the ravine. During the years I had lived there my family and I never stepped foot outside except my dad. I had always wished to see what it was like beyond the ravine's huge, prison like walls. As a kid I would always imagine miles and miles of free space, where there are no walls that can hold you back and where the grass grows as far as the eye can see; where cities stand brave and tall over the land, with big bright, coloured lights to see every night, with new aromas to smell every day and new places to visit anytime and anywhere.

Instead of exploring and finding the answers to the ravine, I had to deal with the one of the most important, yet annoying, things in life: high school. My older brother, at the time, was attending his last year at Small Valley High. He would be off to college after one more school year, out of the house and out of my life. As a younger teenaged sibling you would have to expect my enjoyment of his leaving. Since he's an older brother, he would always find a way to make things miserable for me, especially when I was about to attend the same school. He was trying to convince me that high school is horrifying and strenuous. There's no way I was letting him psych me out before the school year even started. Small Valley High couldn't be as bad as living with an obnoxious older brother like Kyle.

It was the day before school started and three days away from my fifteenth birthday. I only had to wait one more year before I could get my license and drive out of the ravine.

In my bedroom, I was packing up my school supplies for the first day of classes. I didn't really expect much from high school. It's like junior high but with longer classes to attend. Besides, I was always at the top of my class and my two best friends were going to join me at Small Valley High, Sam and Judy.

I never had the perfect clean room; there were still things that needed to be fixed up. I had the common stuff like any other school girl: hope chest, dresser, mirror, closet, bed, nightstand, shelves, stuffed animals and books, but my favourite part of my room had to be my dragon lamp. My dad gave it to me on my seventh birthday. It's really special to me. The dragon lies asleep on the base of the lamp with his eyes open and looking out. My dad always said that whenever I turned the light out at night, that dragon would watch over me and, if need be, it would spring to life and protect me if my dad was never there. The funny thing is, I believed him for the longest time. I stopped believing it after my thirteenth birthday.

I hummed a song to myself as I tried to tidy up the mess of a bedroom I lived in but I stopped to watch my brother barge into my room, as usual.

"Hey, Connie, I wouldn't even bother to pack for the first day of school because there is a good chance you won't survive it," he said, leaning on my dresser.

"Get out, Kyle," I said, trying to ignore him.

"I'm not joking! You won't be able to. There are many things to fear in the halls of Small Valley High," he said in an evil tone. "The ghosts and demons will eat you *alive.*"

"Are you done?" I asked, looking at my ignorant brother. He checked his reflection in my mirror. "Kyle, I know school and you aren't buddies but don't you attend it because of your girlfriend? Your girlfriend who's helping you graduate instead of letting you fail and repeat a year?"

"Hey, I'm not failing gym," he pointed out.

"Gym's not a core subject, genius; it's just an option that only gets you three credits. Remember you need a hundred credits to graduate school."

Kyle was silent. I smiled.

Kyle is your average six foot three eighteen year old with broad shoulders, sandy blond hair and hazel eyes. The thing about his wardrobe that I hated was the old plaid shirt he wore with torn up jeans and worn out sneakers. I never understood him and probably never will. He was obnoxious, self-centered and ignorant.

I, on the other hand, wore a stylish baby-blue tank top and boot cut jeans. I always kept my dirty blond hair back in a ponytail and wore white runners. The only thing the two of us had in common was our eyes. The Whitsburg family's famous hazel eyes.

"Well, to tell you the truth, I was just trying to be a good big brother and warn you about what's going to happen," he said in a baby voice, pinching my cheek.

"Would you just leave, already?" I said, fed up and smacking his hand away from me.

My brother messed up my hair as he left the room. I'll never understand older siblings, always thinking that they are right just because they happened to enter the world before you.

I finished putting my school supplies into my backpack before heading to the kitchen where my mom was cooking dinner.

My mom has sandy blond hair and pale blue coloured eyes. I guess you could say that she still lives back in the 60's because of her pink dress, white apron and high heels. I guess you could call her my retro mom.

"Hey Mom," I said, leaning on the kitchen island.

"Hello Connie. Are you excited for your first day of high school?" she asked.

"Well, I'm a little nervous but, other than that, I'm really excited about it," I answered, " . . . and my birthday, which is coming up soon."

My mom smiled at me as she scooted me towards the dining room table while calling Kyle out to come and join the rest us. Once we were all seated, we began to eat our dinner.

"Mom," said Kyle, "when is Dad coming home from his business trip?"

Mom looked over at him and sighed. "I thought we already discussed this, Kyle. He is not going to be back for another month or two."

My dad is an eco-friendly business man or as I like to call him, my hippie dad, but I guess you can't really call him a hippie because he doesn't chain himself to trees, wears the cotton pants and tie-dye shirts, or grows out his hair to his waist. He looks like a regular man with a tux. For his job, he always has to leave the ravine to go on international business trips. It's been three months since he left. The only thing that doesn't make sense to me is why he wanted us to live in this ravine in the first place. He always treated it like it was something special but I don't get why we're not allowed to leave it. He always likes to keep to himself. It's rare if he tells us anything.

I stayed quiet for the rest of dinner while Kyle and my Mom kept bickering about Dad. They start every fight with normal talking rising to yells and, for the finale they both stand up and slam a fist on something. In this case it was the table. They're both as stubborn as mules. All I can do is stay out of it and wait for things to die down.

After dinner, I went straight to my room, kicking some stuff over and thinking of how things were going to change tomorrow; I just didn't know how much.

When I awoke the next morning I took a peak outside my window and found it cloudy and cold with leaves starting to fall and that's when I knew that summer was over.

"Morning Mom," I yawned, strolling into the kitchen.

"Good morning Connie. I hope you're ready for your first day," she said with a smile.

"Yeah, and let's hope you don't get scared and run off like you did in the mall," Kyle said as he messed up my hair.

I slapped his hand away. "I was five if you recall. Oh yeah, that's right, you can't. Most of your brain is dead. That's why you can never find the soap," I commented.

He grunted.

"Down boy," I teased. "I will never understand how you ever got Kristen as your girlfriend." I sat down and started to eat my breakfast.

Kyle calmed down and turned his frown upside down. "What does it matter to you? You hate Kristen, but if you have to know my secret it's all because I'm a great basketball player. The ladies love an athlete." He stood behind me and started to scarf down some of my bacon.

"Yeah, but you only got onto the team out of pity," I pointed out while drinking some juice.

Kyle got annoyed and started to give me a noogie. I didn't have time to swallow so I turned around and spat my juice on him making him slap me upside the head which gave me a good reason to stand up and kick him in the shins.

"Enough!" yelled Mom. Everything went quiet. Kyle sat down in a chair and just kept staring down at the floor. "You two have got to learn how to behave around one another." Mom rubbed her temples and sat down. "That's why I signed both of you up for the 'Sibling Respect Program' that your school is sponsoring."

"But Mom, I have practice," Kyle whined.

"And I wanted to meet up with Sam and Judy," I protested.

"It's just a half hour every Wednesday after school for a few months. I want both of you there whether you like it or not. I'll be waiting at the community hall for you today. If either one of you tries to sneak

7

out of this, I'll take away everything you own and sell it on E-bay," Mom threatened.

Kyle and I both exchanged nervous looks with each other and then nodded. Mom smiled, gave us our lunches and our school bags, and sent us off to the garage where the two of us got into Kyle's orange Chevy. Mom blew us both kisses and then watched us take off to school.

We were only half way to the school when Kyle started to talk. "You do anything to embarrass me at school and I'll break everything in your room."

He always threatened me if I didn't do anything his way. Like most siblings would do.

"Yeah, yeah, just don't go and embarrass me either."

Once we arrived at school, I met up with Sam and Judy at the front doors.

Judy was energetic, trendy, smart and a gossiper. Every little word she heard she would usually spread it throughout the school in less than twenty-four hours. She had just returned from Florida, showing off her dark tan skin, new high heels, shorts and a white t-shirt that said 'Florida' in cursive writing. She flicked her long dark hair around that went down to the middle of her back and fluttered her brown eyes.

I can't tell you much about Sam though. We started to hang out two years ago and I still don't know him well. All I can really say is that he hardly speaks and blushes a lot, but he's genuine and kind. He has black hair spiked in the back and outlined in red; he has green eyes, a loop earring on his left ear and a silver chain around his neck. He wore loose clothing, and a black shirt with baggy jeans and unlaced sneakers.

"Morning," I called out waving to them both.

"Connie," said Judy giving me a hug. "I wish you could have escaped to Florida with me; it was amazing. No walls, just the beach, ocean and endless stores to shop at."

"That sounds great Judy," I replied, smiling at her. Sam caught my attention by blushing so I went up to him. "What did you do over the summer? I didn't hear a word from you over the break."

"Nothing much," he mumbled, staring down at the ground. "Just went to meet up with some old friends."

I've never met Sam's family, only his guardian who was his older cousin Kamal. As far as I know Kamal was Sam's only family.

"Tell me about your summer, Connie," he said, moving his eye gaze up to my face.

"My dad left for another business trip this summer so I pretty much stayed here," I said.

"-which . . . is why you should have come with me to Florida," Judy interrupted. "You have to get out of the ravine at some point in your young life."

"You know, it's been so long I can't even remember the last time I left this place." I admitted. "My dad moved us here for no reason at all after I was born."

Sam gave me a light pat on the back, "One day, you'll be able to leave on your own."

I smiled at him. "Thanks Sam," I said, giving him a hug. He blushed again but Judy and I just laughed. "You have to stop doing that, Sam, or else your face will remain a permanent red colour."

The rest of day went by smoothly. I was in gym class with Sam and had English and Foods with Judy. So far high school was going great.

At the end of the day, I told Sam and Judy about the 'Sibling Respect Program', that my mom signed Kyle and I up for it and how we were forced to attend or else. They understood as they walked me to the community hall. Once I got there, Mom came over and gave me a tight hug. However, when Kyle arrived, Mom started to pull on his ear.

"Why are you late, young man?" she demanded.

Kyle groaned. "Sorry, but I gave Kristen a ride home."

"Well, I don't care if you gave the queen of France a ride home! When I said I wanted you after school, I meant right after," Mom scolded.

I giggled a bit, which made Mom give me a funny look. "Mom, France doesn't have a king or queen anymore. There's only the queen of England."

"That's what I meant," she insisted, embarrassed.

I chuckled again and looked over my shoulder; I could have sworn there was an old man watching me. He vanished right after a car passed by.

CHAPTER 2

Stranger

I said goodbye to Judy and Sam, thanking them for walking me over to the community hall after school. Kyle and I entered the building, walking through the empty white hallway and entering a room that said 'Sibling Respect Program (S.R.P)' on the door. To our surprise, we weren't the only siblings present. Three more pairs sat before us. The look on their faces made it obvious why they were here; they were forced, just like Kyle and I. We sat down in some chairs that made a circle around the room.

Another man about thirty entered the room. He walked in wearing a hot pink shirt. I've heard of boys wearing pink before but this was too much. Besides that he had a grin that would scare the smile off the Cheshire Cat. I shuddered at the sight of him.

"Hello there," he said in an oddly high pitched voice. "This is the 'Sibling Respect Program' where brothers and sisters learn to respect one another and, in doing so, learn to get along or until, at the very least, someone leaves. Now let's see who we have here," he said, checking his clipboard.

As he did the roll call I took a look around the room. There wasn't much to see. It was empty and white just like the hallway the only thing that made it different was that it actually had a window.

"And Connie and Kyle Whitsburg?" called the man.

"Here," Kyle answered lifting his hand and my hand into the air.

"Great," he said, putting his clipboard down. "I am Glen Castleman and I'll be your instructor for the next few months."

Everyone groaned heavily.

"Yes, this program goes all the way to the winter holidays on every Wednesday of every week till the winter holidays. Isn't that great?"

Everyone grumbled and slid down in their seats asking themselves how they got caught up in this situation in the first place. I know because I was doing the exact same thing.

"No negative attitudes," he exclaimed. "If I hear even one negative thought, you'll repeat this course, giving us more time together."

We were silent but since we weren't allowed to complain out loud, we did it in our heads. (We had the facial expressions to prove it.)

Glen started to babble on about the sessions that we would be doing. I ignored him and started to play with my nails. It was *so* lame. I've had more fun listening to Kyle ramble on about sci-fi movies than being here.

Glen yakked for ten minutes straight, barely even taking a breath in between sentences. I nearly fell asleep. Kyle elbowed me and whispered into my ear.

"Look, I don't like this either. You think I want to waste my days here? I already treat you well enough."

I rolled my eyes.

"I should be with Kristen right now, in my car, making out but if Mom finds out that either one of us is snoozing during a lesson, we might as well say 'just sign me up for next year'."

I nodded slowly and forced myself to sit up in my chair. Glen handed us a sheet of blank paper and a pencil.

"Now, I want the younger sibling to go behind the older one with the pencil," he said.

The other younger siblings and I followed Glen's instructions and grumbled as we stood up and went behind our older siblings.

"Great," Glen said excitedly. "Now, I'm going to put a blindfold over the younger siblings eyes and it's up to the older siblings to help them draw something unique in the next five minutes. As the two of you do this session you'll learn to trust one another with your hand and vision. You two are to cooperate if not you'll not only waste paper but also your time here."

Some people cussed under their breath while others whined.

"It's either this or I'll have you do the trust exercise, when one person catches the other," considered Glen.

That sounded better than this exercise. In fact, everyone raised their hands.

Glen's eyebrow twitched. "We're doing this exercise!"

Once I was blindfolded Kyle yanked my arm over his shoulder. My feet weren't even touching the ground.

"Connie, give me some space. You're way too far into my personal bubble," Kyle whined.

"Then let go of my hand. You've got me so far over your shoulder I can't even touch the ground," I snapped.

"Whitsburg," said Glen, "this session is about cooperation; you're supposed to work together to draw something unique. If you fail this session, you'll fall behind the others."

"What's that supposed to mean?" asked Kyle.

"Weren't you paying attention when I was explaining the sessions?"

Neither of us spoke.

"Wasn't anybody?" Glen asked the class.

Everyone became silent. I heard the pencils scratching stop for a moment before they went back to work.

Glen sighed and refocused his attention on us. "If the two of you fail a session, you'll have to repeat the course making it longer and harder for either of you to pass, which means you'll both be here next year."

Kyle and I gulped. Kyle straightened his body and loosened his grip on my arm. We maneuvered our bodies so that my arm was underneath Kyle's and he held onto my hand with a strong grip.

"That's better," Glen said cheerfully. "Now, you'd better hurry."

I heard pencils touch paper, some broke through the paper and the lucky ones that didn't break scratched the surface of the paper. There was only one problem. My hand wasn't moving at all.

"Kyle," I said, "why aren't you drawing?"

"I'm not good at art, Connie. Never have been and never will be," he said gripping my hand tighter then shaking it.

I remembered something. "Kyle, draw the flower you gave Mom for Mother's Day."

"But that was a cheap paper flower," he said.

"Exactly," I said. "A cheap paper flower that even you would know how to draw."

Once Kyle started to move my hand I knew that he understood what I was thinking. Even though I couldn't see what he was drawing I could help by directing Kyle's hand at some points. When we finished, Kyle took off my blind fold and showed me what we both drew. I couldn't believe it; he drew a basketball with a flower sticking out of it and it wasn't even a good drawing; no, it looked like a four year old scribbled it!

"Kyle," I complained, "it was just supposed to be a flower."

"Well I got nervous and started to think about basketball so that's what I drew," he said.

Glen came around looking at everyone's drawing and then announced, "Sara and Lilly have the best picture."

Both girls squealed and gave each other a hug. Kyle and I sighed as we saw a picture of a bunny being posted on the wall.

"Well that's it for today's session," said Glen picking his clipboard up. "I'll see you all next week."

Kyle and I exited the community hall. Thank goodness Mom was nowhere to be seen. I didn't want to be the one to tell her that the two of us nearly got kicked out of our first lesson. She would have killed us. Not to mention how badly we were humiliated.

"Well, I'm off to Kristen's," Kyle announced, getting into his Chevy. "You want me to drop you off at home?"

"No thanks," I said. "I'll walk."

Kyle shrugged as started up his car and drove off.

I started to walk home but I stopped at the park. It was only a bit after four but it felt like a whole week just went by since I left the community hall. I sat on a swing and watched kids play. Then a man walked by and sat on the swing beside me.

"Beautiful day, isn't it?" he asked.

I didn't know if he was talking to me so I stayed quiet.

"Even though the summer is over the beauty lingers on forever."

Again, I stayed quiet.

"For a girl you're awfully quiet."

"What's that supposed to mean?" I asked.

When I glanced over at him, he actually looked familiar. The hair was grey hair and I recognized his short beard. His eyes were a dark brown and he had the scar on his lip. He had a brown trench coat on, black sweater and pants but the strange thing was that he didn't have any shoes.

"Where are your shoes?" I asked.

"Well, I'll let you in on a little secret," he said leaning close to me. "I left them with my dragon. You know they'll never leave you alone unless they have something of yours with a strong scent," he whispered.

He captured my attention, "A dragon?"

The man stood up and started to walk away. "If you want to know more, meet me back here before the sun sets tomorrow."

I was confused. I just met this old man and already he was treating me like we were friends. He was weird and I mean weirder than weird. He had to have some screws loose. What was he planning? "Wait!" I called, "What's your name?"

He looked at me and smiled. "Its Devonburg the fourth, but you should already know that, Connie." Devonburg walked away in his bare feet leaving me puzzled.

That was unusual, especially for Small Valley. It may be located at the bottom of a ravine but at least all the people down here are sane. I hoped.

There is no way I would know a Devon especially not a Devonburg. He must have been delusional. But how did he know my name . . . and dragon's couldn't possibly exist, could they?

When I got to school the next day I was exhausted. For the whole morning period I kept falling asleep. It wasn't until gym class when I got hit with a dodge ball that I started to wake up.

"Come on, Whitsburg," yelled the Coach. "Get your head in the game."

Sam stabilized me before I fell to the ground. "What's the matter Connie? You're usually great in gym."

"What?" I replied, dazed.

I couldn't help thinking about what Devonburg had told me. Another dodge ball came by and hit me. I fell to the ground when it hit me.

Coach blew his whistle at me. "Whitsburg, it's only the second day of the school year and you're already out of it. If you don't start playing properly, I'm going to kick you out of the game."

"Sorry Coach," I managed to say.

"Connie, did something happen at the session yesterday?" Sam asked after Coach left.

I didn't say anything. Sam helped me onto my feet as another dodge ball came flying at me. I looked up and caught the ball. I gave it to Sam who threw it at another guy on the other team in the jaw with the ball.

I wasn't myself for the rest of the day. People had to repeat themselves several times before I noticed they were talking to me. I avoided Judy and Sam at lunch and after school. My mind was wrapped around the shoeless Devonburg and dragons. After school I ran to the park and stayed there for the rest of the day. When the sun started to set I gave up hope on Devonburg and started to walk home.

"Leaving already?" said someone behind me.

I turned and saw Devonburg. "Where have you been? I've been waiting here for hours!"

He smiled and patted my head. "I really do like you Connie but I told you to arrive before sunset not right after school," he said. "Now, come with me."

He didn't make it easy for me to figure him out, but maybe that's what he wanted. Either way, he captured my curiosity.

At first I watched him leave Small Valley thinking that I should just go home and let him go, but I didn't. He made me frustrated. I wanted to know more about this screwy guy but I didn't want to leave. Nevertheless I followed him out of Small Valley, down the ravine making a single left turn to a dead end that was concealed by trees and huge boulder.

I held onto my backpack as I saw the dead end, ready to make a swing at him, if needed. My heart started to pound hard as fear came over me.

"Now what do we do?" I asked, waiting for Devonburg to make a move.

"Can't you see the entrance?" he asked.

Cautiously, I squinted and focused at the ravine wall. I saw nothing, zero, zilch. This was ridiculous! I was looking like a fool staring at a wall. Suddenly, there was a noise heard.

It sounded like a roar.

Devonburg moved some braches aside allowing light to hit the rock. The rock began transparent and revealed a passageway. "This is an illusion to the human eye. The only way to find the passageway is to know where it already is. But it can only been found in the middle of a sunrise or sunset."

I was dumbfounded. Never in my life have I ever seen something like this.

Devonburg led the way. As we walked through the passageway I noticed that we were ascending. Once I saw the end of the passageway I ran up to it. However I was too curious and that caused me to slip and slide right out into the open. I stood up and looked around the place; it was a bowl shaped area in the ravine. It was so close to the top of the ravine. I only needed a twenty foot ladder to get out of the ravine. The area was covered with grass, trees, and had a pond off to the side. You wouldn't believe what I saw though. It was a real living, breathing dragon.

CHAPTER 3

Nightly

The dragon had to be about forty feet long and twenty feet tall. It had huge wings that had feathers on it like a bird's. Its green scales and cyan eyes flickered in the sunlight. It bared its teeth like it was trying to greet me or smile. I felt nothing other than the utter shock, disbelief and intimidated having a dragon right in front of me. My heart started to pound even harder as I watched the dragon lie down. I notice something though. The way the dragon was lying there made it look like it was curled around something.

"Do you like my dragon?" Devonburg asked, walking towards the dragon. "His name is Skier and he's protecting your egg."

"You know I only followed you here because I thought you had few screws loose and needed help. But this . . . I can't believe you were telling the truth. Dragons don't exist, though!"

"Yes they do. They've just been hiding this whole time. Now, let's go get your egg."

I managed to grab Devonburg's sleeve, "But I'm human! You know: a mammal."

"I don't mean it like that," he laughed, "What I mean is that you're destined to be a dragon's whisperer."

"What's that?"

The dragon hummed and growled a bit.

"I know, I know," he said stroking the dragon scales. "Listen, Connie, I don't have much time so listen well because what you're about to hear is going to be life or death. When your dragon hatches, you'll have to show him your dragon mark, which will be dragon wings like these," Devonburg rolled the sleeve of his trench coat up and on his wrist was a pair of dragon wings on his skin.

"But I don't have a dragon wings mark like that," I said. "Never have and never will. I'm not a tattoo kind of person."

"That's because I have to place mine on you. Things are changing in this world, Connie, and I've done my part, now I need you to step in and do yours." Devonburg removed the object Skier was protecting. He walked back towards me with a fancy looking grey stone with marks swerving and curving all over it. "Touch it."

I stepped forward and hesitated for a moment.

"It's alright," said Devonburg. "This is your choice. If you don't want to you can leave right now and I won't argue."

For some reason I didn't want to leave. I wanted to do this. I touched the stone and saw it turn black as the night. I stepped back in astonishment. I quickly felt a cold, rough hand touch the bare skin on my back. I looked behind me and watched Devonburg's arm retreat behind his back.

"This is now your dragon egg, Connie; it's alive because you gave it energy so now it's a part of you. Treat it with respect and never let it out of your sight. When your dragon hatches you have to give it a name and also something of yours. Once your dragon acknowledges you as his whisperer he will show you his special ability." He quickly glanced up at the sky and then back at me. He looked at his hand that was behind his back and then walked to where his shoes were. "The most important thing is to watch out for mages, but call the Guardians if you are ever in trouble or need help and also . . . *never* under *any* circumstance should you neglect your dragon. They will destroy everything they see, including themselves.

I know you probably don't remember me and you think I'm insane. Believe me a lot of people do too but we have met before, Connie. If you ask your dad he'll tell you. My duty as a dragon's whisperer was to watch over this magnificent ravine and find people to become new whisperers like you. But you? You are a special girl and the only person I can pass on my legacy too."

Devonburg placed the egg on the ground. He held up his hand to his dragon and started to scratch its scales.

"Our part is done now," said the dragon as he hummed and wrapped himself around Devonburg, *"you will become a fine whisperer young human.*

Send my regards to your dragon when it hatches. I've seen so many of my brethren die but never in my life time have I seen a dragon born."

"The dragon just spoke! Why is the dragon speaking?" I asked freaked out. This didn't make any sense. I slowly took in some breaths.

"That's because you're now a dragon's whisperer. No other human can hear them unless they become a dragon's whisperer," explained Devonburg. "Goodbye Connie Helen Whitsburg." As the sun went down the two of them turned into dust and were carried off by the wind. The only thing that remained were his shoes and the dragon egg.

I trotted to the egg and sat down beside it. I stared at it, waiting, watching for something to happen. What was I supposed to do now? I didn't know if I should run and tell someone about this or just stay hidden. I closed my eyes and felt something move over my feet. When I opened my eyes, I saw the egg was already rolling away by itself.

"Wait!" I cried chasing after it.

This thing, this egg, kept rolling and rolling like it was in a marathon. It wasn't until I cut it off half way to the forest that I caught it.

I sighed and picked the egg up. "You know, for a dragon, that's not even hatched yet you sure can roll." I cuddled the egg in my arms trying to keep it warm. I even put it into my backpack where I had an extra sweater to keep it warm. I zipped my backpack closed and tried to look for the same passageway I came in through. "You've got to be kidding me," I said searching the wall. "Come on! It has to be here somewhere." I looked everywhere but no matter how hard I tried the passageway wouldn't appear. The sun had already set. There was no way I would be able to find it now.

"A storm's coming, whisperer," said a voice.

I looked up to the sky and saw clouds gather quickly. "Great," I mumbled, "I'm stuck in a secret part of the ravine where no one knows where I am." Just then, I remembered my cell phone in my pocket but when I tried to dial, I didn't get any reception. I became scared. "Now what am I going to do? I have no way to get home and I still have to babysit an oversized Easter egg."

Rain started to fall so I ran under the trees with my backpack. The wind blew hard causing rocks and twigs to come flying both at me and the egg. I grabbed the backpack and held it tight. I screamed when I heard thunder. I wanted out of this horrific place, out of the stupid town, I just wanted to get out of the ravine.

"Don't be scared, I'm here," the voice said again.

I couldn't help but relax after I heard that voice. It was calm, soothing and it was just what I wanted to hear. I fell asleep.

My dream was odd. I dreamt that I was at my house with my friends and family having a party for my fifteenth birthday. After I blew out the candles on my double chocolate strawberry cake, I saw a word being carved into the table. It said 'MAGES'. I became scared again and watched as my cake turned into the black dragon egg. I looked up and saw that I was in a black room. I heard a low growl as a pair of grey eyes looked straight at me. A cold chuckle came from it and then it broke out into laughter as the eyes closed. Four people stood before me watching the egg.

"What do you want?" I demanded trying to push my fear behind me.

"Your egg," they replied, showing their black hair, pale yellow pupil slit eyes, grey skin and black, cat-like ears.

Then another group of four humans appeared along with a pearl white dragon.

One of them grabbed me while another one grabbed the egg. I was confused. I began to punch the person holding my arm.

"Stop that!" he snapped, "We are trying to protect you."

"Why? I don't know you and you took my dragon egg," I screamed.

The pearl white dragon turned towards me and looked at me with her violet eyes, *"we're your Guardians."*

I panted as I pulled myself away I couldn't help but feel like I was being watched where I was sleeping and what was with those grey eyes?

That's when I awoke to something licking my hand. I looked to my right and saw my backpack all torn up and a small black dragon lying by my hand.

The dragon had small spikes going down the back of his head where his horns were and ended at the tail. The ears were pointed up like a cat's and the wings were like a bat's; both wings were about five feet long. However what really caught my attention were its gold coloured eyes. For a dragon, it was awfully cute. It didn't look like a threat at all, like you would hear in most stories.

"It's about time you woke up," said the dragon.

I rubbed my head trying to see if the lizard in front of me was real. It took me a little while to remember what happened the night before. Everything seemed so vague. "How are you talking to me?"

"I think the better question is how can you understand me? That's an easy question to answer. I learned to speak your language when you gave me energy to hatch. Now you can hear what I say anytime, anywhere."

"But you're lips aren't moving, how can you talk?"

"Well, does a cat or a dog or any other animal talk with their mouths?" It asked.

"I guess not, but was it you who I heard when the storm hit?"

"Yep, you were scared so I thought I would help you calm down."

"But you were still an egg?"

The dragon stretched and sat up. *"A dragon can always recognize their whisperer's presence even if they're still in an egg."*

I looked up into the morning sky and saw that the sun rising over the ravine.

"I totally forgot about the time," I said, racing to my feet. The black dragon jumped back as he watched me grab what was left of my backpack and took out the egg shells. Then, I tried looking for the passageway again. "Oh, come on! I need to get to school before first block."

"Aren't you forgetting something?" the dragon asked.

I thought for a moment and then I snapped my fingers, "I forgot to give you a name and a present," I said. I rummaged through my backpack and found my sweater. It was the only thing in my backpack that wasn't torn up. "Here," I said placing the sweater under a tree. "It kept you warm last night, right?"

"Sure did," the dragon said excited, *"Now what's my name?"*

I studied the dragon. He was black as night, and had bat wings and gold eyes. He reminded me of a starry night sky. "Hey, I know, you're a boy dragon, right?"

"Sure am," he said.

"Then why don't I call you Nightly since you remind me so much of the night sky?"

"Nightly, Nightly, Nightly," he said, happy to have a name.

21

"Hey, Nightly," I said, "Since I gave you a name and present, could you tell me how to get the heck out of here?"

"Not yet," he said, *"You still have to tell me your name and show me the dragon mark."*

"Nightly, I don't have time for this."

"Then I'll check for it myself," he said. Nightly bit onto my pants leg and dragged me over to the pond. He jumped onto my back, knocking me down to a sitting position. He pulled himself onto my back and started to push my shirt down. He chocked me while trying to do that and his sharp baby claws didn't help. I looked over into the waters reflection of me and noticed the pair of dragon wings on my back. It was like the pair Devonburg had on his wrist beforehand. Nightly licked my ear and jumped down off my back. I reclaimed air as Nightly released the shirt from his grasp. *"Now tell me your name."*

"If I tell you my name, do you promise to show me the way out of here?" I asked panting.

"It's a dragon's promise."

"It's Connie," I said. "Now can you please show me the way out of here?"

Nightly trotted over to the wall and casually walked through the passageway and back out.

I was amazed. "How did you know where it was?"

"I was already fully developed in my egg I just wasn't strong enough to break free. While I was waiting for you Skier and Devonburg always described the area to me. I just did what they told me."

"Nightly, you're one smart dragon," I said, walking towards the passageway feeling stupid. "Stay here and I'll bring you something after school."

Nightly trotted away and sat down on the sweater that I had given him. I smiled but before I left I took a rock and carved out a marking that told me where the passageway was. After that was done, I took a running start and went through it, down the pure dark passageway and back into broad daylight once again and put a mark where the passageway started. From there I ran as quickly as I could to school.

I ran to school refusing to stop. It wasn't till I reached the school parking lot when I took a break. That's when I saw Kyle getting out of his car.

"Kyle," I shouted.

Kyle looked over and had a sour look on his face along with bags under his eyes. Once I reached him, he grabbed my shoulders and shook me. "Connie, where have you been? Mom's been worried sick about you."

I knew I couldn't tell him the truth. I couldn't tell anyone about Nightly or about the hidden passageway that led to a secret area in the ravine.

"I went for a walk through the ravine and didn't stop till the storm hit," I lied. "That's when I took cover from the storm. It was such a bad storm that it interfered with the reception."

My brother let my shoulders go and wrapped me in his arms instead. "Idiot," he mumbled in my ears.

When he let go, I noticed Judy and Sam running towards me asking what happened and why I didn't I pick up anyone's phone calls. I just told them the same thing that I told Kyle.

"I can't believe you took off like that," said Judy. "Sam went and gathered a search party for you."

"Really," I said looking at Sam. I went up to him and gave him a kiss on the cheek. "Thank you."

Sam blushed again and looked down at the ground. "Well, it was really only Kyle, Judy, your mom and me." He then gave me a little white box, "Happy birthday."

After what happened, I forgot that today was my birthday. Hey, who would have guessed that one little dragon would make you forget about your own birthday?

I opened the box and found a heart shaped locket inside. It was beautiful.

"Open it," Sam muttered.

I did and inside the locket was a photo of me and Sam together two years ago at the Small Valley parade.

"I love it," I answered.

Sam put the locket around my neck. I couldn't help notice his hands shake as he attached the clasp around my neck. When he was done, he just looked down at the ground trying to hide his flustered face.

Sam refused to meet my eye gaze, but even if he did I still continued to smile at him.

Kyle took me home and Mom cried her eyes out when she saw me. Kyle and I stayed at home for the rest of the day. Mom was reluctant to let me go; she wrapped me up in her arms tighter then a woven sweater. That told me how worried she had been. I felt guilty for leaving them but I had to go. Don't get me wrong, I love my family; it's just that for the last few years I've wished for a way to get out of the ravine and having a dragon might be the way for me. If only there was a way I could still be with Nightly and my family.

After the smother fest I went into my room and dug out an old t-shirt that I hadn't worn in a year. Lucky for me it still fit and with it my identity as a dragon's whisperer was concealed.

CHAPTER 4

Trashed

When the evening came Judy and Sam stopped by the house to see how I was doing. Judy gave me a birthday present which was a nice jean jacket she got me from Florida. We had my favourite kind of cake which was covered in strawberries. Everyone consumed that cake, leaving only one piece. I was going to save that one for Nightly. The one thing I wanted most of all on my birthday was to see Nightly, but Mom wouldn't let me leave for reasons I actually knew why. Do you know what I got for my birthday from my Mom? A curfew, so that she wouldn't have to search for me again. I guess I deserved it.

I was starting worry though. I had to see Nightly. What if he started to destroy things and was now heading here? I needed to find out somehow. Just a sign to tell me he was fine.

That's when we all heard a noise. Sam motioned us to stay quiet as Kyle grabbed a bat and Mom held up her spatula. We quietly walked towards the source of the noise, which was located at the end of the hall in my bedroom. Sam walked up and slowly twisted the door knob. The door opened and all we saw was a ruined room. The mess I usually had in my room was nothing compared to what it was now. My bed, sheets were all torn up. My favourite lamp was broken and the floor was covered in scratch marks, which trailed from my window.

The only thing that seemed untouched and normal was my closet. All of us crept up to the door. This time Kyle swung the door open. When we looked inside, there was nothing there except for the usual mess of sweaters and jackets, but I saw the sweater I gave to Nightly, on the floor of the closet. What was it doing there?

Kyle yawned and relaxed the bat on his shoulder. "It must have been a dog."

"But I closed my window," I said.

"Then you should of made sure that you locked it," he said waving his finger at me.

"Last I checked, no dog can open a window by itself," said Sam.

"You never know," said Judy walking out of the room. "Besides, the world changes every day and so does everything. Maybe tomorrow we'll see a cat doing math equations or a dragon flying through the sky."

Judy didn't know how right she was.

I saw Mom coming down the hallway, still holding her spatula, to see what the ruckus was. I closed my bedroom door behind me and held up my hands in self-defence. "You don't need to go in there Mom. Everything's handled. It turned out be a dog that got lost."

"Connie, out of the way," Mom said reaching for the door knob.

"Really Mom," I insisted. "It was nothing."

That wasn't enough to stop her. When she pushed past me to get into my room she screamed.

"Mom," I said shaking her shoulders, "Mom."

All she did was turn around with a stunned look upon her face and walked away slowly. Kyle covered his face with his hand while Judy and Sam leaned against the wall saying nothing. This was really bad. One of Mom's biggest pet peeves was a mess and the look of my room had to be the worst she had ever seen.

"Awe, crap," I commented knowing this was going to be a long night for me.

Once Judy and Sam left, I went back into my room with the extra piece of cake. I closed my bedroom door and locked it as well as the window. I placed the cake on my scratched up night table.

"Nightly," I called out softly, "are you here?"

The same noise I had heard earlier came from my closet. I went back to it, opened the door, and out rolled my little black dragon.

"It's about time you found me," he said trotting over to the remains of my bed. He looked up at the piece of cake. *"Hey is that for me?"*

"Nightly, aren't you supposed to be in the ravines secret area?"

Nightly leaned over onto the night stand and took a bite out of the cake then looked over at me. *"You didn't come when the sun started setting so I decided to see where you live. I found this place covered with your scent."*

"Then you were the one who trashed my room," I said impatiently.

"Sorry, I thought that thing over there was another dragon," he said pointing his tail at my broken lamp.

There was a knock on my door. "Connie, who are you talking to?" asked my mom.

"Oh no, quick, Nightly, hide," I said crouching down to the floor. I walked over to the door and opened it.

"Is everything alright, Connie? I thought I heard you talking to someone."

I didn't have time to waste so I thought up and quick and easy excuse. "I was talking about the good times I've had with this lamp," I said pointing to the broken pieces.

Mom looked puzzled but that wasn't what I was worried about. "Are you sure you're fine, Connie? I can take you to the doctor if you'd like. Being out in a storm like last night might have left you traumatized."

"What, no! I'm fine Mom," I insisted. "Geez, I can handle one night by myself and a messy room. It's not like I was attacked."

"Well if you're sure. I'll be in the kitchen if you need anything, alright? Oh, and can you please get this room cleaned up?"

"Got it, Mom," I said with a smile on my face.

Mom kissed my forehead and then wished me a happy birthday. Once she left, I quickly shut the door and sighed. The next thing I knew, Nightly appeared at my feet.

"I thought she would never leave. I like it when you can see me," he said with frosting on his face.

"How did you do that?" I asked astonished.

"Easy, I did it like this," he said disappearing then reappearing on my bed.

"Is that your special ability, invisibility?" I sat down beside him while he ate more cake. "That is amazing."

"If that's what you whisperers call it, then yes. When you gave me energy to live you also allowed me to access my ability. It's an ability that you always wanted to do. To disappear so a darkness dragon was brought into your world," he said eating some more cake.

"I don't want to disappear . . . well . . . no! I've never wanted to disappear."

"Maybe at some point in your life, you did. It's just hidden in your heart. You know a dragon was originally born in their element but now we all sleep in stone waiting for humans to become our whisperers. They are the ones who can release us from our imprisonment of stone. Their touch gives us energy to reclaim our element and our power which is based upon what lies within the whisperers own heart."

I looked down at my hands and thought about my past but couldn't think of any time or place that I would want to vanish.

I watched my dragon eat the rest of the cake. He wasn't scared at all to be in a place where he could be exposed. Nightly was calm like the ocean on a clear blue day, relaxed like there was nothing wrong in the world, and happy like one of the kids playing at the park. Still a dragon living in a house was a little risky.

"Hey, Nightly," I said calmly, "right after you're done with the cake, I think you should head back to our secret spot."

"No way," he said shaking his head.

"Come again?" I asked. Nightly turned around in circles, jumped off the bed then went over to my window where he pointed outside. "What?"

"Didn't Devonburg tell you? The passageway is hidden from view to anyone when the sun sets. Only a whisperer can find the way in and find the way out but only when the sun is out. That's one of the magical wonders of the Mystic Realm. Some wonders in this world are hidden from your sight. It's not until you open up that you'll find the thing you are looking for," he said looking around. *"But I like it here except for the mess."*

"That's because you trashed my room!" I said ticked.

Nightly acted like it was no big deal then went back into my closet. I sighed and began to clean up the rest of the pieces of my broken lamp. It was sad to see my favourite thing in my whole room destroyed. I guess I hadn't grown up as much as I had hoped because I still believed that dragon was going to protect me.

After that was done I buffed the scratched up floors with a cloth, Moms cleaners and girl strength. When that was done I pulled out the spare mattress from the attic, by myself, with no help from Kyle or Nightly. Replaced my torn up one with it and threw the old one outside for the garbage man to take away the next morning. I made my bed with clean covers, cleared up the rest of the mess in my room and, by the time I was all done, it was eleven o'clock at night. I glanced over at the closet and saw Nightly still watching me.

"Well, aren't you going to do anything?" I asked sitting on my bed.

"What do you want me to do? I'm a dragon that can't fly yet. If you want I could burn your stuff for you."

"You can make fire already? Doesn't that take time to develop?" I asked.

"No, it's natural for a newly hatched dragon to breathe fire. If there's any danger that we can't fly away from we can defend ourselves with our fire breath."

I shook my head. "It's fine. I don't want a fire started now or ever in this house."

I was exhausted. I slipped into my pyjamas and covered myself with blankets, then stared up at the ceiling. I thought about what had happened in the last two days and how worried I had made everyone. I was now fifteen years old with friends, school, and the 'Sibling Respect Program'. I couldn't handle this on my own. If I were to still live a normal life and have a dragon, I would need the help from the Guardians that Devonburg spoke of.

I felt something, a nudge against my shoulder. When I looked over I saw Nightly staring at me with his gold eyes. *"May I sleep with you, Connie?"*

He almost sounded scared. I smiled at him and moved over. "I don't see why not unless you're a bed hog."

"I'm not a hog! I'm a dragon," he said, with pride in his voice.

I smiled at him as he crawled under the covers with me. I scratched his ears and cuddled him carefully then kissed him on his head. "Goodnight Nightly."

"Goodnight dragon whisperer Connie."

Then we both fell asleep.

I slept in till noon. I awoke and looked to my side. Nightly was sound asleep barely making a sound. The hard thing about sleeping with a dragon is that they keep poking you with their sharp spine spikes throughout the night unless you make them roll over.

I got up and got ready for the day. I wore the new t-shirt Mom had bought me, the jean jacket Judy gave me and the locket that Sam had given me for my birthday.

Even though I'm a year older you usually wouldn't feel different, but this year I did. Actually, I knew that this time nothing was going to be the same.

I walked into the living room and saw Kyle with his girlfriend Kristen on the couch together. I ignored them and went into the kitchen to get some orange juice for myself.

When I walked out, Kristen turned her attention towards me. "Hey, Connie, how was your sleep?"

I silently drank my juice.

"Oh, did you wake up on the wrong side of the bed?" she asked in a baby voice.

I placed my juice down and looked at her. Kristen had red crimson hair, blue eyes and freckles. She wore her short white sleeved shirt with blue jeans and heels. I hated her personality. She constantly teases me on everything. My clothes, friends, attitude and even the way I talk. One thing I'm glad I have better than her, a tolerance for kids.

"You do know I'm fifteen, right?"

"Connie, show some respect," demanded Kyle.

"It's alright, Kyle. If she keeps dressing like a boy, she's never going to get herself a boyfriend."

"What was that?" I yelled. By the time I started to raise my voice, Kyle stood up and held me back while I kicked and punched thin air. "Well, at least I have a life that doesn't require someone to be my personal chauffer," I argued.

"At least I'm well liked in the school, unlike you. It really is a pity," Kristen commented turning back around. I don't know what really happened next but I saw Kristen jump up on the couch screaming.

Kyle quickly let go of me and ran to Kristen's aid. "What's wrong?"

"A snake," she stuttered, "a black spiky snake!"

I smirked, ran back to my room, and waited a minute before I shut the door.

"Hey, Nightly, are you here?" I asked, scanning the room.

"Yeah," he said appearing by my window. *"That human stinks of roses and skunk, and I didn't like the way she was talking to you."*

I went up to Nightly and rubbed his head. "I never liked her either but I did love to hear her scream, thanks."

Nightly stood up tall and proud, while wagging his tail.

"In fact, would you be up for another 'Scare Kristen' mission?"

"You know it. Besides I have to get back at her. She called me a snake; I don't look anything like a snake!" he said, smoke coming out of his nostrils.

I laughed and then whispered my plan into my dragon's ear. He wagged his tail in glee, I opened the door and we both left the room.

We waited in the hall then Nightly went invisible. I pulled out my cell-phone and dialled the house number. Kyle got up and answered the phone, leaving Kristen by herself. Nightly appeared before her and stuck out his fork-like tongue at her. She screamed and threw a pillow at him. Luckily, dragons have good reflexes; he jumped out of the way and turned invisible again. Kristen grunted and grabbed another pillow and started to whack the couch as hard as she could when she saw Nightly sitting beside her. I was distracting Kyle by pretending to be a solicitor trying to sell him sports equipment. The door opened, it was my mom who walked in with an armful of groceries.

She looked over at Kristen who continued smashing things up with her nice pillows. This was another one of Mom's pet peeves, when her furniture was mistreated. She got upset. "Kristen!" she yelled.

I quickly hung up the phone and ran back into my room along with Nightly. When I closed the door I laughed. Maybe a dragon wouldn't be so bad after all. Or so I thought.

CHAPTER 5

Call the Guardians

Nightly and I played all day in my room and then I got a phone call from Judy.

"Hey birthday girl, how was clean up last night?" she asked.

"Pretty good, but I could have used some help from either you or Sam or maybe somebody else," I said, eyeing Nightly.

Judy laughed. "Sorry but you know as well as I do that when Sam gets the call he's as good as gone for the rest of the day. While I had a dance class to go to in the morning so I had to leave early." I tapped my foot in disbelief. "Anyways do you want to get together tonight? Papa Joe's is having an open mike night."

"Really, he hasn't had one of those in forever. Why should I go, though? I have nothing to say," I said sitting down on my bed.

"Sure you do," said Nightly jumping on my shoulder drawing my attention, *"You can tell them how you met me."*

"I can't do that Nightly," I said, scratching him.

"Who's Nightly?" asked Judy.

"Uh, no one. I'm just saying some random stuff. I've been doing it all day ever since last night," I explained to Judy.

Nightly leaned in close to the phone and started to lick my ear. *"That is a pretty neat thing. How do you humans talk through these things? Is it magic?"*

"Nightly, get away from my phone," I said pushing him off my shoulders.

"Who are you talking to?" Judy asked obviously getting annoyed.

That's when I realized that I was the only one who could hear or talk to Nightly. It was one of the things only a dragon's whisperer could do. "Listen Judy, I have to go but I'll see you at Papa Joe's tonight at nine. Bye." I hung up the phone and glared at Nightly. "Alright dragon, why am I the only one who can hear you?"

Remember, you didn't start hearing Skier until you touched my egg. No other human has touched a dragon egg so they can't hear me unless they are either a mage or another whisperer. Why else do you think humans hunted dragons thousands of years ago? It was because they couldn't understand them. Well they couldn't until whisperers came into the world to tell regular humans what the dragons were talking about.

"Let me guess. They thought it was witch craft and killed anyone that claimed they could tell what a dragon was saying," I said, getting up and pacing around my room.

That's right, that's why dragons are hidden away in secrecy. To be only understood by special humans. Humans that don't kill dragons on sight.

"Then, why did you want me to say 'I have a pet dragon' in front of everyone when I go out tonight?"

I meant it as a joke. Come on, it's not like I want to be exposed out into the world. That would be suicide.

"What about the mages and Guardians? When did they start to appear?" I asked.

Good question, Nightly said, as he thought for a second. *From what I was told from Skier and Devonburg, they said that mages were in charge of dragons but then they started to abuse their power so the dragons decided to give the role to humans and make them whisperers.*

"What is the difference between a mage and a human?"

In the old days, I don't think there was much difference in the appearance but there was in the power they held. You see, mages are half dragon as well as half human. They have the strength, speed and agility of a dragon but they looked just like a human. Mages have special abilities as do dragons.

"Then what happened that made the mages want dragons dead?"

Nightly yawned, *After the mages discovered the dragon and human alliance, they did anything to steal back the dragons eggs that were promised to humans. There was one human that stood out amongst the rest of them and he called out to the Great Dragon. From what I was told, the human asked for something to be done about the mages, a way to make it noticeable for humans to trust and each other without being deceived.*

I bit my lip and stared outside my window. "Will I be able to tell the difference between them and us?"

"I can't answer that, Connie," Nightly said sadly. *"All I do know is that their appearance has changed over time and they have been hunting dragons and their whisperers down ever since."*

A cold chill went down my spine. I wouldn't be able to protect myself or Nightly if I didn't know what mages looked like. I bit my lip again and looked up into the blue sky. "Nightly, I want you to go back to the secret area now."

"Why, have I done something wrong?!" he asked.

"No, of course not, I just don't want you to be put in danger. I think it's best if you go back to the secret area in the ravine and stay there till tomorrow." I thought for a second. "Can you tell me anything about the Guardians though?"

Nightly looked sad and tilted his head down. *"Guardians don't have much history since they just started to appear about fifty years ago. Their main job is to train the dragon and their whisperer in case they get into a battle with mages. They're a combination between teachers and body guards. They are also whisperers who have lost their dragons."*

"Then why don't we call them up? That way we'll both be safe from other humans and mages," I said with a smile on my face.

Nightly took on upset look. He backed away and stuck out his tongue at me in a low growl.

"What's wrong?" I asked, reaching out towards him.

Nightly bared his teeth and snapped at my hand while he crawled underneath my bed.

"Nightly!" I said crawling on my stomach. He turned away from me and curled into a ball. "Nightly," I said again, moving away from my bed and standing back on my feet. I didn't know what was wrong with him because he wasn't talking or even looking at me. Why was he troubled?

He stayed under the bed for the whole day. Even when I was getting ready to go out to Papa Joe's, he didn't budge. It didn't matter though because neither of us would be able to find the entrance at this time of night. He would be better off staying in my bedroom than anywhere else.

For my night out I wore a black skirt with high heels along with a turquoise tank top. I clipped on the locket that Sam gave me around my neck and pulled on the leather jacket Judy gave me.

"Nightly, I'm leaving now," I said, looking at my bed. "I'll be back soon." I then left him alone in my room by himself.

I was worried though. Nightly hadn't moved, not even for food. It didn't feel good to leave him but maybe it was a good thing to give him some space. Maybe he needed some time to himself.

Kyle gave me a ride; he stuck me in the back of his car with Kristen's white poodle, Maggie. That rat face wouldn't stop licking or nipping me the whole time. Of course, Kristen and Kyle sat up front pretending like nothing was happening. Once we arrived at Papa Joe's Diner, I raced out of the car and maybe I accidentally pushed Kristen's seat too far forward that she broke a nail on the dashboard.

While she was complaining, Kyle rolled down his window. "I'll pick you up around eleven, alright?"

Kristen glared at me while holding her precious hand. She turned around and put on a pouty face. Kyle closed the window, sighed and drove off with her.

I stuck my tongue out at the vehicle as it drove away in the distance. I turned and entered the diner and spotted Judy right away sitting in a booth by herself.

Once I sat down, Judy sniffed the air and then sniffed me. "Why do you smell like a dog?"

"I'll give you a hint," I said, "what has four legs, a rat face and is white all over?"

"Maggie?" she guessed.

"Maggie," I said in agreement. "Is the smell really that bad?"

Judy nodded and rummaged through her purse and pulled out a pink bottle. "Here, it's perfume. I know it's not really your style but anything is better than reeking up the joint."

"Thanks Judy," I said grabbing the bottle. "I've never seen this in your collection before."

"It's a new one I got from Florida. It's supposed to make you smell like oranges and lemons," Judy said standing up and showing off her hot pink dress with black flats and white scarf. "Now hurry into the bathroom, cover up that dog stench before Sam and his cousin arrive."

"Why's Kamal coming?" I asked, concerned.

"Yeah, it was his idea that we all met up here tonight," she said stretching.

I walked into the bathroom and looked at myself in my mirror and breathed hard. I hardly ever saw Kamal in the past few years and whenever I did . . . it felt bizarre to be around him. Why would he suggest for all of us to meet up here? I looked into the mirror and splashed some water on my face, knocking myself back into reality. Ever since I've known Sam, his cousin has never showed an interest in coming here. It was strange that wanted to hang out with us now.

I sprayed some of the perfume on myself and then left the washroom. When I returned to the booth, I noticed that Sam and Kamal had arrived. I walked up and joined them, sitting beside Judy across from Sam and Kamal.

Sam wore a red shirt with jeans and sandals. He and Kamal didn't look much alike except for their green eyes.

Kamal had short brown hair, a scar on his left cheek that looked like a 'c' and had a strong physique. He wore a black muscle shirt that showed off his tattoo of a straight line that curved at the top with two lines going through it. There was one short line at the top and one at the bottom. In between the two short lines was a single shaded circle. He wore long pants and worn out running shoes.

Here's an odd thing. I hear Sam say he's alone for most evenings because Kamal is off doing something. Often Sam says he's gone to pick up a new pair of shoes but they are always worn down by the time I see them.

But there was always one thing that caught my attention and that was his brass bracelet with five gems on it. There was a spot for two more but they were missing. The gems were blue, brown, green, yellow and red.

"Hey Connie," said Sam in a cheerful voice. "You're just in time the show's about to start."

I smiled at him; Kamal's eyes gazed at me. I looked away and watched the stage.

For the two years I have known Sam I never set foot into his house. I've gone there to ask if he was available but Kamal would always answer the door. Of course Sam would come running out of the house to meet up with me. The house has always creped me out. Every time we left I always felt Kamal's eyes watching me, like I had something he wanted.

The lights faded and waiter and waitresses ca[r]
candles on the tables and in the booths. Once they [w]
and a girl went onto the stage with a microphone,
They introduced themselves as 'News Flash' then
listened to their music and then watched as other
play music, do a skit, tell a few jokes and say poems

Once one of the stand-up comedians were done Kamal got up and
started to walk towards the stage.

"Hey," Sam said as he grabbed his cousin's arm, "you didn't tell me
you were performing."

"Just telling a story," Kamal said in a deep voice. I lowered my
head and played with my fingers as I listened to his light footsteps. "It's
nothing to make a big deal about."

There was a short applause as he took the stage and once he was on
stage I raised my head I saw something enter the diner from the corner
of my eye.

Kamal tapped the microphone; then, he began to talk. "On a
stormy day in the darkest of night a dragon rose to give people a fright.
They burned every mortal along with their village that was in their
sight. The might they carried was exquisite. Thus exquisite that they
held onto it tightly so no one would rise above them and take it." I
heard something rattle around in the kitchen and then returned my
attention to Kamal. He continued, "They howled, growled and roared
as the night went on. Fire burning, lightning cracking and the sound
of human's screaming filled the night, leaving nothing but ashes and
blood."

The noise in the kitchen grew louder and started to draw everyone's
attention.

"No one trusts the powers these beasts hold because it's not even
their own," Kamal continued.

A flame crackled from the kitchen out into the lounge area. The
flame was close enough that almost everyone could feel the heat.
Tables began to flip over mysteriously knocking the candles onto
the floor causing a bigger fire to start. People screamed in terror as
they were knocked out of their seats. Waiters and waitresses brought
out fire extinguishers, they went running around the diner trying
to douse the fire the candles created. Judy seized me in a hug and

er eyes. I looked over to Sam who stared at Kamal. I was too
ocked to do anything. We couldn't move from our seats because of
the people running around everywhere. Why did Kamal continue to
keep telling his story when the diner was being destroyed from the
inside out?

"They will never stop until they realize that everything they see will
always be destroyed. Until they finally know who their real masters are.
Everything that is living will be destroyed if not." Kamal took one final
breath which drew everyone's attention, "dragons." When he stepped
down off the stage everything became calm.

The crashing and banging stopped and everybody calmed down.
Judy released her grip on me and we both slouched in our seats. I
dropped my hand and felt something nudge up against it. I looked
under the table and saw nothing then I realized it was Nightly.

When we got out of the diner, which was heavily damaged by
Nightly's rampage, we all met in the front. The firemen went around
asking people for their opinions on what happened. People honestly
had no idea; they were just glad to be out of there. The four of us
grouped together and began to discuss the situation.

"I would like to know what happened in there," Judy said crossing
her arms.

"The manager said the stove in the kitchen got out of control and
the back door was opened, allowing a harsh wind in that started to
knock everything over," explained Kamal.

Sam said nothing but his facial expression showed that he was
either scared or mad about something.

Judy's mom came to pick her up and offer me a ride but I declined
because Kyle was supposed to pick me up. After Judy left, Sam and
Kamal piled into a red Corvette and drove off.

I watched as they drove away and once they were out of sight, I ran
to the back of the building where I found Nightly sitting on top of a
dumpster.

"Hey, how are you feeling?" I asked in a calm voice as I cautiously
approached him.

"I'm sorry, Connie. I couldn't control myself," he said in a sulky voice.
"I was waiting for you to return but then I sensed something I couldn't ignore. It

controlled me and the next thing I knew was that I was fighting myself. When I finally realized where I was and what I was doing, I saw you."

I hugged Nightly tightly and then slowly let a few tears fall from my face. I left my dragon alone and he hurt himself because of my lack of responsibility. Tear after tear came running down my face as I held my dragon, Nightly, closer to me, making sure he was alright, but really I should have been asking that question to myself.

Nightly broke away from the hug and crawled onto my back forcing my jacket off, he pushed my shirt down, choking me again. He exposed my dragon wings mark. He tensed up as he bent down and touched it then quickly he jumped off me. I felt a surge of pain go through my body. I collapsed. Sweat came down my face and soon enough, I found myself screaming as the pain was released into the air in the form of a bright light. I lost all my vision, my body went numb, and I couldn't even hear myself scream for a few seconds. Once everything returned back to normal, I stood on my feet and straightened out my shirt.

"Are you alright?" he asked.

I breathed heavily, looking at him. "Yeah, but what did you do to me?" I asked touching my shoulders. "That was bright as a solar eclipse."

"Something's wrong, Connie. Tonight was proof of it, I had to call the Guardians," Nightly said sadly.

"Really," I asked excited, but I noticed his sad face. "What's the matter?"

"When you call the Guardians . . . you also . . . reveal your location to mages," he said.

"Oh, lord," I said stunned.

We heard noises. There was no doubt in my mind that people would start to come around the corner to find out what caused that bright light. I grabbed Nightly and slipped the two of us into the building next door. We were lucky that there was no one in the room we were in at the time.

I looked at Nightly as I held him like a baby. It was no wonder that he was scared from the start. That light was brighter than all the lights in Las Vegas put together. I was so stupid. Before I could sulk I heard Kyle call my name. I looked down at Nightly. He stared at me with his big round sad gold eyes.

"You go ahead. I'll meet you at the house."

"I . . . I can't knowing . . . please Nightly . . . be safe," I stuttered. I gave him another hug and a kiss on the forehead, placed him down on the ground then headed out of the building to find Kyle.

CHAPTER 6

Four Humans and One Dragon

When Kyle picked me up, he kept asking me what was with the bright light he saw in the sky. I played dumb and said things like 'how would you see that when we live in a fifty foot ravine?' or 'really, did you see butterflies and unicorns as well?' The second one got me a one way ticket to Bruiseville on my shoulder.

"I'm serious Connie," he said, "There was a strange light. It was like it was trying to notify someone." I looked at him with a curious face. "I think it might be aliens calling their mother ship."

Do you ever have that feeling that when a person says something so absurd you feel like you have just ran into a brick wall? I think I just did. He just had to bring up aliens. It's the one thing he never shuts up about. He has every movie and every poster ever made about aliens pinned up on his bedroom wall or scattered across his bedroom floor.

"Really Kyle," I said, disappointed, "aliens? They don't exist and there is no proof that they ever did."

That comment got me another bruise on my arm. "You are just like everyone else, but I have proof this time. Before I arrived at Papa Joe's, I was going to send Kristen a video message but instead I got that light that blasted up into the sky."

I became curious. While Kyle was watching the road I slowly moved my hand towards his cell phone but then he slapped my hand away from it.

"Shouldn't you be watching the road," I complained.

"I am and you don't touch!" he barked grabbing his phone before I even had the chance to get near it. "This is important evidence that I'm bringing to the TV station tomorrow."

"The station is closed on Sundays, dummy," I said, "So much for your evidence."

Kyle gulped and gritted his teeth in annoyance. He totally forgot about that and the thought of me reminding him about it upset him more. Nevertheless I really needed to see that video Kyle took. If it caught an image of Nightly or me we would be in trouble.

When we got home, I ran to my bedroom and opened my window which had Nightly waiting on the other side of it. We both waited till everyone was asleep before we attempted to sneak into Kyle's room. I quietly closed the door behind myself as we entered his room. I gagged at my brother's horrendous mess that stunk like a pig sty with alien posters scattered everywhere on his floor.

I plugged my nose. "I've always hated coming in here. Let's find that phone quickly and get out of here."

"Agreed," Nightly said, copying my action and covering his nose.

We spent about five minutes kicking things aside looking for the phone but we found nothing. This was ridiculous, but luckily Nightly spotted the phone. Kyle was holding onto it as he slept. Alas, Kyle began to snore. I swear you could almost create an earthquake with the way he snores.

"Great! Humans are not only loud during the day but also at night too," Nightly said, switching from covering his nose to covering his ears.

"Kyle has always snored and when I mean always, that includes the times when we were kids. It's weird. He even snores when he's in a comfortable position. But all you really have to do is roll him over then it gets better. Well, at least quieter." I walked over to his bed and tapped him on the shoulder. "It's also a good thing he's a heavy sleeper or else I don't think we would be able to get out of here alive."

Nightly jumped on the bed and sniffed Kyle's head. *"Why does he smell like wet dog and socks?"*

"Because he likes to work out and then put on a reeking deodorant before he goes to bed," I said, rolling him over making him release his grip on the phone.

"You make it sound like you've done this before."

"Well, let's just say he has taken some of my stuff before that I had to retrieve from this very room." I snatched the phone from Kyle and turned towards the door. "I've got it. Now let's get out of here."

"Way ahead of you," said Nightly, jumping off the bed and running towards the door.

I tiptoed across the floor, trying not to step on any of his pictures of himself with Kristen, him just posing, his fallen alien poster or any of his dirty clothes. Hasn't this guy ever heard of a laundry or a photo album? Once I had actually cleared the room, I turned around for one last look and I thought I saw something move underneath his clothes. It made me jump and run out of that room faster than a jack rabbit.

"Typical humans," Nightly snickered as he led the way back to my room.

I trotted back towards my room grumbling. I had to make sure I wasn't loud enough to wake Mom. Unfortunately, she was a light sleeper and woke up to any noise. When we entered my room, I put on my pyjamas just in case Mom did wake up; she would find me asleep. I crawled into bed and Nightly joined me shortly after sitting by my feet and turning invisible. Mom did happen to wake up and open the door. I shut my eyes tightly but even though they were closed I could have sworn she was looking right at me. Once I heard the door close I sat up and turned on Kyle's phone. I plugged in a pair of headphones so I wouldn't get another visit from Mom.

Nightly appeared beside me and stared at the phone. *"And how exactly do you get these so called 'videos' on something like that?"*

"You see, there's a camera on the back that can record movements that have happened during previous events," I said pointing to the lens on the back of his phone.

"What's a camera?"

I then realized that Nightly only knew the simple stuff of a human's life along with dragon stuff. "Never mind, I'll explain it to you later."

I played the video and it started off with Kyle in his car driving along side of the road.

"Hey Kristen," he said, puckering out his lips like a fish attempting to make a kissy face. "It's your favourite athlete. This video is just to tell you . . ." he was silent for a while. "What's that? It looks like it's coming from Papa Joe's." he lifted the camera which was now facing a light brightening the sky; with what looked like the dragon wings on my back. "Wow, this is amazing. I wonder if it is actually aliens."

And that's where it ended. I closed the phone and faced Nightly.

"So what do we do now?" he asked facing me.

"We can't let the whole world see this. I'll delete the video. That's the only way no one will find out about us. The only thing is it'll be hard trying to find the Guardians when we don't even know what they look like."

"That's the thing about Guardians, you don't go to them they come to you. Just wait and you'll see; they'll come," Nightly curled up beside me.

He yawned and then closed his gold eyes and fell fast asleep. He smiled while he slept. Now that we got the signal out to let the Guardians know where we were, there was nothing in the world for him to worry about. I on the other hand was too tense to think straight. Mages, Guardians and then my own life kept me tossing and turning the whole night.

* * *

A week passed and there was still no sign of the Guardians. Every night I had a restless sleep. This was bugging me and I didn't know why. Even during the 'Sibling Respect Program' I was out of it and Kyle was mad at me that we had lost that week's challenge. Mom told me that when I was bothered by something, I would do my usual routine which was zone out to another world. I didn't think it was that noticeable. Even Nightly noticed it but at least he knew why.

I woke from another restless night. First of all, the whole week I spent with Nightly he continuously jumped on me because he was hungry; second is that my brother kept yelling at me because I 'accidentally' deleted his video of aliens and thirdly I have to live a normal life trying to find people who call themselves the Guardians so they would help me defend myself against mages. Uh, it was driving me crazy!

I collapsed back on my bed right after giving Nightly half of my breakfast. Hey, who knew dragons liked pancakes?

He looked up at me with syrup dripping from his face. *"Still not getting enough sleep?"*

I nodded.

"They'll come; you just have to be patient."

"I need to clear my head. But when I do a new problem comes at me."

"Humans are weird," said Nightly finishing off the pancakes. He then glanced at the window and saw something fly by. *"Hey Connie, wake up! I just saw something that looked like another dragon."*

I stood up instantly. "Then what are we waiting for? Let's follow it!"

I got dressed and headed outside. It was a bright sunny day so Nightly had to turn invisible, which made it hard for me to keep up with him. Once and a while I had to stop just to make sure I wouldn't lose Nightly. He didn't mind because he would come back and reappear in front of me and point me in the right direction. When I lost him for the third time I ended up at the park. I sighed and sat down on the swing. Sometimes I felt where Nightly was; other times he seemed to vanish completely. Next thing I knew Sam sat down on the swing beside me.

"Good morning. You look happy," he said with a smile.

"Ha, ha," I said sarcastically.

"Come on, I know you've been bothered by something all week," he said.

"Is it really the obvious?" I asked.

"Kind of," Sam said, "I bet it was Kamal last Saturday night, when things got out of control."

I bit my lip and said nothing.

Sam sighed and looked up at the sky. "I thought something might go wrong when Kamal suggested that we all should meet up together."

I noticed he wasn't smiling anymore. "Then why'd you agree to it?"

"Because," Sam got up and started to rub his head, "at first, I thought he just meant the three of us. I didn't expect him to come along for the ride."

I bit my lip again even harder.

"I wanted to say this all week but you had your mind on other things, I wanted to apologize. I really am sorry Connie," he said, sounding a bit frustrated.

I then felt a nudge against my hand. *"I found them."*

This wasn't good. I couldn't act like I had to go somewhere right away. Then my phone started to ring. I picked it up and heard a different voice. A voice I never heard before.

"Do not panic. I'm a Guardian but I need you to convince your friend that I'm your mom calling."

"Yeah, I understand," feeling the hairs on the back of my neck stand.

"Your dragon knows where we are, he also knows your number, and he also said you know the place too. It's in the ravine's secret area," said the female voice. "Now hurry!"

I hung the phone up and groaned. I was surprised how they knew where I was and knew about the secret area.

"Is everything alright?" Sam asked, leaning in towards me. He didn't look good like he saw a ghost. His hands were shaking again.

I sighed and looked deeply into his eyes. "I'm sorry, Sam. I have to go and meet up with my mom now. Do you understand?"

Sam smirked and broke eye contact with me; he looked down at the ground and laughed lightly. "Sure, I've seen your mom when she gets angry and I have to agree it's no picnic in the park."

"Thanks Sam," I said with a smile. I gave him a hug then placed the cell phone back in my pocket.

I ran towards home but hid behind a pair of trees until I was sure Sam had left the park. When he was gone I ran past the park; further into the ravine; turned left and stopped at the entrance to the passageway where I saw Nightly waiting for me. He puffed out some smoke and smiled. *"Did you have a nice chat with Sam?"* he said, attempting to make the same kissy face like the one Kyle made on his video.

"Oh, ha, ha," I said ticked. "I wouldn't even need to talk to him if you just told me where we were going."

"Well, how was I supposed to know that they were heading to the secret area? I'm not psychic you know."

"It would help if you were," I mumbled.

"Oh, sorry for being one of the rare dragons in this world who can turn invisible," he said dramatically.

"Are you trying to mock me?!"

"Maybe I am," Nightly said, spreading his wings out and blowing out some fire.

"Nightly," I shouted, running out of the way.

A white dragon suddenly appeared between the two of us. It had feather like wings just like Skier but it was covered in pearl white scales. Like the dragon from my dream the night Nightly hatched. Its voice was deep and strong.

"Quiet, you two," it said in a feminine voice. *"Your bickering is giving me a headache."*

"Sorry Pearl," said Nightly.

The white dragon spread out her wings then folded them back in. Then she looked at me, studying every move I made. She would scare a regular human to death with her intimidating violet eyes. I would say she was eighteen feet tall and thirty feet wide.

"You've got to be joking," she said pulling her neck back. *"You're the dragon whisperer of one of the last darkness dragons?"*

"So what if I am?" I yelled, not even thinking what could happen to me if I took a step too far. "Nightly is my dragon that Devonburg and Skier put me in charge of. I wear the mark of the dragon so I have a right." I took off my jacket, turned around and then pulled my shirt down revealing my dragon wings mark.

Pearl just huffed then started to fly. *"Hurry up and get inside,"* she demanded. *"The others are waiting."*

"There are other dragons here?" I asked calmly.

"Sadly no, there are just humans who were once whisperers who have escaped the mage's wrath." She then continued to fly up till she was out of sight.

I shook my fist up high. "She's like Kristen just in a dragon version."

Nightly sighed as he went through the illusion into the passage way. *"Let's just go."*

I took a calm breath and then followed Nightly into the area. There I found four people waiting for us. Three were boys and one was a girl who was looking up to the sky. Behind them I saw trees cut down. It seemed they were building something.

One guy in a cowboy outfit ran up to me and shook my hand. "I'm so pleased to meet you, little lady. We've been waiting here the whole morning for you." He grinned at me, showing me his adult braces. "The name's James, James Alexander Parkston."

"Oh, quit scaring her," said another guy appearing from behind me. He almost scared me half to death. "Let her relax, after all, she just met Pearl," he said, starting to give me a back rub. Nightly came up to him and peed on him. "Stupid dragon," he mumbled walking away.

I turned around and saw a pretty boy old enough to be in college. He had thick brown hair, light blue eyes and he wore a leather jacket.

"Don't mind him," said the third guy standing by the girl. "That's just how Theodor is."

"I've told you, Malcolm, it's Teddy not Theodor," he said trying to clean his boots off.

Malcolm wore nerd glasses, had red short hair including freckles and brown eyes. He wore a tartan shirt.

Malcolm came up to me and shook my hand. "It's a pleasure to meet you dragon whisperer but you only look fifteen."

"That's because I am," I said, petting Nightly.

"That means you're the youngest dragon whisperer ever," said the girl still looking up at the sky. She turned her attention to me. "My name's Nicole."

Nicole had short black hair with one section coloured purple. She had murky green eyes and her skin was as dark as Judy's.

"My name is Connie," I said looking at everyone.

"And I'm Nightly."

They all studied me like I was the answer to today's test. I actually felt a little violated and embarrassed.

"I'm kind of surprised that Devonburg would have chosen you. Didn't know that he wanted to recruit kids to be whisperers," said Nicole.

"You knew Devonburg?" I asked astonished.

"Of course we knew him," said Malcolm.

"Yep, we all knew him," said James.

"He's the one who gave us our dragon eggs and made us Guardians. After we lost our dragons to mages Devonburg gave us a quest to find the next dragon whisperer by searching the skies for the calling sign. So far we've had no luck until last week," said Teddy.

"Why couldn't you find anymore?" I asked.

"Because all the other whisperers are dead, but Devonburg brought a dragon stone to one of our training sessions saying he knew exactly who to give it to," explained Malcolm.

"From then on we were given orders to be the Guardians for the next whisperer, which happened to be you," said Teddy.

"What took you so long to get here though?" I asked, "Nightly and I gave the signal a week ago."

"We were all separated at the time that you gave the sign. Pearl had to find each of us before coming here," said Nicole watching Pearl land. "She has incredible speed almost as fast as light but even so it still takes time to find people."

"So is that her special ability?" I asked.

"No!" Pearl roared. *"You have a lot to learn, young human, before you can take on a mage."*

"Well, sorry if Devonburg never explained that before he and his dragon passed on," I said.

Everything went silent except for the wind.

"Devonburg's dead?" questioned James.

"He must have wanted to leave this world in a dignified way," said Malcolm.

"It doesn't matter now," said Nicole. "Right now we have to teach Connie here about the Mystic Realm."

CHAPTER 7

Mystic Realm

Pearl and Nightly made a fire together while the rest of us gathered around it. There was one thing that kept bothering me and that was why Pearl was here. Everyone said they had lost their dragon to mages but Pearl looked like she didn't even have a whisperer at all. If a dragon is born from a human's energy, why was she alone?

"So what's the Mystic Realm?" I asked sitting down beside Nightly.

The Guardians stayed standing. They looked down at me and my dragon, studying us. From the looks on their faces they seemed to be having a hard time accepting that I was the dragon whisperer Devonburg was talking about. They then sat down beside me, warming themselves by the fire.

"The Mystic Realm is known as the hidden world. A second world that had to break away from the human race. Ever since the medieval ages ended, mystic beings have created their own world to live in without disturbance. The Mystic Realm contained the seven attributes or seven elements," explained Malcolm. "Those are water, wind, earth, lightning, fire, light and darkness."

"When the world was first created, the dragons were born in their natural elements full of life instead of being encased in stone, waiting for a human to given them energy. When the dragons were born in these elements, it was there duty to breed until they had a big enough population that created a region," said Nicole leaning on Pearl, sounding tense.

"So that means I would be originally from the darkness region, right?" asked Nightly.

"That's right," said Pearl. *"And I would be from the light."*

"Once the Mystic Realm was created," continued James, "it contained the seven elements that the dragons referred to as regions. The water dragons took the seas, the air dragons took the skies and mountains, fire dragons took the desserts and active volcanic islands, the lightning dragons claimed electrical clouds as their region, the earth dragons claimed exposed soil and dirt for their region, light dragons took any place in the world that was filled with light and the darkness dragons took any dark place they could find for their own regions. These regions were once strong, sturdy and stunning until they were destroyed, courtesy of the mages."

"How did mages appear in the world?" I asked.

"Mages have and will always be strange," said Teddy. "Mages were created before humans but after animals. So you could say we're more like evolved humans but weaker."

I was confused.

"What Teddy is trying to say is that dragons and animals were created at the same time but mages, yes, are like humans but they were created with some of the same materials as a dragon which means they have their own ability," said Malcolm.

"Do you know what that ability is?" I asked.

"Dream manipulation," they all said at once.

"*So* combining both dragons and mages would create the ultimate being?" I asked.

"Well, not really," said Nicole, "mages never trained with dragons the way we do today. Back when mages and dragons were partners they were never really that powerful."

"What are mages if they are not human?"

"Mages are part dragon but they are evil, sinister and conniving murderers," said Pearl stretching out her neck.

"The only thing that mages have in common with dragons is their expert hearing, eyesight, agility, strength and speed," said James. "They thought that since they were part dragon, they had the right to be in control and manipulate dragons."

"That's when they started searching the seven regions for dragon eggs. Unfortunately they found some and stole them away from their natural element. The thing about a baby dragon is that they have to place their mark on their home region or for this case a whisperer," said Malcolm. Malcolm took his finger and began to draw in the dirt. "You've probably heard of stories that have dragons guarding treasures, castles maybe even forests, the reason they do that is because they were protecting their mark."

I took Nightly from under his arms and held him close to me, hugging him tightly.

Malcolm continued. "Dragons have no choice but to submit to their masters once they have given them their mark. It's like a contract that is impossible to break."

"You see Connie," Teddy said moving closer to me, "since there are seven regions, there are also seven marks of the dragon. As you've already noticed they are in the shapes of a dragon. The wind dragon has the wings that represent the dragon's flight, the earth, fire, lightning and water dragon's all symbolize a dragon's claw which represent what a dragon can adapt to in the world, the light dragon has the head to lead the way into a brighter day and then the darkness has the tail that is used for a hidden attack."

"Then why did I get wings instead of a tail; after all, Nightly is a darkness dragon?" I looked down at Nightly who shrugged and licked my face. I scratched him behind the ears. Teddy leaned close to me but Nightly bared his teeth and snapped at him forcing Teddy to back away.

"As I said before," said Malcolm, "Devonburg wanted to leave this world in a dignified way. Once a dragon's whisperer passes on their mark, if they chose to do so, it will give the new whisperer the liberty to become a dragon's whisperer whether they have transferred energy to break the dragon out of its prison or not. The thing is that since you have given energy to release your dragon he already knows who you are the mark is just to confirm it. However when a dragon's whisperer has died in a battle or gives their mark away they will disappear along with their dragon. The dragon's body will automatically become a part of the regions they were once supposed be in while the soul follows its whisperer beyond the point of no return." Malcolm finished drawing in the dirt. "My theory is that after the mages were cursed the dragons made sure that humans would be their only whisperers. By only allowing a humans energy release the unborn dragons. Any other creatures touch will be negated. The thing is it has to be a human's skin. Clothing or any other material won't have an effect on the egg. However, numbers started to shrink when mages heard of humans becoming the whisperers. The only reason why they started to kill humans was because of them, their human appearance changed. A whisperer cannot die unless their life is taken or they pass their mark to someone they see worthy of holding it. Now dragons rely on humans, they protect them, watch over them and make sure nothing bad ever happens to them or else they will die because there energy source has vanished."

"Dragons are almost extinct because of mages. I won't rest peacefully till they are gone from both the Human World and the Mystic Realm," said Pearl, puffing out some smoke. *"The balance of the seven regions had been destroyed now only two dragons live on this earth for now."*

"We're the only ones alive?" asked Nightly shaking in my arms. *"Where are the others?"*

"The others that are not dead are still asleep in their stone prisons," said Pearl.

"This means that you have to protect your dragon with your life," Nicole said, "and the same goes for your dragon."

"Why does Nightly have to protect me? Am I not supposed to be the one protecting him?" I asked.

"The mark we dragons place on beings means we were born to protect it. If we fail to protect what we were born to do, then we die too," said Nightly avoiding eye contact.

"Then if Nightly dies . . . will I die as well?" I asked.

"No," they all said again but sternly.

"We are automatically connected to our dragons once they are born. They protect their protector so nothing that happens to you will affect them, because their life line is only as long as their whisperer's," said Malcolm. "Unless they give their own lives to save their protectors, like ours have."

"Is that how you all lost your dragons? Because they were trying to protect you," I asked.

Everything went quiet. Nightly looked up and shook his head.

Pearl huffed and blew more smoke out from her nostrils. *"Well, my whisperer died over twelve years ago and I'm still alive."*

"Pearl," said Nicole in a sad voice.

"No, it's a lie!" Pearl boasted. *"Dragons can still live even after their whisperers die."*

"You seem close to Nicole. If a dragon can't live without a whisperer wouldn't that make Nicole Pearl's whisperer?" I asked.

Pearl huffed again. *"Nicole was the cousin of my whisperer. After my whisperer died, she looked after me after the mages took her dragon."* Pearl stood up and stretched her long neck out to me. *"If you do anything that will hurt the darkness dragon I will personally end your hopeless life."* Pearl stretched out her wings and took to the skies.

I stood up and watched her fly off towards the sun.

"Don't mind her," said James. "She's always been a hot head, even when we first met her."

Teddy stood up and put his arm around me, "Yeah, she sure has problems but you know she was actually really excited when she saw the sign in the sky. She nearly tore the buildings apart looking for us; wanting to leave immediately to find the two of you."

"She was?" I asked surprised.

"Oh, yeah, when she gathered us, we flew for three days straight trying to locate where the signal came from but I think she was disappointed in your appearance."

"What's wrong with my appearance?" I demanded.

"Nothing," Teddy said touching my chin, "absolutely nothing."

Nightly squirmed his way out of my arms and bit Teddy's leg. While they were trying to . . . settle their differences Malcolm pulled me to the side and we went for a walk.

"So what did you want to talk about?" I asked.

"It's more of what do you want to talk about," he said stopping at the wall. "I saw the look in your eyes when Pearl left. You're confused of how she lives but not her whisperer."

I bit my lip. "You just said that dragons live to protect their whisperer and the whisperer lives to protect their dragon. You also said that if I were to die Nightly would too. Why and why is Pearl living when she knows her whisperer is dead?" I asked angrily.

"Dragons live to protect what brought them to live on earth. It's just their way of saying thanks but if they place their mark on something like a tree that gets chopped down a few days later then they would return to stone they were once and then the stone would shatter. Originally when the seven regions still existed they would place their marks all over the place, declaring that they would protect their region with their lives.

As for Pearl, I believe she's still alive because her whisperer is still alive. She might have mistaken a different human as her whisperer. That would explain how she met Nicole and her dragon," said Malcolm. "I do believe that Nicole is keeping something from her dragon friend though. Nicole has never been that honest or trusting to anyone but herself."

"Why would she do that? Isn't she the one Pearl feels the safest around?"

"Even so, there are *still* secrets that you can keep from a friend. I can't unlock those mysteries. They're not easy and it's usually something that's dark in their past, so they hide it so no soul can be hurt."

"If you don't tell someone something about them they are going to find out eventually and it's going to hurt them more. The truth sets people free." I looked up at the sun that started to set. I bit my lip again and then I heard my phone ring. I picked it up and heard Kyle's voice on the other line.

"Where are you?!" he yelled in my ear. "First you erase my video of aliens on my phone and now you're going to break your new curfew, you really are in for it."

"What are you talking about?" I said back.

"Look at the time, idiot!"

I did and saw that it was already ten past seven.

"Yeah, that's what I thought," Kyle sighed. "Just come home or this time Mom's going to send the search party after you."

We both hung up the phone and I placed my phone back into my pocket. "Sorry, Malcolm but I got to go. I'm only fifteen and I have a curfew."

"I understand, but tomorrow when you come, bring something that will make Nightly stay," he said, tracing the mark I made on the wall. The part of the wall that I had marked which told me where the secret passageway was.

"I tried that last time and it didn't really work."

"Ah, but this time you have us."

"Good point, well I guess I'll see you tomorrow. Nightly we're leaving," I called out.

James was holding Nightly back as he snapped and growled at Teddy whom he was still mad at. When he heard me call his name, James released him and he trotted over to me and stuck his tongue out at Teddy who was shaking his fist in the air at him.

As we walked down the tunnel together I started to hum a song.

"What are you singing?" he asked.

"It's a song I made up when I was a kid. It's a song about how you have to break away from history stop looking to the mystery that lies ahead but be grateful for the day what's happening today."

"Sounds confusing but understandable," he said jumping in front of me.

"Thanks, but that doesn't excuse your behaviour around Teddy."

"He was making a move on you and as your dragon I have to protect you as well."

I laughed as we approached the end of the tunnel.

"What's so funny?"

"You," I said still laughing. "Teddy's like a college student whereas I just started high school. I really doubt that I would go out with a guy like that."

Once we exited the passage way, Nightly turned invisible and began to run. I ran after him knowing this little guy wanted to race but of course he would cheat after all he was invisible, but I knew a short cut home.

CHAPTER 8

Flight

I jumped through the front door and danced. I made it in time before curfew hit. My mom heard me, poked her head out of the kitchen, and looked over at me.

"Hi . . . Mom," I said, trying to catch my breath.

"You're lucky you have a kind brother," she said waving a wooden spoon at me. "If he hadn't called you I would have personally gone out looking for you."

"But I'm back and on time," I said catching my breath, "so there is nothing to worry about."

My mom sighed and put the spoon down. "Well, you're right but I never want you to break curfew ever again. Do you understand me?"

"Yes, Mom," I said, "loud and clear."

I sat down at the table and then Kyle came in and joined us. Then he leaned on the table and smirked at me.

"Well," he said.

"Well what?" I asked confused.

"Don't I get a 'thank you' for getting you home before curfew?"

"I would have made it on my own without your help," I said hiding my beet red face. "Besides when did you ever start caring for me?"

"Since I told him I have big news to tell the two of you and that he had to give me a better performance than what he has been giving Glen at the program."

"You bring your girlfriend there once and it's the end of the world at home," Kyle commented.

"And it didn't hurt to put in a little discipline action," Mom added.

I shuddered. The two worst things in my life are getting homework over the holidays and my mom's disciplinary actions.

"So what is it this time?" I asked. "Take the car away, forcing both of us to walk? How about making us sleep outside for a week or selling all of our stuff?"

"Those are all good suggestions, Connie, but no. I just told Kyle that I wouldn't allow him to see Kristen anymore if he didn't watch over you," she said patting Kyle on the back.

Kyle sat up straight and covered his face the best he could, but you could tell he was blushing. You could see the red in between his fingers.

I sat back in my chair laughing. "That's it?"

"Shut up!" Kyle demanded.

"That's enough out of both of you," Mom said placing some stew on the table. "Now my big news is that I got off the phone with your dad about three hours ago and he told me that he's going to be home next weekend. He'll be home for the rest of the year."

"Really, are you sure?!" Kyle and I both said standing up.

My mom nodded and gave us a smile. "No tricks, flaws or delayed trips either."

"But I thought Dad wasn't going to be home for another month?" I said returning to my chair.

"Well . . . things change . . . and I guess he's coming home early," Mom said sitting down. "Now let's eat."

For the whole time we ate, everything stayed quiet for once. Kyle didn't say anything about his past life time stories when we were kids. Mom didn't ask any questions about how our day was or what we did. It was a weird quiet.

Later, I went into my room carrying an extra bowl of stew for Nightly to eat. But thoughts of the weird silence at the dinner table stayed in my head. The news of Dad returning to Small Valley was huge in our household because, ever since I was a baby Dad had hardly been home at all. He would only come around for the holidays but right after that, he would leave us, always sending money. Nightly knew something was wrong when I entered the room.

"Why was it so quiet at dinner tonight?" he asked, jumping to the floor off the bed.

I don't know why but I didn't tell him. I had a gut feeling that it wouldn't turn out right. "It's nothing you have to worry about." My stomach turned. I always got that feeling whenever I had a bad feeling. "Here, I brought you some stew."

I placed the bowl on the ground and watched as Nightly devoured it. I put on a fake smile as I watched him glance back at me once and a while.

He pushed the bowl away and licked his paw. *"What's with the fake smile?"*

I gulped, wondering if he figured it out already. "What fake smile?"

"Something is bothering you," he said raising his head. *"You can tell me."*

Nightly looked so innocent it made it hard to keep my mouth shut but I did. But then Nightly lowered his head and jumped back onto the bed.

"Let's sleep on it," he said circling around like a dog. *"If it's still bothering you tomorrow you should tell me."*

I bit my lip but then got ready for bed. We cuddled up to each other and fell asleep.

In the morning, it was the usual routine. I got up, ate breakfast and gave Nightly his own to eat. Then I got ready for school but I had to get a new backpack to carry my books in since a certain dragon tore up my last one. After that I went to school leaving Nightly at home. I told him earlier to go to the secret area and that I would meet him there after school. He would have the Guardians to keep him company. As I left I couldn't help feel an uncomfortable look coming from him. The school day went by quickly. I hated that I had to lie to my friends just so I could meet up with Nightly. Before Sam and Judy let me go I had to give them an excuse. I broke curfew last night and was now grounded and had to be home straight after school. Lucky for me, it worked.

I ran out of Small Valley to the secret area and when I arrived I got an unexpected welcome. Nightly, decided to jump on me when I came out of the passageway. He knocked me down on the ground. *"Nice of you to join us,"* he said, licking my ear as he jumped off me. *"We have an interesting lesson today."*

"Really, what is it?" I asked eagerly.

Teddy, Nicole, Malcolm and James all looked at me when I arrived, studying my every move again. Pearl then dropped down and stuck her neck out towards me.

"You're slow, whisperer. Next time, show up earlier," she said looking down at Nightly. *"Alright little one, are you ready for first flight lesson?"*

"You bet," he said eager.

Nicole walked up beside me and pulled me aside. "While they're working on that I'm going to teach you how to connect with your dragon's mind. Now you first want to begin by sitting in your most comfortable position."

I walked over by the pond and sat with my legs crossed down on the soft patch of grass. I looked around at the quiet peaceful area. The thing I saw them working on yesterday was now looking more like a house.

Nicole walked up to me but stayed a good distance away. "Good, now imagine you, yourself as Nightly. Close your eyes. Picture yourself having a body of black scales, wings that can make you fly and a hot breath coming from the back of your throat."

I did what she told me to do. I closed my eyes and pictured a body of black scales covering me from head to toe, wings that spread out from my back that could make me feel as light as a feather and hot fiery breath that was ready to be released at any given time.

"Now," said Nicole's voice starting to fade away. "What do you see and hear?"

I concentrated and felt a shiver go through my body. I listened and heard Pearl's voice.

"To fly all you need to do is stretch out your wings and feel the wind start to pick you up," she said.

"I . . . I can hear Pearl's voice. She's giving Nightly instructions on how to fly," I said. "I can feel his wings stretch out, readying himself to fly."

"Good." Nicole's voice turned into a soft whisper. "Now, try to see what Nightly can see. Try to open your eyes."

I tried opening my eyes but I couldn't. Everything was black. That's when I realized Nightly must of had his eyes closed.

"Don't be frightened," Pearl called out, *"Just open your eyes. Dragons can't fear flight, they can only embrace it."*

I could feel the tension in Nightly's body build. He opened his eyes slowly. I could see what he was seeing. He was only two feet off the ground but I could feel a smile appear on my face as Nightly smiled. He started to rise higher and higher till he was ten feet off the ground. The wind felt wonderful underneath his wings.

Feels great doesn't it?

Nightly, how can you hear me? I'm talking with my mind, aren't I?

Didn't you feel it? Our minds are in sync with each other. I can hear what you're thinking and you can hear what I am thinking. It's our private connection that every whisperer has with their dragon and no one else can hear it except us.

Then can you tell me what I'm hearing, seeing and feeling?

No, that's too advanced for us. Right now you're focussing on me. When I try this trick that you're doing right now I'll be able to see things from your perspective of your human life.

Whatever made me see through Nightly's perspective vanished as I watched my little black dragon soar above me. He lowered himself down and grabbed my shoulders with his back feet.

"Nightly, what are you doing?" I asked, looking up at him.

"I'm giving you your first flight lesson."

"Oh, boy," said James.

"It seems every dragon wants their whisperer to fly with them when they first learn how to fly," said Malcolm pushing his glasses up on his face.

"Wait, I can't fly," I shouted.

Nightly had already dug his claws into my shoulder and started to lift me up. I loosened my body and watched as my feet left the ground.

"Have a nice flight," said Teddy, winking at me.

My body started to tense up as we rose higher. I looked down at Pearl who had been ignoring us ever since Nightly flew over to me. I turned my attention back to Nightly and watched as he and I rose to ten feet off the ground, then fifteen feet. There was only five more feet to go before I would be free. When I looked up at Nightly's face I saw excitement as we were only inches away from edge of the ravine. We were almost out—almost free from a place that refused to let me go.

My phone alarm went off.

Nightly freaked out, he lost his grip on me dropping me into the trees. I crashed through branches, scaring birds along the way down. Once I finally broke through the last couple of branches James caught me.

"Thanks, James," I managed to say. As I looked up at him, there appeared to be multiple images of James moving around in the air.

"No problem, little lady," he said with a smile.

James put me down and watched me wobble around on the ground. That fall really knocked my brain around.

"Incoming," Malcolm yelled.

By the time I looked up I was back on the ground lying on my stomach. I lifted my head and found Nightly sitting up on my back.

"Nightly," I whispered breathlessly " . . . get off me!" When Nightly jumped off me I slowly crawled to a tree a used it as leverage to pull myself up. Still feeling a little dizzy, I started to fall over. James caught me before I hit the ground. "Thanks," I mumbled.

"Sorry Connie," Nightly said, walking over to me. *"When I heard the noise coming from your phone, it startled me and I lost my grip on you."*

"I'm surprised you could even lift me," I sighed as I knelt down and patted his head. "That alarm was for me to go home."

"It's only five," said Teddy, looking at his watch. "Why would you have to go home now?"

"It's early on school nights," I said in a gloomy voice. "It's just in case I need to do my homework or have some studying to do." I hated the birthday curfew.

"Talk about an over protective parent," said Nicole. "But we need to do something before you go."

Nightly and I both stared at her.

"That mark on the back of your shoulders is noticeable to other humans. It might even give away your position to mages. That's why we're going to use Nightly's ability to cover it up."

"Do we really have time for this?" I groaned. "If I don't get home soon, I won't even be able to see you guys for a week."

"It'll be quick, I promise," said Nicole.

"Well, even if you arrive late I'll just go to your house and talk to your mom," said Teddy with a grin. "I have always had an interest in older women."

"For one thing, my mom is married; secondly, if she meets you do you really think she won't be suspicious?" I asked.

"She does have a good point," said Malcolm pushing Teddy aside. "It would be best if we never met your family unless anyone wants to give away your secret." Everyone looked at me, "You haven't told anyone, right?"

"Of course not," I shot back at them. "I doubt anyone would believe me anyways."

Nightly walked over and nudged my leg. *"Let's go."*

I looked back and saw everyone sighing in relief. I began to walk away when Nicole grabbed me.

"Hold out your hand," she said.

I did what she told me to do, knowing I couldn't waste any time. Nicole took out a switch blade and cut the palm of my hand.

"What did you do that for?" I yelled, clutching my hand quickly before I could see the blood.

Nicole said nothing and did the same thing to Nightly. I don't know if it was my imagination or not but I thought I could feel the knife go through my hand again when she cut Nightly. Nightly didn't flinch at all. Nicole then started to scratch him under his chin. He hummed and then Nicole stopped as one of Nightly's black scales dropped onto the ground.

She picked it up and walked over to me. "Alright, now that that's done I need you to touch Nightly's paw that's bleeding. Once you do that both of you will be joined not just by mind but by blood."

"Then what's the scale for?" I asked.

"Dragon scales are good for two things," explained Nicole holding out the scale to me. "You can melt them down and create one of the most powerful weapons or armour in the world. Two, for new whisperer's they can use it for training. I'm going to give you this scale and you have to keep it on you the whole time. The scale will hide your mark until you learn how to control Nightly's power yourself."

"That's where the blood connection comes in," said James. "Both of you will be connected to each other, learning how each other works and who each other truly is."

"So, all I have to do is touch Nightly's paw that's bleeding then I will be able to access his ability?" I asked.

Nicole nodded.

I crouched down to Nightly's height, without looking, I opened my hand in front of Nightly. Nightly lifted his bleeding paw and placed it against my bleeding hand. When our hands touched it felt like the weather changed. As our blood met it felt like a storm had approached bringing with it an electric vibe and a cold sensation that went through my body from head to toe. You would think that it would be an awesome feeling but it felt like being tasered. Once we parted our hands I found my hair down in front of my face. I glanced down on the ground and saw my elastic broken. I reached for it slowly and grabbed it.

"Well," went Teddy, "how was it?"

I shook the electric feeling out of my body then looked up at everyone dazed. I stood up and brushed off my clothes.

"Painful, that's all I can say," I said grabbing my books. I pulled out the sweater I left for Nightly when he was newly hatched and laid it in front of him. "I want you to stay here tonight."

Nicole tossed me the scale. I placed it in my pocket along with my broken elastic.

"Why?" he asked in a sad voice.

"I need you to stay here and train while I'm at home. I think my mom is starting to become suspicious about all the food I'm bringing into my room."

"But I want to stay with you," he said grabbing my leg.

I trudged over to the part of the wall I marked with the rock and put my hand through the fake wall. Nightly remained attached to my leg, refusing to let go.

"Can someone please get him off of me?" I begged.

Pearl stretched out her neck and picked Nightly up with her mouth like a mother cat would do to her kitten. Pearl pulled me across the ground for a bit until James came over and grabbed my arms, pulling against Pearl. Nightly refused to let go until he heard me cry out in pain, his claws sunk in past the fabric of my pants and into my flesh.

"I'll be back," I promised, "I'll see you after school."

"Bye," he whispered, in a worried voice, *"I miss you already."*

Then I left, limping down the passageway.

When I arrived home, I took the scale out of my pocket along with the broken elastic and started to fiddle with them. I took the broken elastic and tied it through another one I had making a dragon scale elastic anklet.

I always had a habit of collecting broken elastics. I thought that something broken can always be used to make something better.

Once I finished the elastic anklet I put it on my right ankle, I took off my shirt then glanced in my mirror. There were no dragon wings on my shoulder blades. I sighed in relief. Something was still bothering me. As I pulled my hair back into a new ponytail I asked myself, "Why were the Guardians so persistent to have Nightly with them?"

CHAPTER 9

A Dragon at School

I tossed and turned in my bed that night trying to find the most comfortable spot but there was no use. I've had Nightly for over a week and I was already used to him sleeping with me. I missed him. I stared up at the ceiling and thought about how Nightly was doing. Was he warm? Was he scared of thunder? Did he miss me?

No, I realized that I shouldn't say that because it was really me who missed him. When I finally fell asleep I kept seeing images of Nightly flying through the sky enjoying life. It made me cry.

When I awoke the next morning I saw the path that the tears made down my face. I washed them away quickly so that no one would see that I, Connie, had cried. I have always been the tough girl, never scared. Why? Because I want to protect my friends but I'm afraid if I show that I'm weak, I'm afraid someone will hurt the people close to me.

I followed the usual routine to get ready for the day and then hitched a ride to school with Kyle. When I got to school, I went straight to my locker and found Sam and Judy waiting for me.

"Hey guys," I said in a cheerful voice. "What's going on?"

"I think you know what's going on," Judy said crossing her arms.

I put on a nervous look. "Look, I don't know what you have heard but it's not what you think."

Sam avoided eye contact.

"You've been avoiding us since the school year started," said Judy. "Something's going on and we want to know, here and now!"

I gulped. I was worried that they might have found out about Nightly. I was in trouble.

Judy approached me and then placed one hand on her hips and the other hand was pointing a finger at me. "Who's the guy you've been sneaking off to see?"

"What are you talking about?!" I asked, stunned.

"Who is the guy you've been ditching us for?" repeated Judy.

I burst out laughing. They both stared at me thinking that I might be crazy.

"What's so funny?!" Judy demanded.

I wiped a tear from my eye. "I'm not seeing anyone. I've just been busy at home for the most part."

Sam sighed in relief, I guessed.

"Now, if you'll excuse me, I need to get my books before class starts," I said pushing them out of the way. "I'll see you both in class."

"Well, I still think there is something going on with you," said Judy walking away. "-and I'm going to figure it out sooner or later."

She stormed off, leaving Sam and me behind by my locker to chat.

I turned towards Sam while opening up my locker. "Please say she didn't tell the whole school this already?"

Sam leaned on the locker beside mine and nodded slowly.

I hit my head on my locker door. "Why? Why does she do that? It's not like I have enough on my hands with my dad coming home next week." That's when I realized what I just said. Mom told me to keep my mouth closed till Dad actually arrived at home.

I looked at Sam and he just looked more shocked when I first heard the news. "Your dad's coming back? Well, aren't you excited?"

I bit my lip, grabbed my books and closed my locker. "Of course I am. It's just . . ." I sighed. "The last time he said he was coming home, he never did. Mom said she was absolutely sure he's coming back but I doubt it."

Sam scratched his head then rubbed my cheek. "Don't worry so much, Connie. He's going to come back this time." He then backed away, blushed, and turned away from me. "I'll see you in class."

I watched as he walked off. Then I headed towards my Food's class. Judy and I were at the same station and she was still trying to figure out what I was hiding when I left them after school. I ignored her, but it was easier to ignore her then it was with our other classmates who were whispering about me.

I leaned over to Judy, "can you please not tell the whole school what you assume I'm doing after school?"

"Then tell me what you're actually dong after school and I'll fix it," said Judy.

"Miss Bachor and Miss Whitsburg!" yelled Mrs. Blue the Food's teacher in her French accent. "Quit talking and pay attention."

"Now, today we are going to talk about cheese," she said walking towards us. "And we're going to taste three different kinds."

Some of the kids made gagging noises, which caught Mrs. Blue's attention.

"We're going to start with my personal favourite: blue cheese," she said.

Again, the kids gagged. She went to the fridge and took out three different types of cheese. The biggest one was blue cheese. The others were Gruyere and Edam. She placed a plate at each station.

Judy looked at me and then I knew I had to go first. "I'm not a big fan of cheese so can you . . ."

I sighed then took a piece of the Gruyere; it tasted soft and creamy. Next came the Edam, which tasted like a fluffy cloud. I didn't want to try the blue cheese but then Mrs. Blue stared at me. I picked up a piece, plugged my nose, then took a bite, and you know what? I was running to the sink faster than a Piranha could eat its prey.

"Well, what did you think?" asked Mrs. Blue.

Everyone glared at her and then at Judy and me. If we hadn't been talking, we wouldn't have to do this.

Judy waited till Mrs. Blue wasn't looking and then whispered, "hey, don't you think that Mrs. Blue actually looks a little like blue cheese but with red hair and glasses?"

I glanced over my shoulder taking a good look at her and then turned back around and nodded.

By lunch time Mrs. Blue was known as the red headed Blue cheese. I was actually glad Judy told that story around the school because it kept everyone's mind off me. I went to our regular eating spot behind the school on the bench. I met Sam there and sat down beside him.

"So, the word around the school now is that you're not the only one being talked about," he said, "what happened in Foods?"

"Nothing really except for the cheese tasting," I said, eating a grape. "And don't believe anyone when they say that blue cheese smells worse than it tastes."

Sam broke out into laughter and so did I. He looked at me. We both smiled at each other. Judy then happened to appear out from behind the bench.

"Hey, love birds," she said.

Sam and I both jumped away from each other and blushed. Judy laughed then sat in between us.

"Just kidding guys, but I have to say that you two would look cute as a couple."

"No way," I said, "Besides my mom gave me the 'talk' and clearly stated that I can't date until I'm out of high school."

"Well that sucks," Judy stated, "right, Sam?"

Sam looked at me, blushed and nodded.

I sighed and then looked towards the school's baseball field. There were seagulls picking at the trashcan again. But then I saw a black tail go around the corner of the school. I got up and went after it.

"Connie, where are you going?" asked Judy.

"Just to check out something," I said. I ran around the corner and found nothing. I figured it was just part of my imagination but, just out of curiosity, I ran around the next corner and crashed into Teddy. "Teddy! What are you doing here?"

"Well hello to you, too. We've got a problem though," he said, as he brushed off dust.

"Teddy, did you find Nightly?" James asked coming around the corner.

I could have told you that I was going to burst into tears, I could have told you that I ran from them and started to search for Nightly myself, but then I would be lying. Instead, I stood my ground and took a swing at Teddy but I missed him because James held me back.

"Let me go!" I yelled.

"Calm down, Connie. You'll just draw attention to yourself," said James.

"You lost my dragon! Why should I trust you now or ever?" I demanded.

"Because we want to protect you and your dragon," said Teddy. "We lost our dragons now we're trying to make up for their deaths by helping you."

"If you were with your dragon 24/7 the mages would surly find you and take your dragon's life along with yours," said James.

"Where's my dragon?" I asked more calmly now.

"A dragon will most likely go to their whisperer when they don't believe they're under good care with the other people they're with," explained Teddy backing away. "We knew you'd be in school. That's the only reason why we came out here."

"I haven't seen him at all. It's obvious that he's not here," I said to him slowly.

James rubbed his head and then tipped his hat down. "Fine, we'll leave but if anything comes up, call us."

"Without any violence," said Teddy.

"I only use violence if necessary, like say if someone loses my dragon," I said.

"We'll be leaving now, later, Connie," said James leaving along with Teddy.

That's when the school bell went. Now I had to run back and lie to Sam and Judy again, run to my locker get my English books and go to my class. This day was just getting better and better. Yeah right.

After I got into my English class, I stared out the window the whole time wondering where Nightly was. Judy had to nudge me a couple of times to get my attention back on my work but nothing was working. I sighed and stared out the window again and then turned my attention back to the white board. The teacher looked at me awkwardly.

"Connie, are you alright?" she asked.

I sat up straight and noticed the whole class was staring at me. "Yes."

"Then how come your left eye is gold?" asked Judy.

She handed me her compact and I looked in the mirror. I gasped. My left eye was really gold.

"Miss Twon, may I go to my locker?" I asked.

She nodded slowly and, as soon as she did, I ran out of the classroom. I ran to my locker, opened it and tumbling out of it was my black dragon.

"Hi ya, how's English?" asked Nightly.

"Nightly, what are you doing here? And did you happen to get bigger over night?" I asked noticing that Nightly was almost up to my chin.

"Yeah, Nicole gave me some special food pellets and I grew after I ate them."

"Are you the reason why my left eye is gold?"

"I don't know. Maybe that's one of the side effects from doing mind sequence; besides, your eye isn't gold anymore so there is nothing to worry about."

I looked into my locker mirror and saw my hazel eyes. "Aren't you supposed to be training with Pearl and the rest of the Guardians?"

"Maybe . . ."

"What do you mean by 'maybe'? You can't just come to me whenever you like. Especially during school, Nightly!"

"What's the big deal? You're allowed to come and see me any time you'd like."

"That's because you can't be seen by regular people or else they'll go medieval on us."

"Fine I'll leave, but you have to bring me a treat later, like pancakes."

I heard footsteps coming down the hall and I panicked. "Quick, Nightly, back into the locker!" Before he could respond, I shoved him into my locker, slammed the door shut, and watched as Judy came down the hall looking for me. "Hey, Judy."

"Is everything alright Connie? How's your eye?" she asked.

I looked at her and showed her my hazel eyes. "It's better. Actually, nothing was really bothering me. It must have been the lighting in the classroom."

The locker door opened a little but then I slammed it closed again.

"What's in the locker?" Judy asked.

"Nothing," my stomach turned.

"Well, it's obviously something. Are you hiding someone in there?"

"No," but I could tell that I didn't sound convincing.

Judy pushed me aside and started to decode my lock. "I'm going to find out what you're hiding."

"Judy, please stop," I pleaded trying to pry her away from my locker.

I was able to get her away from the locker but not in enough time that she decoded my lock. We both watched as the door slowly opened. My heart was pounding. I almost thought it would jump out of my chest. When the door opened far enough, all we saw was a normal locker with nothing in it.

I sighed in relief. "See, I told you there was nothing in there."

Judy went up to the locker and slammed it shut. The noise of the door would shake Mount Everest. "Dang it, I was positive you were hiding something in there. I will catch you and him in the act."

"Well, it can't be today. Class is almost over and we still don't understand the old English plays that Shakespeare wrote," I said.

"Fine, I'll go back but you owe me a shopping day," yelled Judy.

"Yes, alright, whatever, just go!"

Judy smiled at me then ran down the hall. I sighed again and then opened my locker door. Nightly tumbled out and landed on his belly.

"Owe," Nightly whined. *"First I was shoved into a locker not once but twice, then the door slams in my face and then the locker vibrates because your friend can't control her strength."*

"Sorry about that, Nightly."

"That's it! I'm never visiting you at school ever again!" He turned invisible and stormed off.

I couldn't help but laugh. Well at least one thing worked out for me today. Nightly wouldn't be visiting me at school ever again.

CHAPTER 10

Dad

Throughout the whole week, I had to stay away from Nightly. It broke my heart as well as his. I couldn't believe we managed it . . . alright, partially. Every now and then, Nightly would appear before me.

I had to send him back every time but you should have seen Glen's face in the last S.R.P. It was brighter than his pink shirt. Nightly bit him in the pants because of the way he was teaching the session. Apparently we had to help each other read a medieval book from when we were five. The point of it was to read the book out loud to your sibling without getting sprayed. The one who wasn't reading had a spray bottle and they had to resist the temptation to spray the other one. It didn't work out so well. The book we read was 'Sleeping Beauty'.

Glen overdid it when he started to babble about how wonderful the scene was when the sword pierced the dragon and he may have mentioned that it was the best part of the book. I bet you could have imagined what Nightly was thinking at that point. Nightly attacked Glen while he was still invisible and bit right down at the rear area and tore off a piece of his pants and stormed out of the room. It was one of the funniest yet scariest things I've ever seen. Even though Glen was humiliated everyone in the 'Sibling Respect Program' we all got a view of the nasty rear end that belonged to Glen Castleman.

I didn't understand though, why the Guardians didn't want me to see Nightly over the last week. I even went to the secret area but as usual Pearl was guarding the entrance from afar and always snapped at me with her pearl white, sharp teeth that could easily kill me. I felt kind of lonely after Nightly stopped coming to me. It was already Saturday and the next day would be October first. No matter what I tried to think of, Nightly would always appear in my mind in one way or another.

I stayed at home that evening just lying on my bed studying for an English test when Kyle barged in.

"Connie, what are you doing?" he asked.

I looked up and glared at him. "What does it look like? I'm studying for a test which helps me get better grades. Try it sometime; it just might help yours."

Kyle laughed sarcastically then started to talk seriously. "Have you forgotten who's coming home today?"

That's when it hit me. "Crap, he's coming today?"

"Yeah, and unlike you, I'm ready to greet Dad into this clean household."

"Kyle, you do know that you're wearing a green alien shirt that still has a ketchup and mustard stain on it from Uncle Frank's surprise hot dog birthday party, and you have not cleaned your room since the fourth grade?"

Kyle made another sarcastic laugh and then walked up to me and gave me a noogie. "Well, at least I'll be the first one to greet him."

I elbowed him in the stomach and ran to the door. "Not if I get there first."

We both booked it for the front door and opened it. We saw nothing. It was a big fuss over nothing. He wasn't even home yet. I plopped myself on the couch and pulled out an old photo album. Kyle wheezed and went to the kitchen eating some of his so called 'private candy stash'.

"You know, that's how a lot of people get acne," I said blowing dust off the album.

"Shut up," he said chewing on a Mars bar.

I ignored him and opened the album. Inside I saw loads of pictures of Mom and Dad when they were first dating. Then it went into their college years, family reunions and their wedding day. I'd seen these pictures a thousand times but I always liked to go through them again and again. As I flipped through the wedding photos, I stopped at a picture of Mom and Dad feeding each other cake; when I thought I saw Devonburg in the background. I went back to my room and quickly grabbed my glasses.

Alright, here's the story. I had the best vision you could get, fifteen-twenty. Then, one day, I got hit in the head extremely hard, not so hard that I had a concussion but hard enough that my vision got all messed up so I needed glasses whenever I had to look at something like a far off object or if I had to examine something.

I put the glasses on and then ran back to the album. To my surprise, it was really Devonburg in the photo. I was curious and then took a look at another album. I flipped through the pages and came across a picture of myself when I was six months old. Again, there was Devonburg in the background. I didn't and couldn't understand why. My head started to hurt. I grabbed it and shook it. Could Dad have known about dragons when he was younger? Then, I heard keys rustling. I put the albums back and then walked to the door. It slowly opened and I found my Dad.

My dad was a tall man who wore a Mexican soccer shirt, black work pants and dress shoes. He was sort of a business man mixed with a soccer player. He had dirty blond hair, hazel eyes and a tattoo of some sort of language on his right arm. I've tried searching up the meaning of it on the computer and it's something that's not even in the books. Whatever it was, it wasn't human related.

I ran up to him and gave him a hug. "Nice to have you back again, Dad."

My dad rubbed my back. "It's nice to be back, Connie. Hey, you're wearing your glasses," he said pushing me back a little. "I hardly ever see them on you and you know what? You really do make them look good."

My brother poked his head around the corner and dropped his jaw. The Snicker's bar he was eating landed on mom's clean white carpet. He walked up to Dad and shook his hand.

"Nice to have you back, old man," he commented.

"Good to see you, little man," Dad replied. "Where's your mother?"

"She figured you wouldn't arrive till late tonight so she decided to go shopping," said Kyle.

"Then let's surprise her by making dinner tonight," Dad suggested.

We all agreed and then went into the kitchen. I got to work on the noodles while Dad and Kyle worked on the sauce. I was happy that we were cooking together. It had been too long since we did this but the moment disappeared when I felt a nudge on my leg. When I tried to ignore it, the nudge turned into shove. I couldn't believe Nightly was here again, of all times. I didn't say anything as I calmly walked away to go to my bedroom. That's when Nightly appeared on my bed.

"Who's the guy in your kitchen and what's that on your face?"

I sighed and took my glasses off. "These are just something I need to help me read things sometimes. The man in the kitchen is my father, Nightly. I know I should have told you about his return but I didn't think it really mattered to you."

"So your dad's back; that's great. If that was all that was bugging you, I would understand but I hope he's better than your brother. If not, I think we're in for trouble."

I laughed. "Of course he's not, but I'm sorry."

"Connie!" cried Dad and Kyle.

I looked at Nightly and he nodded. I kissed him on his head then left the room. For some reason I felt a whole lot better. I went into the kitchen and found the sauce burning.

"Help!" they both whined.

I ran over and turned off the stove and placed a lid over the pot. Dad and Kyle were both humiliated and not for the first time. I shook my head, placed the stove on low heat and then had Kyle stir the sauce. I finished cooking the noodles as Dad set the table. Once everything was finished, we waited for Mom to come home. Luckily, we didn't have to wait too long. When Mom walked into the house she had a stunned look on her face. Silence filled the household as Mom and Dad stared at each other. Usually, this would be the great happy home makers welcome; instead Mom was giving Dad a death, icy stare.

Kyle pulled me aside. As the awkward silence continued the two of us quietly crept back into our rooms and waited.

Uh! I hated this! I wanted to know what they were talking about and, more importantly, I wanted to know who Devonburg was to them.

I paced up and down my room. "Uh, I want to know what they're talking about." Nightly sat on my bed and watched me walk back and forth. It was kind of cute to see his head bob from one side to the other.

That's when an idea struck me. "Hey, Nightly, you want to practice our mind sequence?"

"Sure, I've been trying to do that with you all week," he said, gliding over to the door.

"Good, but I need you to go outside into the living room so I can try the long distance connection."

"In other words, you want me to spy on your parent's."

"Would you do it, please?" I begged.

"Fine, but I get leftovers," I opened the door and watched my dragon vanish. The only way I could tell that he was in the hall was by the footsteps. His nails tapped against the hardwood floor.

I then got into position. I crossed my legs and relaxed. I thought about being Nightly like Nicole taught me to. I closed my eyes and my vision changed to what Nightly was seeing and hearing. I saw my dad sitting on the coach and my mom was pacing up and down the living room.

"I'm actually surprised you showed up this time," she said. "From what you've said over the phone, I was hoping you wouldn't show. Every time you come home, Devonburg's never that far behind. It was already creepy enough that we knew him for a majority of our lives and still stayed connected with him but I've always hated him, especially when he would talk about . . . well you know what." Mom stopped and hugged herself. "I even hated your idealistic thought of actually listening to that madman to move here in the first place. Ever since Connie was born, our children have never seen the outside of this ravine. I just want-"

"Martha, Devonburg's dead," Dad interrupted. "He resigned from work about a month and a half ago and has been missing since." He sighed. "I remember when we last spoke that he would soon be leaving this world and handing his will off personally." Dad stood up and took one of Mom's hands.

Mom was quiet and then leaned on the wall. I had never seen my mom like this. She has always loved living here with me and Kyle. Why did she hate Devonburg so much and what did he always talk about?

Dad wrapped Mom in his arms, holding her as she shook. "You know that Devonburg and I have been friends forever. You were once his friend too. Every decision I've made was to make sure our family was safe; you know that."

Mom looked up at Dad and pushed him away from her. "I don't want our children to feel like they're suppressed by the world. They've been here long enough! Let them out."

"You know why I won't allow that," Dad said, starting to raise his voice.

"What about the times when we were young and ran off doing who knows what? You can't assume our children are going to end up in the same situations we got into with Devonburg."

"True," agreed Dad. "But how many times have we been confronted by strange people, Martha? I don't blame you for hating Devonburg, but don't I have the right to protect my own children from the terrors of the world?"

Mom didn't say anything.

"Our children are still young. They don't know what's out there and now that Devonburg's gone, I'll be staying here from now on to keep an eye on everything just as I did when we got locked in the museum and were accused of stealing from it. Even though it was Devonburg who saved us from the charges and cleared our names, I made sure nothing happened to either one of us, right?"

Mom mumbled something.

"What?"

"Right," she answered.

"Now, I'm going to clear up a little mishap with our children, after that's done we'll finally start living like a normal family for once," Dad said.

'Live as a normal family for once?' What was Dad talking about and what the heck was the connection between Devonburg and him?

The connection broke. I heard Nightly scratch the floor underneath his claws as he made his way to my room. I opened the door for Nightly; he quickly rushed in and hid under the bed. As I started to close the door, Dad called out my name.

"Hey, Dad, how was the talk with Mom?" I asked, opening the door back up.

"Regularly pleasant," he said. I knew he was lying because that conversation didn't sound pleasant at all. "But, Connie, did you happen to bump into a strange man at all in the last month while I was away?"

"Well, that's hard to say, Dad. After all, we do live in a strange place," I said.

"Not strange enough to attract a strange man like the one I'm thinking of," he said.

"Can you give me a description or a name? Maybe that'll jog my memory," I went and sat on my bed.

"Uh, well, tall, old man, beard, scar on the lip, trench coat and no shoes," Dad thought for a bit and then looked at me awkwardly.

"No name?" I asked.

"Devonburg," he said turning his back to me.

I was silent.

"Doesn't ring a bell, huh?" He kept his back turned to me. He shook his head.

I gulped. It was never good when he shook his head.

"It doesn't matter anyways; he died a while ago. I just thought he would have come here to speak his final words."

I bit my lip. I couldn't possibly tell Dad about Nightly, let alone Devonburg giving him to me in the first place. I could sense Nightly shaking. I knew Devonburg's last words too. This conversation was going nowhere. I felt like I was being interrogated; why? "What makes you think he would come here?" I asked.

"Oh, he always had an interest in this place. Are you sure you never met a strange man this past month?" Dad slowly turned his head to look at me.

My stomach turned. "Nope, no crazy people like that around here."

Dad sighed. "Fine, I'll keep it a secret," and with that said and done, he left the room.

Nightly then came out from underneath the bed. *"What did he mean when he said he would keep it a secret?"*

"I don't know," I admitted. "Dad always has something up his sleeve." I looked at Nightly. "Why are you here anyways?"

"Oh, right," Nightly said stretching. *"I can stay with you now. The training for this week was working on our mind sequence. My job was to go to you every day and practice it. But when you sent me back I had to return and work on my flying instead."*

"And how's that going for you?" I asked, ticked.

"It's going great, why do you ask?"

"Because you're going to need it to get away from me," I said jumping off the bed and landing on the floor watching Nightly fly up to the ceiling. "You've got me acting stupid in front of the whole town just because you wanted to train."

"Yes, exactly," he said soaring over to the window.

"Oh no, you don't," I said grabbing his tail and pulling him down to the ground. "You're not going anywhere."

We wrestled for the rest of the evening and even missed dinner because of it. We had fun though. It was nice to have my dragon back in a place where I knew I could keep a close eye on him. When we fell asleep together once again, it made me feel good for the time being. I wish I had never fallen asleep, though.

I dreamt that I was sitting in a chair and my eyes were blindfolded. I could hear two voices talking in the same room with me. It sounded like they were arguing.

"I'm not going to be a part of it," stated the first voice.

"Do you have a problem with it?" demanded the second voice. "You've done this before."

"That's only because you've made me! I've been with you all my life and you've only ruined lives, from what I have seen."

"We haven't ruined lives; we've been helping the humans to be exact."

"Oh, and for you that would be accusing a random person off the streets that they're a dragon's whisperer and torture them until they admit to it."

I heard something that sounded like a fist slam against a face. "Do you even realize what the dragon's made us into, what we look like now?"

"Yes, but-"

"Are you forgetting that our kind was burned at the stake and decapitated at the guillotine?"

"No."

"Don't you want revenge for what they did to ruin your life?"

"Yes . . . but in a whole different way!"

"Does it really matter what way we get our revenge as long as it's done? So you will be there on the thirty-first at nineteen hundred hours, sharp!"

"What . . . what will you do once you have the whisperer?"

That's when I felt a force tightly wrap around my neck and start to squeeze. All the feeling in my body went numb.

"I will grab the whisperer by her neck, wait till her face goes pale and for the dragon to arrive. When he arrives I'll take his life then leave the whisperer to grieve in her own thoughts as she loses a part of herself."

I suddenly woke up, "Nightly?!"

I looked down at my side and Nightly slowly open his eyes. *"What, bad dream?"*

"Something like that except, I think it was about mages planning to try and expose us, and kill us."

Nightly was wide awake a scooted closer to me even though he nearly took up the whole bed. I rested my head on my knees.

Nightly, I said through our private connection, *let's hope it was just a dream and never becomes reality.*

Alright, but try and get some sleep tonight.

I'll try, but who was I kidding? I got up and leaned my head on the window. I placed my hand on the frame and looked up at the crescent moon. I don't know why but I believed that I knew who those people were and what they said was bad news.

CHAPTER 11

Halloween Flood

Weeks passed and soon Halloween arrived in Small Valley. I didn't have a costume nor did I want one. They were way too expensive and the home made ones only worked for children up to a certain age before they became tacky. This Halloween I was going to spend it with Nightly since some people declare dragons as demons I thought it would be a good way to spend it.

As for the Guardians, they were both giving me a hard time. The Guardians had been making me and Nightly practice mind sequence while we were both moving and I have to tell you that it was not easy. I had to focus on Nightly while being out of my comfortable position with my eyes open. I would always get sparks but never a full connection.

Then there was my dad. He came into my room every night asking if I was sure I didn't run into a strange man. After the seventh day of his interrogation, I almost spilled my guts out but I knew that's what he wanted. Instead, I kept myself together and continued to give him the same answer I had given him the first time he asked me. In the end I felt like the villain because Dad would always leave my room with a disappointing look on his face. I hated when I disappointed my parents. It made me feel uneasy.

Nightly and I were finishing up our training for the day when Nicole decided to feed him another special food pellet. Again, Nightly grew until he was taller then I. He was almost as tall as an average basketball player. Now it was time for a different exercise.

James came out of the Guardians newly finished house and placed a saddle on Nightly. The saddle was larger than a regular horse saddle with a few modifications to it. He then beckoned me forward. "Listen up, Connie, from today on you'll be flying Nightly."

"What? Have you forgotten what happened the last time I tried to fly with him?"

"No, but that was when Nightly was up to your knees. Now that he's bigger and stronger than you it won't be as difficult."

"But I don't even know how," I said, patting Nightly. "And why isn't anyone else helping out?"

Nightly stomped his back foot on the ground as I scratched his scales.

James smiled and rubbed his head. "It's because each of us is better at a different part of dragon training than the rest. For me I am the best at flying, Nicole is the best with communicating with dragons; Malcolm's strength is in strategies and Teddy's is stealth and force. Now let us continue," James tightened the saddle and then put a leather belt around me. "This is my old saddle and I've fallen off it plenty of time to know that you need at least two things to keep you on. One is that clip on the belt I placed on you, it hooks onto the front of the saddle to keep you from flying off; the next thing is the leg straps on the side. There are only two straps on each side so it's very easy to put on and take off. They keep you centered on your saddle."

I went up to Nightly and looked at the saddle. "Are you sure it's safe?"

"Absolutely, it's like riding a horse but in the sky. Now, jump on and let's get you started."

James helped me up onto the saddle and strapped my legs in while I clipped the belt onto the saddle.

"Are you ready for the real flying experience?" asked Nightly, crouching down.

"Not really," I said nervously.

"Alright, Connie, you're ready to go. I need you to hold onto the saddle the whole time, lean forward to, and make sure that the straps are tight enough," said James checking them. "There is one more thing I must tell you. Make sure your feet always face outward in your leg straps. Now, don't be nervous."

"I'm not nervous," I stated.

"Relax, every whisperer who learns to fly with their dragon is," said James backing away.

"Now that we're ready, let's get going," said Nightly excited.

"Hey, Nightly, try some flips like what we practiced yesterday," suggested Pearl.

"Alright," said Nightly excited.

"Wait, Nightly, Connie, isn't ready for that extreme flying yet. Take it easy," James said, trying to calm Nightly down.

Nightly had already taken off with me along for the ride. I don't know how to explain it. In the beginning, all I felt was Nightly's cold dark scales on my face as the pressure forced me down on his back. The sharpness of the scales cut my cheek. After we stopped shooting up into the sky; I nearly found myself flying off the saddle if it wasn't for the leg straps and the clip on the leather belt holding me down. Once I got used to the high altitude my head stopped spinning. I took a look around and saw that I was finally out of the ravine. The ravine was right below my feet but something caught my eye and it was the way the ravine was shaped. It seemed like the ravine was curving in different ways making markings. I've seen those marking before, but from where?

"Hey, how do you like the view?" asked Nightly.

"It's beautiful," I replied, "but can you fly a bit higher and to the east more?"

"That's not even a challenge. Come on, Connie, I've been flying for a month now. Can't you give me something more difficult to do?"

"We'll do a flip on the way back, come on, hurry up."

"Fine we'll do it your way."

Nightly flew to the east and up higher. This time I actually remembered to hold onto the saddle so I wouldn't cut myself on the scales again. Once we slowed down I took a good glance at the ravine again. You wouldn't believe what I saw.

"Connie, are you seeing what I'm seeing?"

"Yeah," down below us we saw the ravine, shaped into a dragon egg. I was living right in the center of it. Water took up a huge section of it, mostly the top with two dams holding it back but allowing some water to pass through the ravine making a river. "Let's get back to the others Nightly, we can tell them about our-"

Nightly started to growl.

"What is it?"

"Something's wrong at the top of the ravine. It feels like the same thing I felt that night when I trashed the place you and your friends were in; the night we called the Guardians. We have to go and check it out."

"What, we can't do that!"

"Sure we can, and you want to know why? Because I'm the dragon and you are just simply riding me. I get to choose where to go. Hold on!"

It was no use fighting with him. He would only ignore me anyways. We flew back into the ravine and through it. I couldn't believe how fast we were going. Everything around us was a blur. If I wasn't so worried about being tossed off or figuring out what Nightly was upset about, I would have been having the time of my life. We flew for half an hour dodging rocks and boulders, then stopping at one of the dams. I looked at the small amount of water that was allowed to flow through the ravine. I looked at the dam and noticed something; something was placed underneath the bridge and another thing by the rails. I took out my glasses and examined it closer and saw explosives.

"This isn't good Connie. If that dam goes-"

"So does Small Valley. Quick, we have to deactivate them."

"It won't work," Nightly flew back out of the ravine. *"If you hadn't noticed, we are already invisible. If you jump off my back you'll become visible again."*

I looked at my hands and saw that they were transparent. It was true; I really was invisible. I also saw a few people tending the dam. If we tried to deactivate the bombs, we would be noticed.

"Let's head back and tell the others what we see."

"Agreed, it's better than staying here."

Again we took off. We had no time to do any tricks. This was life or death happening. We had to get back in time. It took us less time to fly back to the secret area than it took to go to the dam. That scared us even more. There was a down draft in the ravine. If those bombs went off, that water would be at Small Valley in no time flat.

We landed back in the secret area, Nightly turned visible and James came over and started to un-strap me. "You were gone for a while, did you enjoy it?" James looked up at me, "I didn't know you wore glasses."

I took the glasses off and put them away. Once James unstrapped me I jumped off and grabbed him by the shirt and breathed in his face.

"There are . . . there are . . . there are explosives at the dam deep within the ravine. It could blow at any time now."

James grabbed my wrists, "whoa, little girl, now what's this talk about explosives?"

That's when Nightly and I got a hold of everyone's attention. We told them what we saw; when I told them that it reminded me of the dream I had a month ago. This is what they, the mages, could have been talking about. I told them about the dream I had, the mages plan.

"That's very peculiar that you've had warning dream and that Nightly could sense the danger from far away," said Malcolm, intrigued.

"I've never heard anything about it," said Teddy, "and I came from Las Vegas, Nevada."

"What's that got to do with this? Anyways, what we need to do is get the town to safety just in case we can't stop the flood," said Nicole. "Malcolm, I need you to think up a plan to stop the water before it can even get near the town."

"From the situation I have two suggestions. Let the dams break and move all civilians out or make two new dam's a little farther away from the originals. I'm sure that they won't just blow up one dam without touching the other." Malcolm said drawing out his plan on the ground.

"Question!" interrupted Teddy, "How are we going to be able to do all this?"

"By splitting up," Malcolm continued. "We'll have Connie and Nightly scout out the dams while Teddy and James stand by on one side of the ravine to create one of the new dams while Pearl and Nicole wait on the other side. I'll be near the town just in case I need to evacuate it."

"But why don't we create the new dams now?" asked James. "It would save us a lot of trouble."

That's when I stepped in, "if we do it too soon, the culprits will know that we are onto them and blow up the new dams as well but if we do it too late, everyone in the town will be washed away."

Pearl looked up towards the sun, *"then we don't have very much time. We have to move quickly."*

"Everyone has to have their cell phones on so, when I call you, you can create your dams," I said.

"Alright, everyone, move out," said Nicole.

I hopped onto Nightly and James strapped me in before running over to join Teddy and Nicole on Pearl.

"Remember," Malcolm said, "these are mages so be careful, especially you Connie. No matter what happens or who shows up stay invisible and don't get separated from your dragon."

"Right," I responded as Nightly took to the sky again.

Once we were high in the sky Nightly turned invisible right away. We soared over towards the dam trying to make sure there were no people in the area. I would kill myself if anything bad happened to anyone. I've lived in the ravine ever since I was born. Everyone who's anyone is my friend or family. Their life was in my hands.

When we arrived at the dam, Nightly hid at the edge of the ravine. I kept glancing back over my shoulder looking at all the free space with nothing but trees to get in my way. You could imagine my disappointment as I had to focus on the situation at hand.

"Hey, Connie, there's someone inspecting the dam down there," said Nightly.

"Can you tell who it is?" I asked as I turned my head back around.

"Not very clearly, but we could go down for a quick look."

"We have twenty minutes until seven o'clock, we better make it fast. Let's grab the person then get out of there before the explosion goes off."

Nightly puffed out some smoke and then leaped off the edge. My face felt like it was rubber being stretched to its limits as we dived down, head on. Nightly landed by a group of trees and we stayed there to observe what the person was doing. From the angle we were at, I couldn't see anything. That's when I decided to take a closer look so I got off Nightly.

"What are you doing? Get back on me this instant!" he demanded.

"Relax," I said looking down at my hands become visible, "I think I know who's inspecting the dam."

As I looked around the trees I saw Judy examining the dam.

Of course it was her; it just had to be her. She always had to stick her nose in other people's business. I went over to her and tapped her shoulder "Hey, Miss Nosey, the town's in the other direction."

Judy spun around and took me by the jacket. "Connie, they're going to blow up the dam. We have to warn everyone in Small Valley!"

"What are you talking about?" I said, playing dumb.

"I saw two bombs through my binoculars. They're near the support beams . . . and how did you get that scratch on your face?"

I felt my face and remembered the scratch I got from Nightly's scales. "It doesn't matter. Lend me your binoculars." Judy handed me the binoculars and I looked through them. She was right; there were two bombs by each support beam and a few more on the edges of the ravine.

"Judy, how'd you get here?"

She crossed her arms and made a pouty face. "I was trying to follow you, but then you disappeared so I continued to walk until I came across the dam here. Why are we talking about this? We got to get out of here and hurry back so we can warn everyone."

I looked over to where Nightly was hiding. We had to stay. My duty was here; to give the others a call when the explosives go off. "You go ahead Judy. I'll catch up with you later," I said, running back into the trees.

"Wait, I can't leave you here," she said trying to follow me but to her it was like I had vanished into thin air. Little did she know I had already climbed back onto Nightly. Judy looked everywhere and gave up shortly after. "Connie, I hope you know what you're getting yourself into."

I wanted to make sure she would make it to safety but it was that or save the entire town.

She'll be fine, right?

Sure she will. That girl is tough and she knows when there's danger.

You've got that right, but I hope she'll be safe.

To my surprise, the two of us were in mind sequence. It was the first time that I had my eyes open that it had been successful but there was no time to celebrate, unfortunately.

By the time I turned around the explosives were being set off. Water started to pore out as piece by piece broke off the forty-five foot concrete dam broke off. A huge piece of concrete came at us. Nightly and I were separated, we both jumped in different directions. A chunk of the dam stood in our way. I crawled around the chunk and towards Nightly. For a brief second Nightly turned visible bent down, allowing me to grab onto the saddle and pull myself onto it. I then clipped the belt onto the saddle. Once Nightly heard that clip click on we flew up quickly before the two of us were consumed by water. I pulled out my cell phone and dialled Nicole's number.

"Is it time?" she asked answering the phone right away.

"Yes," I yelled trying to stay on Nightly.

"But it's only five to."

"Well, apparently they couldn't wait anymore. Listen, I need you to call Teddy and tell him to do his job. I have to save a friend right now."

"What, but you can't tell anyone about-"

I hung up the phone as Nightly dove close to the rushing water. The water was racing quickly down the sides of the ravine. It was a good thing that we were flying faster than the water. We were able to find Judy who was running for her life.

Nightly, go in closer.

Are you sure you want to do this?

Yes, even if our secret is exposed I will not let my best friend's life perish while I'm around and can help.

Nightly did so and that's when I grabbed Judy's arm. She screamed when we lifted her off the ground.

"Help!" she cried. "Someone help me!"

Nightly, turn visible so Judy can see us.

Nightly did so and Judy became shocked when she saw me.

"What . . . what's going on?"

"Judy, I need you to relax and calm down. Also, put those leg straps on."

Water was moving closer, catching up to us. I could see the damage the water had already done by looking at the sides of the ravine. I quickly helped Judy put on the leg straps while trying to move around while being attached to the saddle.

"Connie, are we actually flying?" she asked squeezing me tightly.

"I'll explain everything later, but for now-"

We were then hit by a powerful wind. Judy had her feet pointed in and now I understood why James said that it was bad. The straps became looser if you pointed your feet inward. Judy's right leg came out of the straps and fell over to the left side of Nightly. She screamed as I tried to grab her hand. Nightly quickly dodged another wind attack.

Connie, I can't stay like this, we have to go invisible, now!

But what about Judy, we can't leave her. Her leg looks broken.

Nightly took another hit and Judy went flying out of the saddle. She screamed as she was engulfed by the water.

"Judy!" I yelled. "Nightly, go invisible and cover me."

Wait Connie, what are you doing?

I unclipped my belt and dived in after Judy. Once I landed in the water I could feel my body tumble around as it was carried off by the current. I managed to reach the surface a couple of times but then was quickly dragged back under. I could feel my lungs tighten up as I lost air. 'Why did I dive in?' I asked myself. Then something clicked in my head, after I saw Judy fall, I knew that I was the only one who could save her. I reached the surface one last time and then let the current drag me along with it. As the current carried me I noticed Judy, caught in between rocks. Her leg was definitely broken and was bent in the opposite direction from the rest of her body; you could tell it was a clean break. I caught onto one of the rocks and released a huge breath of air. My vision started to blur as oxygen left me. As I tried to free Judy a small concrete rock hit me on the back of my head. When my eyes glanced back I saw two huge pieces of the dam heading towards us. We had to move quickly. I grabbed Judy's arm and then pushed off the rocks with what remaining strength I had before we were crushed. I was surprisingly able to support the both of us as we rose to the surface. I caught my breath and noticed Judy was unconscious. And what was ahead of us? Only the new dam the Guardians created. If we hit it at the speed we were going we would surely die. I tried my best to swim upstream, but the current was too strong to overcome. We were doomed. I looked at the dam and saw trees, rocks, dirt and some abandoned junk piled up. I couldn't believe I was about to die. For the first time in my life I wanted the world to know the real me.

"Connie," a familiar voice yelled.

I looked up and saw Pearl and Nicole watching us. My hand lifted up towards them then I found that I was being lifted out of the water. I sighed. I was relieved that I was still alive. Nightly took us to the secret area then laid us down gently. I coughed up some water and so did Judy. Nightly made a fire for us as we laid there for an hour till the Guardians returned.

"That was dangerous and stupid thing to do," Nightly scolded me, trying to warm me up with his body heat. *"But I am glad that both you and your friend, Judy, are safe."*

Malcolm ran up to us and placed a hand on mine and Judy's forehead. "You both have a fever and your friend has a broken leg. Not to mention you have a huge bump on the back of your head."

"We have to get them to the hospital," said Teddy.

"Take care of Judy first," I said leaning on Nightly. "Promise me that you'll get her treated first."

That's when I fell unconscious.

CHAPTER 12

Secrets Revealed

I awoke the next morning to find myself in my own bed. I couldn't believe I was still alive after what happened the other night. My head was throbbing like a bowling ball was slowly colliding with the pins. I lied back in bed and fell asleep.

"*Wake up,*" called a voice. "*Connie, wake up, now!*"

I grumbled and turned over. My first thought was 'leave me alone' but then I realized that it was Nightly's voice. I slowly opened one eye and saw my dragon standing over my bed watching me.

"What do you want Nightly? I'm trying to sleep here," I mumbled.

"*I wanted to make sure that you were alright. Once you passed out, I never left your side.*"

"You are a very loyal dragon," I said reaching out to him. "The most damage I would have gotten from last night would be a few bruises, scratches, a cold and this annoying bump on the back off my head."

Nightly, let me place my hand on his scale covered nose. He felt kind of cold but relaxed. "*I'm glad that you are safe.*"

There was a knock on my door. Nightly gave me a smile as he turned invisible. To my surprise I found none other than Malcolm and Teddy walking into my room. What I didn't understand was why they were doing doctor costumes and carrying an old leather briefcase.

"What are you doing here?" I asked.

"Yes, Miss, we are the doctors who brought you here after you and your friend collapsed after playing by the river around the dam," said Teddy in a loud bad acting voice.

"Sorry," said Malcolm hitting Teddy on the head. "We had to come up with a good story that would convince everyone what happened to both you and Judy."

"You didn't have to hit so hard," Teddy complained as he rubbed his head. "By the way, where is Nightly?"

Teddy suddenly landed face first on my bedroom floor. Nightly reappeared and smiled. He tripped Teddy with his tail.

"There he is," I said. "But how is Judy and what happened to keeping my identity as a dragon's whisperer a secret?"

Teddy got up from my floor then sat on my bed. "Malcolm, close the door."

Once the door was closed Teddy sighed. "Judy is fine. She's in the hospital with hypothermia and a broken leg. The doctors said she couldn't leave the hospital for two weeks."

Nightly growled as Teddy tried to put his hand around me, he backed away instantly.

"Judy's going to be fine, Connie, but to answer your question, why we are here is because the mages are starting to move," said Malcolm.

Everyone was silent. I kept thinking back to yesterday, wondering if they saw us when we were visible. It was my fault that Judy was hurt! Why wasn't I the one in the hospital? If it wasn't for me becoming a dragon's whisperer Judy wouldn't have wanted to know why I kept sneaking away, the dam would still be intact and I wouldn't be responsible for all of this. I wanted to wake up from a bad nightmare; but what can you do when you know you're already wide awake?

Nightly put his head in between Teddy and me and nuzzled himself under my hand. *"I will always be here to protect you, Connie."*

"How'd you get in here Nightly? You're taller than most people and you couldn't have crawled through the window." I scratched his head.

Nightly hummed softly before answering me, *"Your brother let me in. He was bringing something in for your mom and I took the opportunity to sneak through the door but it was hard not to bump into anything."*

"I don't think that you can come to me anymore," I said. "You can't follow me to school or home. At least not until the mages lose suspicion of us living here. You're in danger if you stay around me so I want you to stay with the Guardians from today on."

"But your sweater has a weak scent of you. Even from the day I hatched your sweater didn't have a strong enough scent."

"If my sweater can't keep you with the Guardians and away from harm what could—unless you still want Devonburg's old shoes?" I said getting up.

"You still have his shoes? Wait, could I use yours?"

"Well, I couldn't leave them to rot and no you cannot use my shoes; they are too expensive and they are nice. I don't know what you want, Nightly."

"Um, I have a suggestion," said Teddy. "Don't you have something to give Nightly that you haven't worn or washed in years? That way it will have a strong enough scent that will keep Nightly with us."

We all looked at him with surprise.

"What? Well don't look so surprised! It was bound to happen sooner or later. I realized it after my dragon rejected all my playing cards, poker chips and a scarf I got from a girl. Damn, Hercules, would never leave me alone. He even gave me a few shocks while I was playing blackjack." Teddy crossed his arms.

"Then, you should have just given up on your gambling streak," Nightly commented.

"I wish I knew that when I was younger," he said, dropping his head.

"What happened?" I asked, sitting up in my bed.

"I only had Hercules for two years before mages found out that there was a dragon living in Las Vegas. I was careless and reckless. I kept putting myself before my dragon. I went out partying one night when they attacked. Three mages came to the city and I didn't even know it. Usually Hercules would always go and do his thing during the night and I would do mine but we always met back at the apartment." He gulped and clutched his hands. "Hercules was a lightning dragon and his special ability was shocking or electrocuting anything that touched him or anything he touched. I wasn't sure what to do with him after I became his whisperer. I should have listened to him when he said something wasn't right. When we separated for that night he called out for help; he called to me but I ignored him. When I arrived home that night, I saw him turn to stone and when I reached for him he turned to dust. I will never forget that night. There isn't one day that passes that I don't think about it."

I felt a cold shiver go down my back. I couldn't imagine what it would be like to see my dragons dust. Teddy must have felt awful after he realized he ignored his dragon just so he could continue to live his regular human life. It must have been one of the reasons why he became a Guardian. So no one else would ignore their dragon like he did.

"After that, I met Devonburg and the others. I was the last one to join the Guardians and was appointed as the medical Guardian," Teddy continued.

"So, you're not impersonating a doctor?" I asked.

"Are you nuts? With all the extra schooling I was forced to take, I should be ranked as a lazar surgeon," Teddy said acting like his over confident self again.

"Really? I would never trust you with surgery," Malcolm said.

We all laughed at Malcolm's comment. I even had to wipe a tear from my eye but when I heard Nightly laugh it sounded dangerous yet comfortable to be around. My heart leaped when I heard it. My attention was drawn to Malcolm who had laughing immediately. "What's wrong? Is something bothering you?"

Malcolm turned towards my window and shut the blinds. "It's nothing to concern yourself with."

"Oh, come on, Malcolm," Teddy said giving Malcolm a nudge. "I told my story now you should tell yours."

"It's not one I'm fond of," he said turning towards me. "I was in university and I was studying architecture in Egypt. While we were looking at one of the ancient tombs, a dragon egg was purposely left outside the tomb for someone to find. I touched it and it turned red, giving me a fire dragon; I named him Inferno. My teacher, Dr. Franklin saw the egg and wanted to study it and learn why it changed colour. Of course I'd hidden it away from my classmates and teachers. Inferno was kept well hidden because of our strong will and mind. A fire dragon's ability is to heat anything and I mean essentially melt anything it touches as well as control a fire's direction. I always practiced and trained with him, making sure that he was strong but the saying 'brains are better than brawns' is not always true. I spent so much time studying with him that I forgot about the physical part. A female mage disguised herself as one of my class mates and stole my dragon from me. She did her homework and knew he was only mentally strong. It wasn't until I met Devonburg that I realized that the body and mind have to be at equal strength. If not something will always," he looked directly at me, "always fail."

I looked over at Nightly swishing his tail around the room. He knocked over my laundry basket and would have knocked my dresser had Teddy not caught it. I didn't blame him for being scared or nervous. He had just heard two stories of dragons dying by the hands of mages. I didn't want to leave his side. Not now, not ever.

I got back up on my feet and quickly made it over to the other side of the room, avoiding Nightly's tail. I went into my closet and opened up an old box that contained Devonburg's shoes. I shoved it out of the way and then dug around my closet even more grabbing an old shirt I hadn't worn in years. It was a white shirt that was too small for me; it had a maple tree on the front that was covered by a pudding and gelatine stain. It was a souvenir that my dad had brought back after his trip to Ontario.

"Take it," I said. "This should keep Nightly tamed. While you're at it can you take these?" I said handing Malcolm Devonburg's shoe box. "You'll get more use out of these than I ever will."

Malcolm nodded and took the shoe box and shirt from me. He then turned towards the door. "Your condition is fine; you just need a day's rest."

Teddy avoided Nightly's tail but tripped when Nightly purposely went invisible. "I'll get you back one day, dragon," Teddy said.

I heard Nightly laugh as I lied back down on my bed.

"Nightly, go with them," I said.

"Are you sure you'll be alright?" he asked.

"You heard Malcolm. All I need is a day's rest and then by tomorrow you, and I will be flying in the skies," I said with a smile.

"Alright, but get better quick."

"I always do."

"We'll take good care of him," said Teddy.

"You better," I said glaring at them.

"Don't worry, Connie, unlike us you have Guardians to help to take care of your dragon. We exist so you can learn from our mistakes and live on with your dragon," said Malcolm, leaving the room with Teddy.

After I gave him one last kiss Nightly hummed, became invisible and followed them. As soon as they left Dad and Mom came into the room asking me what I could remember from that day. What could I tell them though? 'Thanks, Mom and Dad, for caring but I've been ditching you and my friends just so I can escape to a secret part of the ravine where I train to get stronger mentally and physically with a dragon your good old buddy Devonburg gave me so we don't get killed by these people called mages.' Yeah, that wouldn't be happening anytime soon. Instead, I just told them the story Teddy and Malcolm had told me. We were by the river near the dam but I slipped and hit my head.

They didn't like the version I came up with. They both looked at me with disappointment. Mom left the room whimpering but Dad stopped at my door way and said, "We love you, Connie, and that means we wouldn't let anything happen to you. You can tell us what's really going on."

I put on a fake smile, "nothing's going on Dad, believe me." He shook his head and closed the door. I bit my lip and felt that bad feeling as my stomach turned.

I looked up at the ceiling and thought about how many more lies I would have to tell to cover up the truth. How many more lies must I tell before this whole thing ends? My parents were starting to get suspicious. I covered my eyes and fell back to sleep.

I slept for the rest of that day. When I awoke the day after I got dressed and stared at myself in the mirror. I started to brush my hair. As I was brushing, a feeling come over me. Guilt? Sorrow? It was a feeling that made me start to think about the choices I'd made. I looked at myself in the mirror and, at first, I saw a happy girl who hung around her friends, spent time with her family and kept her grades up. Before it turned into a girl who was exhausted all the time lying to everyone she cared about; her grades had started to drop slowly and she had to run away constantly to her dragon who was making her life more difficult by the day. I hated it! I took my brush and threw it at the mirror, watching as it broke into dozens of pieces. I didn't want to see myself like that as I dropped to the ground. I didn't want to see myself cry.

"I can never go back to my old ordinary life," I realized. "I love you Nightly but I want my old life back," I punched the floor multiple times until I realized that the broken pieces of the mirror were cutting my hand. I held it up to my face, watching the blood drop to the ground. I closed my eyes because the sight of blood made me want to vomit.

The next thing that happened was Mom came barging in to find me on the floor, holding my injured hand. She quickly ran to the bathroom and returned with a first aid kit.

"What happened?" she asked, bandaging my whole hand.

I never really noticed how bad I damaged my hand until I saw the blood seep through the bandage. The blood covered the back of my hand, my palms up to the tips of my fingers. I hated blood but right now I hated myself.

"I got upset and broke the mirror with my brush," I said, wiping the tears away from my face.

"What on earth could have got you that upset?" Dad asked entering the room.

I shook my head. "I don't know," I lied, "I just felt angry with myself."

Mom finished bandaging my hand and left Dad and me to pick up the rest of the broken pieces of the mirror in my room. We didn't say a word to each other. All we did was pick up the pieces and left each other alone. Once he left, I went to my window and started to cry again.

"I . . . I'm sorry," I whispered. "I'm sorry I have to lie."

Later on that day, I snuck away to the secret area and found Nightly darting towards me. Since he was bigger than me I toppled right over when we came into contact.

"I missed you," he said, rubbing his head up against mine. *"I tried to contact you with mind sequence but you never responded."*

"What's with the bandage on your hand?" asked Nicole.

I forced Nightly off me and looked back at the bandaging around my hand. "I cut myself, nothing else." I stood up and looked at my Guardians and bit my lip. "If it's not too much trouble to ask, can I hear the stories how you guys became the Guardians in the first place?"

Everyone looked at me with surprise.

"I would really like to know why you guys are here to protect Nightly and me," I said. "How did you lose your dragons," I looked at Pearl, "or whisperer?"

"Why do you want to know this all of a sudden?" James asked.

"So I can trust you better with your training and the safety of my dragon," I said. "I already heard Teddy and Malcolm's stories."

Nicole, James and Pearl glared at Teddy and Malcolm, who were both red in the face.

James lowered his hat and rubbed his head again. "Having a dragon isn't the easiest thing in the world, Connie. I had a good life of farming, getting together with my friends and having the time of my life. Nevertheless, a stone dragon egg was left on my farm nine years ago to this day. I touched it; it turned brown, giving me an earth dragon. I named him Boulder Dash. Even though I tried to ditch him so I could go hang with my friends in town. He didn't make it easy for me to leave the farm. Every time I tried to bring in the cattle he would scare them off. Every time I tried to harvest or plant crops, he would devour them, making me do it all over again." He looked down at the ground, knelt down and picked up some dirt. "I had him for three and a half years. He followed me everywhere. There was no way of getting rid of him, except for one night I had enough of him ruining my plans. I had to decline Yael's letter of acceptance just for him since he wouldn't last a day in the city with concrete keeping him out of his natural element. I got into a fight with him that night and I didn't realize I was being watched which was why he always followed me. I was so mad at him for ruining my life. I told him to leave and never come back." James dropped the dirt out of his hand. "I didn't know . . . I didn't know he was in danger . . . He didn't come back the next morning. I went looking for him and I found him injured a mile away from my farm. I was then knocked out like a light and never saw my dragon again."

Nightly's eyes gazed down at me. I touched him on the head calming him down. "If I ever do that, I want you to take me away from everything and everyone till I come to my senses."

"That's fine with me. If it takes a thousand years I will do it," he said humming.

"I became a Guardian because I knew the next whisperer would be like me and want to get away from their dragon constantly, not realizing the danger that would be surrounding them. Your old life was great, but what's not to say that this one could be better if you wanted it to be? I wish I had known that when I was younger. You are only going to make yourself miserable if you reject something you're already committed to. It could make your life better if you tried." James stood up and cracked his back.

James just described what my actions were like this morning, perfectly. I wanted to give up on Nightly and was willing to do it so quickly, too. I was making my life difficult, not him. Even though I loved him, I was ready to get rid of him. I was the one who accepted him into my life and I was the only one who could break our bond or make it strong.

I stroked Nightly's head. I didn't want to do that now or ever. There was no one in this world or the Mystic Realm that could make me leave his side now.

Nightly looked down at me and asked, *"Are you crying?"*

I took my hand and found some tears trying to make their way down my face. I quickly wiped them away. "I'm fine and I don't cry."

"That was a good story but I'm afraid we have to get back to dragon training now," said Nicole, walking towards Nightly's saddle.

"What about your story Nicole? Why did you become a Guardian?" I asked.

Nicole stopped with her back towards us. "I'd rather not talk about it," she said in a cheerful voice. "Now let's get you flying."

"No!" I said.

"Nicole, we all told ours," said Teddy.

"What are you trying to hide?" asked Malcolm.

"We know you've been hiding something for a long time now. You've never trusted us from the start. That's unacceptable even for someone like you," said James. "As your fellow Guardians, partners, friends, we deserve to know what you've been hiding for the last several years."

Nicole quickly turned around looking exasperated. "You want to know what I've been hiding? Alright I'll tell you. I didn't freely join the Guardians like the rest of you. I had to join and so did Pearl!" She began to hesitate. "I'm . . . I'm not a human. I'm a dragon . . . trapped within a human's body."

CHAPTER 13

Body Switch

This was unbelievable! Nicole's response, the boys were in utter shock, I couldn't believe it and Nightly had a questionable look on his face. Pearl didn't look surprised. She lied on the ground by Nicole, acting as if 'it' wasn't a major concern. She knew Nicole's secret but if I recall, Malcolm said Nicole was keeping something from Pearl so this couldn't be it, but then what? I became frustrated and wanted to yell at her for lying to us but I kept it under control somehow.

"You're a dragon?" Teddy asked in a squeaky voice. "How did you even end up like . . . well, like this . . . as a human?"

"It's a *long painful* story," Nicole said in a shameful voice. "Pearl always knew it but to tell other people is an embarrassment. That's why I didn't tell any of you."

"We have time to hear your story," Malcolm said looking at his watch.

"Continue," I said, walking towards her in a stern voice. "You want me to trust you, right? Then I need you to trust me by telling me the truth. No lies. I'm your student am I not? I deserve the truth."

Listen here, you insignificant brat. Nicole has had a hard enough time living in a human body, not able to return to old one. If I were you I would close my mouth before things get ugly around here," Pearl said baring her teeth. She snapped at me when I attempted to move closer to Nicole.

"I won't let you talk to my whisperer that way," Nightly yelled, approaching Pearl.

"You dare defy me! Are you forgetting that we are one of the only dragons roaming the earth?" she shouted back.

"How can I when you tell me every day? You'll never let me forget it! Connie is my whisperer and she carries my life around with her own. She is right and has always been. Trust isn't just about the student giving it to the teacher. It has to work the same way around otherwise nothing is done."

Pearl started to growl, standing in an attack stance, with her claws burrowing into the ground beneath her, with her wings spreading out. Was she actually going to attack Nightly?

"Stop it!" ordered Nicole. "Pearl, calm down and Nightly, back away from her," she used a strong and powerful voice, which scared me. Nightly and Pearl refused to lower their guard to one another, though. "Pearl, I'm going to tell them!"

Pearl blew out smoke. *"I wouldn't."*

Pearl finally lowered her guard, hissing slightly at me as she laid herself down. Nicole came over and laid her smooth human hand on Pearl's white scales. Nicole stood there for a bit letting the wind blow her black hair around before she turned around. For a brief second I thought her eyes flicker a creamy blue colour. The colour made me think of the ocean instantly.

"And why wouldn't you Pearl?" I asked. "What do you have hiding behind that thick head of yours?!"

Pearl stood up and snapped at me. *"Don't start with me human! If you're not forgetting, I am a dragon who can tear you apart in an instant."*

Nightly ran in front of me and growled. *"If you want her, you'll have to go through me first."*

"If it will teach you some manners and respect to towards your fellow dragons, then I will gladly accept the challenge," Pearl roared as she jumped over Nicole and charged towards Nightly.

I backed away quickly trying not to get in the middle of their fight. Nightly went for Pearl's neck and started to claw at it. Pearl was strong and shook Nightly off in an instant. She then disappeared with her quick speed. Pearl was too experienced in battle. He had no chance in winning this fight. She reappeared behind him and grabbed him by the neck with her teeth tossing him into the ravines wall. Nightly growled; rising up from the rubble created from his collision with the wall. He turned invisible. Pearl glanced around but only saw humans. She spread her bird like wings out and flew up to the sky awfully fast. By the time she took off a crater was created. It was Nightly trying to attack Pearl while he was invisible. Nightly became visible not expecting to end up lying right underneath Pearl after he let his guard down.

"Idiot," she said, stepping off him. *"I am a light dragon. My special ability is using my own energy to enhance any part of my body such as my wings for faster air speed. It has to be a specific body part or it won't work but at least it prepares me for any sneak attacks you have."*

Nightly growled at Pearl and snorted out some smoke.

"Oh no," went Malcolm, "everyone get down!"

We all dropped to the ground just in time before Nightly let out a huge breath of fire. The flame was huge; the heat was intense it caused severe damage to the secret area. Was this really my dragon, Nightly? He was doing all of this just to get back at Pearl, for me.

"Nightly, stop!" I ordered, standing up after the fire disappeared.

The next thing I knew, Pearl was standing behind me snorting out smoke. Nightly roared and started to charge. I couldn't let this happen I wanted Nightly to stop but he wasn't listening to me. I was willing to do anything to try and stop him. I began to run towards Nightly's waving my arms calling out his name trying to make him stop. Then I tried to use mind sequence.

"No, Connie," Nicole yelled as she rose to her knees.

By the time I heard Nicole, my mind connected to Nightly and the next thing I knew, my mind started to pulse like it was being pulled by a vacuum cleaner. I yelled Nightly's name and he yelled mine before the pain stopped.

I blinked once—then twice—feeling vague. I toppled over onto the ground and when I tried to get up I found it difficult. Once I stood up I looked around and down at my own body?

"Ah," I screamed, returning to the ground. *"What happened to me; why am I looking at my own body?!"*

"I would like to know the same answer," said Nightly looking down at my human hands.

Nicole stood up. *"See,* this is what I was trying to prevent," she yelled looking over at Pearl who had calmed down. "You two just did your first mind body switch. Basically you over did it when you, Connie, were trying to use mind sequence to stop Nightly."

I looked up at her, hanging Nightly's dragon head in shame.

Nicole sighed, placing her hand on her head. "The mind body switch is when a dragon and whisperer switch bodies. Originally called the mind body connection, the whisperer and dragon shared their knowledge and strength with one another; the mind body switch is an overextension of it. The mind and bodies are now switched and it's the same with the roles you play. Connie controls all of Nightly's dragon abilities and Nightly controls all of Connie's human abilities."

"Is that how you got trapped in your whisperer's body?" I asked.

Nicole nodded.

I finally figured out how to stand without Nightly's tail getting in the way and stood by him. As I attempted to stand up, Nightly's dragon tail would keep getting in the way. At least I had it easier then Nightly. I had to work with four legs which felt like crawling, but he had to figure out how to stand on two legs instead of four.

"But how do we get back into our own bodies?"

"You did it already by accident. Try to calm Nightly down. Use the same technique you used to switch back into your own body. Once you master that you can become a dragon or human anytime you like," Nicole said sitting on a boulder. "I'm surprised that you two were able to do it this early. You've only been together for a little more than a month now, but your bond was strong enough to succeed on the first try."

"Nicole is right," said James. "I couldn't connect with Boulder Dash till the sixth month I had him. Even then we still had a hard time."

"It's the same with me," said Malcolm. "I had my dragon for eight months and I was always with him, trying to make him stronger, but there was something I was lacking and we couldn't have a proper connection."

"Same," said Teddy.

"Not that I don't love to be in my whisperer's body, but I want to be back in my own," Nightly whined, still trying to find a way to stand up.

"That goes double for me," I said.

"I already told you to figure it out on your own," said Nicole. "Each dragon and whisperer has a different way to switch bodies. My whisperer's and mine was laziness. If she was too bored to do anything, I would switch bodies with her. Yet at that time, I was called Aqua in my dragon form but this body belongs to my real whisperer, Nicole. You see Nicole was a traveller and decided to relocate her life in India where she found my egg and reawakened me to the element of water. My whisperer and I had a very strong connection, which is why I'm so good at connecting dragons with their whisperers. That's also why I knew how to act like a human really well which is why you guys haven't asked about me in the last four years we've known each other. I had a problem though. I grew attached to the Human World, and the more I lived in it the more I wanted to become a part of it. I even started to develop emotions."

"Dragon's don't have emotions?" I asked Nightly.

"We only have four emotions towards humans," Nightly explained finally standing on my human bodies two legs. "They are either protective and loving or destructive and hating. The other emotions we carry are for ourselves or other dragons like love, happiness, sad, fear, anger and other emotions."

"That's right," said Nicole. "I grew a loving emotion towards a human man."

"A human man?" went Nightly.

Pearl gagged at the suggestion. *"Dragons and humans are only supposed to be partners! If they loved one another like a mate then the whole world would be messed up."*

"I know and that was my flaw," Nicole admitted. "The more I saw him, the more I fell in love with him. Soon I started to sneak out in my whisperer's body just so I could see him. One night he took me to a rose maze and led me to the middle, where I found my whisperer's cousin beaten, tortured and dying. The man I trusted . . . was a mage and had two other accomplices with him." Nicole closed her eyes and clutched her hands banging them on the boulder beneath her. "It was all a trap that the mages set up just so they could kill two more dragons. I tried to run but where do you run to in a maze? I kept running into dead ends and more turns. I got fed up and contacted my whisperer, who came to my aid. I should have known that was what the mages wanted. Once she arrived along with Pearl, the man I thought I could love and trust appeared and stabbed her with his little 'dragon ability stealing/killing' device before we were able to return into our original bodies. Out of frustration, I attacked him, clawing at his face, stabbing him in the eye with his own tool. Pearl took me to another part of the maze, where we found her whisperer Ellen, but that was also another trap. The Lead Mage approached us and flung his tool, aiming at Pearl, but instead it took Ellen's life. She sacrificed herself so Pearl and I could flee. As we retreated into the skies I saw my whisperer in my body turn to stone and then smashed by the mages. I believe that was the first time I cried as a human."

Pearl wrapped her neck around Nicole, trying to comfort her. Nightly stumbled over to me trying to walk properly in my body, but when he made it to me, he hugged his own dragon body trying to make me feel safe.

"So that's why Pearl is so concerned about your wellbeing all the time," Teddy realized. "You both lost a good friend that day so you both carry each other's burdens knowing that you lived and your partners didn't."

"But Pearl, are you not mad at Nicole after the trouble that she got you and your whisperer into?" asked Nightly.

"Nightly!" I said scolding him.

"What?" he asked innocently.

Pearl shook her head. *"I was angry at first but when I realized I didn't die after my whisperer passing, I didn't know what to think then. It wasn't until we both met up with Devonburg that we realized what we had to do with our lives, which is teaching the two of you not to mess around, while keeping the rest of the Guardians safe."* Pearl looked up at Nicole. *"You know if I could, I would switch bodies with you right now so that you could feel what it's like to be a dragon again."*

"Of course I know. You tell me that all the time," Nicole responded.

I felt bad for Pearl. Her whisperer died protecting her and Nicole and now her only dragon friend was trapped with-in her whisperer's body.

Nicole jumped off the boulder and walked towards Nightly and me. "You want to know why I became a Guardian. It's because I didn't know the limits of this body at the time. I was with my whisperer for seven years but I refused to learn human strengths and weaknesses like emotions. You two should spend a day in each other's bodies and try to figure out the limits of them."

"What?" we both said.

I quickly walked over to James and Teddy, nearly running them over, not knowing how to control Nightly's dragon body yet. *"Please, tell us how to get back into our own bodies!"*

They both shook their heads.

"Malcolm?" I said.

"Sorry, Connie, but as I said, I never had the chance to figure that out with my dragon. Besides, you two are smart and you both work better physically than mentally," he said.

I looked over at Nightly who shrugged as my cell phone started to ring. Nightly took it out of my pocket and looked up at me.

"Open it up and answer it," I said.

"But I don't know what to say," he said.

"I'll tell you what to say, just answer the phone."

Nightly flipped it open and placed the phone up to the dragon ear.

"Don't give it to me, put it up to your ear and say 'hello'."

"Hello," he said, bringing the phone up to the human ear and overdoing do my voice.

"Connie?" asked the voice.

"It's Sam," I said, recognizing the voice. "Tell him 'yes, it is' . . . ask him what he wants?"

"Hey, Sam, uh, do you need something?" he asked sounding nervous.

"Connie do you have a cold?" Sam asked.

I bumped Nightly on the back, causing him talk normally. Now it would sound like me.

"No, no, just had something in my throat but now it's gone," Nightly wasn't happy with me.

"Okay, I was just wondering if you wanted to go visit Judy while she's in the hospital?" he asked.

"Say 'no'."

"Sure, why not? I can head there right now," said Nightly.

"Great . . . great, I'll meet you there in ten minutes," Sam said, "bye."

Nightly closed the phone and placing it back into the jacket pocket.

"Why did you say yes?" I yelled.

"Because I'm going to do what my teacher suggests and learn the strengths and weaknesses of your body," he said as he started to walk away.

"Wait, where do you think you're going?" I asked, using his dragon teeth to bite down on the jacket. *"Besides, what makes you think you can arrive at the hospital in ten minutes? It's unheard of!"*

107

"Then, you'll just have to fly me there," he said, yanking the jacket out of the dragon teeth and walking over to the saddle. "Now, let's mount you and get you flying."

"What? I can't fly?" I protested.

"Sure you can, just let the wind carry you around and fly in the direction you want to go."

"Nicole, help!"

"Just go with it," she said, helping Nightly mount me. "Show him the ropes of the Human World but try to keep invisible so you don't get caught or draw suspicion."

Nicole, James and Nightly mounted me; then, James helped Nightly with the straps. They backed away as I opened Nightly's dragon wings and started to flap; rising higher and higher off the ground until we were fifty feet above. Then we made our way to Small Valley's hospital.

"Hey Connie, can I ask you something?" Nightly asked leaning towards the dragon ears.

I looked up at him.

"What are these things?" he asked grasping the breasts on my body. "They don't look useful."

"Ah, let go of those! They are something you should never touch at all while you're in my body," I yelled at him.

Things were silent then Nightly started to whisperer something to me. "You know, to be fair I should tell you something about my body," he bent closer to the dragon ear and started to whisper even softer.

"Ewe, Nightly, that is gross!" I yelled as we continued to fly.

CHAPTER 14

A Dragon for a Day

While flying, I made a few dips and turns, which almost scared Nightly half to death. Unfortunately I did hit a couple of trees, but the thing about being a dragon is that their scale covered skin is so hard that it could not be penetrated by rocks or trees. Sadly, it wasn't the same for the human body Nightly was staying in; it was the first time he ever experienced cuts. There were only a few but it didn't matter; he was annoyed at me and surprised. This was his first time experiencing pain like this.

When we finally arrived at the hospital, I landed on the roof and guided Nightly through the process of getting the straps off.

"You're not allowed to fly anymore," Nightly said, stumbling off the saddle.

"Well, for the record, I never wanted to fly in the first place," I said. *"If you didn't say yes to Sam, we wouldn't be here."*

"Well, excuse me for trying to learn about my whisperer's life," he shot at me.

I groaned. *"Look let's not fight. Just tell me how to turn invisible so you can go into the hospital and see Judy and Sam."*

"Oh, you don't know how to turn invisible? It's actually very easy, think it and it will happen," he said while doing hand gestures.

"Are you sure?"

"Who's the dragon who owns the body you're in?"

I rolled the gold dragon eyes and thought about hiding in plain sight. 'Turn invisible', I told myself. I then looked over at Nightly. *"Well, am I invisible?"*

"Well for the most part yes."

I took a look for myself and saw that the dragon body I was in had a floating head and a severed tail.

"Oh, great," I mumbled.

"It's not that bad, but for a precaution, why don't you stay here where no one will see you and I'll just go and meet up with Sam and Judy? You can stay here and work on being invisible."

"But they're my friends. I want to see them," I whined.

"No! You're not allowed to see them until you've mastered invisibility," Nightly ordered. "Besides, you can use mind sequence to check on things."

"But if I do that, your left eye will turn gold."

"Then I guess you'll just have to wait here or find another way in but I suggest you don't. Now, I'll contact you if there are any problems."

I lied down on the ground in the shadows and watched Nightly leave in my body. I was mad that I couldn't see how Judy was doing. Dang it, I was stuck in my dragon's body and I couldn't even turn invisible. Why was it turning out this way? I sat there and watched clouds pass by.

"There's a bunny, a hand, another bunny," I said to myself. *"It's only been five minutes but it feels like he's been in there for hours."*

I stared at the door, waiting for it to open with Nightly coming from the other side. I continued to watch, then I saw the door knob slowly start to twist and turn.

"Crap!" I said trying to find a big enough place to hide Nightly's body. *"You've got to be kidding me. There is no place to hide this body!"* I looked everywhere but there was absolutely nowhere for a teenage sized dragon to hide. *"Please work this time,"* I pleaded as I attempted to turn invisible again.

The door opened and out came a few nurses carrying cigarette packs in their hands. I watched as they passed by, each of them taking a cigarette out of the pack.

"So, I told Bertha that she has to go out with Dr. Marshal because they had so much in common but of course she said no because her boyfriend in the city is going to come any day now and take her away to Paris. To tell you the truth, she's been waiting for him to come for two months now. He's never going to come," said a red headed nurse.

"Of course, Bertha would say that because she's in love," said a blond nurse. "Hey, do you have a lighter?"

"No, I thought you had one," assumed the brunette nurse.

I smiled. I was completely invisible and no one could see me. Before I could celebrate my throat started to get hot and then my stomach rumbled.

"Did you hear that?" asked the blond nurse.

"Yeah, sounds like an upset stomach, but it came from behind us," said the brunette nurse.

They all looked around seeing nothing before I burped. For a human a burp is only gas escaping through your mouth but for a dragon they let out more than gas, no, fire has to go with it. Luckily the nurses ducked and dropped their ignited cigarettes while running back inside the hospital.

I looked down at the cigarettes and saw them burning away. *"Well, they could have thanked me for lighting their cigarettes. I may as well put them out before a real fire is starts up and burns this whole building down."* I stepped on them, smothering them until the flames were out. Then I got an idea. I was invisible from head to toe. I could visit Judy. The problem was that I couldn't go into the building without drawing attention to myself. *"Then I'll just have to try something else."* At first I thought about flying but when I moved to the edge and spread out my wings I started to become visible where I found it harder to keep the thought of keeping myself invisible in my head. *"Okay, flying is out."* What now? I couldn't fly and there was no way I was taking the stairs. *"Come on Connie; use that brain of yours to get yourself out of another difficult situation."* I grasped the edge of the building too hard and broke off a piece. I couldn't draw any attention to myself. I grabbed the edge of the building with the tail and started to lower myself down until I caught the rubble. I looked into the window before me and saw Judy. I stared straight into the room, where she was lying on a hospital bed with her leg in a cast held up in a sling. Nightly and Sam sat by her talking. I threw the rubble back onto the roof and continued to watch. There was just one problem—I couldn't hear them. *"Crap!"*

I don't know if Nightly heard me or not but he got out of his chair and walked over to the window and opened it up.

"Why'd you open the window?" asked Judy, shifting her body to one side of the bed.

"Well, it was kind of getting stuffy in here so I thought you could use some fresh air," said Nightly.

Judy smiled and shifted her body again. "I'm actually glad you opened it. The three nurses who look after me always smell like smoke but whenever I ask one of them to open the window, they take as an insult, and storm out of the room."

I bet you they were the nurses who I ran into on the roof.

"I've been in this hospital many times for stitches and the hospital staff isn't friendly to me either," said Sam.

Nightly and Judy both laughed but Nightly used his deep dragon laugh instead of a regular human laugh. Sam and Judy both looked at him with an awkward expression on their faces.

"Nightly!"

"Sorry," he said, coughing a bit, "must still have something in my throat."

Sam looked concerned actually, he looked nervous the whole time I was watching the three of them. He got up and walked to the doorway. "I'm going to run out and get us some drinks," he said leaving the room.

Judy grabbed Nightly and pulled him close to her. "Now that he's gone, I want to ask you something, Connie. What was that thing we were on when the dam broke?"

"What? I thought you were supposed to have amnesia from the incident!" he said, backing away from her.

"I lied so I could ask you in person. This is one thing I want to confirm before I tell people. Besides, I doubt they would believe I was riding on a dragon with you." She grabbed the wrist and squeezed it, "now explain what we were on!"

I bit down on Nightly's dragon lip hoping he wouldn't say anything. Heck, I was praying that some kind of distraction would magically occur to break up the conversation.

Then, a miracle occurred and my cell phone started to ring! Nightly picked it up after freeing my human wrist from Judy's grip, "Hello," he said tucking some of my hair behind my human ear.

"Where are you?!" demanded the voice of my ignorant older brother.

"What do you mean 'where am I?' I'm at the hospital visiting Judy," Nightly said in a calm voice.

"Are you forgetting that its Wednesday today, the one day of the week when we have to go to the 'Sibling Respect Program'?" he said.

I forgot about our session today. Nightly had only been to a couple with me but he always told me that he never understood what we were doing.

"Fine, I'll be over there soon," he said closing the phone and putting it away. "I got to go."

"I know, I heard, but you have to come back tomorrow and visit me again!" she ordered.

"Maybe," Nightly said looking a bit nervous. "For now, I have to say goodbye."

"There is just one thing I would like to know," Judy said rubbing her chin. "Were we really on a dragon?"

Nightly was red in the face, and he looked stupefied not knowing how to reply. Suddenly we heard a crash. Nightly ran out the door and noticed something. There didn't look like anyone was there but I knew Nightly could definitely feel something. The phone beeped; Nightly picked it up and he saw a text message. It didn't look like he could read because he closed the phone up quickly and put it away.

"Connie, what was that noise?" Judy asked, trying to get a better look down the hall.

"A cart got pushed over that's all," Nightly replied. "Hey, I'm going now so I'll see you later."

"Fine," Judy said disappointedly.

Nightly ran through the hospital as he left my vision.

Meet you downstairs, I heard.

I crawled back up on to the roof. At first I thought about how hilarious it would be to see Glen and Nightly go through today's session. I shook the thought out of my head quickly as I stood on the edge of the building. I couldn't turn invisible while I flew down. It was already hard enough to fly on my own. I couldn't jump to the ground without causing attention. *"It just had to be hard for me, didn't it?"* I looked around and spotted two trees that I could soar over to and climb down while still being invisible. I opened the wings and jumped high, making sure that I wouldn't crash into anything. It was a good thing the trees were close, but for ten seconds, I was visible to the world. Once I took a hold of the trees, I started to climb down the tree thinking that it was great that I wasn't a full sized dragon like Pearl or else this would have been impossible. I crawled onto the grass and watched as Nightly rushed out of the hospitals front doors. His eyes were scanning the area trying to locate me.

"So, did you have fun?" I asked.

Nightly looked around and stomped towards the trees I was hiding underneath then stuck a finger out, red faced and infuriated. "What were you doing talking?!"

"Wait, why are you mad? I did what I was supposed to do and stayed invisible."

"Dragons never talk unless they are alone or are around other whisperers," Nightly stated, "and I know someone was listening when I was talking with Judy."

"Do you know who?"

Nightly calmed down then he reached out and touched the invisible dragon head. "You need to know how to hide yourself better in a public area, Connie. Otherwise I won't be the only one who can find while you're invisible."

My stomach turned. Funny; I thought I would only have that feeling in my own body, not Nightly's. I almost blew our cover. The feeling went away quickly as I started to sniff something in the air and then sniffed Nightly. There was a sweet smell on the clothes.

"Oh this! I slipped on some juice some idiot spilt on my way out of there. Now I smell like mixed fruits and I'm sticky."

"Well you can't change now. Kyle is waiting for you at the community hall."

"*What!* You mean I actually have to go to that?" he yelled. "I'd rather be captured by a mage, then go through one of your sessions!"

"You make it sound like he's Teddy."

"I would prefer Kyle over Teddy any day."

"Then, let's see it."

"What?!" he said surprised.

"Let's see how long you can stand Kyle compared to Teddy. That is if you can last the whole session without losing your temper. If you can do that, I'll bring you treats after school for the rest of the month."

"What will happen if I lose?"

"Then you'll have to go to the school as me for a whole day."

The cell phone started to ring again. Nightly looked at the phone, then glanced back at me "fine," he said giving in. "Just tell me what to do in these sessions."

I giggled. *"Sure, now let's see how long you can last."*

Once we arrived at the community hall, the fun began. When Nightly and I arrived Kyle came storming out and grabbed my human wrist. He dragged who he thought was me inside but that wasn't the best part. After I found the single window that showed me Glen's room, I couldn't stop laughing. Glen was making everyone dance together. Nightly kept stepping on Kyle's feet and then Kyle would 'accidentally' let go of Nightly or push him into some chairs. Man, did his face ever turn red with anger. I saw Nightly lift the upper lip and let out a small sound. I think he was actually trying to growl at Kyle.

Calm down, I said.

But . . . but . . . he's, Nightly stuttered.

Let it go and follow his feet. You're the one who screwing up.

And how am I supposed to do that?

Just watch his feet and you'll be fine.

"Connie, focus," Glen said, restarting the music. "Now take that gold contact out and dance to the beat, and one, and two, and three, and four."

Nightly broke off our connection and watched as Kyle moved his feet. It took him a little time to figure out Kyle's dance pattern eventually he got it. It was still funny to see Nightly learn to waltz. For the first time I knew what Nightly was talking about when he said he didn't understand our sessions. It was embarrassing to watch this knowing I looked stupid doing it. Nightly must have had a blast watching me. I have officially lost our bet so after the session was done I would take Nightly back to the Guardians and figure out how to return to our own bodies. Once that was done I would have to start emptying out my piggy bank.

When the session was over, Nightly came running out of the community hall so fast that he tripped over my human feet and fell on the ground. He crawled towards me and threw the shoes off and started to rub my human feet.

"Your brother is cruel," he commented. "He was purposely stepping on my feet or should I say *your* feet."

"Well, since I live with him, I think I've gotten used to it," I said.

Nightly made a pouty face then placed a hand on the invisible dragon body. "Can we please go back now and figure out how to reverse this before it becomes permanent as it did with Nicole and her whisperer?"

"Oh come on. From where I was watching it wasn't that bad."

"Then next time you can have the pleasure of dancing with him," he said, putting the shoes back on and climbing onto the saddle. I stood up and started to walk through the town. That's when Nightly slapped me. "I want to be back in my own body today, Connie!"

I threw him off and growled. *"Look, I'm sorry, but I can't fly while being invisible! That's why I was holding onto the roof while you were talking with Judy and Sam."*

"Well, we can't stay here till nightfall. We'll just have to take our chance with you walking around invisible."

"Really, Nightly, you would risk that?"

He sighed. "Of course I would. It's a better idea than having civilians notice us or mages. Also I really want to get back into my body."

I gulped. I had forgotten about the mages. I was focused on hiding from everyone around me. *"Well what are we waiting for? Let's get moving."*

I started to walk towards the park but it wasn't easy to be quiet. From the way I was manoeuvring around, I thought it was impossible for a dragon to stay hidden during the day. Besides that, it was embarrassing to have Nightly guide me through some streets and back alleys after all, I was the one who was born and raised in this place then he comes along and acts like he knows it better than me. It was good thing that I was invisible now. I had to control a tail that kept hitting everything in its path and since Nightly was wider and bigger, it was hard to adjust to the way it moved around.

"You're slow," Nightly would comment.

"Well, your body's not the easiest to control. Besides, we're in a public place, where it is especially hard to hide in," I argued.

"Now you know how I felt every day before the Guardians came," Nightly stopped us in a field out of the town. "Connie, you can become visible now. We should be far enough from Small Valley that no will see you."

I turned visible, feeling relieved to be seen, and I stretched out his wings feeling great that I wasn't cramped up into a small ball. *This feels so much better than being crammed close to buildings.*" I looked at Nightly, who was facing the ground. "*Nightly, what's the matter?*"

He looked back up tears falling down my human face. "Connie, I need to protect you."

"*And I need to do the same for you.*"

"No! You don't get it. Ever since you became my whisperer, I've been following you around trying to make sure that you are safe from harm." He wiped the tears away then looked straight at me with confusion. "How am I supposed to make sure you're safe when you don't tell me things? You'll tell your family, your friends even the Guardians things, but not me. I train every day to fight mages so I can protect you. Sometimes I feel like I'm a burden to you. You're careless, naive and you don't see the danger that surrounds you." He wrapped the human arms around him and began to shake.

I stretched the dragon neck and wrapped it around my human body. He made me feel guilty, but I understood something. Being in his body is confusing. Everywhere I went today felt like I had to hide because I was unwanted. "*Nightly, I'm sorry, but I will always want you around. Every day after school when I see you, you're the highlight of my day. Sure I have to do some risky things to make it there, but I have to make it appear that I'm living a normal life. That's why you're upset because I can't always be with you and you can't always be with me right?*"

Nightly didn't say anything.

"*I love you, Nightly. I always have and always will, even if death were to come between us.*"

Nightly hugged the dragon neck he scratched the scales, making me hum. Nightly tensed up though and pulled a dragon wing over him. "Hide me!" he ordered nervously.

I felt a cold sensation overcome me. Rapidly I had the dragon body curl around Nightly and the wings covered us as a fierce wind came up. The dust and dirt flew into our faces. I refused to be separated from Nightly so I held on tight to him. I roared before I stretched out the dragon wings and blew everything around us away. A low growl left the dragon lips as I smelt something like blood. I glanced back at Nightly and noticed that the bandage that was supposed to cover my human hand was blown off and blood started to emerge to the surface once again. Then I looked up past the dazzling sun I saw them. Two people standing at the edge of the ravine.

"Are they mages?" I asked, grabbing Nightly with the dragon claws.

"Yes we are," said the tall one extending his arm.

"Watch out!" cried Nightly.

He didn't have to tell me twice. We escaped by flying up into the sky before a blast of fire hit us. That fire exploded once it hit the ground. Nightly stayed in between the dragon claws, making sure no one could see my human face.

"Nightly, tell me what to do!" I demanded holding onto him tightly.

"Your best advantage is to keep flying but be careful with what you say. These mages understand and speak dragon tongue."

Worry consumed me. There was nothing I could do except fly, while still being visible. The mages didn't want us to go anywhere. The same tall mage extended his arm again and then a blue light shined from what looked like his wrist. It blinded me. I couldn't fly because of it. Energy started to drain out of me. I looked at Nightly, flying took too much effort we started to fall.

"I'm sorry Nightly," I said ashamed of myself.

Before we had the chance to crash I felt like I was being sucked out of the body I was in, again. It was that same vacuum feeling Nightly and I experienced when we first switched bodies. In a matter of seconds I found myself back in my own body and Nightly was back in his. Nightly was flying, not falling.

"Stay hidden. If the mages see your face, we're done for," Nightly said in his normal voice.

Nightly vanished blending into the sky as we flew out of the ravine.

"You're not getting away that easily," the same mage said extending his arm again and had a yellow glow coming from his wrist.

"NO!" cried the other mage moving the arm in a different position before lightning could hit us.

I don't know why he did it but it made it much easier for Nightly and me to escape. I wanted to look back and see their faces but it was too risky. Nightly flew us into the secret area where Nicole was mounting Pearl, getting ready to take off.

"Wait," I yelled out to them. "Stop! Mages are out there."

"We know," said Pearl. *"That's why we're going to attack before they do. We'll rid the Mystic Realm and Human World of them, once and for all."*

"You can't! One of them helped Nightly and me escape. If it wasn't for his mercy we would most likely be dead," I said.

Everyone looked at us with unsteady faces.

"Are you sure a mage helped you escape?" asked Teddy.

"Yes," I said.

They were all surprised like they weren't quite sure what to make from this.

"Incredible," Malcolm commented.

Nicole jumped off of Pearl and grabbed me by the shoulders. "Are you sure it was a mage and not someone else?"

"Yes," I said shrugging her arms off.

Pearl walked up to Nightly hastily, stood up straight and talked in a deep voice. *"Is this all true, little one?"*

"As true as we are real," he replied.

Nicole rubbed her face trying to figure everything out then she turned her back towards me. "I want you to be more cautious of who you hang around. If a mage let you go, that means that they might already know you and your secret."

"Nicole, we're fine and we switched back into our normal bodies. I don't see the problem here," I said. As I said it I just realized that the only way Nightly and I want to switch bodies was when one of us wanted to stop the other from doing something.

Nicole quickly turned around, twisted her hand around and slapped me. The force she held made me fall to the ground. Blood trickled down my lower lip. Quickly I wiped it away and rubbed my cheek.

"The problem is that you were careless enough to let a mage see your face. From now on I'm sending Teddy to keep an eye on you," she said.

Nightly ran up to me making sure I wasn't too badly harmed. He helped me up to my feet and looked at the small blemish that was on my face.

"Wait, why me?" Teddy shuddered. "Don't get me wrong, I like being around Connie," Nightly growled. " . . . but I think my skills are a better use here."

"Nicole's right," said Malcolm. "Teddy has never seen a mage and luckily, a mage hasn't seen his face."

"Good luck with that," James said, putting a hand on Teddy.

"Well, what am I supposed to do?" Teddy complained.

"Get a job in town and keep an eye on Connie. Observe her life, see if anyone stands out that could be a mage," said Malcolm.

"Stop it!" I yelled taking a stand for myself. "Who gave you permission to bother me during my human life? I'm not just a whisperer I did have a life before this. It's already hard enough to keep my dragon a secret from my two best friends. I don't need a babysitter!" I started to walk to the hidden passageway. I heard Nightly's light steps follow me. I glanced back at him and mumbled, "Don't follow me Nightly. I need some time by myself."

"Connie," said Nightly.

"Leave her be young one. She's right about one thing," said Pearl. *"It's going to be hard for her to adjust to the new dangers in her life."*

With that said I left, I went through the illusion that hid the passage way and when I exited I watched the sky as white snowflakes started to fall down. Winter had arrived in Small Valley.

CHAPTER 15

Christmas Ski Trip

Walking back into Small Valley gave me some time to think. The Guardians were doing their best on my behalf. Signing up to be a dragon's whisperer should have come with an instruction manual. This wasn't how I wanted to have my life to turn out. The park came into my view; no one was there, as expected. My hand slipped into my pocket and grabbed the phone. The time was seven. I took in a breath and when I released in it took form of a white mist. It was so quiet and peaceful out, one of my favourite times to be out. I placed the phone back into my pocket and started to head home, but not without hearing the crunch of leaves and twigs snapping. At first I thought it would be some town's person taking an evening walk, but then again it could have been the mages that attacked Nightly and I earlier. It didn't matter; all I knew was that I had to get out of there. The footsteps that disturbed the peaceful evening started to pick up. The walking soon turned into running. As I entered town I slipped into an alley. The cold brick wall behind me had cracks in it. My finger traced the cracks before the person who was chasing me shadow appeared. I took the chance, but imagine my surprise when I found that Sam was the person I pinned underneath me.

"Sam, what are you doing?" I asked, leaning closer to his face.

His face turned a bright red and then he started to stutter. "Judy . . . Judy told me that you were . . . were at your program today but when I got there Kyle was already gone and you were nowhere to be seen . . . so . . . so I started to look for you." Sam avoided eye contact with me and started to mumble. "Could you please get off me now?"

I did what he asked and even helped him up off the ground. He brushed some snow off and faced me.

"Why were you following me?" I asked.

"When I saw you I stepped on some leaves and twigs while trying to approach you but the next thing I knew I saw you running," he said.

"You know, you could have just called out to me or said my name."

Sam turned red again and turned his back to me. "Hey, do you want to go and get something to drink?"

Sam led the way to Papa Joe's Diner. We were lucky it wasn't a far walk. When we arrived in the repaired diner we sat down in a patched up booth and ordered some tea.

"So, what do you want to talk about?" I asked taking a sip of my drink after the waiter dropped it off.

"I just found out that our gym class is going to the bottom of the ravine where all the best slopes and caves and-"

"Get to the point Sam," I said taking another sip.

He cleared his throat, "sorry, I got a little worked up, but our class is going on a ski trip for Christmas break and I was wondering if you were going?"

I looked down at my drink; then looked at him. "How long is it?"

"Two weeks."

"When do we leave?"

"December 12th."

"Is it only our gym class?"

"No, probably every gym class in the school," Sam said looking out the window.

"Awe, that means Kyle will probably be going," I grumbled.

"Can you go?"

"Sam, you just told me this now. I will most likely have the answer tomorrow that is if my parents aren't being stubborn and hold things off to the end of the week."

"Well I hope you can."

"Thanks, Sam, but I have to go," I slid out of the booth and placed some change from my pocket onto the table. "I broke curfew and knowing my mom she'll sell all my stuff on E-bay if I'm not home soon. Thanks for the drink." I gave Sam a smile.

"Let me walk you home," said Sam.

"No, no, I'm fine."

"I insist, besides its already dark out."

I looked out of the window at the cloudy night sky. "Alright, but it's only to my house, right?"

Sam was confused. "Yeah, of course, it's just to your house. What? Do you think I'm going to steal you away like Rumpelstiltskin?"

"Uh, no, I've just had something else on my mind." For the truth to be told, Nicole's words were finally getting to me. Could it really be possible that someone already knew I was a dragon's whisperer, and is it possible that their a mage? Then again I could cut Sam from the list. Pearl described mages to be monstrous murderers, Sam was the complete opposite from that. He was the kindest, sweetest, shiest person I have ever met. However I still had to consider the other people in my town to be a spy. Nicole was right, even if we had a little argument. "Then shall we go?"

"Right after you," said Sam leaving placing a few dollars on the table over my change. He walked in front of me and held the door open for me.

As we walked I looked at Sam who just stared forward. He seemed edgy, which was like him, but he seemed to have something on his mind. When he noticed me looking at him I quickly turned my head away. He attempted to say something but nothing left his mouth. All he did was blush again.

When we arrived at the front door of my house Sam watched me pull out my set of keys. I turned and smiled at him. Again he blushed.

"Thanks for the walk home," I said pushing some loose hair behind my ear.

He kicked some snow on the ground, dropped his head and shrugged. "It's nothing, really."

My keys went into the lock on the door, but I never had the chance to open the door. Sam turned me around suddenly and kissed me upon my lips. The way he grabbed me, the way he was holding me told me something. He was strong, tense and was upset about something. His face was wet, had he been crying? When he let go of me I reacted by pushing him away from me.

"What are you doing?" I asked stunned.

"I'm . . . I'm sorry," he said. His face was hidden in the darkness then he ran off.

When I opened the door I walked in slowly pressing my fingers against my lips, astonished that he did that. Actually when Sam and I first became friends we kissed that day as well.

* * *

I remembered when I was thirteen was when we became friends and when two of my best childhood friends moved away to Australia. I was so upset when Alex and Romeo left. I even tried to stow away in their car and travel with them but I chose the wrong box to hide in. Instead of finding a box full of clothes I hid in the box that had all of their dog's squeaky toys in it. The toys were uncomfortable to sit on and when I moved even an inch one would squeak. Eventually I got caught and cried my eyes out when they left.

There was nothing to do for that whole day except cry. Judy took it even harder. Instead of crying about it openly like I did she locked herself in her room and refused to come out. Mom thought it would be a good idea if I got some fresh air. I took her advice and went to the park and started to swing on the swing set. An airplane flew by. All I wanted was to escape from this ravine to find somewhere else that would want me. I wanted out of this ravine so bad. On the swing there was nothing for me to do except pump my legs until I decided to jump off. I thought, maybe, just maybe, if I tried hard enough there would be a possibility that I could fly out of the ravine. Unfortunately gravity refused to let me go. It pulled me down to the ground where I landed on a boy. Our lips met for a brief second in the impact.

I quickly pulled away and curled up into a ball and started to cry. "I'm . . . I'm sorry. It was an accident."

The boy got up and walked over to me. He crouched down to my level and asked, "Why are you crying?"

I looked up and wiped some tears away from my face. My words staggered because I couldn't stop crying. "Two . . . two of my best friends just moved away and no . . . no matter how hard I try I will never be able to get out of this place to see them. I wish I could just disappear from the world."

"Why would you say that?" he asked.

"Because . . . because if I just disappeared from the world," I began to choke up again, "no one would have to see me like this and I wouldn't have to feel this way either." Tears rushed down my face again. "Everything around me feels like its collapsing and I'm powerless to do anything about it."

The boy put his hand under my chin and tilted my head up. "I know the feeling but it always goes away. You'll never forget your old friends but you can always make new friends in the years to come."

He cleared the tears off my face with his free hand. When I actually looked at his face he had this expression on it like he was really trying to help me. He made me feel happy. "Do you really believe that?"

"Of course I do. I also believe that everyone that lives has a destiny to full fill in the world."

"Why are you being so kind to me? I've seen you around but never talked to you," I said pulling away from him.

The boy stood and looked up at the sky. "Doesn't everyone deserve kindness even if it seems as if they don't?"

Those were powerful words he spoke, it made me smile. "Then, do you want to be my friend?" I asked standing up next to him. "My name's Connie."

I stretched out my arm ready to shake his hand.

"My name's Samson," he replied.

"That's a little too long, may I call you Sam?" I asked.

"Yeah," he said, "I . . . I would like that. To be called Sam that is." He shook my hand and blushed.

We've been friends ever since.

*   *   *

I walked into my room, kicked over a pile of cloths then reached under my bed for an old box. Once I grabbed it, I placed the box on my bed and opened it pulling out a picture of my two friends who moved to Australia with me and Judy standing in the background on the opposite sides of them. Alex and Romeo introduced me to Judy in grade five. When the two of them left, it broke Judy's and my heart. The pain didn't go away until we met Sam.

That was it. I got a darkness dragon because after Alex and Romeo I felt like I wanted to disappear from the world. That was how Nightly was born.

I took out another picture but this one was of Judy and me when we first met Sam.

After rummaging through the box even more I found a brochure for the resort that was located at the bottom of the ravine. Sam was right it did look fun, I wanted to go.

Hey, said Nightly through mind sequence. *How are you feeling?*

Still a bit annoyed about what happened and yet I'm excited, I said, *putting the pictures and brochure away.*

What are you excited about?

I ran into Sam on the way home and he told me that the school's gym classes are going on a ski trip and I want to go.

The Guardians can't leave the secret area, Connie; mages know their faces, all except Teddy, sadly.

I really want to go Nightly. I've always wanted to ski.

They won't let you.

But-

They still won't. Look, Connie, as long as you or I breathe, they won't let you go unless someone they trust was with you.

So, you're suggesting that I let Teddy tag along. You don't even like Teddy, I pointed out. *You always try to burn his clothes, bite or hurt him in any way possible.*

Yeah, I know but that's only because he's always trying to make a pass at you. I am willing to take the risk if it means you have protection when I can't be around you.

Are you telling the Guardians our conversation as we speak?

Maybe . . .

Are they? I asked concerned.

Alright, they are but I speak for myself when I say that you should do this.

I stood up and looked into the new mirror Dad bought me. I looked at my left gold eye and touched it. *What about you? What will you do then?*

I'll keep watch from afar and train. Earlier today, you told me that I'm the highlight of your day. You try so hard to make it seem that you're normal every day. He sounded disgusted when he said, *even if it means that Teddy has to watch you, I will allow it. You need to train in the Human World as well as in the Mystic Realm.*

Are you sure you want to do this?

He was quiet for a while, and then I heard him say a faint, *Yes.*

Then I'll go with it as long as Teddy doesn't embarrass me or ruin my normal life.

Don't worry; I will personally make sure he doesn't.

I laughed as I lied down on my bed. *I agree to it then.*

I'll go tell the others, they'll be pleased.

The connection broke and I found myself fiddling with my fingers. There was a knock on my door.

"Come in," I said sitting up.

My dad opened the door and smiled at me. "Hey there kiddo, was that Sam I saw walk you home?"

"Come on Dad. We've already had this discussion," I said.

"I know, I know, but I still think he's a little friendly around you," Dad walked into the room carrying two cups of tea. He sat down beside me and passed me a cup. "Did you know that when you first introduced me to him, I didn't know what to make of him? He was different and it was noticeable. When you brought him home to meet me I thought that you had started to get involved with teenage love . . . until . . ." he paused.

"Until . . ." I said, motioning for him to speed up the conversation.

" . . . Until I realized you rejected his first proposal."

"What are you talking about? He never made a proposal," I said.

Dad chuckled and took a sip of his tea. "Oh, you women always think you know everything about love but you can never see it when it's right in front of your eyes."

I remembered Sam kissing me at the door. "What are you getting at Dad?"

He chuckled again. "That day when I first met him, he came up to me and asked if the two of you were allowed to date. Imagine my surprise when you came back into the room after talking to you mother smiling like you were queen of the world saying 'Dad, have you met my friend Sam?'"

"He . . . he asked that?"

"Sure did, but after you said that the two of you were friends, I told him that maybe you would re consider once you were both a little older."

"I can't believe he did that," I said astonished.

"Well, it's hard for a person to see who really loves them until an opportunity reveals itself. That's what I did with your mother." He smiled again and took another sip. "All I'm doing is warning you of what might happen in the future. Be careful of the decisions you make because they will affect your life greatly."

"I know," I mumbled, feeling uncomfortable with this talk.

"Anyways, I just wanted to give you the same chat I gave Kyle before he started dating." Dad got up and started to head into the hall.

"Wait," I called out to him. He turned and looked at me. "Can I go on the school ski trip this Christmas?"

Dad gripped the door handle fiercely. His body tensed up convincing me that he was worried about something. He turned and gave me a nervous look, "you're kidding, right?"

"Why would I kid? Dad, I really want to go." I placed my tea down on my night stand and stood up. "Please, let me go. I promise I'll be careful."

Dad's facial expression told me that there was no way in the world he would let me go, but my facial expression told him that that I really wanted to go. "Who's all going on this trip?"

"All the gym classes in the school," I answered.

"Will Sam be going?" he asked suspicious.

"Yes, but we are only friends."

Dad rubbed his face. I could feel his disappointment towards me.

"Dad, you can let Kyle go along as well. He loves snowboarding and you took him last year. Why can't I go?"

"Well, Kyle is already experienced so of course I would let him go."

"I beg to differ."

"Oh and how so?"

"I saw him tumble down the hill about twenty times in less than an hour," I said crossing my arms. "Joey posted it on YouTube and it's categorized as the most failed attempt in life."

Dad was beat. There was no way I couldn't go on the trip now. He sighed and patted my head. "Well I guess that you're going then."

I jumped with joy giving my dad a huge hug before whipping out my cell and dialling Judy's number. I just couldn't wait to tell her the good news. Dad gave me an awkward smile and closed the door behind him leaving me alone in my room. Before he left I noticed that he was shaking his head, dang it, he left the room leaving this feeling like something was about to happen. A shiver went down my spine while I dialed Judy's number waiting for someone to pick on the other end. The phone had been ringing for thirty seconds and still there was no answer.

"Come on Judy, pick up the phone," I mumbled. It still rung until a weak 'hello' came from the other line. "Judy, did I wake you?"

"No, I needed to wake up. I only fell asleep because my roommate was watching a boring documentary when dinosaurs roamed the earth. I mean, *come on*, if you have the remote at least put on a channel that doesn't have a monotone narrator. Whatever happened to the shopping channel?" She sighed in frustration while I let out a small chuckle. "Anyhow, what's up?"

I told her about Sam's and my little chat earlier that evening, but skipped the part about him kissing me. I finished off my day report telling her that my dad was letting me go on the Christmas Ski Trip with the school.

"Lucky," she whined. "The doctor said that I'll be in a cast for three months."

"What are you complaining about? You're not even in gym. How could you go if you don't even take the class?"

I heard nothing on the other line for a while. Then Judy broke out, laughing. "Then I'll sneak into one of the supply boxes they're moving and make sure there are no dog toys in it."

I grumbled. She still remembered that incident from two years ago. At least I made attempt to stay with Alex and Romeo. Judy didn't even fight or make a peep when she heard that they were moving. She lightened up quickly after she met Sam. Now she can mention old stories of Alex and Romeo any time. Once and awhile she would even put them in some of her jokes.

"Anyways," she said slowing down her breathing. "Don't worry about me. You should go and enjoy yourself with Sam and keep me updated on the events."

"Judy, Sam and I are *just* friends," I said blushing.

"Sure, you're just friends," she said in a sarcastic voice. "Listen, I have to go, I'll talk to you tomorrow about that dragon."

"What dragon?" I asked trying to play dumb.

"Yep, go ahead and say that, I'll talk to you tomorrow, bye."

She hung up her phone. I kept the cellphone up to my ear for a little while before I hung it up, placing it on my night stand and got ready for bed. I took off my shirt and saw my dragon wings on my back as I glanced into the mirror. It was there as plain as day unless one was blind, otherwise you couldn't miss it. "Where's my scale?" I asked myself, feeling around my ankles but found nothing there. It must have fallen off during the flood. I quickly slipped into my pyjamas and fell onto my bed. How could I have let this happen? It was just one more thing for Nicole to get mad at me about. I shut off my light and slowly closed my eyes.

In my dream I could tell it was different than most dreams. Music started to play. Drums, violins, trumpets, flutes and clarinets were the sounds awakening me. When I awoke I found myself lying on a red velvet couch wearing a long red dress with black frills. I moved my hand towards my face only to feel a mask covering half of it. There was no use staying on the couch. I stood up and started to walk down some spiral stairs that led to a dining room with a huge spread on the table. That's when I saw a man without a mask sitting at the head of the table, sipping some red wine.

"Mage," I whispered, looking at his appearance.

He was a tall mage with grey skin, black hair and cat like ears, pale yellow eyes with slit pupils. He was dressed in all black.

"It's about time," he said, staring at me. "I've been waiting for you."

"Why me?" I asked, slowly gesturing to myself.

"I want to talk to you," he said, standing up and walking towards me. "Now, won't you have a seat?"

I bit my lip, not knowing what to do until the mage took me by the hand and guided me to a seat at the table. He pulled out chair and waited until I sat down, then he pushed me in. He returned to his own seat, at the opposite side of the table and sat down.

"I want to make a proposition," he said, taking another sip of wine. "I want you to hand over your dragon to me nice and quietly. That way nothing has to get rough or violent."

"So this is about dragons? I'm sorry but I refuse your offer," I said, standing up.

"Do you know what will happen if you don't hand him over? Everything you love will start to disappear, causing nothing but loss and pain for you."

"You obviously already know who I am. Why don't you just take him now?" I asked.

"I might know who you are, but mages have always had to confirm who they suspect to be a dragon's whisperer. It can be the hard way or the easy way. This is the easy way. I'm letting you wear that mask so we can have a discussion about your fate." He vanished in front of my eyes and appeared behind me. He held a black rose up to me as I turned around. "Did you know that the outside of the flower starts to wilt away before the inside," he put the rose up to my face. "You have until this rose wilts to reconsider my offer or else we start doing things the hard way."

"Wait, you said 'we', who's we?" I asked suspiciously, but by the time the words left my mouth, I was awake in my bed. I panted, looked to my window and sitting on the ledge was a black rose.

PART 2

CHAPTER 16

Pass or Fail

Snow covered the ground. For the last couple of days my mind had been wandering off constantly because of that single black rose. I didn't even tell Nightly about it. There was one good thing that came out of the events. Kyle and I had finally made it to our last 'S.R.P' session. With one last session standing in the way I would only focus on one thing and that was getting out of this ridiculous thing.

"Connie!" I heard a voice call out. "Connie!"

Because my eyes were blindfolded I could not see. I walked down a hallway. It was tight and narrow. When I stretched out my arms they would touch the dry wall, chipping off some of the loose paint and feel the dust on my hands.

"Move it!" yelled a person, shoving me aside and running down the hall.

"Glen," I yelled, "Does this really have anything to do with getting our papers?"

An intercom came on and Glen's feminine voice echoed throughout the halls. "Remember, those blindfolds must stay on your face until you reach your sibling. Everyone is released into different sections of different halls; it's almost like a maze. You must listen and work together with your sibling to find your way out without removing your blindfolds. If you remove it or if it falls off in any way you fail the 'Sibling Respect Program and you'll have to come back next year to finish it off." He took a breath. "Now, once you find your sibling, you must work together to find your way out of the maze. There is a

135

single door open. That is your way out and your one way ticket to your graduation papers."

"Dang it, Glen, we can't see anything! How are we supposed to find the person we're related to?" I hated this. For ten minutes, I'd been walking around, listening to people cussing, tripping, running, shouting and crashing into walls and each other. I'd been toppled over about twenty times.

"Don't just run around. You've only lost one of your senses." the intercom turned off.

Well, it's obvious. We lost our sight. Any moron can see that!

Wow, I didn't know you could get mean and insulting, said Nightly.

Can't talk now, Nightly, I have to find Kyle and get this final exercise over and done with.

Oh, come on, let me help.

Fine, tell me how to find Kyle, I said running into a wall, *and hurry.*

Alright, it's like doing mind sequence. You need to focus and wait for the connection.

Not to rain on your parade, Nightly, I rubbed my face, *but I don't have that connection with Kyle like I have with you.* Someone ran by me and knocked me to the ground.

Just listen! He growled, sounding annoyed. *Do you see or at least notice anything odd about the other people?*

As I rose off the ground I put my back up against the wall and listened as people ran past me in haste. Further down the hall I heard a few kids cuss as they dropped to the ground after running into other people. *Yeah, everyone's rushing; they're running around like lemmings, hoping that they'll end up running into their sibling.*

Exactly, now what should you be doing?

Concentrating on Kyle's voice, I listened. I could feel the others run past me, smashing into walls and other people.

"Connie, where are you?" It sounded distant but I was sure that was Kyle's voice.

Thanks, Nightly. You're a good boy.

Don't treat me like a dog. How many times must I tell you that I am a dragon?

Goodbye, Nightly, I broke off the connection. "Kyle," I called out.

There was no response at first. I carefully walked alongside the walls and every five seconds, I would call out Kyle's name.

"Connie." I heard him call out again.

"Kyle," I said, returning his call. I started to run.

"Connie," he called again, his voice sounding closer and clearer.

"Kyle."

"Connie."

"Ky-" I never got to finish my response. I went head first into another guy. We both went down to the ground.

"Watch where you're going," the two of us yelled at each other.

"Connie?" said the other person.

"Kyle." I felt the face in front of me, recognizing the shape and texture. I wrapped my arms around the person, knowing it was Kyle.

"Yeah," he replied, shoving me off him. "Now that we found each other how are we going to find the single door that Glen was talking about?"

"Well, if the door is open, there might be a draft coming through the halls. The stronger the draft, the closer we are to getting out of here."

Kyle knocked his fist against my forehead. "Hello, this hallway is connected to others and they are full of turns, and let's not forget our good fellow classmates are running around like chickens with their heads cut off."

I giggled. It was funny. My fingers slid into Kyle's. "Make sure you don't let go, I shouldn't be the one having to take care of you."

"Connie?" Kyle sounded surprised.

We held each other's hands firmly, making sure there was no way that we would be separated. We both got up from the floor together and I guided Kyle through the hallway. Listening and feeling a draft. My instincts told me where to go. All Kyle had to do was follow. A few times the other kids kept bumping into us. They yelled at us for getting in there way when it was really them being stupid and running around thinking that it would solve all there problems. Kyle had enough of it. He swung me to the side.

"Kyle, what are you doing?" I complained.

"Wait for it." The next thing I heard was a thud and the crash of several people collapsing to the ground. "I have had it with you guys. I'm not settling for it anymore!"

Kyle continued to walk, pulling me along behind him.

"Kyle, did you just clothesline those people?" I asked.

Kyle remained silent. He just continued to walk. We heard clapping coming from a distance along with a cold breeze of the winter air.

Kyle pulled me aside. "I'm the one who should look out for you, not the other way around," he admitted. "When we step out of this hall we'll be done being forced to work together, but remember . . ." He gripped my hand even more tightly, " . . . I'm older and it's my job to protect this family."

We walked out into the sunlight where we heard our parents calling and cheering our names. Our blindfolds were removed and we saw all the other parents and some of our friends standing together.

"Congrats, you two," said Glen. He lifted our hands up in the air as if we were champions. You should be proud. You two are the first ones out."

I smiled. Before we were run over by all the other kids. Kyle and I were on the bottom of the doggy pile while the other siblings took off their blind folds. I looked back over at Kyle who was still holding onto my hand. We looked at each other and began to laugh. I guess attending those sessions wasn't a total loss after all.

CHAPTER 17

Preparing for a Trip

Snow piled up quickly in November. One of the other good parts of living in a ravine is that you don't get as much snow as the people outside of the ravine do. The school ski trip was one week away and I was nervous, yet excited. My dad had finally caved and allowed me to go on the trip with Kyle. Nevertheless I couldn't shake the feeling that something big was about to happen.

The black rose I had received the other night was placed in a glass of water in my room. If that mage was telling the truth I wanted to make sure that the black rose would never wilt. It was hard not to think about it. I tried to block it out by filling my mind with excited thoughts about the ski trip. It was useless though. If I wasn't thinking about that mage, I was reminded of Dad's words: 'Be careful of the decisions you make because they will affect your life greatly'. Because of what he said I couldn't concentrate on today's exercise.

Teddy was teaching me and Nightly about stealth. We were going at it with a hundred and ten percent of our strength. I made the mistake of telling my Guardians about my encounter with the mage. What was weird was that they knew mages could manipulate dreams but when they told me their stories it seemed like neither one of them had experienced a mage in their dreams. I seemed to be the only one. That might have been the reason they were getting me to train so hard.

The point of the exercise was for me and Nightly to hide in the forest part of the secret area and tag Teddy. However we could never stay in one spot. If we stayed in a spot too long Teddy would find us then electrocute us or at least give us a bad enough shock that we would know that we were failing. We were doing this for two weeks and Nightly and I had no success at all.

It sucked having to do this in winter, my foot prints were visible, Nightly, even when he was invisible, could be noticed because of the cloud trail he would leave behind. It's also sad to admit that we weren't that fast. Even if I ran at full speed Teddy would still be able to shock me.

I slowly crept forward from behind a spruce tree, watching Teddy looking around as he stood in the middle of the area. I moved quickly from tree to tree, praying he wouldn't see me. He looked over in my direction which made me decide to retreat back a few trees. What I've found out that the further away I am the less the electric shocks hurt.

"You're not very good at hiding, Connie," Teddy called out, he tapped his foot on the ground quickly and the next thing I knew a shock hit me.

"Why are we doing this in the winter," I whined looking out at Teddy, "I can be found easily in this weather condition?"

"Which is exactly why we're doing this. You can't expect a mage to attack you on a clear sunny day, you have to be ready. Expect the unexpected. You have to be prepared, Connie, they can attack at any time and you have to be ready. If you learn to hide yourself on a clear winter day you'll be able to hide from them any day." Teddy tapped his foot again making another electric shock hit me. "Use your dragon's power. Connect your mind and body to his. You should feel his power through your body as well as him."

"What if we're separated?" I asked moving closer to Teddy. "As far as I can tell, Nightly and I can contact each other while he's here and I'm at home, but say if we're farther away from each other," I moved closer, "what would happen?"

"You wouldn't have to worry about that. No matter the distance, no matter the situation a whisperer and dragon will never be separated."

I moved up further and rubbed my back against the bark and needles of the pine tree. *Nightly, we can't keep attacking him head on. Let's try what Teddy suggested, connect our mind and body.*

Are you sure you want to do this? It's risky and we haven't mastered the mind body switch.

Just try it, you can't get anywhere without trying things first.

Fine, have it your way.

I ran out of the forest and into the open, sprinting back and forth. I noticed Teddy could only shock people he touched or were straight in front of him. If I maneuvered around it, it would make it more difficult for him to hit me. Nightly's and I made our first attempt to connect our body and mind it failed. I was too focused on dodging Teddy. We tried again but this time Nightly got shocked so we tried it a third time, then a fourth, then a fifth, then a sixth and finally we gave it a seventh. Nothing was working! We were both tired and it seemed we were getting nowhere. Teddy knew where both of us were every time. Nightly and I laid down on the snow in the open, in front of Teddy waiting to see what he would do next.

"Can we take a break?" I begged trying to catch my breath.

"No, you must be prepared; this isn't school where your mom and dad can aid you. You chose this life; you have to know when to pick yourself up. If a mage finds that you are tired they will go for the kill in an instant. Remember, it's not just your life anymore it is also you dragons," Teddy yelled. "Now get up and do it again!"

I slowly rose to my feet and looked at Teddy. My hand wiped the sweat away from my head. If I returned home again, all sweaty like I have for the two weeks Teddy and I have been working on this he would be calling me 'Sweat Girl' for the rest of my life.

James and Malcolm were outside and once and while I would notice Malcolm taking notes while James chopped up some fire wood. During these times Nicole and Pearl would be patrolling the area for any mage activity.

When I'm home Nightly trains privately with Pearl and hasn't spoken a word to me about it. My life has become stressed ever since that dream. Darn mage! Even when they're not attacking they're making my life hard.

Oh, and one more thing, Teddy got a job at my school as a janitor. If he's not trying to hit on girls he is trying to drive me mad with his training methods. As a janitor it's Teddy's job to wax and mop the floors. I don't think the job required a person to forget about putting up 'wet floor' signs to test the reflexes of students. For two weeks I had slid, skidded and tripped on every floor in the school making a complete fool of myself in front of everybody. I thought my training was supposed to be inconspicuous, I guess Teddy had another thought going through his mind when he accepted the job. Luckily, I wasn't the only one annoyed with Teddy's 'work ethics'. Some other student's parents made complaints to the school and the principal banned Teddy off mopping and waxing for the rest of the semester. Thank heavens.

"Connie, watch out!" Nightly yelled, swooping down and grabbing me by my coat. He got me to think back into reality. If Nightly hadn't awaken me from my day dream state I would still be lying on the ground, moaning and complaining like a spoiled child. *"Connie, get onto the saddle."*

That's what I did. I grabbed a hold of Nightly's horns, swung myself over onto the saddle and strapped myself in. Nightly circled the area, maneuvering in and out of clouds trying to copy what I did earlier.

"Now you're getting the idea," Teddy said impressed.

Nightly and I became transparent. When I was with Nightly it made situations like these so much easier.

Nightly, you know what to do from here, right?

You bet I do, he responded. Nightly pulled his wings in and started to spin. He dove down at full speed. It felt like being a bullet, breaking through the wind like it was nothing.

Great, now with both of us together there is no way he can detect us now, I said proudly.

We were going to make it. We were going to pass this exercise and get it over with. As we got closer to Teddy we hit something like a force field that was pure electricity. The shock was so intense it broke my elastic. Nightly crashed landed, digging up snow and dirt as he made contact with the ground. I was lucky that I was strapped in when we crashed or else I would have been crushed under Nightly's body.

"Not bad," Teddy admitted, "but if you take your time to attack the enemy they will take that advantage and build up enough energy to create what I just did which is known as an electric field. If you're lucky, Connie, and train hard you could create powerful attack known as a 'Soul Blast'."

I unstrapped myself and rolled over onto the ground and groaned. "You know, I buy sturdy elastics to hold up my hair. When they break I know you're over working me besides what's a Soul Blast?"

Teddy walked over to us and held out two pink pills in the palm of his hand. "Eat these, you'll feel a lot better and they'll give you your energy back."

Nightly and I both looked at each other exchanging nervous looks. I sat up and waited for Nightly to turn around. When Teddy gave us the pill we placed them in our mouths and crunched down on them. To our surprise it actually did give us energy. The only problem was that it didn't heal the bruises or cuts that we endured.

"There are three different kinds of these things," Teddy explained. "Humans and whisperers created them over the past few centuries. They're known as 'Whisperer Pills'. The one I just gave is called the E.N. gain also known as energy gain which is pretty self-explanatory." Teddy reached into his pocket and pulled out a blue and a black pill, having them lay carefully in his hands. "The blue one is called 4-get, really known as forget. This little guy will make you forget everything you know for twenty-four hours. When the time is up all your memories will come back. Now our last pill here is very dangerous and rare. This black pill, when consumed, it will immediately break the connection between you and your dragon-"

"But why would someone want that?" I interrupted. "I wouldn't want to consume a pill just to separate myself from Nightly."

"Connie!" Nightly said sternly, *"if you were captured by a mage the first thing you want to do is break our connection."*

"We're stronger together though. I don't understand why we should separate ourselves," I said confused.

"Of course she wouldn't understand," commented Peril landing beside us. *"No whisperer understands until they're in that situation."*

Nicole climbed off Peril and whispered something into Teddy's ear.

"You're kidding?" he asked.

"Afraid not, so you better get going," she suggested.

Teddy pulled the collar of his winter coat up, placed the pills in his hand back into his pocket then head out of the secret area. I watched him run through the illusion that was the exit but didn't understand why he was doing it in such a rush.

"What was that all about?" I asked, turning my attention back to Nicole and Pearl.

"Nothing that concerns you, but I'm going to take over your lessons till your trip," Nicole said stretching her arms. "Now, tell me what Teddy was talking to you about."

I looked over at Nightly mouthing to him 'what?' then turned my attention back to Nicole. "We were finishing up for the day. I just needed . . . I mean, I wanted to know what a Soul Blast is and why I should take the black pill."

"A Soul Blast is something you shouldn't worry about. You're too young to learn it. As for the black pill, it is called 'Sear'-," answered Nicole.

"Sear?" I interrupted. "Why does that pill have a different kind of name then the rest of them?"

"Quiet human," demanded Peril.

Nicole sighed and coughed, indicating that she wanted to continue. "Continuing on, sear is known as the death pill to dragons and mages. One pill can kill a full grown dragon or mage if consumed.

'Sear' is another word for burn. The touch of the pill to any creature in the Mystic Realm will burn them. The essence in the little black pill is unspeakably strong. The material to make it is exponentially rare. To humans and whisperers the pill is harmless because they were the ones who made them."

"Wait; are all the pills artificial? Who made them, when did they come into existence?" I was full of questions dying to know the answer.

"Shut it, you're so annoying," Pearl growled.

"As I was saying, sear is made by humans along with the rest of the whisperer pills. They were made around the end of the seventeenth century and the beginning of the eighteenth. At the time the recipe was popular, until the war started up for the control over the recipes. The humans gave the recipes to the whisperer's, hoping they would do good with them, but as society changed mages became more fierce with their attacks. Mages had this idea that if they got a hold of the recipes they could modify the pills so that they would be immune to their effects but for whisperers and dragons, instant death. The war raged on for four years; breaking the recipes up into individual parts. They're scattered across the world and few are looking for them, some have found parts, but not a complete recipe. Devonburg gave us access to his supplier who found a part of the recipe. The ingredients are extremely rare as are the pills. They are to be used wisely and only wisely.

The reason why the others are called something different is because whisperers needed to code them so no mage would expect it to be our secret stash of defence to defeat them with.

As for why we need that specific pill, when a mage has captured a whisperer they can trace the connection between the two partners. They will try anything to find the dragon. Even if you block Nightly out of you mind you won't be able to block him out forever.

Sear will disconnect you from your dragon, so no matter how strong the mage is they won't be able to track down your dragon."

I sighed and shuddered. I'd rather call these things tic-tac. I hated the thought of a drug saving my life.

"The feeling's mutual," said Nicole. "Don't let the thought scare you, Connie. Otherwise mages will find you. They can smell fear."

"I thought those were dogs," I said.

"Where do you think the saying came from?" she asked glancing over at the setting sun behind her. "Go home, Connie, relax and get ready for your trip. You've had enough training. I'm going to give you the rest of the week off."

"Why?"

"Consider it a Christmas present from me, now go."

"Well, thanks," I said, surprised with Nicole. They've been working me to no bitter end and then she just lets me leave. I guess it really was the season to be jolly. I crawled to my feet and stretched out my back, hugged Nightly goodbye and then walked towards the exit. As I walked through the illusion and into the passageway my mind began to think of situations that would have Teddy leave our lesson. He didn't go anywhere in town except to the school or the store. As I exited the passageway I began to walk to the school. Surely that would be the place for me to get answers.

The walk was long, but Small Valley was beautiful at this time of the year. Christmas decorations were on every house, tree and building. As I walked into the park I glanced up at the huge spruce tree that was decorated by everyone. Most people would have a tree in the town square, not us. The one huge spruce tree by the park was all that we needed.

When I arrived at the school I tried to open the front doors, they were locked, as were the rest of the doors that led into the school. There had to be a way in. That's when I heard a ruckus. When I walked around the corner there was Judy. She was trying to pull herself up through an open window. That window wasn't opened when I first went around the school, to look for a way in.

I walked up to her, tapped her shoulder, the next thing I knew was that I was dodging a crutch that Judy was just randomly swinging in the air. She had her eyes closed and didn't open them until she heard me drop to the ground screaming for her to stop.

"Oh, it's only you Connie," Judy said relieved. "I thought you were one of the doctors that were after me."

"Judy," I yelled. "What do you think you're doing? Why are you out of the hospital?"

"Oh," she scratched her face. Why did I get the feeling she did something I'm going to regret asking?

"What did you do?" I asked, standing myself up.

"Nothing, I just asked the doctors to check your locker for me. When they didn't I snuck out to find the proof for myself. When I arrived the janitor guy was here but he wouldn't let me in which explains why I'm trying to enter through a window."

So Teddy was here. "Do the doctors know you're missing?" I asked.

"Well, yes . . . but only after I used a strategic move to get out of there. Before I escaped the hospital I stole the nurse's cigarettes and threw them in the washing machine."

"You actually did that?" I asked stunned. I knew Judy was sneaky, but desperate, not so much.

"What? I hated the smell of smoke in my room. Did you know you can get cancer by smelling the smoke off people's clothes?"

"No you can't."

"Well maybe you could, you just don't know it."

"Judy, listen, I want to get in the school to, even if it's for different reasons. Instead of whining and attacking people with crutches, let's do each other a favour and help each other."

"Fine, but I will find evidence that you are hiding a dragon."

"Good luck with that," I commented, crossing my arms.

I lifted Judy onto my shoulders to help get into the open window. When she was in I handed her the crutches and pulled myself in right after. It was too easy. Someone else came in through this way and deliberately left it open. Teddy had a set of keys of his own, so who was it?

If I had known which classroom we had just entered beforehand I would have head home right away because we were in the science room. I hated experiments and blood. Even in social class when we discuss historical battles I always have this feeling like I was going to be sick. Speaking of blood or seeing blood made me nauseous.

"Hey, Connie, are you alright?" Judy asked, looking at my pale face.

"Once we get out of here I will be," I replied, holding my stomach as I felt it turn.

Judy trudged her way over to the light switch and turned the lights on, revealing all the petrified insects posted on the wall, frogs in tubes and separated hearts, lungs and guts in jars. I wanted to hurl. I kept my eye gaze down at the ground as I walked to the door and unlocked it.

"Judy, I'm leaving. You stay here and wait."

"Why do I have to stay?" she complained.

"Because your crutches will give us away," I argued, walking out of the classroom.

I heard Judy mumble something before I shut the door. Everything became quiet; I took in deep breaths calming myself down. It seemed like I would never get over that fear. Keeping my footsteps light, they moved me down the hall to the principal's office. Through the offices window I saw a computer on. I tried turning the door knob, it was locked. I couldn't tell if Teddy was in there but I knew there was someone at that computer, I just couldn't tell who. A noise was heard down the hall. I quickly ducked behind the door. The door knob slowly turned as I slid up against the wall and curled up into a ball. The door opened and it wasn't Teddy.

Instead it was a shorter man who had a full grown black beard, a green eye and one glass eye. His appearance scared me, was this the guy who came in through the window? There was something that caught my eye, on his neck was a strange mark. It looked like a triangle with three circles surrounding it.

He gave a small grin, looked left and right then he ran down the hall. When the cost was clear I got up and walked into the office and sat down before the computer. The computer was left on and on the monitor was a file of all the adults working in the school including

Teddy. I closed the file and found another one opened behind it, it was about the ski trip. On the file was a list of all the teachers and students that were attending the trip along with adult volunteers. I didn't understand what that guy was looking for? What was his reason for being here? Was this why Nicole grew suspicious and sent Teddy here, to check things out?"

A hand touched me; I reacted by throwing my fist behind me. I hit someone and it felt like a face. I brought my hand back and saw blood on it. My stomach turned and I felt like vomiting again. Quickly I wiped the blood off on my pants.

"Connie, what are you doing here?" Teddy asked, holding his nose.

I turned around and hugged Teddy. "There was a guy in here and he was looking at the staff files."

"I know," he said, pushing me away and grabbing a Kleenex. "That's what Nicole sent me here for."

I glared at him.

"Alright, I also put my name on the supervisor list for the ski trip."

"Well, now that I know what's all happening I'll just grab Judy and get her back to the hospital?"

"Wait, Judy's here too?"

"Yeah, and she nearly killed me with her crutches."

"Get her out of here," Teddy ordered.

"Why?"

"That man that entered school, where did you see him last?"

"In this office then he sprinted down the hall."

"And where is Judy?"

"In . . . the science room," I said pointing outside the office. "Then again she never listens to me."

Teddy grunted. "Do you have any idea where she is?"

"Most likely by my locker," I said looking down the hall.

"Go get her and I'll take care of the other guy."

I nodded and then we split up. I ran towards my locker and saw the door open. Quietly I crept towards it. I took off a boot, raised it in the air then pulled the locker door back to find Judy snaking on my Christmas chocolates.

"Judy!"

"What? I wasn't eating your chocolates you always have in your locker at Christmas time every year," she said cleaning her face and closing the locker door.

I rolled my eyes as I re opened my locker and grabbed an extra elastic, pulling my hair back and tying it back up. As I did that I said, "So, what did you find either then my chocolates?"

She gulped then straightened herself up on her crutches. "Not much just a picture of a dragon printed off from the internet and a funny looking biscuit."

"Can we please get out of here? I think I saw a strange man," I said, walking towards the science room.

"You mean the guy with the glass eye?"

"Yeah," I said stopping in my tracks.

"He seemed nice. He came by, smiled and left."

A cold chill went down my back. A guy with a glass eye that smiles sounds scary. "Let's just get out of here before we get caught?"

"Alright, alright, calm down it's not like it's a life or death situation here."

"It's only a life or death situation for me," I mumbled.

"What's that?" Judy asked.

"Nothing," I said walking down the hall, "let's just go."

Judy shrugged and followed me back to the science room and back through the window. This time I made sure Judy got to the hospital, safe and sound, without any doctors catching us. Once that was done I trudged back to my home trying to figure out what that man was doing on the computer. What did he want from a regular high school computer? The thought stayed in my head until I fell asleep that night.

Another dream fell upon me. Instead of finding myself in a different location I was still in my room. Everything seemed the same like I wasn't dreaming at all, that was until I saw a mage standing in my doorway.

It wasn't the same mage. This one was shorter. He had the same grey skin and black hair. He had a diamond earring in one ear. He had no shirt, no shoes only black pants. There was a strange mark on his chest like the man with the glass eye only it was difficult to make out the shape.

"Who are you?" I asked standing up.

He said nothing.

"Are you here about the flower? My times not up, you can't hurt anyone."

"I'm here to warn you," he said in a deep voice. "Don't go on the ski trip."

"Why?" I asked sternly. Lots of things have happened to me today, but I wanted answers and the only way I would get them was if I made myself strong and fearless.

"You've been warned. If you want what's best for you and your dragon you won't go on the ski trip."

"You're not very specific," I commented, crossing my arms, "and how do you know about my dragon?"

He turned his back to me and walked away. For once I didn't say 'wait' or 'stop' or even 'don't go'. It already felt like I knew him and that's why I let him go.

CHAPTER 18

The Ravine's Legend

The last week before the ski trip passed quickly. Despite the dream I had it still didn't stop me for preparing for the trip. His words never left my mind or his image. I felt attracted to him, but why?

For the past weak Mom argued with Dad about keeping us together, but then Dad worked his charm and assured her that for the two weeks we were gone it would be fine. Thank goodness Dad got her off our backs. I don't think I could handle anymore suffocating hugs, or rivers of tears.

On the day we were leaving Mom and Dad decided to give us one Christmas presents each. We were in the living room and Kyle and I sat down waiting to receive our present. We only got one because the ski trip was well worth over ten presents for each of us.

Kyle opened his present first and received a video camera.

"Sweet," he said, "now I can actually tape real alien activity that happens on earth."

"Or you can upgrade your status on YouTube," I teased. "Why are you even going on this trip? You suck at snowboarding."

"That wasn't my fault," he whined. "Lee and Joey iced the trail before I even got on."

"Sure they did," I commented, "maybe they were also the ones who got you to fail your math test three times."

"Hey, you're not in grade twelve yet. You don't even know how much homework they give you. Not to mention the tests are extremely hard."

"Yeah, how did you get a girlfriend again?"

Kyle closed his eyes and twitched his left eyebrow, he wasn't happy with me. He gave the video camera to Dad and tackled me off the couch and onto the carpet. He pinned me down, becoming cocky with his strength. Why didn't this guy join the wrestling team? I timed my comeback perfectly, I head butted Kyle in the chest knocking the wind out of him. When he got off me I scrambled to my feet trying to get back onto the couch but Kyle grabbed my waist and pulled me back down to the floor. Once he had me in his clutches he started to give me a noogie after putting me in a headlock.

"Kyle, Connie, stop this immediately!" Mom ordered.

"Oh, let them have fun Martha," Dad said video tapping everything. "This is great stuff."

"But Rick, they're wrecking the room," Mom whined.

I bit down on Kyle's arm forcing him to release me from his grasp if he didn't want a big chunk of his skin ripped off.

"Alright, that is enough!" Mom yelled, stomping her foot on the ground. "Connie on one couch and Kyle on the other, move it!"

I moved to one couch quickly and Kyle sat up quickly running to the other couch while rubbing his arm that I bit.

"Now, Connie, it's your turn to open your present." Mom handed me a wide green box then she sat back down beside Dad who wrapped his arm around her.

I tore off the wrapping paper finding a laptop sitting on my lap. I was surprised. Mom stood back up and sat down beside me.

"You've seemed to be busy lately with whatever it is you've been doing. I've noticed that you've been staying up late as well as barley getting all your homework done. So, your dad and I decided to get you a laptop so no matter where you are you'll still have time to do it," Mom explained, showing me the Mac brand laptop.

"Nice," Kyle commented, "You got a present to do work. Hey, Dad, maybe you should have thrown in a broom and dust pan."

I took the laptop out of the box and then threw the box at Kyle's face.

"What was that for?" he complained, rubbing his face.

"Nice shot sweaty," Mom said, giving me a kiss on the head.

"Mom," Kyle whined.

"Oh hush. You'll even have to admit that you had that coming," she said.

Dad looked at the time and saw that it was quarter to twelve. "Well, we better scurry these kids off to their bus or else we'll have to buy them more presents."

Mom got out our luggage and our coats. We were all set for the trip. I was excited. Dad got the family van started. Before we left I got out one of Dad's old brief cases and put my new laptop in it. We piled into the van and drove off to the school. Once we arrived we took our luggage and loaded it onto a bus. When that was done we went inside the gym and listened as Coach and the principal gave us a speech on behaviour, expectations and the rules. When they were done, teenagers from grade ten to grade twelve said goodbye to their families and boarded the busses. Mom and Dad gave Kyle and me a hug, but before we were about to leave Dad pulled me aside.

"Connie, are you sure you want to do this? Your mother won't mind if you stay at home with us," he said.

"I'm sure, Dad. Besides I don't want to come in between Mom and her snookums," I teased.

"I am not her snookums," Dad whispered angrily.

"Come on, snookums, let's go home," Mom called out.

Dad went red in the face while the other parents laughed.

"You were saying," I giggled.

Dad grabbed his head, faced me then gave me a hug. "Be careful. There is something strange that lives deep within the ravine," he whispered. He let go of me and kissed my forehead. "Be safe," then he left with my mom.

A cold chill crossed with a bad feeling filled my body, I shook it off and looked over to another group of kids. In the crowd I saw Sam and Kamal; it looked like they were having an argument. It didn't seem to last long, Kamal gave Sam something, but Sam didn't look happy at all taking the thing and placing it in his pocket. He then looked up and glanced in my direction. I didn't want to look weird so I boarded the bus with another group of student and sat down next to a girl named Britney.

She was a quiet girl who always kept her nose in her books. She had brown hair, blue eyes which were hidden behind her tinted glasses. She wore a pink turtle neck sweater and skinny blue jeans. Her nails were always chipped; glasses crooked and always had missed matched socks.

She was the brainy one in my grade so you can kind of imagine how her life is. She was also in my gym class and English. That's what made me suspicious about her. Britney was shy. She couldn't throw, couldn't catch and couldn't pass. Why was she on this trip anyways?

"Hi, Connie," said Sam boarding the bus and sitting in the seat right behind me. "You excited to start this trip?"

I looked back at Sam's face. Whatever was wrong before was gone now. He smiled at me which made me feel happy. Even after our 'little incident' there was no way I could stay mad at him. "Of course, why would I be here otherwise?"

"Because of the legend of the ravine," whispered Britney.

The bus started up and took off. During the time I was surprised that Britney spoke.

"What . . . what did you say?" I asked.

Britney closed her book, straightened up her glasses and looked over at us. "There is a legend at the ski resort were going to. It's called Black Ravine Lake. About five maybe ten centuries ago, there was a little village built above the ravine. That town lived and prospered for years. Now, this village had two warriors that made it healthy and wealthy. They defended it from bandits or intruders, collecting the money for their ransom."

"Boring," a guy named Sid commented as he shoved Sam aside so he could sit down beside him. "Instead of talking about lame history let's talk about how awesome this trip is going to be when I start showing off my moves."

"Sid, shut up, no one cares," I said.

"Don't worry I'll keep him quiet," said Sam.

"Continue, Britney," I said.

"Well, the warriors that protected the village were named Gregary and Hanry."

"Don't you mean Gregory and Henry?" asked Sam.

"No, it's actually Gregary and Hanry. If you don't believe me its right here in this book," she said opening her book again showing me the page where they were mentioned.

I pulled my glasses out of my pocket and placed them on my face.

"Hey, look everyone, it's another four eyes," Sid commented.

Sid is a big guy who always commented on everything and everyone. He wore a slimy green jacket, black leather pants, and holey gloves.

Sam jabbed him in the side which made him hiccup making him quiet down.

"Thanks," I said.

He blushed and leaned over the seat.

I looked in the book and saw the names Hanry and Gregary. There was no mistake about it.

"Are you sure it's not a typo?" I asked.

"How dare you! Martin Miles does not make typos, Connie. He tells the truth and nothing but the truth with excellent grammar, spelling and punctuation." Britney held up the book and showed us the title of the book 'Martin Miles Guide towards the Truth through Legends'. "He is the master of myths, the researcher through legends not to mention a hot man of seventeen."

"Britney, can we focus on the legend in the book and not the author?" I asked.

"Fine," she grumbled opening the book back up. "Gregary and Hanry were also brothers. They loved defending the town together; you could say that they were the best of friends, for the time being."

"They broke up," said Sid. "Wow, looks like their relationship didn't last long."

Sam jabbed him in the side again making him hiccup again.

"Ahem, continuing, one day the brothers found a strange girl arrive in their town and they both fell in love with her despite her appearance.

She had grey skin, yellow eyes and weird ears. She also had a dragon with her."

A cold shiver went down my spine. That description, even though it wasn't that clear, sounded like a mage. A mage and a dragon, it must have been right when the curse took effect.

"Does this 'Martin Miles' have proof of any of this or is he just writing all this stuff for fun?" asked Sam.

"Why do you care?" asked Sid. "Are you scared this guy might up stage you?"

"Why would you ask that?" Sam asked concerned.

"Oh, because Martin Miles school, West Avenue High, is staying at the same resort as us," said Britney. "I'll finally get to meet him in person."

I bit my lip. I didn't like the sound of this guy and I would hate to run into him.

While Britney ranted on about her dream boy I took the book from her and started to read it for myself. From what I could summarise it said that the two brothers sheltered the girl and kept her safe from the other villagers. The villagers didn't like the way she looked, they knew something was wrong about her and she had a dragon, so who wouldn't be terrified? The brothers both fell in love with her though. Even when they kept her hidden they tried everything to prove themselves to her. The dragon remained outside the village. It didn't move or do anything really. One day the brothers went too far and started to have a battle against each other. It was a battle for the maiden's heart, but their selfish acts, was destroying the village and themselves. Out of desperation the girl ran out to stop the fight to save the village, but she got caught in the cross fire, the attack gave her a fatal wound. Her dragon appeared by her side, slowly dying itself. Upon her death she cursed the two brothers. The dragon took the dying body and flew down into the ravine bringing the two brothers along with him who fell from heroes to villains in a matter of days. As they were dragged down into the ravine the dragon died along with the girl. As they fell something happened. The two brothers fused together with the dragon's body creating a two headed beast that put fear into everyone's lives. The creature fell down deep into the ravine where no one dared to go taking the girl's body with them. No one saw them again, they dared not to search for it, anyone who ventured to find it died but the ones who did make it out alive died shortly after being poisoned.

I closed the book, took my glasses off and slouched into my seat, trying to ignore the people around me. All three of them were arguing about Martin Miles. I glanced out of the window watching the trees pass by quickly. When I raised my head I looked up at the edge of the ravine there was a figure that passed by hastily.

It made me stand and reach over Britney. I pressed my face up against the window asking, "What was that?"

"What was what?" Sid asked after another hiccup.

"You didn't see that figure run by on the cliff?" I asked.

Everyone shook their heads.

I sighed. "Just forget it."

"You're weird, Connie," commented Sid.

It was no use; they wouldn't believe me without physical proof. I wish Nightly was here.

When we arrived at the ski resort, all the students rushed off the busses and grabbed their luggage. Sam and I took our time to collect our belongings. There was no point on beating the rush, besides a lot of people were over reacting when they couldn't find one thing and started to blame everyone else for taking it. It was funny to see their reactions when they did find it though. Sam and I giggled when the teachers made most of the students apologize to the people they accused. After that was settled the students shoved their way into the lodge and waited in the lobby until the manager came out. Coach stood by the front desk and used his big megaphone voice to make everyone quiet down.

"Alright, kids, the manager of the resort will lay down some ground rules before we get you settled in for the next couple of weeks," said Coach.

The manager walked up to the front desk and used a handkerchief to wipe the bell carefully daring not to make a sound. He placed his handkerchief in his sleeve and stroked his moustache. As he did that he walked back and forth, watching each and every one of us as the only noise in the room was the rustle of his fingers against his facial hairs. The manager then stood firm, right in front of the desk and smoothened out his white, silver uniform. "Good afternoon, children. My name is Mr. Corbin Miles. I welcome you to my humble resort with all my heart. Now, for the ground rules, the girls stay on the ground level and the boys get the second floor. No boy is allowed to enter a girl's room and no girl is allowed to enter the boy's room. We have cameras in the hallways that are active twenty-four/seven, so no sneaky stuff aloud.

There will also be a curfew at nine, lights are out by eleven.

Supervisors will stay with students in their rooms. Maximum for a room is eight the lowest capacity is two and be prepared to be squished together because another school is also coming to stay at the resort.

The ski hills are open from eleven am in the morning to seven pm." He stopped to take a breath. When he did that I was dumbfounded on how fast he was talking. It was polite like you would expect, but I didn't expect him to speak fast like we were all on a debate team. "Breakfast, lunch and dinner will be notified through the intercoms which are also placed throughout my resort. 'You miss the call you miss the meal' that is our motto here.

In conclusion we have a restricted area. If you pass it I can guarantee you won't return without harm being done." He rubbed his blue eyes and took out some spectacles. "Now are there any questions?"

Several kids had their hands up but Mr. Miles ignored them. I sighed. This was great; we had an ignorant manager as our host. This should be fun.

"Great, now let's get you kids settled in," he said clasping his hands together.

Mr. Miles stepped away and Coach stepped forward with his big belly leading the way.

"Alright, go pick your rooms and I want everyone to be in the dining hall at six," he said, rubbing his beard.

Everyone ran off to the levels we were aloud on. I ran through a set of doors and found the hall full of girls. There were twenty nine girls on the trip and the rest were boys. Only a hundred and twenty-five kids from our school came on the trip. Of course there would be fewer numbers of girls in a gym class. I picked room one, zero, eight and when I opened the door I found Britney already setting up her stuff on a bed. She didn't notice me until I the door closed behind me.

"Sorry, I didn't know this room was taken," I said.

"Wait, please, I need someone else to stay with me or else I'll have to go in another room where they'll ignore me," she said.

"Then it'll be a pleasure to stay with you," I said putting my bags down.

Just then we started to hear screaming outside our door. Britney stood up and ran to open the door.

"Aren't you coming?"

"Where are we going?" I asked.

"To the man who directs and plays in his own movies, not to mention writes his own books," Britney said holding the door handle with a firm grip.

"Please don't say who I think you're going to say."

"Yep, it's Martin Miles."

CHAPTER 19

A Drop into the Dark Lake

Britney grabbed my arm and forced me into the front of the hall where a small crowd of seventy-five people were. The boy's stood at the top of the stairs and the girls in the doorway. They were all giggly and excited while the boys were just waiting to see what the big deal was. I agreed with them. I didn't get what everyone was so excited for. If it's only one guy what is the big deal? It's not like he's a movie star or a famous stand-up comedian.

"Oh, I can't wait," said Britney holding onto my arm. "I hope he likes me. On his website it says he likes girls either a year or two older or younger than him, with a great attitude and beautiful eyes."

"He has a website?" I said.

"Yeah, it's called www.martinmilestruthvs.legends.com."

"Wow, that's a mouth full."

"It tells how old he is, when and where he was born, where he goes to school, what he likes and the legends he has unveiled onto either DVD or as a documentary."

"I'm guessing you're on their a lot," I said fighting for my arm to be free from Britney's killer grasp.

"It's the best way to pass the time on the computer," Britney said clasping her hands together. "He's my knight in shining armour and he reads, writes, and knows almost everything about computers."

I could have sworn I saw her eyes sparkle. She really wanted to meet him. The next thing I saw was Britney taking her glasses off? She pulled out some lipstick and started to smear it on her face. She handed me her glasses and then smacked her lips together.

"Wish me luck," she said pushing her way through the crowd.

Once Britney left all the other girls trampled over me to meet this one guy. After I got up off the ground I brushed off the shoe prints that were left on my clothing. The only thing I could hear were high pitched screams which nearly drove me insane. The next thing that happened were big black men pushing the girls back over me.

"We love you Martin," called one girl.

"Martin Miles, you're the greatest," called another.

"Martin, don't let them take us away from you," said Britney.

Again girls screamed as the men pushed them through the doors trampling over me with their high heeled boots, again. They all awed and sobbed as the doors were forced closed in their faces.

I had enough of this ridiculous, desperate, romantic obsession, drama! "GET OFF ME!" I yelled pushing the girls off me. "FOR GOODNESS SAKES IT'S JUST ONE GUY."

All the girls stopped screaming suddenly. They all gave me cold dead eyes as I stood up. I felt like I was surrounded by the predators and I was its prey.

"Are you kidding? Martin Miles is so hot it's like he's the sun," said one girl.

"Then remind me to bring sunscreen whenever he's round," I joked.

No one laughed.

"Connie, this man is a legend in the ravine," said a grade twelve student.

"Yeah, you don't even know him," said another one.

"Neither do you," I said.

I regretted saying those words the moment they left my mouth. Every girl in the hallway was barking at me of how much they knew Martin Miles. I needed to get myself out of there. It took all my energy to push past all the drama queens and force my way through the door where the big men from before were standing. When they saw me I ran for my life. One of them nearly got a hold of me but then he had a mob of teenage girls to deal with, who were screaming again and trying to fight their way to get out of the hallway. While they were busy I was running and not watching where I was going and you know where I ended up? On the ground along with Mr. Miles who had been explaining the rules to the students from the other school. He landed on his face and I on my butt.

"Ouch," I whined.

I was then dragged to my feet by one of the big men. "Girl, you have guts to charge in here and knock over Mr. Miles uncle in broad daylight," he said in a German accent.

"Look, I can assure you I didn't do it on purpose . . . it was just an accident," I said.

"Sure, and those glasses you're holding weren't going to be used as a weapon to hurt Martin Miles," he said tightening his grip on my wrist.

I winced as the circulation in my hand was cut off.

"Enough, let go of her," a voice called out in a British accent.

Out of the crowd walked a tall, handsome boy. He had to be the same age as Kyle. He had fine-looking blue eyes, his hair was a raven black and he wore a neat, clean sweater vest that I found attractive.

The second that boy approached me was the very second the big man released his grasp on me. He backed away slowly and then turned his attention to Mr. Miles who was yelling at the other big men who were trying to help him up.

"You okay?" The boy asked.

I rubbed my wrist glanced back at the whinny old man then turned my attention back to the boy giving him a short nod.

"Will you allow me to treat you to dinner tonight? To make up for the rudeness of my men." The boy grabbed my hand and gave it a kiss. He smiled at me, acting all charming in his British accent.

"Who are you?" I asked, pulling my hand away from him and crossing my arms.

Everyone began to laugh at me.

"What, what is so funny?! I demanded, turning around to see everybody laughing.

Even the British boy started to laugh. "I think I'm going to like you. My name is Martin Miles."

In my room Britney was freaking out, she was *way* too over excited. She kept lecturing me on Martin Miles, telling me that it was 'extremely rare' that he would just pick up some 'random girl'. Then she talked on and on about his high class status and while doing that she found that it was her obligation to go through my suitcase to look for an 'appropriate outfit that would make me worthy of going out with Martin Miles'. She was driving me nuts.

"Britney, do we have to do this? It's only dinner," I whined, while lying down on one of the bunk beds.

"You don't get it, Connie. You're living my dream . . . uh; sorry . . . I mean most girls' dreams. You get to meet with Martin Miles, in person, for dinner," she said crumpling one of my shirts into a ball. "I wish I were you."

"No, I don't think you would like it," I said, sitting up on the bed. "Oh, I forgot, here are your glasses."

I handed the glasses over to her and she didn't hesitate to shove them on her face. It was really weird to see her so giddy and excited. All she talked about was his adventures, looks and past relationships. When she went to the bathroom I took the opportunity to escape into the lobby. There, I spotted a waiting couch and decided to sit down on it, taking my shoes off and placing them on the coffee table that lay before me as the warmth of the fire slowly dragged me into slumber. It was so nice to be out of my room, to be in the empty lobby, and relax without my roommate stressing me out. Everyone was off unpacking there stuff leaving a nice quiet evening for me.

"What are you doing?" asked a familiar British voice.

At first I thought I was in trouble for having my feet up on the coffee table, but when I turned around I found out that it was just Martin Miles. The guy almost gave me a heart attack.

"What's wrong with you?" I asked him, trying to slow down my heart pace. "Couldn't you tell that I wasn't expecting anything?"

"Yeah, that's what made it fun," he smiled at me while leaning on the arm on the couch. He leaned in close making my heart pace speed up again, "but what I really wanted to ask was if you were excited for tonight?"

"Yeah . . . I guess . . . shouldn't you be unpacking like everyone else?"

"I got people to do that, you're interesting, I want to know more about you."

"There's nothing to know," my face started to heat up, I was becoming flustered. "I'm a girl that lives in a low class town with a

162

low class family. We're not rich and we're just considered as a regular family."

"Leave her alone, Miles," Sam said, cutting in. He walked over from the dining room carrying two mugs. "You already have her for the evening, so leave!"

"Alright, I'll go, but not without leaving a present," Martin said, he left a kiss on my cheek before he strutted upstairs.

Sam didn't keep his eyes off Miles until he was out of sight. After he stopped scowling at him Sam sat down beside me and handed me one of the mugs that was filled with white hot chocolate. I scooted myself close to him and slouched into the couch.

"How are you feeling about tonight?" he asked.

I took a sip of my white hot chocolate. "You know, I'm actually okay with it and it's only for one night, right? It's not like he's going to transfer to our school." I took another sip of my drink then slouched further into the couch. "How do you always know what I like?"

He blushed and smiled. "I remembered from last Christmas, when you were first introduced to white hot chocolate you specifically said that the taste, smell and colour all matched the season. From then on you declared that no matter what, you would only drink white hot chocolate during the winter season."

He was right. Being around Martin made me feel nervous but being around Sam always seemed to relax me. Maybe it was because he knew me longer or maybe it was because he was just the one person I felt the most comfortable around. I smiled at him as I drank the rest of my white hot chocolate. The feeling of a warm drink going down my throat made me feel warm. The heat of the fire and of the drink made me lean my head on Sam's shoulders and shut my eyes. In my head I pictured Sam and me racing down the ski hill while Kyle wiped out and Teddy was trying to flirt with the school girls and chaperones. Everything was almost perfect. The only thing that was missing was Nightly. I wished he was here then I wouldn't have anything in the world to worry about.

"You little tramp," someone called.

My happy dream broke away as I opened my eyes and turned my head to see a tall buff girl standing in the center of the lobby. I didn't recognize her from my school. She had to have gone to the same school as Martin Miles.

"And you are . . ." I asked, gesturing to her to fill in the blank.

"I'm Celina Cortez, and how dare you cheat on Martin Miles after everything he's given you," she said in a disgusted way.

"Look, Celina, I don't even know the guy. He just invited me to dinner and that is it, okay?" I said.

"Oh, but I saw him give you a kiss. That is very valuable for a commoner like yourself," Celina said sticking up her nose.

I rolled my eyes. "Go away, you're annoying."

"You better watch out, girl, and I'm only going to warn you once," then she stomped off.

"Wow, what would you rate her as, the Scrooge or the Grinch? Sam asked.

"Neither, she's just a hot headed girl who goes to the other school." I jumped to my feet and began to walk.

"Where are you going?"

"To change my shirt then off to the dining room."

"I don't trust that guy."

"I don't either," I stopped and looked back at Sam, "I'm only going because he got the thug to let go of me. Not to mention I got a bruised wrist from his grip." I pulled my sleeve up and showed Sam my purple wrist.

He whistled. "Wow, that is one nasty bruise."

"Yeah, but it's a good thing I heal fast," I covered up my wrist and smiled. "I'll see you later Sam." I continued to walk leaving Sam in the lobby by himself.

I walked back to the room where I found Britney asleep on a bunk. I shook my head as I grabbed a black sweater and headed into the bathroom. When the door was closed and locked I took off my jacket and shirt noticing my dragon wings mark. My dragon wings were visible to everyone, but as long as I kept them covered no one would know what I was. To be honest, I hated looking at my dragon mark. Every other part of me said human but not my back. I loved Nightly and everything but I hated that reminder that embedded me with a task I wasn't a hundred percent sure I could do. I touched my mark then traced the wings with my finger. I pulled the black sweater over my head covering the mark back up.

The intercom came on, "attention, attention, dinner is now served. I repeat dinner is now served. Thank you."

I walked out of the bathroom, placed my shirt and jacket I wore before back into my suitcase and woke up Britney. Immediately, she jumped up and hugged me when she woke.

"I had a dream of me and Martin Miles. We were eating dinner and then he took me out onto the dance floor. After that we went into a library where he knelt down and proposed to me," she giggled. "Oh, I hope one day it will come true."

"I hope so to."

She glanced at me. "Why?"

"Because I'd rather it be you then me on this date. Personally, I don't know anything about the guy."

"But after your date you will."

"Yeah, lucky me," I said sarcastically.

"Come on, we don't want you to miss your date," Britney said, trying to make it sound like she was excited for me.

I shook my head then headed out the door with Britney following. The hallway was packed full of girls once again. They were all trying to get into the dining room before the line got too big. Almost every girl was waddling like penguins trying to talk to with friends, talk on phones, put on makeup or text. I couldn't believe this. I wondered how the boys were doing. I bet they didn't have traffic like this.

Finally, when we got through the corridor we lined up to get our food in the dining room. The smell was incredible and the spread was almost a mile long. They really went overboard with this stuff. There was turkey, roast beef, scalloped and mashed potatoes, rice, stuffing, red cabbage, fresh cooked bread and more. This was one luxurious resort. I didn't figure they could afford this kind of stuff, but I've been wrong before.

Britney and I stood in line for twenty minutes before I felt a tug on my arm. When I turned around I found Martin standing behind me.

"I've found you," he said, giving me a smile, "we can have dinner now."

"What about the spread that's already out?" I asked.

"Don't worry I have plenty at my table. Shall we go?" he asked, taking me by the hand and guided me out of line.

"I guess I have no choice now," I said, looking back at the crowd of students staring at us.

"Then let us go to our arranged table," Martin guided me to a long rectangle table, placed in its own separate room with its own spread.

It reminded me of my first encounter with the mage all that was missing was the dress I wore and the mask that hid my identity. It was creepy, the spread on the table was the exact same as the spread the mage had prepared for me in my dream. Prime rib, creaser salad and cabbage rolls. Everything was the same including the placement.

"Is everything to your liking?" he asked.

"I honestly don't know what to say," I admitted, my eyes widened with surprise.

"Then instead of words allow me to fill your mouth with the delicacy that is my chef's cooking," he said wrapping his arm around me.

There was nothing for me to do. I watched Martin as he walked to the table and pulled out a chair for me. I gave him a small smile and took my seat. He pushed me in, sat himself down at the other end of the table and watched me very carefully as we ate. It was awkward for me to see him, staring at me, not saying a single word and sifting and sipping his wine just like the mage from my dream. I refused to meet his eye contact throughout dinner, there was only a few times when I actually glanced up to see if anything changed, nothing did. Once I was done eating I sat up straight giving him another small smile.

"Was the food to your liking?" he asked.

"Yes," I answered.

"What would you like for dessert, Connie?"

"Wait, how did you know my name? I don't remember telling you it."

"My uncle insisted that I should stay on the same floor as my fellow classmates. So, I'm staying in my own room which happens to be right beside you friend Sam's and Sid's. While I was having my room prepared I asked people from your school a few questions about you."

"And what did you find out? Surprise me," I challenged him, hoping the tension in my body would loosen if he made mistakes.

He gave me a smile of delight, "your name is Connie Whitsburg. You live in Small Valley and go to Small Valley High."

"That's not very impressive," I said, slowly relaxing my body, "you have anything else?"

"Alright," he placed his elbow on the table and laid his head on his hand, "let's try this, you only like white hot chocolate, your brother is Kyle Whitsburg who is the same age as me, you're staying in room eight, zero, one with a girl named Britney Shine."

"I'll have to admit, that's not too bad," I said, under the table I was gripping my knees with my fingers. "Do you do this often?"

"Let's just say I like to find information about the people I date."

I bit my lip. "It's not a date!" I stated.

"Then what is it?"

I thought for a second. "Alright, it's a pity date," I sulked crossing my arms.

He laughed as he grabbed his wine glass and filled it with red wine. It was then I was convinced that Martin Miles could possibly be the mage I encountered in my dream.

"I'm sorry," I said standing up, "but I need some air."

I walked out casually and once the doors were closed behind me I ran outside, shut the doors behind me and let out a big breath of frustration while stomping my feet and throwing my fist out at the air. This was not happening. It was no wonder the other mage warned me not to come. Then again, why did he warn me in the first place? None of this made sense to me. "Oh, God, tell me what to do?"

The door opened behind me and out walked Teddy.

"Are you alright, Connie? I saw you run out after your date. As a supervisor and as your Guardian it's my duty to see what's bothering you," he said closing the door behind us.

"I'm fine, Teddy, really. I just needed some air," I said rubbing my arms. "That Martin Miles scares me."

"Yeah, I'm going to keep an eye on him. You shouldn't worry though, Connie. I'm going to make sure nothing happens to you." Teddy started to wrap his arms around me.

"Get your filthy hands off her," said a familiar voice.

"Nightly?" I whispered, breaking away from Teddy. Nightly became visible and was standing by an ever green tree. I ran up to my dragon and gave him a hug. "I missed you."

"And I for you," he responded.

"Great," Teddy said throwing his arms in the air, "I have one moment where a girl doesn't over react while I'm comforting them and you have to appear."

Smoke came out of Nightly's nostrils. *"If you ever do something like that again I can guarantee you that you'll have an early cremation."*

"Fine, I'll back down, but you should get out of here before your temper burns this resort to the ground," Teddy argued. He gave Nightly a dirty look as he looked in all directions, making sure there was no one around.

"Where should I go?" Nightly asked, his gold eyes shimmering in the lights.

"This place is filled with crevasses and caves, you can hide in those, just don't go into the restricted area," I said scratching his scales. "Go, I'll contact you in the morning."

"You better," Nightly stretched out his wings and flew into the night sky.

"Bye," I said, watching him blend into the pitch black night sky. "I miss you already."

"The two of you sure have a strong connection don't you?" Teddy said approaching me.

"We sure do," I said closing my eyes, feeling my heart rate beat slowly as my body relaxed. "I don't think anything could come in between us."

"That will be a challenge for the mages." I opened my eyes and looked at Teddy, curious to know why. "Whenever a whisperer and their dragon have a strong connection it strains a mage's power. Separated, the two partners are weak but together they are like one being that has the ability to overpower the mages."

"No matter what happens, I'll make sure not one single mage will lay one sinister finger on Nightly," I stood up brave and tall to Teddy. My confidence was fully restored.

"You should get inside, I'll cover up Nightly's tracks," Teddy grabbed my shoulder and shook it.

I smiled at him. Teddy released his grasp on me and started to push snow over Nightly's footprints and his own tracks. I looked at him and then went inside shutting the door behind me. A sigh left my mouth as my body welcomed in the warm heat. I strutted up to the couch and lied down. My evening for the night was confusing, but in the end I was happy because Nightly was here. I closed my eyes again and felt the locket around my neck. It was only eight days till Christmas and I didn't have anything to give anyone. I thought maybe I could find some construction paper and markers I could make a nice card for people, but seriously where would I find that stuff around a fancy resort?

"So, how was the date?" asked Britney leaning over me.

I opened my eyes and slowly sat up. "It wasn't a date and the dinner was fine. He's not much of a conversationalist."

"That's because he saves his words for directing, acting, writing or blogging."

"He has a blog to? All right, that's it, come on," I jumped to my feet and stomped my way back towards the room.

"What are you doing?"

I glanced back at Britney and smiled. "We're going to do some researching of our own."

I dragged Britney back into our room and spent three hours with her trying to look up things on Martin Miles.

The first thing we went to was Martin Miles website. It had information about where he had lived, his previous relationships and his high class life style. On his website we found that he had researched unicorns, trolls and goblins but now he was researching dragons. This guy had interesting hobbies from school switching all the way to travelling around the world on search of 'finding the truth'. The information was easy to find but if the Miles were the nineteenth richest people in the world, why would they bother with a place like this? There was nothing interesting here except for the ravine being in the shape of a dragon egg.

"Attention, attention, it is now eleven o'clock. Lights should be out and students should be in bed and asleep, goodnight," came a voice from the intercom.

"Well, I'm off to bed," said Britney, stretching her arms.

"I'll join you in a moment." When Britney shut off the light I continued to scan my monitor. It was hard to believe that this website had so much on it. Martin was only seventeen and he had already done so much in his life.

As I scrolled down the webpage I found facts of unicorns living in eastern England. Apparently, they only appear in front of virgins or pure good souls. They ride rainbows and their horn is what gives them their power. If they lose their horn they die, if you find it you gain their magical abilities. It's convenient for them to live in England because they receive lots of rain. If other people couldn't find them, how did Martin?

The more I scrolled down the more I found out about his research. He explained that goblins are greedy gold lovers who live in the Caribbean and the Philippians islands. They hide in the coves and deep within caves. Goblins love to cause trouble and wait for pirates to come and bring their gold with them.

Then there was a page on trolls. Trolls lived in the swamp lands. They were ugly and dumb creatures always carrying huge wooden club not knowing how to use them. Trolls live near fresh tampered water areas and feed on insects and small animals. Never approach one. Trolls like to attack anything that comes near them.

I kept thinking why would anyone want to approach them? They probably attack everything because they're scared and don't want to be bothered. Exposing creature's whereabouts will get them hunted and killed. Why does he do this?

As I was about to click out of the website I noticed a link. A link that took me to an article dated twelve years ago. It was about the city above the ravine. It went up in flames on New Year's Eve. Drake and Shelley Slayer were both killed on the night of the incident, the only people that died, all the other survivors had permanent damage. The fire started at their house and spread to the neighbourhood before it was extinguished. Citizens who witnessed the event said that one man left as another one entered into the Slayer's household. Police believe the man who left the scene caused the fire, no physical evidence has been found to who caused the fire or the survival of the young families son.

This was interesting, but Sam's last name is Slayer. It could have been his parents that were killed in the fire, was he the young boy the police never found? Too many questions filled my mind. I closed the computer then hopped into bed. It took a while for me to fall sleep, all I could think about was Sam.

The next morning, I went straight to the dining room to grab a bite to eat. After that I went to the rental shop and got a snowboard, helmet and boots. I met up with Sam at the top of the lift. We looked down the hill and saw a lot of obstacles in our way. Twists, turns, jumps, ice patches and trees were everywhere.

"You ready for this?" he asked, putting his snowboard on the ground.

"With all the skateboarding lessons you've given me, I sure am." I copied Sam and dropped my board on the ground then strapped myself on it. "Race you to the bottom."

"You're on," he said taking off.

"Hey, cheater," I called out going after him.

We went through the twists and turns, trying to avoid the people in our way. Sam had been giving me skateboarding lessons since spring last year. I hated those twelve months. All I got for the first six months was cuts and bruises all over my arms and legs. For the last six months, well, let's just say I'll never criticize action movies again. Skateboarding was kind of like snowboarding just without the wheels and your feet are attached to the board.

Sam pulled ahead but it wasn't for long. I caught up to him quickly but he only pulled ahead again because he hit an ice patch. At first I thought he was going to wipe out because it looked like he lost his balance but he recovered.

"Come on, Connie! You can do this. It's not a problem," I kept telling myself.

All of a sudden, I felt a strong force start pushing me.

"Hey, what's going on?" I said, trying to stay balanced.

"Calm down, relax and have a good time," said Nightly.

"What are you doing here?" I asked. "Stop it!"

"Why? You're winning the race," he said pushing me faster.

I noticed how fast we were both going. We were definitely wining, but I didn't like the look on everyone's faces while we were passing by.

"Nightly, we're going too fast, we're drawing attention. We have to stop!"

"Alright," he said casually letting go of me.

"Thank you," I said, not realizing the jump I was heading for. When I saw it I turned my board sideways trying to stop but it was no use. The trail was too icy. "Nightly," I cried, flying through the air. I must have reached twenty feet before crashing into a pile of snow. "Stupid dragon," I muttered, sticking my face out of the snow.

Sam finished the run and stopped in front of me. "You took on a jump on your first time out."

"Shut up!" I held out my hands. "Help me out of here," I ordered.

Sam unlatched his boots, grabbed my hands and helped me up onto my feet. I brushed off snow and unlatched my boots from the snowboard.

"Let's go inside," I whined, "it's too windy out here."

"Hey, tramp, nice wipe out," called Celina as she had her ski's blow snow in mine and Sam's face.

"What do you want?!" I demanded, brushing the snow off me again.

"Just to tell you that your wipe out beat your brother's by a long shot," she said sticking her nose up.

Everyone was laughing. My face became beat red with embarrassment. I turned and looked to my right where I saw Nightly, hiding in the forest, snickering at me before he turned invisible and took off.

"I'll be right back," I said to Sam before I chased after my dragon in the woods. It wasn't until I was deep within the pine trees that I knew no one would hear me if I started to call for Nightly.

"You stupid dragon," I yelled. "Show your face so I can give you a piece of my mind."

"Dang, Connie, you can't take a joke," he responded, refusing to show himself.

"I only laugh at the jokes that are funny, not embarrassing," I stated. "What are you doing here, Nightly? You're supposed to be at home with the Guardians and Pearl."

"Oh . . . well . . . I kind of flew away," he said.

I placed my hand on my head and shook them. "Why would you run away?"

"I flew away, I didn't run away! Human's run, dragons fly and I wanted to be with you for my first Christmas."

"Why don't you become visible and we can talk about it?"

"Nah, I'm going to explore the area, but don't worry, I'll be back," he said.

"Wait, Nightly!" I said, trying to find him. All I could see were a few broken branches and a couple burnt trees.

"Who's Nightly?" asked a familiar British voice behind me.

I tensed up. There wasn't supposed to be anyone here, that's why I ran deep within the woods, so that no one could hear my conversation with Nightly. I slowly turned around and saw Martin leaning on a tree.

172

"What are you doing here?" I asked surprised.

"I saw your little stunt back there. Then you took off so I decided to follow you," he said walking towards me. "But who's this Nightly person you've been talking too?"

I had to think up of something fast. It was a good thing that at that time I had been practicing lying. "*Shoot*, you caught me! Whenever I'm humiliated, I run off and talk to my invisible friend."

"Really?" he said intrigued. "Then what was making you go down the hill so fast that you were shouting 'stop'?"

"It was really windy and I hit an ice patch," I said, becoming nervous. "What's with all the questions?" I crossed my arms.

Martin approached me, stretched out one arm out and grabbed my face with his hand. Then he started to whisper into my ear. After he was done, I gulped, feeling my body tense up. Martin grinned as he walked away. I slouched down into the snow. It felt like an arrow pierced my heart. He whispered to me his knowledge of dragons and that he knew I had one. Apparently when I ran off the other night he caught a glimpse of my dragon mark and spotted Nightly threw his rooms window.

Nightly, can you hear me? I asked, trying to use mind sequence.

Yeah, I always have my mind opened to you.

I need you to stay away from me for a couple of days.

Why?

I bit my lip. *Just lay low till Christmas, promise?*

I will promise, but I'm going to keep an eye on you. This place has an unusual aura.

I agree, I told him before our connection broke. Once I calmed myself down I stood up and headed towards the resort, but I couldn't help feel like something or someone was watching me.

*   *   *

For seven days I had been trying to avoid Martin at every turn, but he always seemed to be at the exact same place as me if I wasn't forced to go look for him with Britney. I had to hide in the room or spend unnecessary hours on the ski hill just avoid her and Miles.

At the times I wasn't avoiding people I would usually meet up with Sam. Sam was the only person that made this trip bearable for me. If

Sam wasn't there for me to talk to I would check in with Nightly. He seemed to have a great time exploring the area, but he never gave me anymore detail than that.

As for Kyle, he and I pretty much avoided each other. There was one time when the two of us actually did make contact but that was when his friends convinced me to film Kyle as he snowboarded down a trail his friends messed up. It was hilarious that is until he caught me, but Joey still managed to upload the video on YouTube.

Teddy kept an eye on Martin ever since I told him what happened when Miles confronted me in the woods, but occasionally, he would fall behind on his work and start flirting with our school's nurse.

It was Christmas Eve and I finished my last run down the hill for the day. So far, the day was great until I made the mistake of running into Celina while returning my snowboarding gear to the rental shop.

"Well, well, if it isn't the tramp. Made any more of your pathetic wipe outs lately?" she said, leaning on the counter.

"Would you shut up," I snapped. "I am here to enjoy my vacation but I can't with snobs like you ruining it."

"I don't like your attitude, tramp. Maybe I should teach you a lesson," she said holding both of her ski poles up.

I looked around only seeing two of her friends. There wasn't anyone else because the announcement for dinner was already announced. Everyone must have been in the dining room. Celina took a swing at me with her ski poles, forcing me to fall to the ground with my board. She raised her arms, prepared to bring her ski poles down on me. Luckily my snowboard was beside me; I grabbed it and used it as a shield. Celina was strong though. I couldn't recover my ground with her overtop of me.

"What is your problem?!" I demanded.

"Martin Miles could of had any girl he wanted, but he had to pick you. A girl who doesn't even appreciate the kind of guy he is. Not to mention you went straight to another guy before and after your date," she lifted the ski poles up again. "For the rest of the trip you'll be resting in bed."

I became scared, my eyes widened in terror. I was going to be beaten up for just turning down one guy. My body wouldn't do anything, I had never been in this kind of situation. Then something happened that I couldn't believe. My body was filled with strength, my fear left me, and I was able to kick Celina off me. She stumbled backwards into the box of ski poles.

"Ha, is that all you can do?" she asked.

"No," I stood up, used my new strength to strike both of Celina's friends in the chest and on the back. I turned my attention back to Celina and swept her feet out from under her. As she started to fall I hit her in the face with the snowboard. Celina slowly fell to the ground with blood coming out of her nose. "I win," I said taking in a deep breath.

I placed the snowboard back in the wall, feeling the power drain from me, I looked back down at Celina and her friends and noticed the blood. I felt sick looking at the red liquid.

Nurse Jacqueline walked in. "What happened?" she asked.

"It . . . it was an accident," I said, backing away.

"Connie, there are three girls down on the floor bleeding," she said, helping Celina up. "You better get out of here. I'll take care of this problem."

I was relieved. "Thank you, Nurse Jacqueline, you're life savour."

I ran out of the rental shop, ran across the snow and entered the lodge. Sam was there holding two mugs. He invited me to sit down on the couch and I did. With what had just happened I was relieved when I saw Sam.

I collapsed on the couch. "I am so glad that you're here. You wouldn't believe what happened."

Sam sat beside me, placed the two mugs on the coffee table and stretched his arms out. "Yeah, well, why don't you tell me about it then?"

I told Sam about my encounter with Celina, how we got into a fight, how the nurse came and saved me. He was the only one I could open up to.

I sat up, looked at the mugs in front of us. Sam took one and gestured for me to have the other one. I was excited to take a sip from it but when I looked into the mug I knew something was wrong. "Sam, this is regular hot chocolate."

"Yeah, so," he said, putting his arm around me.

I tilted my head a little and took a good look at Sam, there was something in his eye, like it was glass. This person wasn't Sam.

"Listen Sam, I'm going to head to my room," I said standing up.

"Then I'll walk you there," he said.

I had to be cautious of this imposter he made me feel uncomfortable and I knew Sam. He was always nervous when he asked me things and he knew I liked white hot chocolate. Who was this guy?

"I can manage on my own," I said sternly, backing away from him.

"But I insist, Connie," he said in a creepy voice.

I began to walk away, but the imposter followed. He followed me all the way to my room's door. I pulled out my key card slowly. I should have kept an eye on the imposter. He turned me around, making me drop the key card and pinned my hands above my head.

"What are you-" I started to yell but he muted me by pressing his lips on mine.

The imposter used his free hand and moved it across my body. He started from my shoulders then moved slowly down to my legs. My heart pace sped up. He was too strong to fight against. Where was the strength I had when I fought Celina?

"Where is it?" he asked, slowly moving his face away from mine. "If I can't find your mark, I'll find your scale."

I took in a breath and released it. My heart pace slowed down and the strength returned to me. When the imposter was down near my feet I kneed him in the head. Once his head flung back he released my arms and I took the opportunity and crotched him. When he went down, I grabbed my key card off the floor. Quickly unlocked the door and then shut it. The imposters head collide with the wooden door. I sat down on the floor and listened as he banged on the door.

"Connie, let me in!" he yelled. "You can't stay in there forever." I heard him struggle to get up. "After all, I do know everything about you. Even the stuff you think I don't know."

He left. I curled into a ball asking myself, 'Why was this happening?'

That night I couldn't sleep. My mind was wrapped around Sam. Where was he, who was that guy that impersonated him and how did he know about my scale and dragon mark? Lying down didn't make things easier for me. I got out of bed and went to the window. That's when I saw someone leaving the resort. The way the person acted; nervously, cautious, making sure no one followed him. It had to be

Sam. I forced the window opened and climbed out, following the foot prints that Sam left behind. He went deep within the forest and into the restricted area. When I caught up to him I hid behind a boulder and listened.

One person collapsed on the ground. "You know, you could have taken this better," he whined.

"What do you think you're doing?" demanded the other voice I believed belonged to Sam. "You disguised yourself as me and could have ruined everything."

"Hey, if you think it's that easy then you should have been doing your job from the start. Instead you're off in another word thinking of that girl 'Connie'," the other person stated.

I stepped back and slipped on some snow. That mistake brought me closer to the cliff's edge. Someone approached me as I tried to escape. Then I saw Sam's face.

"Connie, what are you doing here?" he asked.

"I can ask you the same thing, Sam. What happened to you today? What's going on?"

"Listen, I can explain, just come away from the edge."

I wasn't sure what to believe. My body was acting on its own, forcing me to back up more.

"Connie, please trust me," Sam said, extending his hand out to me.

I couldn't do it. I didn't trust him; my thoughts and actions told me not to trust him. My fear made me lose my footing and the next thing I knew I was falling.

"Connie!" Sam cried, still trying to reach for my hand.

I was falling, falling into a trench to my death. I looked up and saw Sam jump off the cliff; he dove down and he caught me. Sam tucked my head into his chest and wrapped his arms around me. During a short time I noticed something on his chest. We were falling together, to our deaths. I closed my eyes scared to no ends. I should have kept them open. Something caught Sam. He released his hold on me and when I opened my eyes I found myself bouncing off the icy edge of the cliff. A cold sensation covered my body.

"NIGHTLY!" I yelled, knowing if anyone could save me it would be him.

That's when a fire broke out beneath me. The fire melted the ice that covered a black lake. I saw the fire again and it created steam, when I fell in it the water. The freezing cold water numbed every part of my body. I squinted my eyes and realized I was drowning. Then someone jumped in and tugged on my shoulders. As I started to reach the surface I lost consciousness.

CHAPTER 20

The Forgotten Whisperer

I felt warm, wet but warm. It took a while for me to wake and realize that I was in a bathtub. When I actually focused on my surrounding I noticed the little cottage I was in. Beside me was a chair that had fresh dry clothes for me to put on. All I really wanted to know was who the person was that saved me? I went out on a search to find Sam but ended up falling to my death but instead fell into a lake which I almost drowned in. Someone had been watching me and it wasn't just Teddy or Nightly. I got out of the bath, dressed myself in an old purple night gown and exited the bathroom and entered a small sitting area that had a fire going in a fire place.

"Oh, good, you're awake, Connie," said an old woman entering the room with a tray of tea and crackers.

She was in her late sixty's, with some grey in her brown hair. She wore a purple shawl and had wrinkles on her forehead.

"Excuse me, but who are you, where am I, and where is my dragon?" I asked.

"All in good time, but first you need to get your strength back. Take some tea, eat some crackers and listen to what I have to tell you," she said harshly. I sat down on the couch behind me. "For your first question you asked who I was and my name is Baboline. Your second question was where you are, you're in my home far off in the restricted area. I make sure the centagon stays at bay."

"Centagon?" I asked, concerned.

"Don't interrupt," she snapped at me. "Now for your third question you wanted to know where your dragon is." Baboline walked over to the window and opened it up. Wind blew in and when it did I noticed a mark on the back of Baboline's neck. It looked like the head of a dragon. "He's right outside, waiting for you to recover."

I sighed in relief.

"But my question is why were you falling?" Baboline asked, as she leaned over the fire place.

I bit my lip. "I followed a friend to that area, we . . . we had something, like a fight. The next thing I knew I was falling only to be saved by you and Nightly. He jumped off to help me though." Baboline became interested in what I had to say. "But something caught him before I reached the lake. I had my eyes closed; I didn't see what it was." A thought came into my mind. "Could it be possible that the creature you mentioned before could have got him?"

"It's possible. The centagon loves to eat fresh meat especially around this time of the year." Baboline rubbed her chin as she sat next to me. "A centagon is a two headed beast that was banished to live in this land. To my surprise, people do not care of their own safety. They rather enjoy themselves at the resort instead of living," her voice turned into a whisper, "far away from here where no damage can be done to them." Her voice turned back to normal, "the centagon is as big as the resort that you're staying in, it carries razor sharp claws and has a swift double tail that can cut through a glacier

I gulped. Sam got scared when a mouse crawled over his foot once. If he would freak out at that I don't even want to know what his reaction would be toward that beast.

"I have to go," I said standing up.

"Girl, a centagon isn't something you would be trained to fight against. He will kill you on sight. The one thing a centagon hates is a whisperer and their dragon. It was because of a mage whisperer and her dragon that the centagon was created," Baboline explained.

"I need to save him!" I yelled. "If the legend's true, if that beast exists I *will* go after it and I *will* save my friend." I calmed down a bit and ran my finger through my pony tail. "Wasn't it a mage and a dragon that created the monster?"

"No one knows," Baboline said annoyed, "no mage or dragon had the power to do that. The brothers who were heroes met a cruel fate. They became villains in the eyes of their own village," she got up, grabbed clothes above the fire place and walked back over to the open window and beckoned something forward. "Here are your clothes and talk to your dragon."

"Why?"

"You need to save your friend, correct? Well, I'm going to give you some whisperer pills," Baboline paused quickly and gave me an awkward look, "you do know what they are, right?"

"Yes," I said in a drowsy voice.

"Well, then it saves me a whole lecture. Oh, how did that fight go with . . . uh, Celina?"

"How'd you know about that?" I asked, taking my clothes.

"I told her and I helped," Nightly said, laying his head on the window frame.

"How'd you help out? I was the one fighting her," I stated.

"I gave Nightly an E.N. gain pill. He said you were in trouble." Baboline walked over to a picture frame and grabbed it. She quietly whispered a name and then placed the picture frame faced down. She then quickly walked over to a cabinet.

I looked over at Nightly. He gave me wide open eyes and I gave him a shrug.

Baboline got a ripped piece of paper and walked back up to me. "Have you been taught about the original recipe and how it was lost during the war?"

"Yes," I answered.

"I have a part of it," she whispered. "Took forever to even come across some of the ingredients, but I found some. Not the original, but substitutes. Substitutes that make the pill weak but affective."

She must have been the supplier for the Guardians.

Baboline looked back at me while I was thinking. She must have got the wrong idea of what I was thinking of because she started to raise her voice to me, explaining what the pill that she gave Nightly did. "If a dragon or a whisperer consumes an E.N. gain pill, the energy between the two partners will be divided evenly so you both obtain the same amount of strength. Are you sure you know how these work?"

"Yes," I whined. She made quick decisions and wasn't afraid to speak them.

Baboline pulled me to my feet and pushed me towards the bathroom. "What are you waiting for? Go change and get your mind set for battle. I will guarantee that you and your dragon will encounter the centagon."

She shoved me into the bathroom. When the door was shut behind me I took a minute to think. Her temper and attitude reminded me of Pearl.

I pulled off the gown I wore and placed my dry pyjamas on. As I prepared myself for the search of Sam I tied my snow boots on tightly. I'd made mistakes before but this time I was going to make sure everything went right.

Nightly was already mounted when I exited the cottage. He was ready to take off. When my eyes looked upon my night black dragon a smile crept across my face. Too long I went without speaking or even seeing my dragon. As I took one step onto the snowy ground I raced towards my dragon, hugging his head. Nightly hummed, moving his tail side to side.

I've missed you my dragon, I said.

And I've missed you, he replied.

"How'd you meet Baboline?" I asked, scratching his ear.

"When I told you I was going to explore the area. I ran into her by the cliff. She was collecting ingredients for the whisperer pills. I remained invisible at all times, but she could detect my whereabouts."

"How did you know she wasn't a mage, as a matter fact, how did you know she was a whisperer?"

"Because I was sure she wasn't going to let me save you after spending a week with her. She's not a mage or else she would have revealed her true form and I would be dead, but no dragon has shown up either. My best guess is that she is a whisperer who has lost her dragon, like the Guardians."

"That's where you've been for the past week, was here?"

"Yeah, but she's strict, mean almost kind of reminds me of-"

"Pearl," I said finishing off his sentence.

"Yeah," he said.

"Nightly," I let go of his head and stepped back, looking deep into his golden eyes. "We've barely spoken to each other in the past week, do you know why?"

"Is it because of the centagon?"

I shook my head. "No, I wanted to avoid contact with you because someone found out our little secret. Apparently he did his research on me."

"Sounds like a researcher," said Baboline, coming out of the small cottage. "Researchers like to expose life of any Mystic Realm creature they can uncover. They call it exposing the truth within our world."

"Yep, sounds like Martin Miles *exactly*," I said.

"It's best to avoid those people at all times. They will go to any length to expose the truth." Baboline handed me a box big enough to fit in the palm of my hand and had it filled with pink E.N. gain pills.

"These pills, how'd you get a hold of the recipe Baboline? If they were lost in the war how is it possible that you could obtain the human made pills?"

"A good question, the artificial pills recipe wasn't easy to come by." Baboline took me by the shoulder and held it firm. "My brother sacrificed many things to obtain the recipe I hold. The E.N. gain pill is the easiest one for me to make but the others are difficult. Sear especially. If it wasn't for my brother, who had been taught by a legend, I would have never known how to substitute the original ingredients and make my own. The legend was incredible."

"Wow, that legend must have been something," I commented.

"Yeah, he was," she said. "Now, what you want to do is go back to the cliff you fell off and go into the cave above the lake. Stay invisible at all times until you find your friend, then get out of there. The centagon cannot fly that is your biggest advantage. Have Nightly stay in the air, and if not get ready to take off at any moment."

"Got it," he said.

"And Connie, I want you to be extremely careful. The two souls that are held prisoners inside the centagon fell in love with a whisperer. They will not take too kindly to new visitors such as yourself. Listen to your surroundings and keep an eye out for anything. This is an old creature that hasn't died in ten hundred years so keep your guard up."

"Hey Baboline, you remind me of a dragon I know back home." I wanted to know something. I removed her grip on me. "Her name's Pearl. She's a light dragon; I think she would really like you. That and your kindness reminds me of the man who made me a whisperer. His name was Devonburg."

Baboline's breathing became unsteady.

"Sorry, I didn't mean to offend you in any way."

"No," she said, getting a hold of herself. Baboline rubbed the back of her neck. "Devonburg was my younger brother. When I heard about his passing I never expected to hear his name again."

Nightly and I were shocked.

"Devonburg was committed to being a whisperer. The legendary Gabriel Whitsburg and his darkness dragon Nix were his teachers."

"Whitsburg?"

"Yes, the legendary Gabriel Whitsburg was Devonburg's mentor. Devonburg became a whisperer before I did and he loved it so much. He and his wind dragon, Skier, were the best of friends. He gave me a dragon egg while I was travelling through India. When the egg changed colour I knew I couldn't take care of it. I left it, a decision, no, a mistake I made. Before I could leave it for someone else to find it, it hatched and placed its mark on me." Baboline pulled her hair up and showed us the light dragon head mark on the back of her neck. "I couldn't do it and didn't want to do it."

"So what did you do?" I asked.

Baboline let go of her hair. "I didn't want her to see me but she hatched quicker than others. I guess she was eager to see her whisperer, but I just left her, left her alone, all by herself."

"You never leave a dragon alone. They'll go out of control."

"She was found by someone else! Apparently, my dragon was accepted by a human and believed that she was her whisperer. To this day she's been with a human and I regret letting her go even though she was with another dragon and whisperer."

"Your dragon's, Pearl," I pointed out.

Nightly nodded, *"There is no doubt about it."*

Baboline placed her hand on her heart. "Thank goodness. I never told Devonburg that I got rid if my dragon since he loves his so much. Gabriel Whitsburg was the person who taught me to make the pills and assigned me here. It was a punishment for abandoning my dragon. He told me to keep the monster at bay and to keep people away from its lair, but I would never believe that I would run into Devonburg's legacy."

"What about Gabriel Whitsburg, am I related to him? I want to know more." I said.

"We've wasted enough time talking already you better get going," said Baboline grabbing me and helping me up onto Nightly's saddle.

"All I'll say is that he's your great-grandfather. He and his darkness dragon were given the nickname 'angle and demon pair'. Now go!"

I strapped myself onto Nightly's saddle. He bent down low to the ground, readying himself to take off.

"I need to know who my great-grandfather was," I cried as Nightly took his big leap up into the sky.

Baboline just smiled as we flew into the dark winter sky.

CHAPTER 21

Attack of the Centagon

We flew through the cold dark night for at least an hour. The black lake that I fell into lay still, motionless. Nightly flew over it then began to fly up near the cliff's wall. In the middle of the wall rested a ridged cave that went deep into the ground. We entered the cave feeling a draft of freezing cold air hit us, like it was a warning to turn back. Nightly ignored it as did I and continued forward hiding him and myself from every creature's eyesight. As we glided through the cave obstacles stood before us. Multiple passageways stood before us, all shaped exactly alike. The whole cave had to be twenty-five feet high and long. If I were to ever compare this to any other maze I had seen this one would definitely win first place.

Stalactites hung from the ceiling and stalagmites stood on the bottom. Ice covered the rocks and covered something else. Bones of all different beings, Mystical Realm and Human World related. This place was huge, the look of it represented a prison like the ravine was to me. It was no wonder the centagon would be testy. It had been trapped in a prison for a thousand years.

As we traveled deeper within the cave things started to get more challenging. We started to hit dead ends, the amount of bones grew and there was no sign of Sam or the creature.

I bit my lip. *How are we going to find him?*

Maybe they're at the center of all these tunnels.

Why do you think that?

If you think about it, in a maze all the passageways are connected to one place, the center. That would be the best place for the centagon to rest, because it would have all the access it needed there.

But how do we find it?

A majority of these tunnels have to connect to the center. If we can just find a clue that would lead us to it we'll find the beast.

The freezing violent draft hit us again.

Follow the draft, it has to come from somewhere.

But a draft like that wouldn't come from the center of this maze.

What if it's not the wind making it? What if the centagon's making it?

Let's find out then.

Nightly flew against the draft. The frozen air made me lie down on the saddle. Once and a while I would feel Nightly shake, he would also blow some fire to keep him warm.

Are you sure you want to do this, Nightly? We can stop if you can't handle this.

I'm not a wimp, I can do this. I can do this as sure as you are willing to risk your life for a friend.

I blushed. Maybe I did have some feelings for Sam, everyone knew he had something for me I just didn't know if I had the same thing for him. He was a great friend, an irreplaceable one. That's why I was so determined to rescue him.

Nightly flew low and landed behind some stalagmites. We had arrived. There in the center of this ridiculous maze prison was a twenty foot beast sleeping soundly. A head was breathing heavily. It created the cold air that led us here.

A feeling came over me as I looked over at the beast. When Nightly first hatched I had a dream that a pair of grey eyes were staring at me and I had the same feeling here, in the centagon's lair, I could feel its presence as if they were watching me.

The sleeping creature really did have two heads. The body was ice white with no wings. The tail was wagging back and forth as if it was trying to sweep something away. It was truly a beast to fear!

Where do we start looking?

Anywhere. We just can't wake the big guy.

Then I'm getting off. I unstrapped myself and stepped onto the cold ground. I became visible as did my dragon.

Be careful, this guy looks like he's still partially awake.

I will be if you quit worrying. Besides, if he does wake up, I'll just take an E.N. gain pill so he can't catch me.

Remember, that energy with in that pill is equally divided amongst us. Don't expect that you'll get the full dose.

That is why I am giving you an E.N. gain pill too. That way we'll each get the full amount of energy from one pill.

I took out the little box and placed one of the pills in Nightly's mouth. I watched as he carefully positioned the small pill underneath his tongue. I placed the small pill box in my boot, right near the heel.

Quietly, Nightly and I walked into the center. It was twice the size than the tunnels. I walked across the ground; carefully going around the centagon while Nightly began to search the other tunnels.

"Sam," I quietly called out, "are you here?" I looked all around. He had to be here somewhere. I dared not to think what the centagon could have done to him. I just wanted to find something of his that would tell me what happened. It got hard when I searched near the centagon's tail. "Sam, where are you?"

Connie, be quiet. I thought I heard something.

Is it Sam?

I can't tell, I'm going in for a closer look.

You be careful now.

That's my line for you. Don't worry I'll be right back.

Nightly flew into a tunnel that was in the ceiling leaving me alone with the sleeping centagon. I stared at the beast noticing that one of the heads had a scar on the mouth as if someone took a sword and slashed open the mouth from one side. As I moved myself around the gigantic body I noticed something. Below the centagon rested a frozen body. Was it something they wanted to protect?

The frozen breeze from the beast's mouth suddenly stopped and its tail began to speed up after every swing. I found myself ducking more often than I should of. As I looked at the double tail a low, deep growl was heard. I bit my lip and turned around; widening my eyes as I looked upon the two heads slowly rise. A blue fire left the head without the scar's mouth.

"Well, well, well, what do we have here, Grags?"

"Looks like a little girl who's gone astray, Hans," said the head without the scar named Grags.

"Sorry to disturb you, it was an accident, I'll be going now," I said, backing away slowly.

The double tail stopped swinging side to side. It slid across the icy ground and stopped me. It moved quick and made no sound. I didn't even realize it was there until I backed up into it. The tail pushed me forward, close to the centagon. Sweat began to emerge from my body as terror began to spread through it.

"But you just got here."

"Yes, you have to stay for breakfast, whisperer."

Both heads licked their lips with fork-like tongues. The heads leaned in closer to me and took a sniff. They both hissed with delight.

"Wait, Grags, we're missing something," said the head with the scar named Hans.

"You're right, we need to find the whisperer's mark first. They taste better when their identity's been exposed."

The tail moved away for a brief second before it returned, whacking me in the side. I smashed into a tunnel, gasping for air as the impact made me lose all of mine. My shoulders ached along with my right side. It was hard to stand but I did it. That thing had no intention of letting me live, but for now it just wanted to play, and it did, it played rough.

I leaned up against the wall, trying to figure out what to do next. As long as Nightly stayed in the other tunnel we could escape without no further harm being done. It sounded like a great plan, but I didn't expect to hear hesitant footsteps approach me. My head turned slowly. My thought's kept telling me to ignore it and move but my body refused.

"Sam, is that you?" I asked, hoping it was then this mission wouldn't be for nothing, but it wasn't. It was the same mage who warned me about this place. I recognized him from his height, the strange mark on his chest and the earing he had on. "You! What are you doing here?!"

"I could ask you the same thing," he said leaning on the tunnel's wall next to me, his arms were crossed and he had a serious look on his face. "I told you not to come here."

"I had to," I stated. "My friend is here somewhere."

"What?" The mage's slit pupils became round with surprise. I stared at him not knowing what to do. He didn't look like he was going to harm me but then again he might have something else planned.

"My friend, Sam, was caught by the centagon earlier this evening. I feel responsible! I have to rescue him, if he's not dead already." I dropped my head and held a hand over my face. I kept telling myself he was alive but my mind still held that possibility that he was dead.

A roar exploded through the tunnels and I recognized it. I dropped my hand back down and forced my body to run out of the tunnel back into the center. There I watched Nightly and the centagon fight. Black scales, broken stalactites and stalagmites were scattered everywhere. Nightly was flying around the center and the centagon lay below him striking the air only when Nightly got close to them. The mage joined me and looked at the battle I was watching.

"Nightly!" I yelled.

The mage covered my mouth and pulled me back further into the tunnel.

"What do you think you are doing? Do you want that thing to come and eat both of us?" he asked in a viscous voice. I looked up at him. His ears were up and I think the slit pupils in his eyes grew thinner with his anger.

"The centagon eats mages too?" I said removing his hand.

"The whisperer was a mage that cursed them along with the dragon."

"So what are you going to do now?" I said, separating myself from him. "Are you going to stuff me in a bag now so you can take Nightly's life?"

"No."

"Then are you going to kill us right now?"

"No."

"What are you going to do?"

"Your friend Sam, he's alive. I helped him get out of here and I'm going to do the same thing with you," he grabbed my hand. "Now let's go!"

"I can't. Nightly is still out there! I won't and will not leave him," I said, pulling my hand away.

He sighed and rubbed his head. "Then you're going to need *this* to get around him." The mage tossed me my anklet that I had lost in the flood.

"Where'd you get this?" I asked putting it on.

"You should be aware of the things you carry with you. If you lose them, you never know who will pick them up," he said, leaving.

"Where are you going?" I demanded. "I need help."

"Figure it out yourself, because I'm not helping a dragon." The mage had his back turned to me. He then travelled further down the tunnel.

"You jerk," I called out clenching my fists. "I'll show you! Nightly and I will survive."

I faced back down the tunnel where the roars were getting more violent. I sat down with my legs crossed trying to connect my mind with Nightly's.

Nightly, if you can hear me, I'm coming to help you. Try to connect your body and mind with mine.

I'd rather you not, Nightly insisted in a weak voice. *But I will try.*

Right then and there, I felt it. Our minds connected. I stood up strong and brave. I walked out into the center only to find Nightly under the centagon's claws.

"Oh, looks like the whisperer is trying to save her dragon, Hans," said the head called Grags.

"Let's eat them both," suggested Grags.

One head launched at me but all I did was take a breath in and jump up to twenty feet in the air. The head crashed into the tunnel I came out of, caving it in. It was amazing how much power I had when we connected both our mind and body. I had Nightly's speed and agility. The only thing that was missing was the enjoyment of having this power. Nightly was so serious in training all the time and the only thing he feared was losing me. He shared those emotions with me while mine were buried away within my heart. The one thing we both shared at this point was determination to survive and win the battle.

"Brat!" roared Grags.

When I came back down I landed on a neck and began to run along it trying to draw the other heads attention. It worked. The head called Hans came at me with full speed, the breath I took was released. I jumped back to the ground and watched as the Hans teeth sank into Grags neck. Blood poured onto the ground and the Grags screamed in pain.

"Idiot, why'd you bite me?" It yelled.

"It wasn't my fault! I was, after all, trying to catch the whisperer."

The centagon may have been a huge and scary but they still were brothers, and brothers fight. What sibling couldn't resist a good fight with the other?

"We haven't eaten for a year and you want to eat me instead?"

"Idiot, if you die I die. You should know that since we're sharing one body."

As they bickered, I ran to Nightly, he squirmed his way out of the centagon's grip.

"Let's get out of here now!" I said, pulling myself onto Nightly's back.

"But what about your friend Sam?" he asked, preparing to take off.

"Don't worry, he's safe," I said.

"Are you sure?"

I bit my lip as the image of the mage appeared in my mind. There was something about him, something that made me say, "Yes."

After my reply Nightly took off, flying in close to the stalactites. I searched the area, looking for the same tunnel we first came out of. My gaze was drawn upon the centagon though. The blood leaked out of the neck, some of it dripping on the floor. My fear of blood was gone, I could look at it and there was no sickness, no queasiness it was all gone. I loved being connected to Nightly, he wasn't scared of anything and when he wasn't scared I wasn't either.

Then something caught my eye. The thing the centagon was laying on was in view. It was the frozen woman trapped beneath the ground.

"Nightly, look!" I said pointing to the frozen woman.

"That must be the mage who turned them into the centagon."

"She's beautiful," I said as I looked at the mage in her eternal slumber.

Long flowing black hair and cat ears, ruby red lips and pale grey skin that almost matched her blood stained white dress.

As I was observing her I could have sworn that I saw her eyes open and hiss at me. I screamed and fell off the saddle, I was lucky enough to grab the leg strap. My little mishap drew the centagon's attention. They watched me dangle in the air. They straightened up and rose off the ground. A grin appeared on both their faces. That's when they started to snap at me trying to make me fall. I hung onto the leg straps, struggling to pull myself back up. The connection between Nightly and I broke.

"I want the whisperer," called Hans, snapping at me.

"That means the dragon's all mine," said Grags.

"Connie, use the E. N. gain pill now," said Nightly, as he flew in and out of the stalactites trying to use the unbroken rocks as cover.

"Eat yours then," I said grabbing the box out of my boot. It was hard to open and when it did half of our pill supplies spilled out. I managed to grab one and swallow it.

Nightly crunched down hard on his pill, soon there was twice the amount of energy filling both our bodies. Nightly flew faster and I had enough strength to pull myself back up onto the saddle, but a claw reached up, it hit the chain around my neck breaking it off.

"No," I cried as I jumped off Nightly. One of the heads came at me; I landed in between its eyes and then slid down the centagon's neck grabbing the locket, "Gotcha!"

That's when I noticed the sides of the centagon move. Four pairs of extra legs broke out. I slid down one and was grossed out by how slimy they were.

"We haven't had to use our extra set of legs since the angel and demon pair came here," said Grags.

"The dragon and whisperer here, they almost look like them," commented Hans.

I gripped the locket and began to run.

"The girl almost looks like the angel that was here."

"Only this time, they won't be leaving."

A leg came down trying to stomp on me but missed. I was already scratched up and bruised from their last attack. I kept running pointing to a random tunnel to Nightly, hoping that it was our way out. Both of the centagon's heads had their attention on me. They both hissed in anger as they failed to stomp on me. I kept on running, waiting for Nightly to get in the tunnel. The head called Hans caught the back of my shirt and pulled me up off the ground.

"I caught her," it boasted swinging me around.

"Quit swinging the food around, idiot," yelled the other head, head-butting its brother.

During the impact Hans dropped me but not without exposing my mark to them. The back of my shirt ripped and on my flesh that was revealed was the dragon wings Devonburg had given me. When I hit the ground, Nightly stood behind me helping me up to my feet. I looked down at my ankle wondering why it hadn't hidden the mark, was it because the pills might have been disrupting its power?

"Thank you, Nightly," I said, looking back up.

He growled as he knocked me back to the ground. Nightly then blew fire trying to buy me some time. It didn't work. Both heads began to blow their blue fire against Nightly's flame. Nightly's flame was too weak and there was only one of him.

I rose to my feet and watched as both fires died down.

"Impressive," said Grags. "Usually when something touches our ice-fire they freeze then burn."

"You're the second pair able to stand your ground against the attack."

I stepped forward and touched Nightly on the snout. "The other pair you are talking about was my great-grandfather and his dragon. I don't know why he was here but I'm guessing it has something to do with your frozen girlfriend."

"The angel and demon pair were related to you? Ha, don't make us laugh. They were strong and smart and would have killed us if we hadn't taken the whisperer's wife's life. Compared to them, you two are just new hatchlings. Besides, like all whisperer's, dragons and mages they only came here to hunt us."

"Yeah, now you can die like the rest did." said Hans.

Both heads went back as they dug their claws into the ground. As they were taking a breath, I gave Nightly another pill and I took one as well. The centagon then attacked with its ice-fire. I quickly swallowed the pill and felt something hit me. No, it wasn't the ice-fire, instead it was a power that I didn't believe I had. Nightly touched my back and the energy that was bottled between us was released through my body. I forced my chest forward.

"Soul Blast," I yelled as the power took the centagon right off its feet.

"Impossible," they both said landing on their back.

Nightly turned around and started to sprint into the tunnel that was our way out. I followed him but as I walked the tips of the centagon's tail hit me in the back. I flew off in the opposite direction only to be caught by the mage I ran into earlier. He slid across the ice floor for a short bit then stopped as he held me like a new born baby.

"Why are you here?" I mumbled

"I'm surprised you're still conscious, whisperer. An attack like that isn't easy to live through," he said holding me tighter.

"Shut up," I said coughing.

Nightly watched the whole thing. Fumes escaped from his nostrils as he ran up to us ready to attack at any moment.

"Mage," he growled.

"Relax dragon, I just saved your whisperer's life. I'm going to treat her wound first, then both of you can leave." The mage set me down and turned me over onto my stomach and lifted my clothes up. He whistled. "Wow, that's some cut, are you sure you didn't do this on purpose?"

I groaned. "It was an accident," I said.

The mage reached into his pocket grabbing a small bottle of disinfectant. He took out a cloth from his other pocket and cleaned my wound. The feeling felt like a thousand knives going through my back. I did a blood curling scream. Once my wound was bandaged, Nightly stayed in his attack position waiting to see what the mage would do next.

"There, done," he said, lifting me up into his arms. "I recommend that you get that wound treated right away when you get back to the humans."

He placed me on Nightly and strapped me in. "I thought you left."

"Let's just say I came back to help a friend," he said.

"You better leave before I start biting," said Nightly stepping away from the mage.

"I would hold your tongue because I am not alone," he said. The mage looked at me and gave me a small smile I recognized, "but before I go I want to leave a present."

He grabbed the side of my face and kissed me on the lips then ran off.

Nightly growled, *"Why did you let him kiss you?"*

"I don't know, I thought it was sweet," I said sitting up ignoring the pain. "Usually when I get kissed I back away in shock thinking they kissed me by accident but that was on purpose and it felt nice and familiar."

"I think that wound is messing with your mind," said Nightly.

"Oh, hush," I said swaying side to side as Nightly moved.

Nightly went through the same tunnel as the mage, trying to get out of this place as quickly as possible. The tunnel took us back to the lake.

Nightly then flew me back to the resort. The sun had just started to rise in the sky and I didn't want to be caught by the cameras or by anyone else. Nightly stayed invisible with me as we approached my room's window. Quietly and quickly I snuck in. Nightly gave me a sadden hum as he left me. Before he left I gave him a kiss on his forehead. My dragon then vanished from my sight. My thoughts weren't about him though they were about Sam. We failed trying to find him, I hope what the mage said was true, that he helped him get out of there. I changed my pyjamas. Pain filled my body as I climbed back into bed. The feeling of being warm underneath the covers reminded me what it was like to be held by that mage. He had no shirt or shoes on yet he was warm. My eyes closed slowly as the Christmas sun slowly rose in the air. I liked the sunrise, it was my first time seeing it, and it was beautiful. My last thought before going to sleep was 'did I really have feelings for Sam?'

Britney woke me up for breakfast and was the first person to say 'Merry Christmas' to me. We went to the dining hall finding it nearly bare. There were only a few other groups who were eating breakfast. I figured everyone would be opening gifts in their own room or sleeping. I know that I wanted to sleep in. Being up all night made my body ache. Britney pulled me to the same table as Sam, Sid and Kyle.

"Merry Christmas," they called out all excited.

"Merry Christmas," we said in returned along with smiles.

Pain surged through my back as I sat down. It went away after a while but I was just happy to see Sam safe. I guess what that mage said was true. Maybe they weren't all evil like the Guardians said.

After breakfast, we went to the ski hill. We were the first ones to snowboard down the hill for the day. I was so happy and excited. I was able to come back alive from the centagon's lair with one serious wound and a few scratches and bruises.

I took my board and surfed down the slopes. It wasn't until I was halfway down the hill that the pain returned. I wiped out and slid the rest of the way to the bottom twitching violently.

"Connie!" yelled Kyle as he came to my aid. "Someone call the nurse."

My back turned cold and something was coming out of it. That's when I knew my wound had reopened and blood started to pour out. I became dizzy and weak, losing consciousness.

CHAPTER 22

Saliva

My eyes opened very slowly. It took a while for me to figure out where I was. My hearing was shot for the first few seconds and the same was with my blurry vision. It occurred to me that I was in the nurse's office lying on my stomach. I looked to my right and saw a clock that said two o'clock. My back was exposed to the cold open air. I could still feel the pain. It was worse this time. Instead of knives digging into my back it felt like someone was taking a weed whacker to my flesh. Something you would find in a horror movie. I clutched the blankets and shut my eyes hoping that the pain would go away.

"Oh, Connie, you're awake," said Nurse Jacqueline entering the room.

I opened one eye and released my grip. The pain vanished for now. I sat up straight to greet the nurse as she placed a hand on my head. My temperature was high, and my head was soaked in sweat.

"You were found unconscious right after your run down the hill. When I examined your body I found that nasty gash on your back. If you don't mind me asking, how did you get that?"

"I really don't want to talk about it," I said, running my hand down to my mouth carefully placing my fingers on my lips. The pain came back and I screamed "Help!"

Nurse Jacqueline got a bottle and some pills. She put her hand out in front of me filled with some pills, but I pushed them aside and screamed for my life. Nurse Jacqueline was forced to shove them into my mouth. Her hand stayed over mouth until she heard me swallow.

The pills acted fast and relieved me of the pain. I coughed after feeling drowsy.

"The pills I gave you are pain killers. They don't last long in your condition," she said placing the bottle on a side table.

"Wait, in my condition? How long have I been asleep?" I asked, curious.

"Let's see, it's been five days now."

"Five days!" I said shocked. "You mean to tell me that today's the day before New Years Eve . . . and that I missed Christmas?"

"Yes."

She answered that very quickly and a bit harsh to. I had been asleep for five days with this wound on my back that hasn't started to heal but get worse instead.

"We called your parents and they wanted to know your progress as soon as you awoke, I guess I have a phone call to make tonight." Nurse Jacqueline paused. She reached for me but I hit her hand away. For a reason I don't even know why. Then she continued to talk. "For the days you were asleep was when I inspected your wound. I've checked all the medical records and couldn't find the animal that would make that kind of wound," she said pulling out a book and flipping through pages.

"What's the wound look like?" I asked.

"See for yourself," Nurse Jacqueline closed the book and walked over to the other side of the room, in her high heels, grabbing a full length mirror, bringing it to my bedside.

I turned around finding that my shirt had been cut up. There was only enough of it left that covered my shoulders down to my ribcage. On my lower back was the wound. It was graphic, bloody and had these bluish purple colour veins that were spreading across the rest of my back. I knew I wasn't hit with the whole tail only half, or else I would be in two pieces. A thought hit me. I looked down at my leg wear, a fresh pair of pants; quickly I ran my hand down my leg and found the scale placed up to my knee. Someone moved it, but who?

Nurse Jacqueline pushed her dark hair back into a ponytail and rubbed her brown eyes. The sleeve of her nurse's coat was covering a blue splotch on her hand; it almost looked like a burn.

"Is something wrong?" I asked, lying back down on my stomach.

She turned to face me slowly. "It's nothing really. I just forgot to take my allergy medicine." She brushed off her red shirt and did the same thing with her black pants.

"What are you allergic to?"

She didn't make eye contact with me. All Nurse Jacqueline did was look over at the door knob and watched it turn. In entered Sam and Kyle.

"Hey, she's awake," said Kyle walking up to me. He forced me to sit back up and hugged me. "Oh, you scared me. Mom and Dad would have killed me if anything were to happen to you."

Yep, that was the same old Kyle. He's just being nice so he won't get into trouble with our parents or any other adult.

"Kyle, let go! You're hurting me," I said.

Kyle released his grip on me, turned around and sat down in a chair. Sam came up to me and put something in my hand.

"Sam, I can't accept a Christmas present when I have nothing to give you," I said, trying to give it back.

"Just open your hand and you'll see," he said stepping back.

I opened my hand to find the locket Sam had given to me for my birthday. I felt around my neck to find my necklace missing.

"It broke off your neck when you were taken to the nurse's office," Sam got another chair and sat right next to me.

There was a knock on the door and in walked Teddy with a bouquet of roses and a box of chocolates.

"Hey Jacqueline, I brought you some flowers," he said, blushing.

"That is very nice, Teddy, but I need to go to my room and get my medicine." She left with her lab coat flapping through the air.

Teddy sighed and placed the roses on the counter. "That's the third time she's made an excuse to leave the room while I'm around. I've tried everything from surprise mistletoe to the original box of chocolates and roses."

"Don't worry, janitor dude, I'll give you some tips on how to win a girl's heart. I've done it a hundred times," Kyle boasted, grabbing Teddy's shoulder.

"Kyle, you do know that ninety-nine percent of the time you win girls is in your dreams," I commented.

"You better be glad that you're injured," he said, clenching his fists, a faint smile appearing on his face.

Sam laughed as Kyle and I argued. Unfortunately, the conversation broke up when the intercom came on, the voice asked for both Teddy and Kyle to report to the front desk. They both looked nervous, they obviously knew what they were being called down for, but it was still funny to make fun of their facial expressions as they exited the room, closing the door behind them.

Sam was the only person left in the room with me. He chuckled but then became serious. "Connie, how did you survive that fall?"

I bit my lip and then rubbed the back of my head. "Well I'm sure if I told you, you wouldn't believe me."

"Try me," he said, touching my hand. "I won't make fun of you and I won't tell anyone."

I bit my lip even harder, ready to tell him, but then I held my tongue. "I'm sorry, Sam, but I can't even tell you." I took my elastic out of my hair and hid my face with it. I gave him the elastic and kissed him on the cheek. "I'm so happy that you're safe though."

Sam let go of my hand and felt his cheek. He blushed and scooted out the door. That was Sam for you. He was a typical guy who hides most of his feeling under his warm cheeks. I flopped down on my bed and went to sleep.

My dream took place in the centagon's lair with me above the frozen woman.

"So, you made it out alive," said the same mage from before, "but you strained your wound now it's worse then before."

"I don't like to worry my friends or family," I said, kneeling down to the woman. "All she wanted was for the fighting to stop and now look at her."

The mage moved closer to me, he held out his hand over the woman. The ice underneath his hand began to melt as his hand took on the colour of red.

"What are you doing?" I asked standing up.

Once the woman's face was unfrozen she hissed at me again. I backed away, startled.

"Why are you afraid?" he asked, covering her face. "She's already dead, she can't hurt you."

I sighed in relief. "I'm sorry, but when I was battling the centagon her eyes opened and she hissed at me."

The mage removed his hand and then the woman opened her eyes. "You just said that she opened her eyes and so she did. You're the one who's in control of your dreams. If you don't want her to do something then she won't."

"How do you know that?" I asked scared.

"Are you forgetting that mages are part dragon? Remember we also have a special ability, we can appear in other people's dreams and manipulate them if we please." The mage stood and took me by the hand. I rose up and looked into his eyes. "Dreams are weird; you can go a whole night without one or have one so realistic that you feel that it's almost like real life. We mages make you feel conscious in your dreams; to make sure you feel everything and never forget it." I looked at him. He took his hand and raised it to my face. I quickly shut my eyes, fearing what he would do. At first nothing happened. Everything became silent when I felt his hand rub against my head. I opened my eyes again and watched as the mage rubbed the hair on top of my head. "Your dreams are your own creation. Humans don't realize that they have control over their dreams. If you wished to leave one you would simply wake, even if someone is controlling it. Don't let anyone control what you have created."

"I don't get it, why you're helping me," I asked confused.

The mage moved his hand down my hair and moved it all the way to my chest. "I told you before, I'm doing it for a friend," he said, letting go of my hair. He started walking away. "Think about it, Connie, I would have already killed you and your dragon if I wasn't helping."

I looked down at my feet and saw the scenery change back into the nurse's office at the ski resort. The mage was still there but he stayed in the door way. I looked up to him and watched a smile appear on his face. I knew that smile, but from where? He then approached me and kissed me again.

"I envy the guy who ends up with you," he said leaving.

"Wait, what's your name?" I asked.

"Call me . . . Amson," he said as he left.

I awoke sitting straight up feeling my lips. He kissed me again and it felt better than last time.

"Amson," I whispered. "I will never forget that name but who do I love, you or Sam?"

I stood up and began to walk until the pain returned to my back. I tried to return to the bed but the best I could do was reach for the blanket and pull it off the bed as I collapsed onto the ground twitching with unstoppable aggravating pain running throughout my entire body.

*   *   *

A day later Kyle and I drove back to Small Valley. We never got to finish that final week at the resort but I doubt I would even like it, especially when Martin Miles kept hanging around and I sure didn't want to stay around knowing that Celina would swear revenge against me. The resort kindly lent us their car to drive back home. Kyle stayed by my side the whole trip home. He was really worried about me. When we got home I was taken straight to the hospital where the doctors examined my back and tried to find the cure for my wound. They knew it was some kind of poison but a kind they had never seen in their life. When they asked me what happened, I just told them that I was attacked from behind and I never saw what the beast looked like before I fell unconscious. It was a believable story to most people except for Dad and Sam. They both knew that there was something else that I wasn't telling them. It didn't matter to me though. All I wanted was for the pain to vanish; the longer the wound remained on my back, the more the pain grew. By the third week; nobody slept, I cried. Every tear that would fall down my face I would say "I'm sorry" in the quietest whisper. The veins had spread to every inch of my body, the wound on my back had darkened.

Doctors had no idea what to do. There was no cure, the creature that had caused my agony was unknown to them. I had been given until Sunday, the day after tomorrow to prepare myself, I was going to . . . die.

That night, at the hospital, I fell asleep again on my stomach anything that touched my back made me cry out in pain. I was going to die at the start of the forth week. I didn't want to die and I said that over and over again, crying tears of fear.

I dreamt of Nightly at Baboline's cottage, he was talking with her. Nightly looked terrible, his night black scales started to lighten and his gold eyes started to lose there colour. Then I saw him do something that I never thought Nightly would ever do, beg.

"Please, you have to help her," he pleaded.

"I can't do much if I haven't seen the wound, Nightly. I'm afraid I can't help you." Baboline replied.

"No, you have to help her," Nightly growled. *"She's your brother's legacy, it should be your duty!"*

"I'm sorry," she turned away from Nightly and started to head back inside her cottage, but someone stopped her. "Who are you?"

"My name's Amson," he said stepping out of the shadow of the door way.

Nightly started to growl.

"Calm yourself, dragon, I've come to help." Amson approached Baboline and showed her a picture of my wound. "Connie has been scratched by the centagon's tail."

Baboline became shocked. She snatched the picture away from him examining it closely. She pushed past Amson entering her cottage.

Nightly stood up and slowly approached Amson. *"Just because you helped us last time doesn't mean I trust you."*

"I don't expect you to," Amson replied. "My friend asked me to do one last favour for him. He has a crush on her. Besides you don't look well yourself. You're probably feeling the effects of her body weaken."

"My body and my whisperer are my own business, not yours!" he roared.

Amson knew Sam, I realized. This dream was strange. I've only been the one in my dreams but this time I was seeing things through Nightly's perspective.

Baboline came running out, holding a purple jar with a fire and ice symbol on it. "If Connie really has been scratched by the centagon, the poison must have contaminated the whole body by now."

"Not yet, she's a fighter and she's still breathing. Now, how can we cure her?!" demanded Nightly.

"The centagon was given its name because the two brothers weren't just fused with the dragon but also with a little insect they made contact with. The insect was a centipede. A centipede has poison in its little pinchers, but the centagon carries it in its tail, claws and fangs." Baboline took a breath. "No human has successfully brought back the antidote. Hey have either died trying to obtain it or were too cowardly to even venture into the centagon's lair to collect it." She walked over to Nightly, climbed up onto the saddle then strapped herself in. "We have to go back to the centagon's lair, the antidote lies within its mouth, collect it and you'll save Connie."

There was silence nothing but silence. It was insane to go back in there and it was a death sentence to go up against the centagon. Even though I was only watching, I could feel my heart start to race.

Nodding his head, Nightly prepared for takeoff. Baboline tucked the jar under one arm, and held onto the saddle as tight as she could. As Nightly traveled back into the tunnels that led to the centagon's lair he started to get sloppy with his flying. He seemed to regain control but he was pushing himself too hard. By the time they reached the center, it was bare. The centagon was nowhere to be found.

"Where is he?" asked Baboline. "He is usually here sleeping, protecting the frozen girl."

"It's hunting," said Amson.

"When did you get here?" demanded Nightly.

"I've been here for ten minutes now. You're starting to lose your ability to fly, aren't you?" Amson eyed Nightly, he growled in return. "We need to get that antidote or else the dragon and his whisperer won't live another day."

Amson, a strange unpredictable mage. He managed to beat Nightly to the centagon's lair. It was no lie that mages still had a dragon's speed and strength with them. It was unbelievable.

"The centagon doesn't hunt. The food always comes to it," said Baboline.

"We should think up a battle strategy while we wait for him to return," suggested Amson leaning on a tunnel wall. "The quicker we do so the better."

"Wait just a second," said Nightly, *"what is wrong with the idea with finding it?"*

"There are multiple tunnels. Each one will lead you to a different place. We have no idea where they go and if we're lucky we'll manage to find the one that will lead us out of here. Even if we were to take one there is no guarantee that the centagon will be there." Amson looked at Nightly's displeased face. "Let's say if we did find him, within a tunnel, there would be no use fighting. The centagon created these tunnels and it is the only one that knows where each and every one goes. We'll, most likely end up killing ourselves just trying to find him. I'm sorry Nightly, but I'm going with the mage on this one," said Baboline.

Nightly let smoke out of his nostrils and growled. *"Do as you please but don't come crying to me when the mage betrays us."*

"Tell me everything you know about the centagon," said Amson.

"You've already faced off with it, there isn't much more that I can tell you. The two head's bicker about anything but watch out when they actually do work together. When you're in their sights they will try everything in their power to kill you. The extra arms are something else though. Once they come out they won't just attack with their heads and tail anymore, those arms will be constantly moving; waiting to crush whatever is underneath them. They aren't there for show," said Baboline.

"Is that all?"

"No, there is one more thing I want both of you to know. I've told you that the centagon carries poison but I never said what was in the poison . . . its sear. If the two of you are poisoned you'll die. I don't know how that creature obtained it but it did."

Both Nightly and Amson faces went pale and fear came over them.

"You both have to be extra careful. For a human and whisperer sear is rendered harmless but for a mage and dragon the slightest touch will burn and kill you, slowly," said Baboline.

That's right. Whisperer pills are artificially made. The recipe has been lost for years now. This wasn't going to be easy for Nightly or Amson. I prayed they would be safe.

"Then I will be the distraction," said Amson, getting a hold of himself. "If the dragon could hide in the stalactites I think we can end the centagon for good."

"What are you planning?" asked Nightly.

"I get it," said Baboline, impressed.

"Get what?!" asked Nightly irritated.

Baboline turned to Nightly. "Amson is going to draw the centagon's attention while you hide yourself in the rocks above us. I will be waiting in our escape tunnel till I know that the centagon is dead then I'll collect the saliva."

"While you're hiding in the stalactites wait for the right time then cut the rocks down so they'll land on the centagon, understand?" asked Amson.

"Yeah, I got it and don't treat me like an idiot," Nightly said, stretching out his wings and flying up to the ceiling.

Amson and Baboline hid, listening to slithering and hissing growing louder and louder by each second. The centagon emerged from a tunnel on the ceiling. They slithered their way down not even noticing Nightly. All their legs were out. They seemed very agitated and distracted. In one of the creature's mouths was a carcass of a cow. They dropped the dead animal down on the ground making loose rocks jump into the air.

"Give me some of that already. I'm starving," whined Grags.

"Relax, and settle down. We have to protect Veronica before we can eat," said Hans.

The centagon laid down over top of the frozen woman and started to tear at the cow. They ate every morsel of meat on the poor animal. The flesh, meat, organs, anything really. Broken bones laid on the ground. When the creature was done it sniffed the air.

"You smell that?"

"Yeah, smells like a human is in our lair."

Nightly looked down at Baboline, she was all big talk, because what I could see through Nightly eyes she was shaking, holding the jar close to her chest and sweating. Baboline shut her eyes and started to relax but Amson had already sprung the plan into action. He walked out and looked up at the centagon.

"Hey, which is the worthless head? Is it the one who can only speak human or the one who can only speak dragon tongue?"

The creature growled.

"It's that mage from before," said Hans.

"Let's end what we started," suggested Grags trying to stomp on Amson.

Amson was fast. When he started to run it looked as if he was a blur. Both heads had their focus on Amson for a while until the head called Hans stopped attacking. The head called Grags noticed and became infuriated.

"What's wrong with you, Hans? If you don't move your half of the body, we will never be able to catch the annoying mage."

Hans stood his ground and sniffed the air again. *"Grags, don't you find it odd how we smelt a human but only a mage appeared?"*

Grags stopped and looked around. "You're right. It must mean he's not alone."

Amson stopped above the frozen woman as the centagon stood up and talked amongst itself. Nightly took action. He used his tail and claws to break the rocks around him, making them fall on top of the centagon. The beast roared as stone broke against its body. The strange thing was that the centagon hardly bled. The creature looked up seeing a black dragon hiding amongst the rocks.

"You think rocks will hurt us?" Hans chuckled. *"You are mistaking us as a dragon when we are far from that."*

Grags then struck at the ceiling, forcing Nightly to move and more rocks to fall. Nightly dodged, making sure he was still in the air. He was weak though, flying took too much out of him even I could see that. Then Grags noticed where Amson was standing. It attempted to strike him but missed as he dodged the attack.

"Stay away from Veronica," it spat.

Amson then got a strange look in his eyes as if he knew exactly what to do.

"Hey dragon," he called out, weaving in and out of the centagon's extra pair of legs. "I bet you can't breathe fire from there and reach me down here."

"This guy needs to be taught a lesson," said Nightly as he took a big breath and released a huge flame.

The centagon took cover but Amson stood his ground above the frozen woman. At the last second he moved only feeling the fire burn the tips of his fingers. Nightly's fire made contact with the ice. The centagon grunted and then roared in pain as their extra legs began to burn up. When Nightly stopped blowing fire he noticed that only the top layer of the ice was melted and there wasn't much damage done to the woman.

"Stay away from her!" demanded Grags swiping the mage away with the back of his hand.

Amson hit a few stalagmites then slid down to the ground coughing up blood.

I wished I could scream for him, trying to make sure he was alright but I was just observing; there was nothing I could do. I felt so useless, weak, wanting to cry.

To my surprise Amson stood up with his hands on his legs. "Is that all you got?" he asked glancing up at the centagon with a grin on his face. His pupils growing thinner.

"Does this mage even know how to die?" asked Hans.

Nightly came down and stood over the frozen woman. He winked at the mage then started to break the ice away with his tail. The centagon noticed it quickly and charged at Nightly. Nightly jumped back up into the air and soared over to Amson. Amson grabbed hold, swinging himself up onto the saddle. The centagon watched carefully as Nightly circled above them.

"Hey centagon," called Amson. "I bet you ice-fire is weak and pathetic. You wouldn't even be able to hit a regular human."

Amson was crazy. It was like he wanted to die by provoking the centagon. I noticed what he was doing, finally. When Nightly's fire hit the frozen woman it did damage to the centagon. Was the frozen woman the whole reason why the centagon's lived for ten hundred years?

"I'll burn you to nothing," shouted Grags.

"And I will assist you brother," said Hans, taking in a big breath.

They took a step back and out of their mouths shot the blue flame they called ice-fire. The flame hit everything except Nightly and Amson. Amson steered Nightly in the direction of the centagon. They got closer and closer till the base of their tail hit Nightly making him and Amson crash land onto the icy ground. They both staggered to their feet and looked up at the centagon, which grinned as it took another breath. Nightly straightened himself up and also took a breath. Amson stood by his side and held onto the saddle. My dragon and the centagon released their flames. Like before they collided with each other. Amson guided Nightly over to their left and then stopped him. My dragons flame died as did the centagon's. I'd never seen Nightly pant so viscously, if we weren't going to die because of me being poisoned then my dragon would die just trying to save me. He was already weak enough as is but he wouldn't give up, he refused to give up.

"Die," it said together breathing out their ice-fire once again.

Nightly rolled out of the way with Amson and then watched as the centagon's fire hit the frozen woman. The centagon stopped as they collapsed to the ground, grovelling. The woman began to burn, opening her eyes and screaming. She was still alive after ten thousand years. That's why I kept seeing her scream I was seeing what happened before she was frozen and what she would do after she was killed. As the woman burned, the centagon burned along with her. They spat out a clear liquid and roared. Both heads looked at Amson and Nightly and shrieked at them as if they were calling out for help. Then they curled into a ball dying by freezing then burning up in their own flames.

I heard a voice that filled the room after they died. I heard two men and a woman say "thank you."

Amson and Nightly trotted over to Baboline to find her scraping the clear liquid into her jar.

"*Is it over?*" asked Nightly lying down.

"Yes, now with the centagon gone there will be no need for my services here." Baboline then looked over to Amson who was covering his arm. "You're hurt, aren't you?"

Amson knelt to the floor and panted. "It's nothing that concerns you! Just get the antidote to Connie."

Baboline sighed. She placed her hand in the jar and when she pulled it back out her hand was covered in a clear liquid that was the centagon's saliva. She then approached Amson, removed his hand from his arm revealing a scratch like mine. The centagon must have made it before Amson collided into the stalagmites. On his arm was blood covering a bluish purple wound that was smaller than mine but had a whole other effect on him. The veins slowly started to creep up his arm, trying to spread the poison throughout his body. Amson went down on his hands and knees. Baboline placed her hand on his wound, making him roar just like a cheetah. When she removed her hand there was no more blood, veins or wound.

"Now that that's over, let's get out of here," she said, closing the jar and climbing back onto Nightly's back, "there's just one more thing we have to do."

I awoke crying out in pain again. Every time the pain returned my forehead would become sweaty, my throat dry, my head would feel as if it was being pounded by an anvil. Every second the wound remained on my back the more intensifying the pain would become. The bluish purple veins nearly covered my body; the poison flowed through my blood as if it were eating at away at me slowly. Dad stayed at the hospital to watch over me. His presence was the only thing that kept me calm.

"It's going to be alright Connie. Daddy's here and as long as I am around, I will protect you from harm," he said, grasping my hand.

A memory came back to me of when I was three and my dad was in the hospital. I developed my fear of blood that day. Dad had just come back from a business trip, but he made a stop in the city above the ravine. When he returned I saw him before he was rushed to be treated. The burns had almost eaten all his flesh away, he was covered in blood. It scared me. I could never look at blood again after seeing my dad nearly covered in it. When he was bandaged up Mom took Kyle and me to visit him. They left me in the room alone for a minute. During the time I asked him why he was injured and why he hadn't avoided getting hurt. He answered me by grabbing my hand, giving me a faint smile and said that he had acted before he could think. To make quicker decisions in life, sometimes requires you to take action instead of waiting around for an idea to come to your mind. With that kind of thing you never know if you might save someone. I asked why he would do that. His answer was simple. He said to let instincts come to you and tell you what to do was the Whitsburg way. Apart from that I could never forget what he said that day. "Don't worry about me, Connie, because as long as I am around no harm will come to you."

I knew he was a brave man and I believed I took after him. I made the quick decision to take responsibility for Nightly, I saved Judy from the flood and I didn't let anything stop me as I entered the cave to rescue Sam. Dad was right. Whenever I went by my instincts, I increased the chances of survival and the protection significantly for me and my friends and family.

Dad gripped my hand more tightly as the pain left my body. He got up and I looked at him leaning over me.

"I got a call," he said. "I'm taking you home."

Dad packed my stuff and shoved it into the car. He carefully placed me in the backseat, rolling me onto my stomach. The road home was icy and slippery from all the salt that people put on their sidewalks. It was four in the morning when we got home. Mom was in the city trying to find new remedies that would help me. Kyle was at home watching his alien movies until we walked in. Dad took me into my bedroom and Kyle followed with my stuff and the bottle I saw in my dream. He placed my stuff on my bedroom floor. Kyle then opened my underwear drawer, grabbed a ball of socks and told me to bite down on it. I didn't understand what was going on. Dad delicately placed me on the ground and turned me over onto my stomach. Kyle put the socks in my mouth and instructed me once again to bite down on it. I wondered why until the pain attacked me. It wasn't the usual pain I'd been feeling but more of a piercing sensation that dug through my entire body. I bit down fiercely on the socks, but the pain was hard to ignore. I began to flail my arms and legs in the air trying to escape the horror.

"Hold her arms down and I'll get the legs," said Dad, grabbing hold of my legs and placed himself on them.

Kyle did the same thing with my arms. I was scared, what were they going to do to me? Kyle was acting responsible, but violent as well as Dad. Dad touched my wound pouring some stuff that made it burn. I bit down harder on the socks, crying. I head butted Dad in the face, Kyle took me by the hair and held it firmly, forcing my face to press against the cold floor. The unbearable pain continued then it went away. Kyle and Dad released their grip on me as they stood up. Dad took the socks out of my mouth and cradled me in his arms once again before he placed me into my bed. I moved my hand slowly across my body, the veins had faded, and nothing hurt as I moved my limbs once again until I reached my back. There was a thin scar across my back leaving a light sting and nothing else. I was relieved. For the first time this year I fell asleep peacefully.

"Thank you," I whispered as a tear of happiness ran down my face.

CHAPTER 23

Two New Teachers

I awoke the next morning feeling incredible. No pain, no suffering and I had all my energy back, maybe even more than I usually had. The only thing that was weird about that morning was that my hair was down. I never have my hair down unless I'm sleeping or depressed. I was out of elastics so I had to go the day with my hair down. I got dressed, and then met Dad and Kyle in the kitchen, trying to make breakfast.

"So what's for breakfast?" I asked pushing my hair behind my ears.

"Connie, you're awake," said Kyle, dropping a pan and spoon on the ground. "You slept like a bear for two days. Heck, I almost though you were a bear."

I picked up the spoon that he had dropped, annoyed with his comment and whacked it on his shins. He started to hop on one leg while grabbing the other.

"Look, now you're a bunny," I said walking over to Dad.

"How does the back feel?" he asked clasping one of my shoulders.

"Great, I only feel a light sting when it's touched but its way better than before," I answered. "Where did you get that antidote, Dad?"

"I have many friends in many places, don't worry about it, Connie."

Kyle stopped hopping around, grabbed me from behind, put me in a headlock and started to give me a noogie.

"Get off," I yelled.

"Not until you apologize," he said, rubbing his fist harder into my head.

I bit my lip out of pain. I've experienced enough pain for a while, so I started to elbow him in the gut. He groaned as he let go of my head, clutching his stomach while sitting down.

"I'll just have an apple for breakfast," I said grabbing my backpack and walking towards the garage. "I'll meet you in the Chevy Kyle."

I entered the garage and opened the door watching as the sunlight entered. It blinded me for a second, when my eyes got used to the sunlight I noticed the snow level had gone down quite a bit. It was hard to believe that the snow had melted so much while I was asleep. While waiting for Kyle I started to go through some old boxes that we always stashed in the garage. There were old baby toys, clothes and pictures. In one box were baby photos, my favourite out of them was when Kyle was two and was holding me as a new born. He smiled like a monkey. It was dated September third on a Tuesday morning. I moved the box aside and went to a book case of old memories. The higher you reached the older the stuff got. On the fifth shelf were older boxes that held memories from when my mom and dad were dating. On the same shelf was a book with flowers pressed in it. It was only roses though. Every page was a red rose except for the last five pages. From then on it was pink roses. I tried to reach even higher only to knock down another box.

"Darn it," I said picking up the papers.

I turned some of the papers over and found an old family picture with a young boy about my age standing with a grandpa. The grandpa's hands were on the young boys shoulder.

The grandpa looked about eighty. He had a strong feature despite his age; he still had a full head of hair that grew all the way down to his face making chops and he had this long narrow scar running along the side of his face. He wore a purple dress shirt with a black dragon tattoo on neck. What really caught my eye about the picture was the dragon tail mark on his hand. It was there for everyone to see. Was the grandpa a dragon's whisperer?

"Alright, Connie, let's go," called Kyle entering the garage and tossing me an apple. "You forgot that."

I quickly cleaned up the rest of the papers, putting the box away but I took the picture and placed it in my bag before I got into the car. As Kyle started the vehicle, I took the picture out again.

"Hey, Kyle," I said, "who are these people?" I asked showing him the picture.

He thought for a bit. "That's Dad and our great-grandfather Gabriel."

"How come I've never seen this before?" I asked.

"Because Dad doesn't like to talk about it," he said, backing the car out of the driveway. "Dad never met his mom. She died while giving child birth and his dad died when our Dad was only ten years old. He doesn't like to talk about his past though, so don't ask him."

"Then how'd you find out?" I asked, taking a bite out of the apple.

At first Kyle was silent. "A year ago I found Dad's old journal with some of our great-grandfather's notes in it. I asked Dad about it and he started freaking out at me. I'm warning you for your own good: Don't approach Dad with that subject!"

I had never seen Dad get angry. He's hardly angry and he doesn't even show the slightest sign of worry in his voice. What was in his past that he wouldn't tell his kids about? Could it have something to do with his dad's death? Either way I was determined to find out my family heritage. I was going to learn about the Whitsburg family tree!

Once we got to school and Kyle parked the car I watched as Judy hobbled over on her crutches. Sam followed behind; making sure Judy wouldn't fall at the speed she was going. She only fell once throwing one of her crutches and denting a vehicle.

I winced as the car alarm went off. "What are you so anxious about?" I asked holding out a hand to help her up.

Judy accepted the help and stumbled back onto her feet, leaning on her only crutch to stabilize herself. "I need to show you something," she said, grabbing my hand. "The whole school's talking about it."

"Talking about what?" I asked, while slowly walking with my one crutch friend up to the school's front doors.

Sam stopped us. He blocked us from the doors and handed Judy her other crutch. "Our friend from the ski resort decided to switch schools."

"Is it Celina?" I asked nervously.

"No, even worse, Martin Miles," Sam corrected. "He also posted something about you on his website."

"Oh, no," I forced Sam to move and opened the doors. A cold wind entered the hall as the doors opened wide. Every student in the hall became dead silent as their eyes were averted to me. They refused to speak; you could see there was surprise and utter shock in their faces. I didn't see what the big deal was. "Would someone please tell me what's going on?"

Again, everyone in the hall refused to say a word. They turned their attention away from me and began to whisper amongst themselves. I became annoyed as my fellow classmates continued to ignore me. It wasn't until Kyle pulled out a picture of my back that I finally realized why.

"Yeah, what's the big deal about my wound?" I asked. "I know I had to be hospitalized because of it but there are a lot of people going in and out of the hospital."

"Turn it over," said Sam flipping the picture for me.

My eyes widened as I saw a typed out page of Martin Miles opinion on my wound.

Connie Helen Whitsburg endured a gash that weakened her will to move forward. During her stay at the Dark Lake Ski Resort she had been attacked by a creature that is unknown to the animal kingdom. A common wound that many other people have received but had never survived.

The symptoms are blood curling shrieks, hallucinations a bluish purple coloured veins spreading across the body and severe pain is felt throughout the entire body even to the most delicate touch. It is only a matter of days till the victim demise.

I call it 'Laceration Toxin'.

No cure has been found, the longest anyone has survived is a week.

I tore the paper up immediately, this guy really wanted to get on my nerves. I dropped the pieces on the ground letting them scatter. "What is with that guy?" I asked. "I'm alive and better! See," I pulled my shirt up slightly showing the small thin scar that ran across my back to Sam and Judy.

"Don't worry about it," said Judy. "At least you're in better condition than I am."

"That still doesn't make me happy," I said, walking over the pieces of paper I tore up.

Everywhere I walked; I heard whispers and saw glares. I wanted to hurt them. I hadn't trained in the longest time and this could be just what I wanted if Sam and Judy had let me. They knew what I was feeling by just looking at the expression on my face. They knew me well, so well that it kept my anger at bay. Nevertheless I told them continuously that if I ever saw that Martin Miles again I swear he is going to be one dead man.

Kristen pranced down the hallway and hooked her arms around Kyle's while also giving me a strange look. Kyle noticed my ticked off face and decided to leave me alone with my friends. A sigh of relief left my mouth as Judy and I headed to our Foods class. It was hard enough to deal with all the other kids in school but I had no tolerance for Kristen right now.

In Foods Mrs. Blue looked at me the same way everyone else did, surprised and shocked that I was living and standing in her classroom. You'd think she would act more mature then my fellow classmates, but no. She did the exact same thing they did; they avoided me; pretended I didn't exist; gave me looks like I was a ghost. Judy was the only person who stayed by my side. It was good to know that I had a least one friend who wouldn't dare leave me in the state I was in. Next block wasn't so easy though. For Social Mr. Nook, the teacher, made me sit in the corner where he said I wouldn't hurt anybody. I felt like a miscreant that should have been wearing a dunce cap, but I didn't even do anything wrong. This had to be my worst day at school!

When lunch came around Judy, Sam and I ate by the front doors. People were constantly coming and going. It wasn't the best spot to eat lunch but anywhere else would have made me uncomfortable. I had enough of the dirty looks, Lunch was the only time during the school day that I could relax.

"Uh," I said frustrated, "why does this have to happen? What did I ever do to him?"

Sam slouched, leaning on the rail near the door. "A guy like Martin Miles always seems to get under people's skin. He's like a bug that flies around your head, trying to find a way in."

"Are you jealous that Martin's interested in Connie, Sam?" Judy asked nudging him.

He didn't say anything.

I sighed, pulling out the picture of my dad and his grandfather.

Judy leaned over my shoulder, trying to see the picture. She didn't have a very good balance though. She landed on me and the picture flew out my hand making its way to the door. Sam reached out and caught it before it had the chance to escape out the door.

"Who's this?" he asked examining the picture.

"My dad and great-grandfather," I said pushing Judy off me and standing myself up. As I rose I helped Judy to her feet as well. "I found it this morning while I was waiting for Kyle."

"Let me see," Judy said snatching the photo from Sam. She looked at it carefully then gave it back to me. "They don't look much alike."

"I know," I said looking at the picture again. It wasn't until I looked at the picture a third time that I noticed the black tail in the background. I wondered what it was doing their?

The bell rang. I said goodbye to Sam, then went with Judy to English. I opened the door for her and helped her sit down in her seat. When everyone else came into the classroom they all eyed me. Sitting on the other side of the room from where I was.

"Are you alright?" Judy asked, watching me sit down in the seat next to her.

I sighed. "It'll be fine, besides Martin Miles isn't in our class so there's nothing to worry about."

"Take your seats," said our teacher entering the room. "Today we are going to finish off 'Romeo and Juliet'."

Then there was a knock on the door. We all turned to see Mrs. Blue enter.

"Sorry to intrude," she said, "but I need to borrow you for a little cooking experiment."

Miss. Twon sighed and followed Mrs. Blue out of the class room, assigning us the last few pages of 'Romeo and Juliet' to finish off. As for me I had to read the whole book, by myself, from start to finish.

Most of the class goofed off but I was already far behind in my school work. I picked up my book, put on my glasses and started to read. A few people started to snicker and laugh, talking as loud as they could. I was so frustrated with them. The only way I could drown them out was with my iPod. It was easier to read and I managed to finish the book in one class with just a few minutes left before the bell would ring. Once I put my book down I saw Miss. Twon back and talking with Martin Miles in the doorway.

"Connie, come here," she said.

I got up and walked to the doorway, where Martin Miles pointed to the hall. I followed him out. He closed the classroom door behind me making sure I wouldn't back out. I glanced back at the classroom and watched as Miss. Twon grabbed everyone's attention.

"What are you doing here?" I asked.

He pulled out the picture of my back still wounded at the time. "I came by to ask you something about your wellbeing. You're the first to ever recover from the laceration toxin. Now, why don't you tell me what made that mark on your back or should I ask how'd you survive?"

"You interrupt my class just to ask me about the wound I received at the ski resort?"

"Yes." Martin raised his hand and grabbed my face, forcing me to look into his dark blue eyes. "Let me tell you something Connie Helen Whitsburg, I always get my story."

"Like I said before," I knocked his hand off my face, "I was attacked from behind. I don't know what gave me that mark let alone how I survived it. It was a miracle. That's all I can say."

I wanted to walk away but Martin trapped me in between his arms. "Yes you do. Don't lie to me."

I blushed a little. No boy had ever paid that much attention to me. I looked at the picture. All that remained on my back was a faded scratch. The colour was gone, but seeing what it actually looked like . . . it scared me. The bluish purple veins stretching out across my back as the scratch darkened. I reached and touched the picture. I could have sworn that I heard the centagon's roar. My finger moved off from it and I turned my head away.

Martin leaned in close and began to whisper into my ear. "No one would have missed an animal that could have made that mark. What was it?"

I faced him again. "I must have got amnesia then, because I don't remember it," I snapped. "If you'll excuse me, the bell is about to ring and I need to get my books from my class."

Martin dropped his arms. I speed walked away from him and back into the classroom. Once I sat back down in my desk the bell rung. I grabbed my books and rushed out of the there, forgetting about Judy.

The centagon was dead, there was no proof of it ever existing, even if I told Martin Miles what actually happened there was no proof for him to distribute.

When the school day ended, I ran out to the orange Chevy, waiting for Kyle. I wanted to go home and think. Being around people that day, it made me want to isolate myself. I looked over at the school and saw Sam walk out.

I looked over at him. Judy must have told him what happened in English.

He walked up to me and kicked some snow. "I heard that Miles gave you a tough time today. I'm sorry."

I sighed. "Why are you sorry?" I asked wrapping my arms around myself. "I let Martin get the better of me. I was the one who nearly lost it."

"Even so," he said, "I wish I could protect you."

"If only you could." A cold shiver came over me. It was still cold out; my jean jacket didn't keep me very warm. A coat was then placed over my shoulders. I turned to see Sam's bear arms. I gave him a small faint smile. "Thank you."

I heard fast, almost soundless footsteps approach. I was hoping that they belonged to Kyle but it wasn't. His footsteps were heavier and he always dragged his feet. Those nearly soundless footsteps belonged to Kamal. I turned to see him walking towards us.

"Hey girl," he said smiling, "I heard you made a miraculous recovery the other day. I'm assuming your backs all better."

I lowered my head, gave Kamal a quick nod than grabbed the ends of Sam's jacket and closed it a little. Kamal reached out his right arm, attempting to touch my back. I didn't let him. I backed away from him as fast as I could only to prick my lower back with one of side mirrors of the car. Pain surged through my body.

I gasped then slid to the ground. I panted while looking up at Kamal. He took one small step back and held both of his hands behind him. Sam guided me off the ground.

"Why'd you do that?" Sam barked. "She's still sore."

I got a hold of myself and slowed down my breathing. That pain was fierce. It was definitely not the sting I had felt earlier that morning.

Kamal bowed in a formal way and took my left hand. He kissed it. "My deepest apologies," he said. "If you'll excuse me, Sam and I must be on our way." Kamal straightened up, turned around and walked away. As he did that I could tell he was grinning.

"Sorry about that Connie," Sam said, blushing as he realized he was holding my hand. He released it immediately. "I hope the pain goes away."

"Samson!" called Kamal.

"I got to go but I'll be back . . . I mean I'm always here. Got nowhere else to go . . . uh, bye," Sam stuttered as he backed up.

"Uh, Sam, watch where you're-" I started to say but then Sam tripped over the sidewalk landing in the snow, "-walking."

Sam face turned an even darker red. He staggered to his feet then ran towards Kamal. I held onto Sam's jacket and smiled. He really was the sweetest guy I knew.

After fifteen minutes, Kyle decided to show up with Kristen. "Connie, whose jacket it that?"

I looked at the two of them. "It's Sam's. He forgot it."

"Oh, looks like your finally getting involved with teenage love," Kristen teased. "By the way, how's your back?" she asked. "I overheard some people say that you actually died and came back to life. Your scar is proof of it."

I tried suppressing my anger but it wasn't easy. Stupid rumors being spread across the school like a common cold. "Kyle, do something about her."

"Kristen, you shouldn't believe everything you hear," said Kyle. "Now Connie, you're on the back."

I grumbled as I climbed into the back. I couldn't believe how stupid people were. Even if I told them what really happened there was no proof. The centagon was dead and his lair was deserted. Not even Martin Miles could use that piece of information to its fullest.

Kyle jumped into the driver's seat and Kristen took the passenger side. We drove off to Kristen's house where she and Kyle took half an hour to say good bye. I had to honk the horn to get Kyle back into the car. He had a stupid grin on his face when he returned. I shook my head in disbelief. Once we got home I immediately started to look through the boxes. Slowly I worked my way up from the bottom shelf up. Searching through boxes, trying to find the journal Kyle was talking about that morning.

Kyle tossed his keys up in the air. He continued to do so until he noticed what I was doing. "Connie, are you actually looking for Dad's journal?"

I went from on my flat feet up onto my tip toes, quickly giving Kyle a nod then turned my attention back to searching for the journal. At first my thought was 'it had to be in the same box the photo was in' that was until Kyle spoke.

"Well, just to let you know, Dad moved it. At first it was in that box you are trying to reach but ever since I found it he moved it."

I quit trying to reach the top shelf and turned to face him. "Do you know where it is?"

"Maybe," he said, pushing in a code to close the garage door.

I sighed. "What do you want?"

"My car cleaned out every month till my graduation." He had this stupid grin on his face like he was waiting for this to come up. He probably was thinking about it all day since he saw that I took an interest in it.

"Fine! Alright! Just tell me where the journal is." I couldn't believe he wanted to strike up a deal, even after what we went through with the 'Sibling Respect Program'.

"It's in his forbidden drawer and the key is in his pillow case."

"Great, thanks, bye," I said rushing out of the garage.

"Wait, what about my car?" he whined at me. I ignored him and shut the door behind me. The door slowly reopened but I was too excited to close it again. Kyle gave me a lead on our family's heritage. There was no way I was going to pass up this opportunity.

I ran to my room, threw my school bag and Sam's jacket onto my bed then hastily walked to Mom and Dad's room. I quietly opened the door and saw Dad passed out on his reading chair with a newspaper covering his face. I smiled. Kyle got his heavy sleeping ability from Dad. Carefully tiptoeing towards the bed, I took up Dad's pillow and shook it until the pillow fell out of the pillow case. There was nothing. I even looked inside the pillow case just in case I may have missed it but no key. That annoyed me. Kyle wouldn't have lied though. He loved his car and wouldn't have me clean it knowing that I wouldn't get anything out of our deal. I started to put the pillow back in its case. Something fell on the ground. On the ground laid a stubby key with tape stuck to the back of it. Dad's wasn't stupid. He wouldn't have made it easy for anyone to get the key. He must have stuck it to the pillow for extra precautions. I grabbed the key, crossed the room to the dresser that was beside Dad's chair. I looked at him once and he didn't stir or even move. My attention turned back to the key. It fit perfectly in the lock. The drawer opened and lying at the bottom of the almost empty drawer was a black leather journal. Once I placed the book under my arm I closed the drawer, locked it, put the key back in the pillow case and speed walked back to my room. I was so glad to be out there. I jumped onto my bed and stared at the leather book in my hands. I didn't get to open the cover though, no, because a little voice started to talk to me in my head.

Greetings from the secret area, said Nightly.

What do you want, Nightly? I'm kind of busy at the moment, I said putting the journal down.

Is it more important than your dragon?

Well, no, but-

Great, because I think you should get over here, he interrupted. *I have a surprise for you.*

Do have to show me right now? I complained.

Yes, I'll be at your house in five minutes, he said, breaking the connection.

I wanted to pull out my hair. I just risked a lecture and a grounding just to get an important book that might help me figure out the situation with my family. Besides that I had to clean out Kyle's car for the rest of the year till his graduation. After complaining, I pulled on Sam's jacket but the journal was still in my hands. Where was I going to put it? I used to have a diary but not anymore because Kyle found it. I tried hiding it all over the house but he still managed to find it in one way or another. I looked at my bag on my bed. That's when I realized that no one ever checks my bag. Reason being is that I only use it for school. No one would look in there and besides it would be with a bunch of other school books. I placed the journal in my bag. When that was done I ran out into the living room where I told Kyle I was going to be out for a while. He didn't care. I went out the back door where I found four fresh dragon footprints. I went up to Nightly and climbed onto his back, becoming invisible myself. When Nightly heard the clip attach to my belt he bent down and took off into the winter sky.

"How are you feeling?" he asked.

"Much better thanks to you, Baboline and Amson," I said, reaching around and touching my back.

"How'd you know about that?"

"Please, who else would risk their life for me? Besides, I saw what happened through mind sequence."

"Really?" he asked, astonished.

"Yeah, I even saw the part where Amson was riding you," I teased.

"That was for one time and one time only," he stated.

"You still let a mage ride you."

"Shut up," he grumbled.

We flew onward and landed in the secret area no later than five o'clock. Nightly became visible and that's when I saw them: Judy and Baboline standing together and talking with my Guardians.

"Alright," I yelled, getting off Nightly and grabbing everyone's attention. "What kind of joke is this?"

"This isn't a joke Connie," said Teddy. "Believe me, if this was a prank yours truly would have been the master mind behind the whole thing. I remember this one time we pulled a prank on my uncle Larry and-"

"Yeah, no one cares Teddy," interrupted Nicole.

"We would like to introduce you to your two new teachers," said Nightly.

I didn't say a word. I was trying to wrap my mind around the situation. Judy, my best friends and Baboline, a forgotten whisperer, were here together.

"Wait, teachers?"

Judy brought out her crutches and trudged over to me. "I knew you were hiding something from the start. Ever since we entered high school you've been acting weird. Some people thought you were on drugs with the way you were acting. You know, coming to school exhausted, disappearing and your skins gone a little pale but not me. I knew it was something bigger. Who would have guessed that I would run into an old woman who recruits me to help you and your dragon?"

I looked past Judy and over at Nicole, confused. "Are you playing a trick on me with your special power?" I was hoping she would say yes but instead, she shook her head.

"A water dragon's special ability is manipulating the water particles in the air to create an illusion. The thicker the water density in the air, the more powerful the illusion is." Nicole walked over to Pearl and stroked her scales.

Baboline approached me from behind and felt my back. That freaked me out and I jumped away from her.

"What do you think you are doing?" I asked.

"Just checking if your back is all healed up." Baboline lifted up the jacket and my shirt to see my scar. She dropped the shirt and jacket back down and smiled at me. "I also wanted to thank you," she said lowering her hand.

"Thank me for what?" I asked.

"For defeating the centagon of course," she said.

"But I didn't—" then it hit me. Baboline didn't want the others to know that we were helped by a mage. No whisperer in their right mind would admit it, I played along. "That's right," I said. "It was mostly you and Nightly, though. I was in the hospital during the final battle."

"Uh, what are you guys talking about?" asked Judy.

I smiled then looked at her. "Sorry, about the lies, Judy, but believe me, if I told anyone outside the secret area any of this . . . they would have thought I was crazy or like you suggested, drugs."

"But I'm your best friend. You shouldn't keep secrets from me."

"Well, I'm sorry to say this but you can't keep a secret. Never have and never will," I pointed out. "Remember the time I told you that I had a crush on Alex? The very next day you found him and blabbed to him what I thought you could keep to yourself."

"If keeping this all a secret is the problem then we'll have her do the dragon oath," suggested James.

"What's that?" Judy asked in a snotty brat voice.

"A dragon oath is a way that whisperers use to make sure humans don't tell anyone about their secret," explained Malcolm. "It is very simple. Connie, you'll take the scale you got from Nightly and have Judy swear upon it."

I did as Malcolm said. I knelt down, pulled up my pant leg and slipped the elastic anklet off. When I rose I saw Judy stared at the coat I was wearing. She mouthed 'That's Sam's coat'. I rolled my eyes and gave her the scale. Judy looked at the black, smooth scale with amazement.

"So this is a dragon scale." Judy laughed. "Now I've seen everything."

"Now, repeat after to me," said Nicole. "I vow to keep all dragons and all mystic beings a secret."

"I vow to keep all dragons and all mystic beings a secret," repeated Judy.

"I vow not to tell friends or family, even if I'm in danger," said Nicole.

"I vow not to tell friends or family, even if I'm in danger," repeated Judy in an awkward voice.

"And if I break this vow, I allow any whisperer or dragon to strike me down where I stand," Nicole finished.

"What?!" yelled Judy. "I just met you people and now you want me to swear upon this scale that if I reveal your secret . . . you're going to kill me?"

"Judy, please just say it," I begged. "I really need your help more than ever right now."

Judy glanced back at me; she sighed then finished the oath. I ran over to her and gave her a hug. I felt relief and acceptance. The back of her hand glowed, a diamond shaped scale appeared on her skin and was outlined in a faint yellow colour. It then vanished after a few seconds.

"Great, now let me tell you one more thing," said James. "If you ever do come close to telling our little secret, that mark will reappear on your hand and give you a little pinch as a reminder. If you break the oath you'll see the image on your hand become permanent and there will be no pain. That is until you're hunted down by dragons and there whisperers." Judy gulped, "So no worries."

I felt her shiver, but she started to talk again. "Connie why didn't you tell me sooner?" she asked pushing away from me.

"I can answer that," Teddy said cutting in. "As you know, Connie here is a dragon's whisperer. She has a destiny to protect the dragon that has hatched from her energy from the mages who have already turned up in this town."

"So, what's that got to do with me?" demanded Judy.

"Since we don't know who the mages are we have to be cautious of everybody," Malcolm continued. "We need you though. Connie is drawing too much attention to herself-"

"And we need your help to train her but in a way that mages wouldn't expect it," interrupted Teddy.

"How can I train her?" she asked, bringing her cast into view and shaking it. "If you haven't noticed I'm crippled here."

"Yes, but we had Teddy, A.K.A your schools janitor, look at your school records," said Nicole. "You have represented your school for the gymnastics tournament three times when you were in middle school."

"Yeah, what's your point?" Judy responded rudely.

"Can I eat her?" Pearl asked bending down to Nicole.

Judy looked at Pearl and studied her, "well?!"

"Well what?" asked Nicole confused.

"Well, is the dragon going to do something or not?"

Pearl would have burnt Judy to a crisp if Nicole hadn't stopped her.

"The whole reason we called you out here, Judy, is to have you train Connie in gymnastics. When she does that the mages suspicions will lower and they will think that she's just a normal girl, with a new hobby. If she keeps disappearing like she's doing now the mages will declare her as a dragon's whisperer. In other words, there next target," said Nicole.

"Question," said Judy, "how do I train someone when I have crutches? What are mages? And why can't I understand dragons?"

"This girl is too hysterical for me," Nicole said walking away with Pearl following behind.

"I like this girl," said Teddy. "She's managed to tick off both Nicole and Pearl in less than ten minutes. That's a new record. Anyways, since I'm the janitor at your school I'll give you two a set of keys each. That'll give you access to the gym and the school at any time of the day. As for the crutches you're going to have to figure that out yourself."

"Then why don't you train Connie?" suggested Judy.

"You don't think that I haven't been training her? I've been teaching her and her dragon 'stealth' but she has a problem with keeping her movements quiet and she doesn't have the flexibility to dodge my attacks," explained Teddy.

That's when the argument began. Judy is good at arguing, I should know, we've gotten into plenty and she's always came out on top. She can go on for hours, beside she has to come out on top; she had to deal with three younger siblings.

I sighed. It was my first day out of bed since the centagon incident and all they cared about was getting me back on my feet to train.

Nightly walked up to me and rubbed his face against mine gently. *"Don't worry, when I returned the Guardians had me continue my training. Despite the fact that you were dying they wanted me to train. It paid off in the end, if they didn't make me do it I wouldn't of had enough strength to fight the centagon and I wouldn't have you right now."* Nightly rubbed his face against mine again and I smiled.

"I know, but it feels like they want to kill us before the mages do," I whispered to him.

James appeared behind me, startling us. "For the record, we aren't trying to kill you we are just making sure you're ready at any place at any time for a mage attack."

Malcolm joined us. "Well, it looks like your friends a little bit dumb, and that's saying a lot since I've been training with Teddy for four years." He sighed "Looks like we'll be waiting a while." Malcolm grabbed a cigarette and a lighter from his pocket. He placed the cigarette in his mouth and lit it.

"You smoke?" I asked, stunned. I didn't think Guardians had any bad habits. They always seemed to be focussed on training and survival.

"I stopped when I met Inferno; he always gave me heck for smoking, arguing that it was a dragon's job to smoke not a human's. The habit came back when I found out Devonburg died," Malcolm said, blowing out some smoke.

"Speaking of Devonburg," I said, changing the subject, "Did you know Baboline was Devonburg's older sister and your pill supplier?"

James and Malcolm looked at each other and sighed. James scratched his head and Malcolm continued to blow out smoke.

"The only family Devonburg ever mentioned was a selfish older sister who wanted nothing to do with dragons. It's surprising to see her now co-operating with us. As for the pill part we never knew who was behind it. Devonburg always picked them up from a person he called 'a special source'," said James. "Heck, I'm surprised Nightly knew where she was."

"Yeah," I said, nervously looking back at Nightly, "that's very weird."

"We've only heard stories about her," explained Malcolm, "nothing more and nothing less."

Then why did she come here? I asked Nightly. *She hated dragons from the start and even got rid of Pearl because of her fear.*

Maybe she changed her mind when she noticed that you looked like her brother's mentor . . . well that and you are her brother's legacy, suggested Nightly.

"Where is Baboline?" I asked looking around.

"Last I saw, she was following Pearl and Nicole," said James.

That's right. Pearl doesn't know that Baboline is her real whisperer, but I bet Nicole does. That's what she's probably hiding from Pearl, I told Nightly.

Should we tell them?

I don't think it's our right to tell them. They'll figure it out on their own, and while they do that we'll focus on our training.

Teddy and Judy stopped arguing and joined us. They both had beet red faces. It had to be from all the yelling they were doing.

"So, does she understand now?" Malcolm asked.

"For the most part, yes," said Teddy.

I smiled. My phone rang. I picked it up and heard my dad's voice.

"Hey, Connie, where are you?" he asked, concerned.

"I'm hanging out with Judy right now," I answered.

"You went out without telling me?!"

"What's the big deal?" I whispered into the phone, walking away from the group, "I told Kyle before I left. There shouldn't be a problem."

"You did?" he said sounding confused. "Anyways I need you to come home. Your mom's back and she wants to tell you something."

"Can it wait till later?" I asked, looking at everyone from distance.

"No," he said sternly.

I sighed, again. "I'll be right there. Just give me ten minutes."

"You better make it five." Dad hung up the phone.

I hung up my phone and placed it back into my pocket and walked back to the group, grumbling.

"You have to leave?" assumed Malcolm.

I nodded.

"You should go and bring Miss Gymnastics here with you," Teddy said, pointing at Judy. "She'll tell you when you should be at the school to train."

I rolled my eyes and grabbed Judy's arm.

"What are you doing?" she asked, yanking her arm back. "I came here through a hidden passageway and now it's gone. How are we supposed to get out of here?"

I smiled at her. Nightly let out a small roar and stretched out his wings. "We fly of course."

"Fly?" she asked.

"You've flown on Nightly before," I pointed out, walking over to Nightly.

"Yeah," she snapped, "and last time we did that I got this broken leg."

"Would you rather walk home?" I asked. "It's a lot longer than flying and you would take twice as long since you have crutches."

Judy glanced back to see the three male Guardians waiting to see what she would decide. Judy sighed and climbed on Nightly's back. I helped her up and strapped her legs in and made sure that they were pointing out. I gave her the crutches, which rested on her lap, before I climbed on and attached the clip to my belt.

"I'll be right back." Nightly jumped into the velvet sky.

Judy hugged me as tight as she could as we rose above the snowy clouds. Her grip loosened as Nightly opened his wings a glided through the air. I looked back to see Judy's eyes widen with surprise as she saw the beauty of the ravine from the sky. Her expression made me smile.

"What do you think, Judy?" I asked.

She didn't say anything.

"Is she alright?" asked Nightly.

I think she's just stunned of how beautiful the scenery is, I said through mind sequence.

I remember when you first flew with me.

Yeah, and that was the day when Judy broke her leg, remember?

Wasn't my fault mages attacked us that day.

A thought came to me. *Nightly, what does a dragon oath do?*

Well, after the human says the oath every dragon and whisperer is connected to that human. That way they'll know if they break the oath or not.

So, I'm also connected to Judy?

Yes.

I smiled. Judy didn't know it but we were both connected with each other. To me, it felt like we were sisters. Sometimes I wished I did have a younger sister or brother.

CHAPTER 24

Hello Journal, Goodbye Amson

We dropped Judy off at her house. She couldn't believe that she had just flown on a dragon. That kept her mind off Sam's coat that I was wearing. I didn't want to explain why I had it or anything, I wanted to go home. Shortly after Nightly flew me home. I unclipped my belt and jumped off my dragon, becoming visible once again. Before I had the chance to run inside my house, Nightly bit down on the coat I was wearing, stopping me.

"Nightly, let go! I'm already late as it is and this coat isn't even mine," I said trying to find my invisible dragon.

"I was just wondering about that guy, Amson, he seems to be close to you, doesn't he?" asked Nightly letting go of the coat.

"What about Amson?"

"Don't you think it's strange that he knew about your wellbeing?"

"He cares for me Nightly, like you do. Besides, why do you care? He's doing it for a friend," I said, raising my voice.

"Yeah, a friend you know."

I didn't say anything. My face went cherry red as I imagined Amson carrying me like a baby in his arms. Then I remembered watching him risk his life to get me the antidote from the centagon. The one thing I could never forget was the warmth of his body and his soft lips.

"Connie, are you even listening to me?!" demanded Nightly knocking me to the ground.

I snapped out of my day dreaming and stared up at where I thought Nightly was. "Oh, shut it. You and Amson made a good team and I don't have to take this anymore." I the stood back up brushed off the

230

snow on my clothes and walked inside slamming the door behind me. I ran my hand through my hair still finding no pony tail holding it up. It was weird to have my hair down. I never had it down, not since the fifth grade when I met Judy. I loved my hair long, but the problem was that no matter how I styled it always seemed to get in my face. Judy introduced me to elastics and ever since then it's been rare that I have my hair down.

"You're late," Kyle smirked as he leaned on the kitchen island.

"Where's Mom?" I asked.

"Waiting for you in the living room," Kyle replied.

I dropped my head, starring at the floor. I walked into the living room and lifted my head slightly when I saw my mom waiting on the coach.

"Mom," I said slowly raising my head a little more.

"Connie, have a seat." She patted a spot beside her.

I sat down beside her. She pushed my hair out of my eyes and smiled like there was nothing wrong in the world.

"So, what's the news you wanted to tell me?" I asked.

Her smile grew then she mouthed the words 'I am pregnant'.

My eyes widened then I hugged her tightly. "When are you due?"

"Either late September or early October," she replied.

"So I'm going to be a big sister?" I asked.

"You sure are," Mom said crying. "Just like Kyle is a big brother to you, you're going to be a big sister to our new family member. I just know you're going to be an amazing big sister with no secrets to hide when this baby arrives."

Mom hugged me again and while she did my smile dropped. Mom always had high expectations for everything even me. I've kept so much from her. She's my mom, for crying out loud! The woman you are supposed to trust when your life hits a rough patch.

"Martha, come her," Dad called from the kitchen.

"Coming, Rick," she let me go after kissing me on my forehead. Then she skipped off humming a merry tune.

"Thanks Mom," I whispered as I went into my bedroom. I broke down. Tears fell down my face. No secrets to hide from the baby, I'm the perfect big sister. Yeah right, who was I fooling, with the way things were I could never be the older sister my mom wanted me to be. I took Sam's coat off and jumped onto my bed, knocking off my bag. I looked at the floor and saw the journal stick out of the bag. I cleaned my face and began to read it.

> March 2
>
> My father, Mitchell Dwight Whitsburg, gave me this journal to fill out. He said that it's good to write down knowledge of both worlds just encase anyone needs something to look back on. For any of the next generations to come, they will read my journal as I embark on my journey of being a dragon's whisperer.
>
> Sure I might be only fifteen but I'm the youngest to ever receive a dragon egg in the Whitsburg family. I just received her today and she is breathtaking. I named her Nix (means goddess of the night) she's also a darkness dragon. I can't wait to see what's about to happen next.

Oh the page beside it was a sketch of the baby dragon, Nix. She looked exactly like Nightly all except for her wings, spikes and eyes, they were all shaped differently. Nightly had sharp, straight wings, pointed spikes and his eyes were circular while Nix had more of a curve to her wings, her spikes had no shape and her eyes were more of an oval shape.

I flipped through a few more pages finding notes, drawings of dragons, a dragon's egg and some of the scariest sketches were of mages.

He made him look like a regular human with a friend beside him. He made them both look friendly. I didn't feel nervous or scared. But the one thing that caught my eye was that the mage had the same mark on his chest that Kamal had on his arm. But there was something about the mage that reminded me of Amson.

I continued to read but stopped when I found a picture of my dad with Nix standing in front of dozen of dragon eggs. They were all still stone like with different markings on them. In the background it was all rocky and rough, the eggs must have been hidden somewhere underground. I looked over at the page beside it and began to read the entry.

> July 30
>
> We went to the dragons nest today where I counted five thousand, seven hundred and sixty-two dragon eggs. My dad took me here when I was Rick's age and his father did the same with him with his dragon.

I stopped reading. Rick was my dad's name, this was supposed to be his journal or so I thought before I flipped to the inside cover to see the name Gabriel Mitchell Whitsburg written on it. This was my great-grandfather's journal, not Dads. Why did Kyle say it was Dad's journal? I shook the thought out of my head and continued to read.

I even showed Lucas this when he was younger but now his son can enjoy it. This nest is sacred to the Whitsburg family. After our ancestor, Bowen, became the very first human dragon whisperer. When he received a dragon he took the name whisperer to be his last name. Bowen Whisperer. It didn't seem to work out too good, though. Mages went after anyone who bared the title whisperer or carried it as a last name. In the thirteenth century our family changed there last name to Whits and a few centuries later it became Whitsburg. That's the history behind the family name.

Bowen also met the Great Dragon, who allowed him to see the new nest for the dragon eggs. After mages stole the eggs out of their realms, the Great Dragon decided to hide all the eggs in one place. The Great Dragon also had the eggs only hatch when they were touched by a human and only a human. The dragon then would take that humans energy and break free from their stone prison. The Great Dragon made a law though, one dragon for one human. It didn't matter how long the dragons waited, they knew they would only hatch when a human shared their energy with them. Nix waited for me and Angelia waited for my son. It's too bad Rick never wanted to become a whisperer. Ever since his father died he has never wanted to be a whisperer only a knower. All he does is sulk and tries to shun out the Mystic Realm that he's already apart of.

"Our last name was Whisperer? What's a knower?" I asked myself out loud.

There was a knock at my door. I freaked out. I threw the book up in the air and watched as the journal hit the wall and slid behind my bed. Dad then entered my room.

"So, Connie, are you excited for the new family member?" he asked leaning in my door way.

I smiled at him and nodded.

"You know when I told Kyle that he was going to be a big brother he assumed you would be a boy so he decorated your room with his toys, green finger paint and alien stickers. When you arrived he was shocked and grumbled in his room for days."

"Even as a kid he was an annoying brat," I commented.

"Connie," Dad snapped.

I raised my hands in defence.

"Anyways, as you grew he started to like you. And you want know something? Behind your head rest are still the alien stickers Kyle put up." Dad walked over and pointed to one of the stickers that stuck out from behind my bed.

"Why'd he keep them there?" I asked.

"You don't remember?" Dad said surprised. "Well you were still a baby. He said that they would keep an eye on you just in case he couldn't."

"He really said that?"

"Don't act surprised," Dad said messing up my hair. "We Whitsburg's may be thick headed and ignorant at times, but we are always . . ." he let go of my head " . . . always are people to trust."

I looked deep in his eyes. They were filled with sad and loneliness. As I looked at them I almost saw myself. One person, having to do things on their own, baring the burden of a secret life.

"Anyways, I know you'll be a terrific big sister when the baby comes," he said looking away.

When I knew I was outside of his eye gaze I let out a sigh of relief.

"Don't stay up late," Dad warned. "I know exams are coming up, but you still have a week of school to finish."

"Alright, Dad, I'll see you in the morning."

He left the room, closing the door behind him. I wondered what was in his life that made him reject the life of a dragon's whisperer. What was the huge burden he carried alone?

Hey, Nightly, you there?

Give me a second Connie, I'm hunting right now.

I was curious when he said he was hunting. I concentrated my mind on Nightly and found myself looking through some woods with Pearl. They found a few deer wandering about. I felt Nightly lick his lips and watched as he pounced at the deer with quiet and deadly speed. I broke out of his mind and back into my own.

I stared at my dresser and watched as three of the black rose petals fell onto the ground. There was too much going on in my head. One thing after the other was nothing more than another question.

Sorry about that, I needed to get my dinner.

So I saw, I responded.

What's bothering you?

I just wanted you to ask Baboline what she knew of my great-grandfather before she ran away.

What got you interested? He asked, intrigued.

I found his journal, I said, reaching for it behind my bed trying to find it.

What have you found out?

Well, my family's name dates back to the medieval ages where it used to be Whisperer and I know where to find the dragon nest.

What?! He said, surprised.

I grabbed the journal and flipped over to the page that had the picture of my dad and Nix standing in front of the dragons nest. I took the picture out and looked on the back.

There's a picture of it in the journal. On the back it says that it's here, in the ravine. It's just a few miles away from Small Valley somewhere underground.

That's correct, Nightly responded, stunned.

Nightly, tell me what you know of that place.

I can't really tell you much, Connie. A dragon takes a few years to develop in an egg. After we're developed we just lay in the nest. Waiting for our whisperer to arrive and free us. Devonburg didn't want to wait. Instead he would talk to us always saying things like 'one of you is going to leave today' or sometimes he would say things like 'one of your brethren has died'. When he took me out from the nest, I was scared but he described you to me from time to time.

And what did he say? I asked.

Nothing much, just that you knew right from wrong, you were intelligent and a beautiful young girl who was worthy to be a dragon whisperer.

My body began to shake. I placed the journal back into my bag, and hid the picture in my nightstands drawer before I curled up hugging my legs. "Am I?" I whispered. *Am I really worthy to be your whisperer?*

Why would you say that?

I said nothing.

Don't doubt yourself Connie. Once you start to doubt yourself your connection with me begins to weaken. You and I are one. If I were to die a part of you would too. If you never became a dragons whisperer there would be no Guardians, Baboline would had never come back to find her dragon, the centagon would still be alive terrorizing the ski resort and there would be no me.

I started to cry. Nightly spoke to me in a serious, calm voice and yet I could tell he was frightened.

"Nightly," I said.

I'll ask Baboline what she knows but you have to remember that I need you more than anything in this era. Good night.

The connection broke and I continued to cry. I tried to stop but I couldn't. That night was the night I cried myself to sleep as thoughts of the past ran through my head.

"Where am I?" I asked, sitting up on a red velvet couch. I looked around and saw that I was wearing the same red dress trimmed with black lace, my hair was down but pulled back with a painful headband.

"It's about time you got here," said a voice behind me.

I felt my face, noticing that the mask wasn't there. I prayed that it wasn't the same mage that gave me the black rose.

"Please," I begged, "I still have time."

"Turn around," said the voice.

I stood up and turned around to find Amson. He wore a tux and had a white rose pinned to his jacket.

"Amson, what's going on?" I asked.

He snapped his finger and music started to play. "I want to dance with you."

Amson carefully lifted my hand into his and led me down spiral stairs onto a black glass floor.

"Why do you want to dance with me? I thought you were done helping me and my dragon," I said, taking my hand back.

"Can we please just dance before this dream ends? You probably don't know this but a dream travels fast through time. That's why it's so hard for people to finish a dream."

"Alright then," I said.

Amson took my left hand and place it on his shoulder; he placed his right hand on my hip and grabbed my right hand with his left. We then started to dance. The music died down a bit. Amson pulled me closer to him. My head was pressed against his chest.

The music became quieter. My heart started to race and my face turned a light shade of pink. I closed my eyes to find everything return back to normal. I was happy.

"Are you having fun?" Amson whispered into my ear.

I opened my eyes and looked up into his yellow eyes. "You've make me so happy Amson. I'm glad my friend told you about me."

"Connie," he said, "I can't see you anymore."

I pushed myself away from him a little. "What do you mean by that? You're here with me right now."

"I can't keep doing this," he explained. "I'm risking so much to help you, I can't do it anymore."

"Why did you bring me here?"

"I wanted to say 'goodbye' in a proper manner."

"What kind of manner?" I asked nervously.

"Alright, I wanted you to remember me in a special way."

"Amson, you are always going to be in my mind. You saved me from the centagon and risked your own life to get me that antidote."

"That's because you're an extraordinary person. I've been watching you and I noticed something. The way you trust people, not knowing if they are friend or foe, is interesting. The more I saw you trust people you didn't even know the more I began to see why you were made a whisperer."

"Don't say that," I said pushing myself away from him.

"Connie, are you starting to doubt your decision?"

I didn't say anything.

I stopped dancing with him and took back my hand. I turned my back to Amson. I could feel him looking at me.

"Don't . . . If you start doubting now, things will just get worse." He grabbed one of my hands and held onto it tightly. "Do you remember back in the centagon's lair you and your dragon did a Soul Blast?"

"Yeah, what's the big deal about that though; my Guardian did it once too."

"I bet he hasn't," Amson said. "A Soul Blast is created when the body and soul of the whisperer and dragon have a huge, enormous connection. It usually takes years to learn it. I personally have only seen it once and it's amazing."

"Who showed you a Soul Blast?"

"You," he answered as he turned me around.

I smiled. "You really are an interesting mage."

"And you're one special whisperer," he responded, leaning in close. "I wish this dream would never end."

He kissed me and I kissed him back. I ran my fingers through his hair and stopped at his pricked up ears. Amson pulled me in close as he released our lips. We ended our time together with a hug. My head on his chest slightly turned and his head rested on my head.

"I'll miss you Amson," I said trying not to cry.

"And me for you," he replied taking off the white rose from his chest. He pushed me back a bit and held up the white rose. "For you, so you'll always remember that you are a whisperer and no ordinary one, either."

That was my breaking point. Tears started to come down my face as I accepted the rose.

"I better let you return to your own home," he said, releasing his grip around me.

"Don't forget me," I said dropping my arms around him.

"I don't think that's possible," he said fading away. His last words to me were, "I'll always be there to protect you."

"Goodbye," I mumbled as I awoke in my bed. I stood up and walked to the window where I found the white rose. I grabbed it along with a familiar band on it. It was the elastic I had given Sam.

CHAPTER 25

Training with Judy Begins

The next day, every student in the high school was studying for the exams. Trying to cram every morsel of last minutes notes in before the test actually arrived. The same thing went for me. It drove me nuts how much I had to catch up on after missing two weeks of school because of my stupid scar, which people still continued to spread rumours about. I was behind everyone on everything and to make it harder, I still had to train.

Sam and I were in the library, late that afternoon. We tried to study, but kept getting distracted by the new books that had come in.

"Hey Connie, they got the new world record book in," said Sam, leaning back in his chair.

I yawned. "Can't look at it now, Sam, I'm reading the 'King Arthur' books. In this one, he encounters a dragon with his wizard Merlin."

Sam put his book down and looked at me. "Another book with dragon's in it? Connie you've been obsessing over dragons lately."

"What can I say?" I asked, shrugging my shoulders. "It intrigues me."

"Then, you'll really want to take a look at this book," Sam got up from his seat and climbed onto a book ladder reaching for the biggest, oldest book on the shelf. He tucked the book under his arm, grabbed the sides of the ladder and slid down. He placed the book in front of me while creating a huge amount of dust to fly into the air. "If it's dragons you're into, then this book will tell you everything you need and want to know."

I looked up at the shelf he got the book from. "Has it always been up there?"

"Longer then the librarian," he whispered, making sure Mrs. Gem, our schools librarian, wasn't looking over at us. "And that's saying a lot for a fossil."

"Sam," I said, hitting his shoulder. "Mrs. Gem is only in her fifties."

Sam glanced over his shoulder. "Yeah, she hasn't aged well." I smacked him again. "Alright, I'll stop," he laughed.

I sighed and sank into my chair feeling stress cover me like a thick handmade quilt. "How am I supposed to catch up on everything by next week? Ugh, there is too much to do in the little amount of time I have."

Sam leaned over my shoulder to see the English essay assignment I had to write. An essay on the play Romeo and Juliet which was due tomorrow.

"Then why don't you ditch this dragon stuff and focus on your work?"

"If only I could," I said, twirling my fingers through my pony tail. "Unfortunately it's another project I'm working on for myself."

"What's with you and picking up useless assignments?"

"They're not useless and they're fun to research. Only problem is that there is just too much to do."

Sam scratched the back of his head as he sat back down in his seat. Once he did, the chair broke right underneath him. Sam blushed, I laughed then we both grabbed the books we were reading and booked it out of the library. If there was one thing we both knew it was that if you got caught breaking anything, you'd get expelled. We ran to my locker and stayed there.

I looked up at Sam's beet red face. "It's alright Sam. Justin Tools broke one of the janitors waxing machines."

"Yeah," he panted, "you're right."

I smiled he blushed then we both sighed. I opened my locker and gave Sam his jacket back. "Thanks again, it really did help."

"Connie," called Judy from the other side of the hallway.

"Coming," I replied. "I'll see you later Sam." I ran up to Judy who was wearing a different jacket. "What's with the new clothing?"

"It's our team logo. Every gymnastics team has a school or gym to represent, but in your case were going to represent dragons." On the heart of the jacket was a dragon head, and on the pockets were claws. Judy Turned around and showed me the wings on the shoulder blades and the tail a little further down.

The jacket was black polyester with the dragon body parts outlined in dark silver. Judy held out a jacket to me. It looked cool. The only problem I had with it was that it said 'Connie Dragon Whisperer' on the left shoulder.

"Judy, is this really necessary?" I asked feeling kind of embarrassed while holding the coat.

Judy showed me her left shoulder 'Judy Human Coach'. She had a jacket printed up just for me. I had to wear it because she also gave me her 'you have to' look.

"Fine, I'll wear it," I said, folding it up, "now what?"

"We go to the gym and start warming up," she responded, leading the way to the gym.

I followed her to the separate building, which was the gym. Everyone complained when they had to go from the main building, the school, all the way to the gym which was only ten feet away. Once we got into the gym Judy had me take off my shoes, jacket, socks, and jewellery. Then she got me to do some yoga stretches. (My legs aren't meant to go behind my head.)

"Now release," Judy said, releasing the stretch easily.

I was stuck. I couldn't put my legs behind my head so Judy decided to 'help'. She got both my legs behind my head, but once she did I rolled onto my stomach, where I could only move my arms.

"No, no, you're doing it all wrong," Judy yelled, crawling towards me. She sat me up like a new born baby and got my legs out from behind my head.

I groaned in pain.

"You really aren't that flexible," Judy commented sitting up straight.

Once I'd adjusted myself I started to talk. "What was your first guess? The groans of pain, or the fact that you have to move my arms and legs around because I can't? That's why I need you to teach me how."

"Alright, you want to learn gymnastics, let's get started then."

For the first hour Judy was talking about doing flips, showing me videos on the best techniques and then came the worst part. She was about to teach me about response time. At first it wasn't too bad. I stood at one end of the gym while Judy stood on the other and threw dodge balls at me. In her condition she could only throw a ball half way across the gym. That I didn't mind, it was when she took out the pitching machine that I became nervous.

"Judy, this can't be legal!" I said scared what she was going to do next.

"Relax," she said loading the balls into the machine, "they're tennis balls. They should be better than any old baseball."

"Define better?" I asked her, crossing my arms.

"Look, all you have to do is dodge them and try using a few of the techniques I showed you. You'll improve in a matter of seconds or maybe a few days."

"Judy!" I yelled, throwing my arms down to my side.

"Now, how do you turn this on?" she asked herself, inching her pointer finger to a red button.

The machine started up and started to shoot tennis balls at me like there was no tomorrow. I dodged and weaved but it wasn't enough. The machine was on full blast.

"Judy!" I yelled, taking a few hits to the face and the stomach, "turn that thing off!"

Judy began to panic. She pushed several buttons, none of them made a difference. I sprinted towards the machine and Judy, taking on fiercer and stronger hits to my body. I dived down and went for the plug. The machine turned off.

I sighed.

"Well, at least we are making progress," she said standing up and leaning on her crutches.

I laid dead on the wooden gym floor. There was a bit of the tennis balls fuzz in my mouth. I took it out and glared at Judy.

"I'll see you tomorrow," she said, like nothing went wrong.

"Tomorrow, you mean the day after today?!" I whined.

"Yes, tomorrow, that way we can start working on those flips you forgot to do today. Then we'll get to work on the flips where you only use one arm."

I had a blank expression on my face when she told me about her plan. "You're going to kill me before the Guardians and mages do," I whined again.

"No I'm not," she stated. "Besides the janitor guy even told me and I quote 'make sure Connie can bend, stretch, jump, flip and if possible, make her soar through the air. Nothing too hard because I still need to break her into battle training'."

"I'm going to kill him," I said, clenching my fists.

"He also said that I'm going to be the one training from this day forward until you can master all of my techniques."

I grumbled to myself as I sat up.

"Now, I'll leave you be."

"Wait, what about you? You can't walk home by yourself," I said.

"Don't worry about me, Connie. I get my cast off in two weeks. Which means I need to get to the doctors so he can inspect it."

"But the hospital is at least a block away."

"Stop worrying, Connie." Judy grabbed her bag and trudged all the way to the gym doors but then stopped. "You know, when the Guardians told me about you being a dragon whisperer, I figured you didn't want us to know for some reason, but then James and Malcolm told me why you kept it all a secret. So you could keep everyone safe that you know and love.

Instead of you protecting me, I want to protect you now and so do a lot of other people but only if you open up. Sam and I are your friends. We deserve to know something as big as this."

She left me alone in the gym thinking about what would happen if I actually told my family and friends about what I'd been up to for the last couple of months. On the other hand I might be thrown into a rubber room along with meds that would force me to act normal. If that happened I would be a burden to my family. No, it would be better kept a secret.

I looked to my right. There were my books I took from the library, but I had forgotten my bag and the journal in the library.

"Dang it," I jumped to my feet, put on my socks, shoes, jacket and placed the locket back around my neck then took off out of the gym back into the school and into the library. I went to the front desk where Mrs. Gem usually was, reading. "Excuse me, but did anyone return a bag to the front desk?"

Mrs. Gem lowered her book and looked at me with her pale blue eyes. "Yes, just one moment." She got up and looked under her desk.

"Connie?!" asked a familiar voice. I turned around to see Britney with a bunch of books in her arms. "What are you doing here?"

"Well, Sam and I stayed after school to catch up on some work at first but then Judy dragged me away and then I realized I forgot my bag here. What are you doing here?"

"I volunteer here," she answered. "Mrs. Gem needs help putting books away so I help her and I get to skip gym and still get a good mark because of my volunteer hours."

"Here you are, dear," said Mrs. Gem, handing me my bag.

I grabbed the bag and hugged it tight. If I had lost it, I don't know what I'd do.

"Oh, that's your bag?" asked Britney.

"Yes," I said, in a worried voice.

"Martin Miles brought it to the front desk," she said.

I gagged at the mention of his name. "He touched my bag?"

"Only to hand it into the front desk, that's all," she said. "By the way do you know who broke the chair at the back table?"

I bit my lip. I pretended to look at a fake watch on my wrist. "Oh, darn, look at the time . . . I should be going. I'll see you tomorrow." I ran out the door carrying my bag close to my face.

I ran through the hallway, out of the school, across the baseball field, past the park and into my house. I was exhausted from running, and gymnastics training.

Mom was up watching 'Titanic' crying her eyes out and eating triple chocolate fudge ice-cream. Dad was reading the weekly newspaper and Kyle was doing who-knows-what. Either way, they were all doing their own thing. They didn't even notice me walk in. I went straight into my bedroom, locked my door and shut off the light. I was too tired to do anything. I decided to do my essay in the morning when I got to school.

Sleep? I wondered. If we don't have enough of it we as mortals would over exert ourselves. If that happened we could collapse at any time. However, if you slept forever you'd be either in a coma or dead. With what I had to put up with sometimes I wished I could sleep forever.

I awoke at six in the morning. My body felt so sore. I had to take it easy with the training. That is if anyone would let me.

I went into the kitchen and started to pour myself a bowl of 'Lucky Charms'. Dad walked in shortly after, wearing his old housecoat and coffee stained coloured pajamas.

"Connie, what are you doing up so early?" he yawned while tying his housecoat up.

"I have to get to school early. I need to finish my final essay for the semester," I answered placing the bowl of cereal on the kitchen island.

"Doesn't school start at 8:30?" he asked, taking another lion roar of a yawn.

"Yeah, but I can't risk it," I said shovelling some cereal in my mouth. "It's already late as is. I need all the time I can get."

"Understandable," Dad agreed trudging over to the coffee machine.

I finished my cereal then grabbed my bag.

"Bye Dad," I said giving him a kiss on the cheek.

"Have a good day," he replied.

Before I left I watched Dad take a sip of the cold coffee he had just poured into his mug. He was disgusted. He stuck his tongue out and squished his face together. I giggled then ran off out the back door.

When I got to school I went straight to the library spending an hour and a half finishing up my English essay. After proof reading it a third time I rested my head on the desk, wrapped my arms around my head and dozed off. It wasn't a long nap. I was woken up to the sound of a book cart being pushed. When I opened my eyes I saw Britney putting books away.

"Morning sleepy head," she said pulling up a seat next to me. "How's the essay going?"

I blinked a couple of times before letting out a yawn. "I've finally finished it. Now I have to study like crazy for the exam."

"Well, at least when exams are done we'll get to relax with the school dance," said Britney.

"What dance?" I asked, propping my head up with my hand.

Britney went back to the book cart and pulled out a flyer. The flyer had two people on it dancing below the title 'End of Semester Dance'. I took the flyer and noticed it was the last Friday of the month.

"Who came up with this?" I asked.

"Martin Miles," Britney replied in a love sick puppy voice.

"Why am I not surprised?" I whispered to myself, putting the flyer down. "So, are you going to the dance with him?"

"Of course," she said certain of herself. "I have a strategy that will get him to ask me."

"You're just as capable of asking him out as he is asking you. You should ask him out," I suggested.

"Are you insane? I can't do that! It ruins the tradition of a boy asking a girl out. It ruins the romance, and . . . and-"

"You don't have the guts to do it," I cut in.

Britney lowered her head.

"Honestly, Britney, you can do a lot better than Martin Miles. He's just a cocky know-it-all."

"But I dreamt of him last night, and that proves it."

"Proves what?"

"It proves that the two of us are meant to be together."

When I heard Britney say that, I thought I was going to throw up my breakfast.

Britney looked up at me, pushing her glasses closer to her face. "Connie, did you know that if you dream of someone it means that the two of you are destined to be together in some way?"

I lowered my gaze as I thought about Amson again. Then again, mages controlled dreams. They can make anything happen to you.

"I'm sorry Britney but I think that can never happen."

Britney then stood up. "I'm going to prove you wrong, Whitsburg, by showing you that Martin and I are supposed to be together at the dance."

"No, Britney, I didn't mean it like that," I said, trying to reason with her.

"Too late Connie, I've already made up my mind. You're looking at the future Mrs. Martin Miles." Britney stormed out of the library, determination gleamed in her eyes.

I sighed and laid my head back down on the table trying to figure out what had just happened. I rubbed my eyes, sat up straight, stretched as far as I could, gathered my books together then headed towards my locker.

I yawned the whole way to my locker. I opened it and started to put one book in after the other. Originally, I had seven books in my bag. Four were library books, two were textbooks and the one was the journal. The journal wasn't in my bag though. I began to freak out. I kept it in my bag all the time. How could I lose it?

"Morning, Connie," Sam said, leaning on the locker next to me.

"Sam, did anything drop out of my bag the other day while we were studying?"

He thought for a second. "Sorry, I don't remember anything falling out. Did you lose something?"

"It's my dad's old journal. I took it without telling him. I need to find it."

"We'll go back to the library then, and start looking from there," he suggested, grabbing my hand.

Our time grew short as the bell rang.

Sam looked down at his hand that was still grasping mine. He quickly let my hand go and blushed. "Sorry."

"What are you sorry for, Sam? Trying to help me find something that's important to me?" I blushed. "You're so sweet . . . I love how you're concerned about me."

Sam hugged me. For once neither of us backed away from one another or was surprised to be in this situation. It felt nice. I closed my eyes. Sam was one of the best people I knew. He always seemed to have my best interest at heart. I tilted my head up and opened my eyes seeing Sam still blushing. I blushed as well. He moved his hands up to my face and felt my soft skin with his thumb. We heard doors closing as our faces got closer to each other. Words couldn't explain what we were both feeling right now. Something at the back of my head told me to stop, but I ignored it. I believed for a short moment that I really did love Sam.

"Hey, love birds, class is about to start," Judy yelled from the end of the hall.

Sam and I quickly separated, still blushing. The picture perfect moment was lost thanks to Judith Bachor.

Judy smirked. "Come on."

Sam ran off to his classroom and I shut my locker, following Judy to our Foods class.

"So what was that about?" she asked.

"Nothing," I stated, still a little embarrassed.

She nudged me. "Come on, you don't have to keep secrets from me anymore."

"What you saw was nothing, it was a misunderstanding. All that happened was me thanking Sam for helping me study for exams."

"Sure you were," Judy replied patting my shoulder.

"Look, can we just get to Foods and drop the subject?" I asked speeding up my walking pace.

"Looks like someone still has a secret to tell me," she mumbled to herself.

Foods and English went by slowly. I didn't mind because I was relieved to get my essay in on time. When lunch came around, Sam and I searched the whole library and even asked the librarian Mrs. Gem about the journal but she claimed it never turned up. I was upset for the rest of the day. In Social, all I could think about was the journal. In Gym, I decided to release my anger. I threw a ball so hard that I broke a guy's jaw. He was sent home for the rest of the day, heck the rest of the week. I felt sorry and all but I was having a hard day, could you really blame me?

At the end of the day, I was banging my head against my locker door trying to remember places that journal could be. It wasn't at the library's front desk, not in the lost-and-found in the office and it sure wasn't with me.

"If you keep doing that you'll put a dent in you locker," said Judy, standing beside me.

"Uh," I groaned. "Judy, I lost my dad's journal and he is going to kill me if he doesn't get it back," I said, continuing to hit my head on my locker.

Judy snapped her fingers. "Who handed in your bag to the library's front desk?"

I suddenly stopped banging my head and looked at Judy. Worriedness covered my face and I slowly took in breath releasing the words, "Martin Miles."

Judy regretted asking the question.

I knew Miles took a limo to the town's hotel after school every day. I had to hurry if I wanted to catch him. I ran down the hall passing hall monitors, teachers and other students. I ran through the schools front doors and saw him entering his limo.

"MILES!" I yelled, running up to him.

He turned around and smiled at me like he knew why I was there.

"Well what do we have here?" he asked getting into his car acting cocky in his British accent.

As I approached his limo he lowered the window and studied me with eager content. This guy was too cocky and unpredictable.

After straightening myself up and releasing a few pants from my mouth I glared at the arrogant researcher. "Where is it?!"

"Where is what?" he asked, innocently.

"Where's my dad's journal? You were the one who handed my book bag to the library's front desk and I'm sure you went through it, too."

"Oh, you mean this book?" he asked holding up the old leather journal. "Here," he said handing it to me. "I've already finished reading it."

"You read it?!" I asked, concerned, holding the book close to my chest.

"Yeah, you've got a very interesting family history there, Connie. I never knew there were people called whisperers or that dragons and mages still lived amongst us."

"What are you going to do with the information you have?"

"Nothing," he replied.

I sighed in relief.

"At least not yet."

"Why won't you leave me alone?"

"Why would I? This is too much fun. Tell you what though, I won't put this on my website or tell anyone as long as you go to the dance with me," he said.

I was shocked. "Why would you want to go with me? There are plenty of other girls who would love to go with you."

"I know that, but I want to go with you. The journal was unclear about some things like where the nest was, or who mages really are."

"And you assume that I know something about them?"

"In a word, yes."

"And if I don't?"

"Then I expose you and your family's secret and all that I know about dragons from your journal."

"Why are you doing this Martin? I only met you once and that was at the resort. Does that give you rights to barge into my life? When I tried to leave you alone you come after me. What are you trying to prove?"

A crowd formed outside the school. In the crowd I noticed Judy and Britney standing side by side. Further in the back I saw Kyle by Teddy and at the doors I saw Sam standing, waiting to see what was going to happen.

Martin leaned out of his window then said, "I'm trying to uncover the truth hidden in the world."

"Sometimes the truth hurts people," I said, trying to state a fact.

"You believe what you want to believe and I'll believe what I want to believe." He leaned back in his seat and continued to give me that British smile. He was expecting something.

The crowd stood restless. They were waiting for something big to happen.

Miles leaned out of his car and then raised his voice loud enough for everyone to hear. "Connie Whitsburg, I accept your invitation. I'll be going to the dance with you."

My face turned red. Whispers started up and cries were heard. I looked over at Sam who went back inside the school. When I tried to run after him to tell him it wasn't true Miles caught my wrist and pulled me in.

"You say anything and I'll go public with the information I already have. Face it, Connie. We got our second date set, and I will get my answers in one way or another."

I pulled away from his grasp and watched his limo drive off. This couldn't be happening, why did it happen?

When Miles was out of sight Britney stomped towards me and slapped me across the face. I didn't even hesitate to dodge. When her hand met my face I knew I deserved that. She ran off as the crowd scattered leaving me standing alone. Kyle and Kristen left and Teddy continued his janitorial work. Judy limped towards me and passed me a cloth to hold against my face. I took it with gratitude and held it on my red cheek. The two of us then walked to the gym.

CHAPTER 26

Prepare for the Dance

When we arrived at the gym there was nothing to do either than talk. I felt terrible, and Sam witnessed the entire thing along with half the school. My stomach turned like crazy. Sam and I had a great morning together and I was ready to confess my hidden feelings to him, but with what just happened I wouldn't blame him if he wanted to avoid me for the rest of our lives.

I hate Martin Miles. He knew I would make a big deal out of this entire thing and he used that to his advantage. I expected he would be planning something to get information from me, but nothing like this. He really is unpredictable and one day I will beat him at his own game.

Judy leaned against the gym wall. "That dirty British punk thinks he can get away with everything just because he's rich and famous. I've only saw half of what happened and I don't think I need you to tell me what already happened. What did happen though?"

"Judy!" I yelled.

"Sorry, I'm a gossiper. Have to keep up my rep; this broken leg has already brought my popularity down quite a bit."

"Judy!" I yelled again.

"Sorry," she looked at me watching me rub her cloth on my wounded cheek. "You really do have it rough for a dragon's whisperer."

"Tell me about it," I said, sliding down onto the floor. "You can't tell anyone that's close to you anything."

Judy coughed.

"You're acceptable," I said. "After you accepted the terms and conditions of being a whisperer you start to regret it."

"Why would you do that?"

I looked up at her. "I'll . . . sorry, *we'll*, never be able to go back to our old lives of just you, Sam and me hanging out at the park or at Papa Joe's Diner."

Judy looked down at me. "You've been through a lot today. You can go home and rest, take a bubble bath and curl up with a good book."

"What about you?"

"Quit worrying about me, Connie," Judy said, giving me a scowl. "I'm getting my cast off, so I was going to end the today's lesson early anyways."

I got up and smiled at her. "Thanks, I really appreciate it." With that said I gave Judy her cloth back, a hug goodbye and left the gym, swinging my bag onto my back. When I opened the gym door I found Teddy salting the sidewalk.

"What, done already?" he asked.

"Judy's getting her cast off and I need to study for my exams next week."

"You know, I saw what happened with you and the Miles kid. For an old book, I suggest it's not worth the trouble going to the dance with him. Besides . . . you got it back, there's no point in going with him."

Teddy didn't know anything about the journal, Nightly hardly knew anything about it. I never told my Guardians of the secrets that my family kept hidden in that journal, maybe if I did it would have helped everyone out.

"You don't understand. It doesn't matter if I have the book or not, I have to go with him." I rubbed my face trying to avoid the subject. "Besides where have you been? You're not doing a great job of keeping this place orderly," I stated.

"Are you serious?" he yelled. "Your dragon keeps appearing on school grounds and I have to get Pearl to come and take him back before mages notice him."

"Really, Nightly comes here to see me?" I said, happily.

"Well, yes, you are his whisperer, after all. I would expect that you would know that already."

"Sorry if I've had other things on my mind, but you guys got your dragons during college." I sat down on curb. "If you hadn't noticed, I have no time on my hands with making up excuses for my family and friends, homework, studying, going to school for eight hours a day, and spending the rest of the time training."

"We didn't have it easy either Connie," Teddy said, sitting down beside me. "Unlike you, we didn't have Guardians and we had to train on our own. I will admit that it was easier to keep it a secret since we lived on our own but we still went to school. Sure, it wasn't as bad as going to high school but we had to get jobs and a dragon who doesn't know how to hunt is a real money grabber."

"A dragon is a money grabber?" I asked.

"They're *real* expensive, especially when you only have a grocery budget of fifty bucks a week."

I began to laugh.

Teddy faced me and smiled.

The feeling of being surrounded by love and support still felt the same from back when it was just Judy and Sam and me. I never lost that feeling. Actually, I gained more than lost. Nightly and Amson were right when they said I would become weak when I doubted myself. As long as I had people who understood me, like the Guardians, and the support of others like Judy, I knew I could do this.

That's when I felt it. I could never feel or sense it before. I'd been so busy complaining and being frustrated with myself that I never realized I could feel Nightly's presence.

I stood up and walked to the back of the gym. At the other end was another pair of doors. I walked up to them and then placed my hand out, it touched something cold.

Found you, I said.

Nightly became visible and nudged me to the damp, snowy ground.

I laughed as I stood up. I hugged Nightly's head and kissed him. *I love you.*

"And I for you," he replied, humming.

Teddy came around the corner and saw me with Nightly. "You finally noticed."

I looked over at him as I released Nightly from my grasp. "You knew Nightly was here already."

"We needed to know that the connection was still strong between you and your dragon," said Teddy.

"Well, as you can tell, my connection with Nightly is stronger than before."

"So I see," Teddy confirmed.

"What made you so cheery?" asked Nightly.

"You know how I've doubted myself lately? I finally let go of all my worries. You're the only thing I should be worrying about."

"Good, because it's been awhile since we flew together. What do you say?"

I looked around to see no one anywhere then gave Nightly a smile. "I say, let's go." I scrambled onto his back and strapped myself onto the saddle.

"Be back before the sun sets," warned Teddy.

"Chill," I said, tightening the leg straps. "We'll only be gone for an hour or two."

Nightly turned the two of us invisible and flew up into the sky.

It was nice to be on Nightly's back again. The air flowing through my hair always made me feel happy and just flying with my dragon was fun.

Nightly flew above the ravine, which was covered by clouds. He dove back down close to the ledge and even scurried down the wall a bit. He showed me his flying movements which included diving, speed and agility in the wind currents, and then he did a move which I am proud to call my favourite. He called it a guard spin. It consists of the dragon tucking their head, arms and legs in. The dragon then begins to spin through the air and once they get to a certain speed they wrap the wings around the body, the tail is the only thing that remains out because of its used for directing where the attack goes. It saves a dragon from a fire attack and also delivers a frightful blow.

After he was done showing off his impressive moves, Nightly took me above the ravine and landed near wide spread of spruce and pine trees with no locals around. When I climbed off Nightly's back, I felt free for once. The last time I was out of the ravine was before the dam burst. It felt so nice to see an actual wide open space. I spun around and fell down on the snow making a snow angel.

"You really are happy," Nightly commented, becoming visible.

I flipped over onto my stomach and smiled at him. "This is my first time I have ever been outside the ravine. I finally get to see wide open space of the world with my own eyes. I don't have to look in a picture's or listen to descriptions anymore. This time, I get to experience it for myself."

"How long have you been in the ravine?"

"My whole life," I said, sitting up and listening to the wind whistle through my ears. "I've been so occupied that I forgot that you could of flown me out of here."

"That's one of the perks of having a dragon."

"Oh, are there more?"

"You'll have to figure that out on your own."

"Meany," I commented.

He smiled. Nightly blew out a little flame that melted the snow off the ground. He lied down on the warm patch of dirt. I crawled over him and laid against his scales. They were warm like an electric blanket. I swung my bag off my shoulders and pulled out the journal.

"Is that the journal?"

"Yep, and since I got it back, you and I are going to study the Whitsburg family origin."

"Are you sure you should be looking through it?"

"Well, aren't you curious?"

"Well, maybe a little."

"I love my dad, Nightly, but he's keeping something from me and Kyle and I want to know what. I'm reading it whether you're with me or not."

Nightly puffed out some smoke as he laid his head down on the dry dirt ground.

"October 3rd

Summer's gone and fall is here. That's a dragon's favourite time of the year. When their whisperer is cold, a dragon's eternal heat keeps both of them warm.

A dragon's fire is basically their soul letting out their warmth for the people they care about. However, their fire can also be fierce and aggressive when engaged in battle. A dragon's first instinct is to attack with fire when the enemy is in range. The minimum temperature a dragon's soul can burn at is 250 degrees and the maximum temperature it can burn is 15, 000 degrees.

However there are three ways a dragon's soul can be extinguished. They can be extinguish when their whisperer dies, abandons them or when they're treated like a beast."

"Makes sense," said Nightly puffing out more smoke. *"Remember the day you received my egg, Devonburg told you that if you abandoned a dragon, they'll destroy everything and themselves."*

"Yeah, I do remember," I said, placing the journal down on my lap. "Didn't Baboline abandon Pearl though?"

"I will have to admit that it is odd. When a dragon's born they know who their whisperer is because they share the same energy. As a dragon hatches they can see the energy of all beings and it's that energy that confirms them as their whisperer, the mark is just to confirm that you are a dragon's whisperer. My best theory for Pearl is that she was on the verge to destroy everything, but when Nicole and her cousin found her she had no need to."

"She was lying to herself the whole time then. Her real whisperer never wanted her, but she refused to believe it. Pearl lived through life knowing she wasn't with the right human, why?"

"Maybe because she wanted to feel like she belonged to someone, even if it wasn't with her true whisperer."

I got to thinking. Devonburg said never abandon your dragon or else they'll go insane but he never said that the dragon couldn't be reasoned with.

"I guess we can't really tell Pearl who her real whisperer is if she doesn't believe it. What's done is done, you can't change the past, but do you think it could have worked out, if Baboline kept Pearl?"

"We'll never know."

Nightly blew out more smoke. I continued to read the journal. Another thought came to me though. Baboline shouldn't have touched the egg if she knew that she never wanted to be a dragon's whisperer. Then again, she might have wanted to but got scared after she exchanged her energy with the egg. Pearl must have also saw her, or else she wouldn't have the dragon mark on the back of her neck.

> January 16th
>
> Nix discovered a mage family living nearby. They don't seem to be doing much. They wait around, socializing with humans, not even acting like regular mages. Rick's become very fond of them to.

The one thing my father and grandfather told me was never start the battle. It's true that mages hate dragon's for what they've done to them, but that was in the past. It doesn't really matter what happens now in the present. Why should we repeat what has already happened? A person who steps forward into the future, towards new goals and knowledge is a brilliant being. An idiot is a being that stays where they are and always moves back. Staying in the past and keeping what knowledge they have. They'll never learning, and never growing.

I bet mages, humans and dragons could get along if they only tried. Then the Mystic Realm would finally be at piece.

"Your great-grandfather tells great knowledge in his journal."
"Agreed," I said closing it up. "I wish I could have met him."
"And I for his dragon Nix."

For the rest of the month Nightly and I would meet after gymnastics training to read and study the journal. As for Sam, like I had predicted, he had been avoiding me the entire time exams were going on. Britney was worse. She would scream at me whenever we met, saying that I stole her guy and that I was worst person in the world. If I could tell them the truth I would. Judy was the only one who knew exactly what happened and why. She was the only one who would listen to me without freaking out franticly. Exams past and soon it was the night before the dance. That night I was talking with Judy, listening to her recite the same speech of how great it was to get her cast off and how happy she was that she wouldn't be crippled at the dance.

"So what are you going to wear to the dance tomorrow?" I asked Judy, while lying on my bed.
"Oh, Connie I have the cutest dress. I found it a week ago after the English exam. I'm so excited to wear it," Judy giggled. "What about you?"
I was silent, shifting the phone to my other ear.
"Oh, that's right; you've been busy every hour of every day. You wouldn't have been able to shop around for a dress."
"It's fine, I don't think I'll be going anyways," I said.
"What are you, crazy? You have to! What about Martin Miles, he'll expose you and your family."

"Well, what's the point if I can't go looking good?" I said, sitting up. "I'll be the laughing stock of the whole school if I just show up in my regular clothes."

Then have I got a surprise for you, said Nightly.

"Nightly," I said annoyed.

"Oh, I get it. It's 'dragon talk time'. I'll let you talk to him now. See you tomorrow—or not—but I do hope you come." Judy yawned, "good night."

"Night," I said hanging up the phone. *Nightly are you always going to cut in on my conversations?*

Just come outside, the Guardians have something to give you.

I grunted. *If it's another lecture your dead.*

I'll see you outside.

"Uh, what am I going to do with him?" I asked myself, rubbing my temples.

I put on my jean jacket, shoes and ran out to the back yard. I felt Nightly's presence and when I found him I climbed onto my invisible dragon.

You were quick, I said, strapping onto his saddle.

And you were slow. Now that we got that straightened out, let's go.

I rolled my eyes as we took off. As we flew through sky, I felt the warmth of the setting sun. Then a nice spring breeze came though, it felt so nice.

Spring's finally here, I said, raising my hands up and tilting my head back.

Good because I'm sick of the snow, said Nightly.

You only hate it because I got hurt during the season.

And you better not do it again. I never want to go through that again.

What are you talking about? I was the one dealing with the pain.

Yeah, but I had to team up with a mage.

I sat up and giggled. I hadn't talked to Amson in so long. I missed him. He said he would always protect me, was he watching over me like a vigilantly?

When Nightly landed I noticed that the Guardians were standing in a circle. Including Pearl which meant something had to be happening.

"What's going on?" I asked getting off Nightly's back, becoming visible.

"Do we have to do this?" Pearl complained.

"It's fine Pearl, we're just giving Connie something that she deserves," said Nicole stepping out of the circle and up to me. "Okay Baboline, show her."

Baboline pulled out a gorgeous white dress that shimmered in the light. It had to be one of the most beautiful dresses I had ever seen.

"It's beautiful, but why?" I asked.

"You've been working so hard with your studies," said Malcolm.

"Training," Teddy added.

"And keeping this all a secret from everyone," James added.

"You deserve it," said Baboline.

"I don't know what to say," I said, amazed.

"Just take it already," Pearl snapped. She sounded like she was ashamed of doing this. Was I really that bad?

Baboline approached me and gave me the dress. It felt soft, almost like silk. Nightly walked over and rubbed his head on the dress showing that the fabric was strong enough to withstand dragon scales.

"You guys really are amazing. I could never ask for better Guardians . . . ah, who am I kidding? I could never ask for better friends."

"Oh, don't start getting sappy on me," snapped Pearl, turning her head away.

Nicole laughed and walked over to Pearl.

James walked up to me and handed me pair of black gloves with Velcro straps by the wrists.

"What are these?" I asked curious.

"Every dragon whisperer needs a weapon to defend them self with. For you, I thought I would forge gloves. You're too young to handle a weapon," James said, turning the gloves over. "They're made out of dragon's scales. If you land a hit on someone they'll rip through the skin like nothing."

I strapped the gloves on and felt the silk material on the inside and sharp scales on the outside. They were loose, soft, but dangerous. I clenched and released my hands. The only part that wasn't covered with any material were the palms of my hands.

"The palms of my hands are bare, why?"

"Your dragon wouldn't shed anymore scales," said James, eyeing Nightly.

"Hey don't give me that look. I didn't grow like a usual dragon, remember? Otherwise I would have shed more scales."

I scratched Nightly's head. "It's perfect."

"Now that we've got that settled, we can go to the dance," said Teddy wrapping his arm around me.

"She's not going to the dance with you," Nightly growled. "She's going with that know-it-all boy, Martin Miles."

"Martin Miles . . . a name I know too well," said Malcolm.

"You know him?" I asked.

"Know him? That little brat followed me across Africa while I was still in university. I've met him face to face before in a crowded hallway and he'll stop at nothing till he gets the information he's after," said Malcolm.

"Believe me I know," I said.

"Just be careful when you're around him, okay?"

"Yes," I said walking back to Nightly.

Baboline ran up to me and grabbed my shoulders. "Wait Connie," Baboline pulled me aside and spoke to me in a sketchy voice.

"Baboline," I said, happy, "I've wanted to ask you something."

"And I know what it is. Never ask me it."

I was confused. "I don't know what you're talking about. I was just wondering if you knew anything about my great-grandfather. What were you talking about?"

"Nothing of your concern," she said turning around.

Yep, her and Pearls attitude sure were the same.

"I didn't become a whisperer, like Devonburg. He was the one who gave me the dragon egg and at family reunions he would always rant about his mentor. I've only heard stories of your great-grandfather. I don't even remember what they were about anymore. The only time I actually saw him was when he assigned me to watch over the centagon. I'm sorry I couldn't help."

I can't tell you that I wasn't upset, but I could tell you that I was heartbroken. The one person who accepted the Mystic Realm and knew of my family couldn't help me.

"It's fine, thanks anyways," I said walking back to Nightly and strapping myself in.

"Come on Connie. It's time to go," said Nightly.

I climbed back onto the saddle, laid the dress on my lap and waited for Nightly to shoot up into the air. I held on tight to the saddle, making sure the dress wouldn't fly off, and kept the gloves strapped on. They gave me a funny filling, it felt like a need to fight, they wanted to hit something. The gloves were meant for battle and I feared that I would be forced to use them one day. As the two of us soared, we glanced back down at the Guardians as watched as they waved to us. I waved back before Nightly went invisible.

"They really are the best," I said.

"No, you're the best. Ever since you regained your confidence, you've really impressed them," said Nightly.

"All of you are great," I said, wrapping my arms around his neck.

Nightly hummed with gratitude and did a flip with excitement.

I love you, I said kissing his scales.

And I love you.

After Nightly dropped me off I snuck through my window. I didn't want my parents to see the dress just yet. I hung the dress up in my closet and grabbed an empty shoe box. The gloves felt nice on, but they needed to be put away for the time being. A weapon in the house was dangerous, but now I had a weapon that was hidden. It wouldn't hurt anyone as long as they didn't go looking for it. I slid the box to the back of my closet then I closed it and got ready for bed. My mom and dad came to check on me a little later. All they saw was their teenaged daughter, sleeping. I heard them whisperer among themselves. They were worried about me, I could tell. I couldn't blame them though. Between school, exams, Nightly and training with Judy there wasn't any time for my family. I was going to protect them though. Protect them, no matter the cost.

CHAPTER 27

The Dance

The night before the dance I had another dream. I was wearing the same red dress and the mask. The dream was placed in a dressing room; I was sitting in a hair dresser's chair staring into a large mirror in front of me. There was no doubt in my mind that I was about to be visited by mages.

"Why am I here?" I asked.

"Just to talk," said a new voice.

I looked in mirror and saw the image of a new mage. It was a female mage. She was beautiful just like the one frozen in the ice in the centagon's lair. She had long black hair, a blood red dress, the same yellow eyes with slit pupils, grey skin and black cat ears. Her presence seemed familiar.

"Talk about what?" I asked.

"Your dragon; what else is a mage interested in?" she asked, approaching me.

"Why?"

The mage looked stunned.

"Why go after dragons that aren't harming you?"

The mage stopped behind me and pulled out a brush from behind her. "Because we need, and have to stop them."

"That was in the past. Why continue this when you just hurt people?" I saw her raise the brush and began to stroke her hair. "Why continue something that's worthless now?"

The mage struck me with the brush. I fell to the floor tasting the red liquid that lingered in my mouth. Amson didn't lie when he said that mages made the dreams feel like they were real.

"Worthless! Pointless! Are you an idiot? Look at us! Look at what the dragons turned us into. Why should we continue hunting dragons because if we can't exist, neither can they," she barked at me.

I sat up and watched the mage continue to brush her hair with the blood stained brush.

"I've never seen a mage out in public. It's obvious that you're doing fine now, why continue the slaughter?"

The mage turned to me with disgust in her eyes. She raised her hand ready to smack me with the brush again but her wrist was caught. The mage who gave me the black rose appeared; he held the other mages wrist firmly.

"Never strike a guest," he said forcing the brush to drop out of her hand. "You are dismissed."

"You put me in charge of this," she complained.

"And now I'm dismissing you. Go!" He ordered and she obeyed. "I apologize for my assistance behaviour."

I looked up at the mage. He didn't change. He still wore the same black suit as before.

I stood up and faced the mage, one on one.

"Maybe you can answer my question. Why continue the slaughter?"

"You ask a lot of questions," he said forcing me to sit back down in the chair. "Let's go with this . . . our lives will never be used to their fullest until every single dragon is dead."

"That makes no sense," I said trying to stand back up. The mage pushed me back down in the chair; he wasn't going to let me stand.

He turned the chair around to face him. He stared at me with his yellow eyes. He held my wrists down, daring not to give me the chance to fight back. "To you, it might not but to a mage, it makes perfect sense. Now, why don't you tell me where your dragon is so we can end this little game?"

"You think this is a game? A life isn't something to toy with like a doll."

"Are you sure? What I've heard was that you've been toying with a young mage down at the ski resort." He released one of my wrists only to reach into his pocket and held out a doll that looked exactly like me. "If you can toy with him why can't we toy with others? Like you."

"We helped each other and saved each other's lives. I never toyed with anyone!" The mage let go of my other wrist and tossed me the doll. It squeaked when I caught it. It had a painted smile on, the same painted smile I had on when I lied to my friends and family. How did he know?

"Do you want your old life back?" the mage whispered in my ear. "Do you want to forget the troubles that dragon got you in?" he whispered in my other ear. "I can make it all go away if you just tell me where he's hiding." He said grabbing my shoulders.

"No," I whispered.

"What did you say?!" he asked, retreating a few feet back.

"You heard me," I said, standing up. "I will not give up my dragon. He is a part of me just like I am a part of him. We both have become strong together through mind, body and soul." I tossed the doll back at him. The doll squeaked again when it came into contact with the floor. "I'll die before I even let you lay one finger on Nightly. You'll have to pry him from my cold dead hands." I ripped the mask off my face and revealed my identity. "My name is Connie Helen Whitsburg and I am a dragon's whisperer. Bring on the battle, mage, because I'm ready for you." I didn't know why I said that. I knew I wasn't really ready, but I hated to be pushed around. I wanted to leave. "Goodbye."

"What, no!" he said running towards me.

I remembered what Amson told me. I was in control of my own dreams and because of his advice I wanted to leave and so I did.

The following night was the dance. Before I awoke from my encounter with the mage earlier that day I remembered someone sitting next to me and say 'That's my girl'. Someone knew I had contacted a mage, but who? Was it Amson?

The phone rang and I heard Kyle pick it up and I could hear Kristin's high pitched voice, all the way on the other side of the house.

I couldn't believe it. She was having problems already.

There was a knock at my door. "Connie, are you almost ready?" asked Kyle.

"Yeah, I'm coming," I said stepping out into the hall, "Tell your over excited girlfriend that we're on our way."

I walked to the front door and saw Dad waiting for us.

"You look beautiful Connie," he said, pushing some hair behind my ears. "Where'd did you get the dress though?"

"A friend made it for me," I answered feeling the delicate layout of the long strapless dress. It was outlined with a silver trim with black diamonds. The black diamonds were really Nightly's scales that were shaped into diamonds. The white fabric ran from the back of the dress onto my wrists. My hair was curled and put into a pony tail at the top of my head. To end it I put on some makeup. "She's really good at making things."

"So I see," Dad said with a smile.

"Alright, Connie, let's go to the dance," Kyle said popping up the collar of his coat and slid his hands over his slick hair.

He wore a white coat with matching pants and a black tie.

He actually didn't look half bad. We both looked at each other and smiled.

"Okay kids, it's time for a photo," Mom said, entering the room with her belly leading the way.

"Awe, Mom, do we have to?" Kyle and I whined.

"Yes, now get together so I can take a picture," Mom said, pulling out a digital camera.

Kyle and I sighed as we stood next to each other. Mom had to take three different pictures before one of them actually turned out nice. For the first picture, Kyle bumped me forward. In the second picture, I elbowed him in the stomach and for the third one, Dad had to stand in between us so we wouldn't fight.

"Great, thank you, Rick," Mom said rubbing her head.

"Can we go to the dance now?" I asked impatiently.

Dad walked behind Mom and wrapped an arm around her. "Go ahead and have fun."

"Thanks Dad, we will," Kyle assured him while spinning his keys around his finger.

Once we were in the garage I crawled to the back seat. Kyle had to pick up Kristen. I was thankful that Miles never insisted on picking me up. We picked up Kristen and drove off to the school. The three of us walked to the gym together. I looked up at the partially cloudy night sky. A crescent moon shined bright next to the stars. The night sky was beautiful, like always.

Judy exited the gym right when the three of us were about to enter. Her cast was off, she had no crutches and the way she moved her feet so carefully, making sure they wouldn't break, made her look like a ballerina.

"Connie, you actually came," she said twirling around in her short glittering purple dress. "I'm so glad you're here."

"I'm really excited too. How does it feel to be dancing again?" I asked.

"Incredible, I missed dancing so much, Connie. It has to be my calling, because nothing can stop me from going onto the dance floor."

"Hey," I said in a soft voice, "have you seen Sam at all? I want to apologise."

Judy stayed quiet. I knew she knew something. She looked nervous.

"Come on you two," called Kyle.

"Uh . . . well, Sam went to the dance with Britney since he couldn't go with you and Britney couldn't go with Martin Miles." Judy spoke really fast and she always did whenever she didn't want to confess something.

"Oh," I said upset.

"Well, there you are." Martin Miles came out of the gym and stood beside me. "You look beautiful tonight, Connie."

I rolled my eyes and grunted as he wrapped his arm around me. 'Help' I mouthed to Judy.

She nodded and ran back into the gym. Martin dragged me along with him as he entered the gym. He kept his eyes and hands on me, making sure I wouldn't do anything that he didn't like. I needed to get away from him and find Sam.

The gym was lit up with lights of all different colours. The lights flashed continuously, music was almost as loud as the music you would hear at a rock concert and there was a huge disco ball hanging from the center of the gym.

"Wow," I said amazed.

"Yeah, I made sure it was all perfect," Miles said, guiding me underneath the disco ball.

The whole gym was crowded with kids of all ages. I looked at them then at the supervisors who watching from afar. For a second I spotted

Judy but she vanished in the crowd. She seemed distracted though. She was looking for someone or something.

I tried to follow her but Miles grabbed my wrist. He held onto it with a strong grip. "Where do you think you're going? We haven't even had a chance to dance yet."

A slow song started to play and Miles didn't hesitate to pull me in close and place his hands on my hips. He pulled me in closer only allowing me to press my hands up against his chest.

"Do you know how to dance?" he asked.

"Yes, I do and I could dance better if you loosened your grip."

"If I loosen up you'll escape and I won't find out what I want to know."

"What do you want to know? By the way, your way of getting information is selfish and arrogant. Black mailing people will only get them to hate you."

"I can live with that, after all, I have more people that love me then hate." I gave him a dirty look. "Don't give me that face. Now let's get down to business. I know your great-grandfather, Gabriel, had a great idea of what he wanted to happen with the Mystic Realm and the Human World but when I read your dad's half I got a bit confused."

"My dad's half?" I asked confused.

"Oh, you didn't know?" he asked surprised. "I was intrigued with how much emotion and feeling he put into that half of the journal."

"I haven't been able to read very much of it because someone happened to snatch it away from me before I even had that chance to."

"Then maybe you can tell me the location of the nest. There was a picture that was missing from a page."

"So, it's old. A lot of things are crumbled and torn off."

"It was half way into the book so you must have noticed it," he said as he pulled out his phone and held me close to him with one arm.

"What are you doing?!" I demanded, trying to pull away.

"Just tell me the location or I update my website with the information I've already collected from the journal."

"You wouldn't!"

Miles opened up his phone and pressed the buttons with his thumb. He then held his thumb over the send button ready to update his website.

"Well?" he went with his British accent.

I bit my lip and shook my head.

He inched his thumb towards the send button. I felt sweat come down my face but then the lights went out. A loud buzz filled the room making everyone cover their ears. I took my chance. I hit Mile's hand, knocking his cellphone out of his hand and escaped his grasp. I ran into the crowd of people, making sure I was far away from Miles. Once the sound passed by the lights came back on and the DJ started to talk.

"Sorry about that folks," he said into the microphone. "It was just a short fuse nothing to worry about. Now let's party."

The crowd cheered as the music started up again.

"Connie," Judy yelled running towards me. She pulled me out of the crowd where we could talk to each other, without screaming so loud.

"Judy, I'm glad to see you," I said. "What happened?"

"I cut the power after I noticed you fighting to get free from Miles," she said lifting up his phone.

"Thank you," Martin Miles said taking his phone back. "Now I can finish what I started."

I was about to walk up and hit Miles, but Judy stopped me.

Martin Miles opened his phone and then closed it back up. "You erased everything," he yelled, eyeing Judy. "Do you even know how much information I stored in there?!"

"Yeah, I actually do because you're not the only one who researches other people. Apparently, on your website, I noticed you always updated it by phone," Judy said with a smile. She held up a small black chip, "and this is the only back up file you have." She dropped it on the floor and stepped on it. "That loud buzz you heard was magnetized meaning every electronic device in here is whipped clean of data."

Martin scowled at her. "I could report you."

"Same goes with me. After all, you did steal Connie's journal. You should leave. You're not getting any information tonight."

"You must know then," he said, "I'll be back, you haven't heard the last of me." Martin stormed out of the gym, opening the gym doors all the way, drawing everyone's attention. When the doors shut everyone went back to dancing.

I turned to Judy and gave her a hug. "Thank you so much. How'd you do that? You're no computer whiz."

"Hey, after that course my step dad forced me to take I'm surprised I'm not a nerd." We laughed. "Anyways, no one bugs you unless it's Kristen, Kyle, your dad, maybe me and-"

"Alright," I said annoyed.

Judy laughed as she threw her arms up in the air. "Now let's go find the person you actually wanted to the dance with."

"And you know who it is?"

"Sam, of course," she said grabbing my hand.

I blushed a bit as I joined her to find Sam. We were looked for five minutes until we saw a crowd circled around someone. Judy and I pushed past them and found Sam and Britney watching a fellow student of ours break dance. Sam saw me and gave me a faint smile. I looked away. I still felt terrible not telling him the truth.

"Sam, Britney," Judy called out.

I faced the ground as they approached us.

"Judy, Connie, where are your dates?" Britney asked smoothing out her orange spaghetti strap dress.

"Uh, well I came alone and I saw Martin Miles taking off. I'm sure he's really lonely and needs someone to talk to," said Judy.

Britney didn't hesitate to leave us to go and look for Martin Miles.

"Well, that was easy," Judy said, flicking her long dark brown hair back. "Now I think I'll leave you two alone."

"What, why?!" we both asked nervously.

"I don't like intruding on people's love besides, you two need to talk and you might as well do it now or else this could be it for you two. See ya," Judy ran off, leaving awkward tension between Sam and me build up.

"So how was it with Britney?" I asked.

"Annoying," he answered. "As you can tell, she talked the night away about your date and then ran off once you left him."

"To tell you the truth Sam, I never wanted to go to the dance with Miles. I wanted to go with you," I said, looking at his black dress shoes.

"Then why didn't you?" he asked grabbing my hands.

"Because he blackmailed me," I answered.

"Oh, I should probably apologise for my rude behaviour over the past two weeks then. I actually thought you liked Miles," he confessed.

I raised my head a little but stopped as my gaze stared at Sam's dark red dress shirt. It was half covered by his black vest and a tie hid behind the buttons.

"Shall we dance?" he asked.

"I would like that," I said taking his hands and placing them on my hips.

I wrapped my arms around his neck and we began to dance. All music started to quiet down. Dancing with Sam felt so familiar. The whole dance felt like a dream but it wasn't. I was so happy but sad too, why? I'm with the man I want to be with but I felt like something is going to upset me and soon.

Once we stopped dancing Sam tilted my chin up. I lowered my hands down to his chest and pulled myself forward, matching my lips with his. I did this of my own free will. That wasn't an accident. I kissed Sam on purpose, it made me happy. That's when I remembered where I had this feeling before. It was the last time I saw Amson.

Sam released our lips and tried to pull away but I held him firmly.

"Please," I begged, "don't leave."

"I'm sorry Connie, but I have to go for the time being," he said removing my hands and leaving me.

"Sam, wait!" I yelled as I ran after him.

I lost him in the crowd for a second but I caught a glimpse of him running out of the gym doors. I followed him, remembering that there was only one place where Sam would go: the library. When I entered the room, it was empty only a few lights were on. Walking up and down the aisles enclosed with bookshelves. I heard a low growl and groan. I walked past a few book cases until I came across a person curled up in the corner. I walked up to him and touched his shoulders.

"Sam?" I whispered.

"Stay away from me," he hissed grabbing his head. "I never wanted you to see me like this." The person stood up and faced me, showing me a teary face Amson.

I covered my mouth in disbelief and backed away.

"I don't blame you," he said, looking at his grey skin. "I'm disgusting, a freak."

"I never said that." I removed my hands away from my mouth. "I should have known you were Amson. You just took away the 'S' from your full name to create Amson."

"Yeah, when you asked for my name I hesitated and all I could come up was Amson."

I bent down, pulled up my dress slightly and slipped off my dragon scale anklet. I made sure Sam saw it in my hand before I dropped it on the floor. When I heard the scale hit the floor I turned around and showed Sam the dragon wings mark on my back. My head turned slightly to see Sam's reaction. He was definitely shocked.

"I'm Connie and I am a dragon's whisperer," I admitted. "You showed me that you were a mage and now I've shown you what I really am."

"Connie," he whispered, approaching me. "The reason why I was always distant was because I was afraid you would see me as a mage. That's why I hardly talked or showed my true emotions. True emotions bring out the real me, in other words, my mage form." He scratched his head, "but I've grown to love you."

I raised my hand and felt his cheek. It was wet and soft. "You know it took me awhile, but I finally figured out that I love you too."

He smiled, holding my hand against his face. "Sometimes I thought that you could never accept me for me since I'm . . . well-"

I placed a finger on his lips. "I can accept whoever I want in my life. I accepted Nightly, and I accept you."

Sam let go of my hand and waited for me to remove my finger before he bent down and picked up my scale. "You really are something different."

"That all depends on how you look at me," I said, poking him on the forehead.

He wrapped his arms around me and held me tight. I giggled as I felt his cat ears. Sam's smile dropped as he hurried me to the libraries storage room.

"What's going on?"

"Another mage is coming and she will rip your head off if she finds you," he said. "Do you know how to turn invisible?"

"A little bit, I guess," I said.

"Concentrate on the scale and stay hidden till I return," Sam closed the door trapping me behind it. I placed an ear on the wooden door, trying to listen to the conversation that was about to start.

"What are you doing here?" I heard Sam ask.

"I could ask you the same thing, Sammy," the mage asked him.

I saw a piece of the door's edge was broken off. I managed to see what was going on once I stepped onto a bucket. The female mage from my dream was talking with Sam.

"I needed to get away from everyone," he lied.

The female mage placed her hand on his shoulder and bent down to his ear. "She's here, isn't she?"

"No, she isn't," he said refusing to move.

She gripped his shoulder and shoved him aside smacking him across the face. "Do not lie to me! I saw her follow you and I don't think you want me to report this to the Lead Mage."

The Lead Mage, I remembered hearing that name before. If Sam was a mage and his blood relative was Kamal, would that make him a mage to? I didn't pay attention to my surroundings as I thought. My clumsiness accidentally knocked a broom over.

"What was that?" the female mage asked. "You're hiding something from me," she slapped him across the face again.

I focused on the scale and kept telling myself to turn invisible. I continued to tell myself as I stepped off the bucket and backed into a corner.

The footsteps began to get louder. I held my breath hoping she wouldn't hear me. The door swung open as the female mage stared into the dark storage closet. She looked around but didn't see anything. Her face was full of anger, she knew I was in here, she just didn't know where. My heart rate sped up, it felt like it wanted to teleport out of my chest with fear. The mage reached her arm out. I backed away further into the corner almost feeling the tip of her fingernail touch me. She kicked the bucket I stood on over and slammed the door shut, causing all the cleaning supplies in the closet to fall on me.

I listened from where I was. I dared not move, fearing that the mage would return and find me.

"Are you satisfied?" Sam asked.

The mage said nothing. I heard high heels begin to walk, their sound faded and when I heard the library door shut, I knew she was gone.

Sam came to the door and slowly opened it up, forcing a bunch of the cleaning supplies aside. "It's alright, she's gone."

Sam reached out his hand helped me stand up as I became visible. "Who exactly is she?"

Sam scratched his head. "She's Nurse Jacqueline," he guided me out of the closet.

"What, I don't understand?"

"Yeah, well Kamal is sort of the leader of the mages. Basically she's a spy who's supposed to keep an eye on you and me."

"So I was constantly being watched? What are we going to do now?" I asked, nervously. There was blood on Sam's lip. He noticed my awkward expression. He felt his lip and removed the blood.

"We'll go back to gym and go our separate ways," he said. "Pretend this whole night never happened. We were both at the dance with separate dates and we danced the night away with them."

I lowered my head. I put my scale anklet back on and walked with Sam outside onto the baseball field. Most of the snow was gone but the ground was still damp. Sam brought me to home base.

"What are we doing here, Sam?" I said shaking.

"Your dragon's coming," he said.

When he mentioned Nightly, I felt his presence. It was like mind sequence, but instead of us talking to each other we would feel where each other was. Nightly was flying and he was approaching us fast, too fast.

"Oh, no," I said.

"What, Connie?"

An invisible Nightly swooped down, pulled me over his neck and grabbed Sam with his claws. Nightly then began to rise out of the ravine. I nearly fell off at the speed we were going.

"Nightly!" I yelled as we rose up out the ravine and flew over the trees.

"Connie, control your dragon," Sam yelled.

"I'm trying," I whined as Nightly lowered himself closer to the trees. "Nightly, put us down."

"Fine," he snapped, landing in a clearing of spruce trees. He dropped Sam. I watched as Sam rolled in the snow. *"Mage, you dare to show your face around my whisperer!"*

"Nightly, wait, its Sam," I said, get off his neck.

"I know, I've always known," he growled. *"That day I spent in your body, he spilt the juice in the hall while Judy and I were talking about dragons. He was the*

273

only one there and the only one with enough information to tell the Lead Mage where we were that day. Mages wouldn't help a human unless it benefitted them and he was someone you knew. It had to be him."

"Well, I'm sorry! I made up for it by letting the two of you escape." He stood to his feet. "I was the one who helped you find that antidote for Connie. I've never mentioned a word of your secret area to the Lead Mage and I've kept my distance for a while now."

I approached Sam, cautiously. "How long have you known?"

Sam scratched his head. "Since the second day of school, you were acting weird so I followed you to the secret part of the ravine with that old guy who didn't wear shoes. Unfortunately, I wasn't able to find the passage way . . . I wanted to stop you . . . I was too late. When I found the secret area I saw you sleeping with your dragon sitting beside you. I want to help both of you."

"Yeah right, since when?"

"Since . . . since . . . I love Connie. She accepted you and me into her life. That tells me a lot about her."

"Sam," I whispered, walking up to him and touching his face. "I don't care if you're freakishly tall or as small as a mouse, a mage, human, dragon or whatever, I'll always love you."

"Connie, step out of the way. He needs to disappear," Nightly demanded, smoke came out of his nostrils.

"No, I won't let you hurt him," I said, turning around.

"CONNIE!" He roared, releasing a bright flame into the sky, *"Move, now!"*

"What if I took the dragon's oath?" Sam suggested.

Nightly calmed down and strutted forward. He reached his neck out and looked at Sam. *"Will you actually do it with no deals, questions or tricks?"*

"If it means I can be with Connie and have you not kill me, then yes." Sam knelt down and took my scale anklet off.

"Really Sam, I don't want to force you to do something you don't want to do," I said nervous.

He nodded. "Like you said before, I can accept anything I want in my life and I accept the conditions of the dragon oath." He took the scale and slit his hand open, across his knuckles. I backed away as I saw the blood. "I vow to keep Connie's identity as a dragon's whisperer a secret along with the whereabouts of her dragon. No matter what I may go through, I will not tell, show, or speak a word to any living thing about them. If I dare to break this vow, I allow any dragon and their whisperer to strike me down where I stand." The same mark of the diamond dragon scale appeared on the back of Sam's hand as it did Judy when she said the oath.

"Thank you," I hugged Sam refusing to let go. His hand still bled. I backed away and asked, "Sam, why did you cut yourself?"

"For a mage to do a dragon oath they have to cut themselves with a dragon scale or else they can break free from it. After all, we are part dragon."

"Great, now that we've got that settled we can go."

"Sam, shouldn't we tell Judy about this?" I asked looking back at Nightly.

"What's Judy got to do with this?" Sam asked, wiping the blood away on his pants.

"Judy knows that I'm a dragon's whisperer, actually she's been helping me with my training too. She's a good friend and she has kept my identity a secret this long. We can trust her."

"Listen Connie, I know that the three of us are friends but I need you to keep my identity a secret like I'm keeping yours." He tore a bit of his shirt off and wrapped it around his hand. "It's difficult for a mage to hide their identity from humans. Why do you think we disguise ourselves like them? I can't have other people know, especially humans. I'm fine with you knowing it but no one else can find out."

I walked up to him and slipped my fingers into his hands. "I understand. I will do as you ask and so will Nightly."

"What, no way, I'm not doing it!" Nightly stated.

I glanced back at him, giving him cold eyes. Nightly looked away and remained quiet.

Sam turned around and smiled. He knelt back down and slipped my anklet back on my leg while returning to his human form. His ears lost their soft touch while they shrunk and took on the shape of a human's ear. The skin tone lightened and his eyes returned to their emerald green with the slit pupils widening into a circular shape.

Nightly gave Sam a low warning growl. Sam stood up and smiled at me.

"Come on, we'll take you back home," I smiled.

"Why are we taking him back?"

"Hey, if you didn't want to give him a ride back you shouldn't have kidnapped him in the first place." I shook my finger at Nightly. *No complaints got it!*

Yeah, I understand.

Sam sat behind me on Nightly's saddle wrapping his arms around my waist. Nightly walked to the ravines ledge and tilted over it before diving down. He didn't even pull up once. Nightly was mad at me and so he decided to make the ride back 'bumpy'. He jumped from one wall all the way to the other, gliding along the way. After he was done jumping he would climb down the wall, making it hard for Sam and me to hang on. He mostly did it because he wanted to knock Sam around.

When we finally settled down on flat land, Sam toppled off the saddle, stumbling around like he had just gotten off an amusement ride.

"You're cruel, dragon," Sam said, dropping to his knees.

"I'm sorry, Sam," I assured him as I got off the saddle. "He's just a little nervous."

"I am not, he deserved that!"

"Shut it," I said, annoyed.

"Fine, I get it," Nightly turning invisible. *"You want to be alone with him. I can tell and I'm gone."*

I heard him flap his wings up and down, as he took off, leaving the two of us behind.

"Stupid dragon," I muttered, brushing myself off.

Sam got back up on his feet and grabbed my hand, guiding me back into the gym where almost everyone had left. I couldn't believe how long we were gone.

"Connie, is that you?!" Kyle asked looking at me and Sam holding hands as we entered.

"Awe, how cute," Kristen teased, hanging onto Kyle's right arm.

Sam quickly took on a cherry red colour and let go of my hand.

"Come on Connie. It's time to go home," Kyle said, leaving the gym with Kristen.

Sam turned towards me, watching as I pulled some of my hair back behind my ears. He smiled and so did I. We both leaned in, ready to kiss each other, but Sam stopped. That sudden creepy feeling came over me like someone was watching us. I looked over my shoulder to see Kamal and Nurse Jacqueline staring at us.

Sam got my attention by grabbing by the shoulders. "Go," he let me go. "I'll see you after the weekend in the new semester."

I nodded and ran out the door, my heart pounding hard against my chest. That night had been a magical thriller. However my body was shaking—but why? Sam wouldn't betray Nightly and me, would he?

Even if he was a mage, I should have been more cautious because that night when I went to bed, the final petal on the black rose fell.

CHAPTER 28

"Attack"

As I woke to a Saturday morning, it didn't turn out like a usual morning. Everything that happened the night before all felt like a dream. There was something about that whole day I was about to go through. It felt strange, like either something good or something bad was going to happen, I just didn't know what.

When I rose to my feet I went and checked my closet, there it was, my moonlight white dress, hanging up. That dress was the only proof that the other night was not a dream but reality. Well, it was that and Kyle wouldn't stop bragging about him and Kristen being awarded the dance King and Queen. It got so bad that I had to stuff one of his shoes in his mouth to make him shut up. Before I left my room I took out my dragon scale gloves and placed them in my bag. When that was done I walked out into the hall.

Still in my pyjamas, I walked into the hall, listening to a frying pan lifting up and down off the oven. As I entered the kitchen Mom stood at the stove cooking pancakes.

"Good morning, Connie," Mom said in a welcoming voice.

"Morning," I replied, yawning as I sat down at the kitchen island.

"You're up early, is there anything happening today?" she asked, placing a plate of pancakes in front of me.

"Not that I know of," I said yawning again. "I might get together with Sam and Judy or just hang out at the library."

"Or have a family night with us?" Mom suggested.

"Excuse me?" I asked.

Mom grabbed a cup of coffee off the counter and sat in the seat next to me. "You and Kyle are both in high school. Kyle is graduating this year and in two years, you'll be graduating too. For the next little while would you come home on time and spend two hours with your mom and dad while we're still together like this as a family?"

I had a bad feeling about this. I didn't blame her for wanting to spend time with her family. She was just worried and didn't want to let any of her kids go off into the world. I think that's a mother's worst fear.

I sighed. "Alright, I'll be there."

My mom jumped up and hugged my head while also spilling her hot coffee on my lap.

"Ah, Mom, hot, that's hot!" I cried out in pain.

Mom let me go, allowing me to get up. She got a rag damped in cold water and started to dab my pants. When she finished I ran to my room and changed into my everyday close. When I came out of the room, I guess Mom was talking to Kyle about the same thing. He sat there looking nervous and guilty. He was acting the same way I did when Mom was talking with me. Kyle sighed, agreeing with Mom, and she got all excited again, spilling her refilled cup of coffee on him. This time it was a lot funnier. Kyle ran past me into the bathroom and screamed his lungs out.

"Martha," Dad called out entering the room. "Be careful, or else you'll hurt the baby and our kids."

"Too late," I said, leaning on the door way. "She already dumped hot coffee on both Kyle and me."

Mom giggled and blushed.

"Well, she has done worse," Dad kissed Mom on her forehead. "When she was pregnant with Kyle, she would fall down every step and knock everything over." He walked towards me, "and when she was pregnant with you she had muscles spasms every day and night. She was more violent at night then she was in the day. I still have the scars to prove it too."

"So basically Mom is a klutz when she's pregnant," I said.

Dad tapped his nose.

"I am not," Mom said, out ragged as she swung her arms up in the air franticly. Her over reaction knocked the mug over and broke on the floor.

"I'm sorry, sweetheart, but you are," Dad said, cleaning up the broken pieces.

"Alright, I'm off," I said, grabbing my bag from my bedroom and walking out of the front door. "I'll be back at seven." I closed the front door and ran down the street. It was a Saturday and everyone was about, enjoying the weekend. As I ran out of Small Valley and came across the hidden passage, I started to talk to Nightly. *Nightly I'm coming.* I pushed past the tree branches and looked for the mark I placed near the illusion. When I found it I walked into the dark tunnel.

I heard him yawn. *What are you doing up so early?*

I was thinking about last night and how Sam's trying so hard to keep us a secret. I don't want him to regret it. From now on, I'm going to train as hard as I can.

Ah, I was really hoping that it was all a nightmare, Nightly grumbled. *You just want to train to impress him. Can I go back to sleep now?*

Nope, not going to happen and since you we're a witness, you have to train with me. Besides there is one thing I found in the journal last night that I really want to try.

And what's that? He asked, yawning.

I want to try something my great-grandfather rediscovered and that's a mind, body and soul fusion. Basically you and I will become one and share one mind, one body and one soul.

Uh, Connie, I've heard about that one. It's the hardest things for a whisperer and dragon to accomplish. It's nothing like us communicating right now. The mind, body, soul fusion is when a dragon and whisperer have mastered all the other techniques. We haven't even mastered the mind body switch.

Then we'll have to work extra hard, I said, walking up to my half sleeping dragon. "I'm willing to break every bone in my body to make this work. We will train and we will become strong enough to defeat a mage. Oh, and if you talk about Sam that way again I'll never let you forget what happened last night."

"The way you're talking sounds like you don't trust your boyfriend."

"No, and he's not my boyfriend! I just want to be prepared for anything."

"And that's why you're my whisperer. Never bring up that night again though. Let's get started." Nightly said eagerly.

"You took the words right out of my mouth," I said, placing my bag on the ground and strapping on the dragon scale gloves.

Nightly rose off the ground and charged at me. I did the same thing, except when we met I flipped over him. That was the first time I did a successful flip. Nightly growled and I smiled. We charged at each other again. Nightly blew a small fire. It singed my right arm as I spun underneath it. From then on, we battled while being invisible. The hard thing about battling your dragon was if you tried to connect your mind with theirs you could both read each other's moves. Nightly brought down a few trees and I managed to put a dent in the rock with the gloves. Nightly roared and I yelled as we attacked each other the whole morning. The whole reason we were attacking each other was to see where each other's weaknesses were. Mine was reaction time. I could dodge Nightly's tail, but when he would place it on the ground he would be able to sweep my feet right out from underneath me, he usually succeeded. His weakness was speed. Nightly wasn't that quick when it came to running on land, and he knew that he needed to improve it or else his life could be taken in a matter of seconds.

Nicole and Pearl got up at the same time we arrived. Then they went out to patrol the area. The rest of the Guardians didn't come out of their house until Nightly almost burnt it down. Teddy came running out like a mad man to see the remains of our training. I made the mistake of stopping to look at Teddy's stupid expression, and that's when Nightly pinned me. We both became visible.

"*I win,*" he said, lifting his foot up off me.

"You just got lucky," I commented while trying to catch my breath.

We heard clapping from behind. While Teddy was freaking out about their house, James and Malcolm came out and noticed Nightly's and my little battle.

"Very impressive Connie, but a dragon will always have the upper hand in the battle as long as their whisperer is safe," Malcolm said.

Teddy joined us, still a little frantic with what happened. "Either than almost burning down our home, those weren't bad moves you had there. I trust the training with your friend Judy is going well."

"Well, what do you think?" I asked, panting as I sat up.

"Good. Not great, but good," Teddy grinned.

"*She improved exponentially,*" Nightly growled. "*Don't you dare say that about my whisperer again!*"

"Take it easy dragon. I'm only kidding."

Nightly continued to growl at Teddy, he was tempted to bite his head off.

"If you don't mind me asking Connie, why did you come here to train?" asked James.

"I discovered something that I want to accomplish with Nightly. Have you ever heard of the mind, body, soul fusion?"

"Nope," said James.

"Yeah . . . kind of . . . no," said Teddy.

"Not if there aren't any books about it," Malcolm commented, lighting a cigarette. "I don't even recall Devonburg mentioning anything like it."

"I've heard of it," Baboline yawned, coming out of the house. "It's the merging of the body, mind and soul between whisperer and dragon. It's pretty risky though. There's only a fifty percent chance on living if it's not done right. That's why no one's heard of it."

I gulped but smiled. "Then I guess we'll have to make sure we do it right, what do you say Nightly?"

He hummed with delight. *"We want to try it."*

Baboline looked surprised. "Then you're going to have to double your training time because from what I can see you're nowhere close."

"I can make that work." I was determined. Nothing was going to stop me. "One day I want to use it to protect the people I love."

"Then we'll help you to the very end," said James.

I nodded. "Shall we start?"

For the rest of the day all we did was train. For once, we actually beat Teddy at his drill and we knew why. Nightly and I both noticed that Teddy had to wait ten seconds to recharge before he could strike. The more time he took to recharge the more time we had to strike him down.

Next, I worked with Malcolm with tactics and strategies. He showed me that if I were ever trapped by an enemy, I should make it look like I would lose but essentially return with a strong hidden blow once they dropped their guard. Movement, time and attitude were the key features to winning a battle. Know when to move, make sure everything is timed right and be sure to keep yourself intact with the right attitude. If not you have already lost the battle as well as yourself.

There was also one other thing Malcolm taught me that I found intriguing. If there was ever the opportunity that would have me choose a battle field I had to take it. He also said that it was best to bring the fight to a place that you would feel familiar with and area where, if there were traps, I would know where they were. The last thing he taught me was even if I never had the chance to change the battlefield he said to be aware of my surrounding, because they might just help me. If I remembered all that he taught me, the battle would become easier to win.

While Malcolm and I worked on strategies, James was flying around with Nightly teaching him to maneuver through weather conditions. Nicole and Pearl supervised our status while Baboline went off to collect ingredients to make more whisperer pills.

Night drew near and that weird feeling came over me again. I felt a need to try something this particular night.

As James and Nightly ended their training for the day, I approached James, feeling excitement take control of me.

"James," I called out as I watched my breath took shape in the night air.

"What is it Connie?" he asked, getting off Nightly.

"Can I fly with Nightly tonight?"

"You want to do night flying?"

"Yes."

"You want to do it tonight?"

"Yes, oh please, please, allow us," I begged.

"Yes, let us fly together tonight," begged Nightly

"Uh, fine, but don't fly too long, there's a song lingering in the air," he warned us. He helped me up on the saddle and said, "Stay invisible at all times."

"Why, it's a new moon tonight and I've never flown visible." I pulled my bag onto my shoulders. "Come on James. There is no way we can be seen on a night like this. I'm wearing black and I'm on a black dragon. No one's going to notice."

My dragon hummed and nodded his head.

"Alright, go," said James, "I'm sick of your begging." He watched us take off but he appeared worried.

"What did James mean when he said that there's a song lingering in the air?"

"Who knows? I just want to fly!" Nightly rose higher and higher into the sky. *"How high do you think we can go?"*

"Let's find out," I said, gripping onto the saddle.

We flew out of the ravine, past the first set of clouds, and continued to rise. We rose higher and higher until I found that it was getting hard to breathe and colder.

"Nightly," I gasped, "Nightly, turn around. I can't breathe."

"Wait, we can go a little higher," he said. He continued to fly higher, but I could hear him start to pant.

"Nightly . . . we're going up into the atmosphere . . . we're going to run . . . out . . . of . . . air."

"We . . . can . . . keep . . . going!"

I couldn't do it anymore. I unstrapped and unbuckled myself with my remaining strength and fell off the saddle. If I stayed any longer I would have passed out.

"Connie!"

I was falling straight down aiming back towards earth. I slowly took in the air before turning myself around to catch the saddle as Nightly flew over me. He opened his wings up as we drifted down. It gave me the time to pull myself onto the saddle and strap myself back in.

"Never do that again!" he growled.

I coughed a bit. "Then next time don't try to kill me. We can't go up that high or else we'll lose air. Space is an oxygen free zone."

Nightly was silent.

I sighed. *What am I going to do with you?* I heard something, music? It sounded violent but peaceful, and it played by only one instrument, a flute. "Nightly, do you hear that?"

"Yes, it's beautiful."

I didn't have to say anything to get him to find the source. It was so beautiful almost hypnotic. It had to be one of the most beautiful songs I had ever heard. We flew closer and closer to the sound hoping to find the source. Soon, it was the only thing I could think of. Nightly flew down further and further past the clouds and back into the ravine. However, we landed on the east side of the ravine where the caves were. Nightly stopped in front of one and let me get out of the saddle to check it out. The cave in front of me held the source of the music and all I had to do was go in and find it. I was five feet away from the cave entrance when Malcolm and James tackled me to the ground.

Malcolm covered my mouth and picked me up, moving me to another cave that had a dazed Nightly and angry Pearl hiding in it. James held out a knife and hammer and hid himself behind a boulder.

"Nightly, turn us invisible," Malcolm ordered in a whisper.

Nightly did as he was told and turned the four of us invisible. I looked over at James who remained visible; the only thing that covered him was a rock that was just bigger than him.

Two figures exited the cave. The female mage from my dream held a flute in her hand and the other was male mage with one eye made of glass.

"You ruined our plan, Guardian," said the mage with the glass eye.

"If you don't come out, we're going to get violent," said the female mage. "Come on James. We know you're there."

James stepped out from behind the rock, tightening his grip on the tools.

"What's with the hammer and knife?" asked the female mage. "You're a fool to think those are going to kill us."

"They were all I needed on the farm and they're all I need tonight," said James.

The mage with the glass eye ran at him holding a cane and started to swing it at James. James went on the defensive side and blocked each attack.

Will James be alright alone? I asked Nightly.

Let's hope so, he answered.

Blow after blow, it seemed like the fight would never end. Then things changed when James was pressed up against a rock. What surprised me was that when the mage attempted to hit him again, James took up his brown hammer and brought it down on the cane, shattering it into two.

"Hey, that was my best cane!" the mage complained.

"Leave now, you're defenceless!" James warned them.

A gun went off. The bullet hit James's hat and knocked it off his head.

Another mage, I realized.

"Oh, you think we're defenceless? You should look again and notice it's not us but you who should be on the run," said a familiar voice. "As long as I'm here you're going to die tonight! Not escape but die!"

Out of the cave stepped out another mage. Right away my jaw dropped as I saw Kamal. I wouldn't have recognized him if I didn't see the odd tattoo on his arm and the brass bracelet he always kept on his wrist.

"You've taken too many lives as it is," James yelled. "I'm not going to let you take anymore."

"Unless I take yours first," Kamal said holding up his gun. "Jacqueline, Edgar, restrain him so I can get a clear shot."

"With pleasure," said the mage with the glass eye.

The mage named Edgar used what remained of his cane as weapons. Jacqueline ran up behind James and knocked the hammer out of his hand. Edgar managed to put a few splinters in his shoulder as he stabbed one half of his cane in James's arm. James grunted as he slipped behind the female mage, Jacqueline and hit her shoulder, popping it right of place. She screamed as she watched James pull out the cane from his arm. Edgar managed to run up and knock the knife out of his hand. James backed up against the solid rock wall. Edgar and Jacqueline stood before him, waiting for the command to strike and kill.

"You know what I'm going to do to you, James?" Kamal asked, walking towards him while playing with his gun. "You are going to die right here in this ravine before you even have the chance to make the young whisperer a legend. You're forgetting one thing."

"And what might that be?" James asked.

"Once you die, the other Guardians are next. There will be no one else to protect your whisperer or her dragon. The next things to vanish will be this ravine, the unborn dragons and every other human being," Kamal said, rubbing his gun.

"Not if I have anything to say about it," James said, disappearing into the wall behind him.

"Where'd he go," demanded Edgar. Edgar didn't even know what happened next. He saw fist appear, it hit him in the face and he dropped to the ground groveling over his broken nose.

"He's using his dragon's ability," said Kamal. "Earth dragons can hide in the earth up to hundred feet deep but they always have to surface after two hours or else they'll become part of the earth."

Become a part of the earth? I asked, trying to watch the fight without reacting to the blood that was being spilt.

286

Think about it as swimming in water. You can only hold your breath for so long. It's the same thing for an earth dragon. They can only last a certain amount of time underground before they die, explained Nightly.

James pulled Jacqueline's feet down into the ground. When she lost her balance he grabbed her wrists and trapped them beneath the ground as well.

"Come on out," Kamal called, readying his gun. "If you don't, I'll shoot."

Nothing happened.

Kamal shot down at the ground. Nothing happened until I saw James rise above the ground with a bleeding leg.

"What . . . what kind of gun is that?!" James asked holding his leg.

"It's a special gun that I finally found after centuries. It can take anything and convert it into a bullet that will shoot through anything and cancel out special abilities. This includes dragons," Kamal reloaded his gun and then shot it at James's other leg and arms.

James yelled in pain every time the bullet pierced through him. His hat caught my attention. It flew over to us. I retrieved it and held it close. My heart pace sped up.

"Face it Guardian. You never stood a chance against me." Kamal held the gun up to James's chest. "You'll never win."

The bullet was released and went straight into the chest of my down to earth, loving Guardian. I watched him try to yell something but the words never left his mouth. That's when I watched his body go limp.

"No!" I cried out, drawing Kamal's attention. He looked over at us.

"Time to go," said Malcolm, jumping onto Pearl. "Connie, get on Nightly and let's go."

I couldn't move. Watching one of my Guardians die right in front of me made my body freeze.

Nightly bit my jacket and tossed me up onto the saddle. I shook myself out of it and strapped myself in. Pearl held onto Nightly's tail so she could remain invisible. He then started to fly away just before a bullet hit either one of us. Kamal reloaded his gun but didn't seem too concerned.

"You see whisperer, you're only causing suffering to the ones around you. Hand over your dragon to make it stop," Kamal said in dragon tongue.

"Don't listen to him," said Pearl.

Nightly took off and picked up speed but the gun went off again and it hit Nightly in the leg. He roared in pain. I looked over and saw the blood drip down and outline his foot. Apparently not everything remains invisible.

"Nightly, land," I ordered.

"Why?" he asked.

"She's right," agreed Malcolm, "if we don't treat that soon, they're going to find us. You'll lose too much blood if you keep flying."

He grunted and crashed landed on a cliff. Nightly turned visible and I saw the bullet would. Malcolm came over and tore up his coat.

"Pearl, disinfect the wound."

Pearl bent down to Nightly's leg and started to lick it clean with her tongue. Malcolm wiped the blood clean off Nightly's leg and used his torn up coat as a bandage. I turned away. So much blood was shed and I couldn't bare it any longer.

"Pearl," said Malcolm. "You know what to do."

I watched as Pearl nodded as flew away. "Where's she going?" I asked.

"Dragon blood is very flammable," he explained. "Each of us carries a bottle of dragon blood. When fire hits the body, it will destroy the bottle, and then the blood will burn whole body before anyone can get information from the corpse and find the dragon mark.

Connie, take Nightly, go home and stay there," he said in a weak voice, "go now!"

I was scared. I did as he told me and had Nightly bring me home. Nightly was weak, but he survived the flight back to my place. If he could survive the flight to my place I knew he would be able to fly back to the secret area. Before he left I gave him James's hat. It didn't belong with me, not with what had just happened.

My Guardian was dead, Nightly was injured the only thing that made the night even worse was when I walked through the back door I found my angry family waiting for me.

"Young lady, do you know what time it is?!" asked Dad.

I said nothing.

"Where have you been?" asked Mom, grabbing my hands and feeling the dirt on them.

Kyle was sitting down with a royal flush in his hands.

Again I said nothing.

"Connie Helen Whitsburg, you owe us an explanation," said Dad.

"No I don't," I said walking to my room.

"Connie!" he yelled.

"Well, what do you want me to say, Dad? You know I wouldn't have skipped out on a *family fun night* if I didn't have a good reason," I said, turning around. "I wanted hang with some friends alright, but we got caught up in something the cost him his life." Tears started to trickled down my face. "Look, I'm sorry. I regret what I did but now that we got that settled, I want to be alone."

"Connie," Dad whispered, "I know what you're going through."

"How could you possibly know what I'm going through?" I asked. "Times have changed and they are nothing like they were in your day." I walked down the hall and into my room, locking the door. I fell on my bed. Why did it happen? I just wanted to see what it was like to fly at night. I didn't want James to lose his life for me and Nightly. I sat up on my bed and threw a pillow at the door. That's when I noticed the black rose still sitting in its bottle of water with no petals on it. I was so stupid to ignore the signs. The Lead Mage showed himself the night before the dance and on the same night, the last petal falls. Now they're going after everyone I care about. "Not this time." I pulled my bag off my back and took out the journal and began to the half that my dad wrote.

> July 6
> Why do I have this book? I don't know why. Why do dragons exist? I still don't know. Why was my father killed? That's a question I have an answer for. My father was killed because he became a dragon whisperer. Grandfather always wanted everyone in the family to be a dragon's whisperer but ever since my father was killed by that mage. I wish none of them ever existed. They ruined my life just by existing. But the real person I'm mad at is me. I was the one who had to be captured by the mage and used as bait. It was me who

got my father and his dragon killed. I don't care if they
are going extinct. I'm never going to become a dragon's
whisperer EVER!

After I read that entry I couldn't help feeling that he actually did
know what I was going through. Then again, he abandoned the life of
living with a dragon so there is no way I could talk to him about this. It
would just upset him and maybe bring back bad memories. I curled up
into a little ball and felt tears go down my face. "I'm sorry, everyone."

* * *

It had been two weeks since the attack. During the time I'd only
talked to Nightly twice to see how everyone was taking it. They hadn't
taken the loss of their friend to good. Nightly told me that the only
thing that was left of James was the cowboy hat that I managed to
recover. I don't even think they gave him a funeral. No mages followed
us and Nightly seemed to be healing fine even though it was slower
than usual, but there was still something lingering over me and it
wouldn't go away. Whatever that gun was it made sure that the wound
would take time to heal.

I met up with Judy at the library studying for our science test before
spring break that started next week. I'll have to admit that it wasn't
the only reason why I wanted to meet up with her. Home was rough;
Dad kept pondering me with questions, questions I couldn't deal with
because I was still feeling horrible about James's passing. It was nice to
have at least one human friend that knew about my secret. It was easy
to tell her about my slip ups and how I really felt. She was the only one
who would talk to me and listen at the time.

"Uh, why does Mr. Yen like to give us so much homework?" Judy
complained, erasing her work again. "I'm telling you, he hates us ever
since you let the frog escape in class."

* * *

Last week Mr. Yen wanted me to clean the frog tank during class.
Sadly amphibians don't take kindly to people sticking their hands into

their tank. Once I placed my rubber gloved hands in there he got out with one jump. I tried to catch him but he slipped out of my hands and down Judy's shirt. It was funny to see her dance though. Even the class was laughing and clapping all except for Mr. Yen.

"Connie, Judith, get the frog back into the tank, now!" he yelled.

I ran up to Judy and caught then frog once it jumped out of her shirt. I quickly put it back in the tank and closed the lid before he could escape again.

"You two girls, stay after school for your spring break home work."

We both gulped.

*   *   *

"Well now it's official. I hate blood and frogs and they hate me," I said.

"Says the girl who has a dragon as a pet," Judy snickered.

"I wouldn't say that anymore," I said putting my head on the table. "Judy, I told you about what happened two weeks ago, right?"

"Yeah, you said one of your Guardians died protecting you." She looked over at me. "I'm guessing nothing's being done other than avoiding each other. Is that including your parents?"

I nodded.

"Did you check your great-grandfather's journal? Maybe that will help."

I shook my head. "I've already tried that and all I got out of it were my dad's whiny words of how he avoided my great-grandfather ever since he was emancipated at the age of fifteen. He did mention what his tattoo said though. He got it on his sixteenth birthday and had it written in the dragon language. That's why I could never find the language on the computer or in any books. It says 'I will never become a dragon's whisperer as long as I live'." Judy sucked in air between her teeth. It was a harsh thing that my dad did. It must have broken my great-grandfathers heart when he saw it. I pulled the book out and opened it up, hoping to find something else. "My great-grandfather wrote an interesting entry after the commotion with my dad."

"And what's that?"

"When my dad lost his dad he actually befriended a couple of mages and one of their names was Drake Slayer."

"Slayer, you mean like Sam's parents?"

"Maybe . . . I'm not too sure," I was glad I caught myself. I still had to keep Sam's identity a secret but it wasn't easy with the researching I was doing. "I also found this article," I pulled it out of my bag. "I printed this off Miles's website a few days ago after I found the entry."

Judy took it and began to read. Her eyes widened as she finished it. "Sam's parents died in a fire?"

"I'm still not entirely sure if they're Sam's parents, but apparently those people went to Ravine College. It's the exact same college where my parents graduated from." I pulled out the year book and flipped through the pages. "See it's my mom, dad, Devonburg, Shelley and Drake."

"You've been doing a lot of researching," Judy said impressed.

"That's not all," I said pulling out another book, "my mom has roses in here each representing a year she and my dad have been together. Look, up to six years it's been only red roses but then they turned to pink."

"So what's that supposed to mean?!"

"Look here in my dad's entry," I said reopening the journal. "A red rose means human, a pink one means knower and white a whisperer. It means my mom knows about the Mystic Realm as well, she's just been hiding it. My whole family except for my mom's side knows about another world, why would they keep that from their kids?"

"I don't know, maybe it's for protection. You have to admit, the Mystic Realm is more dangerous than the Human World."

"That all depends with what you grew up with. Maybe mystical beings think that the Human World is worse than the Mystic Realm, we don't know. I want to know though."

"Well, I want to know what the black rose means? You said you received a black rose and apparently every other rose categorises people, so what does the black rose mean?"

"The journal says it means mage," I said. I immediately thought about Sam. I even whispered his name.

"What was that?" asked Judy.

"Oh, nothing, I just thought that I should be going." I packed up all my books and stood up. "See ya, Judy."

"Bye Connie. Hope everything turns out better for you."

"You and me both," I left the library and saw Kyle waiting for me in the parking lot. "Kyle?"

"Hey Connie, hop in," he said.

"Uh, alright," I said, entering the vehicle.

He got in and drove all the way to the other side of Small Valley and parked on Crescent Avenue, the steepest street in Small Valley. He parked downhill.

"What are we doing here, Kyle?" I asked putting my bag on the dashboard.

"We need to talk," he said turning off the car. "Mom and Dad are worried about you and I think I am to."

"Since when did you become the responsible brother?"

"After we passed the 'Sibling Respect Program'. You remember when we got our papers after Glen's shirt was ripped off and everyone saw his tattoo of a motor home he lived in." A cold shiver ran down his back. That was one part of that day we both could do without remembering. Nightly, just had to appear and torture Glen one last time. "Anyways, working together with you actually made me look at you differently."

"Why now?"

"Because I know my little sister is being bothered by something."

I bit my lip.

"What's going on Connie?"

"Nothing," I lied, feeling the web of lies I'd spun become larger. "Everything's fine, I'm just getting used to high school and you're right, it's not easy."

Kyle smirked. "I really wish you could have said that before the second semester started." He dropped the smile and sweet voice. "Connie, ever since you started high school, all you've been doing is running off somewhere making everyone worry about you. You lie about it all the time just so we won't know where you really are."

I shut my eyes, trying to drown out his voice but it found a way back inside my head. "Please, Kyle, stop!"

"No!" he stated. "Not until you tell me what's going on." He turned towards me. "You act so strange, more than usual, ever since you found Dad's and great-grandfather's journal. You have been obsessed with our family and dragons."

"I am not obsessed with it!" I yelled.

"Oh, yeah right," he said. "Look, I've gone through your book bag." He grabbed my bag off the dashboard and started to pull out books. "Mom and Dad's college year book, the journal, Mom's date book and printed off articles."

I grabbed my books back and stuffed them into my bag. I stuck my tongue out at Kyle. "So, it fascinates me besides, you like aliens and basketball."

Kyle sighed and leaned back in his chair. "You really don't want to make this easy for me do you?"

"I wasn't planning to from the start," I admitted while tapping the dashboard.

"You're just like Dad, always kidding, trying to keep secrets from everyone. All you let people see is the peaceful side of things instead of the dangers."

"And you're a worry wart like Mom."

"Connie, I see you every day saying goodbye to your friends, leaving to go to either the library, gym or someplace else you never tell anyone about."

"And you're with Kristen all the time and eating chocolates."

"Connie, quit it!" he demanded springing up. "Do you even know why Kristen bugs you?"

I said nothing.

"Kristen is an only child and her dog is her only company besides me. She does it because she's jealous that I have a sister and she doesn't. She tries to treat you like her own sibling."

I couldn't believe what I was hearing.

"Kristen tries to treat you the same way I do, but in a girl's way. Do you know what we talk about?"

I remained silent again.

"We talk about what colleges and university we want to attend. She wants to go to Europe and study aroma's, perfumes where I want to stay close and go to Ravine College. I want to stay close to my family, especially with the baby on the way."

Right there I wanted to spill my guts out about everything I was involved with. However, I couldn't. Kyle opened up to me but I couldn't do the same with him.

I lowered my head.

"Now, is there anything you want to tell me?" he asked.

I mumbled something.

"What?" he said.

I tried again. "I can't tell you."

"WHAT?" he said again.

"I SAID I CAN'T TELL YOU UNLESS YOU WANT TO DIE," I yelled.

Everything went quiet, but I had enough. I was about to break and I didn't want to do it in front of him. I unbuckled my seat belt, grabbed my bag and got out of the car.

Kyle rolled down the window. "Connie, let's talk about this. Get back in the car."

"No!" I screamed. "I don't want to hurt anyone so you shouldn't get involved."

"And you don't think what I'm doing is dangerous," he said getting mad. "I try to be honest with you, Connie, I'm actually trying. Being the oldest isn't that easy and I'm actually trying to take on the responsibility for once. If you don't care, especially through what the two of us have worked on, I won't bother you anymore."

"Good, Kyle," I said, raising my voice. "Maybe you shouldn't. You'll have a great time without me being in the way."

"Fine," he said, fed up and started the car. "I'll tell you one more thing before I erase you from my life. What you're doing with this researching might hurt someone or yourself. So unless you are willing to sacrifice the things precious to you, you better hope that you're ready to take on whatever is coming your way."

Kyle sped off. I watched as rubber burned on the road. I sighed. I felt horrible and asked myself 'was it worth it?' I started to walk up hill where I noticed a vehicle coming down the street. As it drove past me I saw no driver inside. I turned around and watched as the steep hill made the empty car accelerate. Kyle was at the bottom of the hill and on the verge making a U-turn. I ran back down, trying to warn him of what was coming his way. I was too late. By the time Kyle actually noticed the car it had already crashed into him.

"KYLE!"

PART 3

CHAPTER 29

Guilt

I rode in the ambulance with Kyle. I watched as the paramedics stabilized his heart. I couldn't cry or speak; all I could do was stare at the blood that covered Kyle and my hands. The paramedics asked me questions, checking me to see if I was in shock. I didn't answer them, the blood was too distracting for me. When we arrived at the hospital I was checked out by a doctor and then was escorted to the waiting room. The doctor told me that Kyle needed surgery, his rib cage was collapsing and he was punctured in the side. Kyle was then prepped for surgery and went into the room.

I called Mom and Dad as well as Sam. I couldn't handle this alone. They arrived quickly and found me in the waiting room. Mom and Dad ran to the surgery room, trying to get information on the matter at hand.

I ran up to them, trying to explain myself. "Mom, Dad, please listen to me."

"Quiet, Connie," Dad yelled, scaring me. "This is not the time. I have no interest listening to your lies."

"But Dad-" I said.

"No! Just . . . go wait over there," he said, pointing to the chairs.

I turned away from them. I already felt guilty as it was, but Dad's tone of voice was what frightened me the most. He had never talked to us like that before. I wanted out. I ran to the doors at the same time Sam entered. He stopped me and watched as I hugged myself, shaking to no end. I began to cry, I probably looked like a mess, but I didn't care. I grabbed Sam's shirt and cried in it. He hugged me and listened to my cries of sorrow. Sam sat me down and got me a drink of water. From there we both watched as my parents were led into the viewing room to see how the surgery was going.

"Connie what happened?" he asked.

"Sam, mages are starting to attack the people I care about," the cup of water shook in my hands. "James was one of my Guardians and I saw him killed by Kamal. Not even an hour ago I witnessed an empty runaway car crash into Kyle's on Crescent Avenue. They're making me witness their crimes and they know I can't do anything about it."

Sam was silent.

I sniffed. "Sam, everyone I know is being hurt. I can't stand watching it anymore." I put the water down and covered my eyes with my hands hiding my tears.

Sam was quiet. He grabbed my hands, removing them from my face. "Then let's run away together."

I looked up at him, confused.

"I hate the idea of making you suffer. Kamal's obsessed with killing dragons. I'm miserable being with him and I know there is no purpose staying."

"Do you really mean it?"

He nodded.

"What about Nightly, Judy and my Guardians?"

"We'll take Nightly and Judy but the Guardians will have to stay. If they find out about me, I'll be killed."

I was silent. "Can I have time to think about it?"

"Yeah, of course, uh," he blushed and removed his hands off mine. "Call me or use the flash light signal that we created." He stood up and gave me a peck on my cheek. "Talk to you later."

I watched him walk out of the room, leaving me alone to wait for the results of Kyle's surgery. As I waited I began to drift asleep.

Lightning flashed, thunder roared, wind howled, the earth cracked and screams echoed through the night. That is what I heard as my world fell apart all around me. I fell through the crack of the earth seeing previous decisions I've made in life. The first thing I saw was hiding Nightly away from my family when I could have been up front with them. Then next image was me avoiding my friends just so I could go and meet up with Nightly. Leaving them behind was the hardest thing I could ever do. The night of James murder replayed in my mind, over and over again.

"Please, stop it," I begged, rolling up into a ball preventing myself from seeing the death and pain I had brought onto him.

Then, the crash Kyle was in came into view. I remembered running to him, calling out his name to see if he would respond. Nothing happened. I ran to the car and forced the driver's door open. Kyle was badly hurt even though the vehicle that crashed into him was on the passenger's side. I unbuckled Kyle's seat belt and pulled him out of the air bags and onto the pavement.

"It's alright," I said, "I'm going to get you help." I whipped out my phone and dialled a few numbers. All I heard was the dial tone. "Come on, pick up already!"

That's when I felt fingers slip into my hands. It was just like at the last session of the 'Sibling Respect Program' he was holding my hand. It was different though. Kyle was shaking like crazy. "Connie," he coughed, "who's after you?!" He then fell unconscious leaving me with a shock impression on my face. I took my hand back and stared at the blood he had coated it with.

"9-1-1 what is your emergency?" asked an operator.

At first I didn't and couldn't speak. My stomach turned, but then I forced myself to talk. "Yes, my brother was in a car crash on Crescent Avenue. Please, send help immediately," I begged in a shaky voice.

"An ambulance will be there in a few minutes," she said.

"Thank you," I said, hanging up before she could ask me anything else. I looked back at Kyle. His head and arms were slowly being covered in blood and the way his leg looked it had to be at least fractured. I had to look away. The sight of my brother was unbearable. I held myself, crying. "Kyle," I whispered.

I awoke still in the waiting room. I looked up at the clock and saw that it was already ten o'clock at night. Not much was happening. I walked up to the nurse at the front desk.

"Excuse me; has my brother come out of surgery yet?"

"What's his name?" she asked.

"Kyle Whitsburg," I said.

The nurse typed away at her computer. "Oh, yes, he was out of surgery about an hour ago. He should be in room forty-nine," she said.

How ironic. That was Kyle's unlucky number.

I thanked the nurse and walked down the hall to his room where I found my dad and mom waiting by his bed. They saw me and stood up.

"How is he?" I asked.

"He survived the surgery but . . . he's in a coma," said Mom.

"He'll be fine, after all, he is a Whitsburg," said Dad wrapping his arm around Mom. "Come on, let's go home. All we can do now is pray and wait."

I walked up to Kyle and watched the monitor. I listened to the beeps of his heart rate. One last time, before Dad dragged me out of the room, I slipped my fingers into his hand. I wanted him to grip it; I wanted to hear him yell at me, saying that it was his job to protect me not the other way around. I felt so guilty. I should have told him what was really going on, but I didn't.

Later, after an awkward silent car ride home the three of us sat down at the table. A silent car ride home always meant that it was time to sit down and have a serious talk.

"What happened, Connie?" asked Mom.

"Kyle picked me up from the school library and drove to Crescent Avenue. We talked and it turned into a fight. I got out of the car before he drove away and got hit by a runaway car," I answered.

"Why are you telling us the truth now?" asked Dad.

"Richard!" yelled Mom.

"No, Martha," he said, "I want to know why our daughter has been lying to us since the beginning of school year." He eyed me. "Well, Connie, what do you have to say?"

"I say, I've been protecting you and the reason I lie is to keep you safe," I said, raising my voice.

"Do not speak to me like that young lady. I am your father."

"What do you want me to say then, Dad? That I screwed up, so you can feel better? Fine I screwed up, but why are you allowed to hide secrets from both me and Kyle?" I raised my voice even louder. "You call me a liar when really you are the one who's been lying this entire time."

"My life has nothing to do with yours," he replied.

"Yes it does," I said, frustrated. "Your life is a part of mine, Kyle's, Mom's and the baby's. If you weren't so stubborn and ashamed of your grandfather, things might have actually turned out better."

"Connie Helen Whitsburg, you know nothing about my past, you know nothing about what went on in my time and you definitely don't know what it was like for me."

"Because you're a stubborn old man who can't and won't open up to anyone," I yelled.

"Connie, Richard, enough!" Mom intervened.

Silence filled the room. Dad rubbed his hand over his face. He removed it once and looked directly at me. He gave me a look of disappointment and then started to speak in a quiet harsh tone. "Connie, hand over your phone. From here on out you are grounded until further notice."

"That's perfectly fine with me," I said in the same tone of voice. I gave him my phone and stormed off to my room slamming the door behind me.

That was the last straw. For once, I tried to be honest with my parents, but did they understand? No. I wanted out of the ravine, out of this family, out of this life. I opened my closest door and grabbed a flashlight.

It had been two years since I had last signaled Sam or Judy with a flashlight. The only reason we came up with it was to plan what we wanted to do on our free days. It died after we all got cellphones.

I crossed the room, grabbed the code sheet from my nightstand drawer and went to the window. I signaled to Sam, telling him that I did want to run away with him. If it would make the guilt stop then I would do it.

Sam signalled back. If I read it correctly it said to meet him at the baseball field. That was all I needed to know. I dumped my bag out and began to fill it with clothes, food I've stashed in my room and a bag of whisperer pills Baboline had made me. I thought about taking the journal but then I threw it under my bed. The only other thing I took was the picture of my dad and Nix at the nest. I got it out of the nightstand drawer and placed it in the same pocket as the whisperer pills and the school keys Teddy had given to Judy and me. Once the bag was all zipped up I threw it onto my back and then opened my door a little bit to hear my parents arguing.

"Richard, you can't keep hiding things," said Mom. "You're hurting our kids."

"Hurting them? Martha I'm trying to protect them from what I experienced."

"Richard, our son is in the hospital because Connie was scared to tell him something. Kyle is in a flipping coma, Connie's lying to us constantly because you can't show our kids that it's alright to open up to others and now she is using the same excuse you do."

"But Martha," he took a breath, "I really am trying to protect this family."

"Protect? You don't realize it but you're actually hurting them. Connie was lucky to come back after what had to her at the ski resort, but now another one of our kids is in that hospital fighting for his life. Do you want our unborn child to experience the same thing our other children have because I sure don't."

I closed the door. There would be no way for me to sneak out of the house unless those two were asleep or if I went through my window. I grabbed my shoes, slipped them, opened up the window and crawled outside. Once I landed on the foggy ground I closed the window and walked away from my family. If I could I would have said goodbye as I was about to leave forever.

I took my time before arriving at the baseball field. I wanted to remember all the good times I had in Small Valley. To be honest, I never wanted to come back. When I reached the baseball field, I stood at home base surprised that Sam wasn't here yet.

"Where is he?" I asked myself, taking out a flashlight and aimed it towards Sam's house. It wasn't too long before I received a signal telling me to run. "I don't understand. What's going on Sam?" I asked, trying to signal back to him.

An image emerged from the fog. It was walking towards me.

"Sam?" I whispered.

It wasn't Sam. As the figure approached me I recognized the nearly silent footsteps and the shape of the person. It was Kamal. The school wasn't far from where I was. I turned and to ran towards it. If I've learned anything from Malcolm it's to pick an area you know well just so you could have an advantage on the situation.

"Come and get me Kamal. You are going to pay for James's death."

CHAPTER 30

Capture

I ran to the school, using the set of keys Teddy had given me to enter. Once the door shut behind me I looked down the dark hallways. It was rare for them to be so quiet. I reached into my bag, pulled out the whisperer pills and ate an E.N. gain pill. Energy filled my body the instant I swallowed the pink pill. I locked the door behind me and ran into the room I hated the most: the science room. It may have not been my best choice, but I had to choose something that would have my enemy never expect I would hide in.

I hid under of the teacher's desk and turned myself invisible, listening to those carful footsteps getting closer and closer until they stopped.

I held my breath. Out of the corner of my eye, I saw the class frog sleeping peacefully. The doorknob began to twist. I threw a pebble at the cage just knocking the lid out of place by an inch.

The door broke down and in Kamal walked carrying around the same brass, multi-coloured gem bracelet. He looked around, seeing nothing, only hearing the frog's croaks.

"Whisperer," he said in a sick cheerful voice, " . . . a dragon's whisperer. I knew getting close to you would lead me somewhere."

I grabbed a fallen pencil and threw it at the cage giving away my position but it made the frog mad enough to jump out at Kamal.

I took my chance and ran out of there. The frog started to scream then there was nothing. I ran to the library and climbed up the ladder onto one of the book cases breathing slowly, trying to keep myself calm.

Kamal entered the room and began to look around.

"You think a frog will stop me," he said, blood dripping from his hand.

I covered my mouth and held my stomach as the sight of blood made me want to hurl.

"Come out, come out where ever you are."

I stood on the bookcase swallowing my vomit as I watched him go around every isle in the library.

"What is it you want?" I managed to say.

He turned around but continued to walk to the end of the library. "You know you could have made it easier for yourself and family if you had given up your dragon. Think about how much you're hurting the people all around you by keeping your dragon a secret. Think about how much you're just hurting yourself."

"Hurting myself?" I questioned him.

Kamal pushed a bookcase over with only one arm. The case collapsed against another until all the book cases were acting like dominos. I didn't have much time. I jumped off the book case and grabbed hold of a ceiling light but my weight was too much for it. As soon as I grabbed it, we fell onto the ground. I crawled on my hands and knees. Looking down at my body I noticed my invisibility was going on and off. My hand was bleeding. The light had cut it when we came into contact with the floor. I forced myself to run out the door and down the hallway towards the auditorium.

"Come on! Come on! Stay invisible," I said, trying to control my powers. I finally turned invisible.

"Where are you running to?" Kamal asked, still following me. "Where can you hide that I can't find you?"

"Unlike you, I know this school like the back of my hand," I said entering the auditorium.

I ran past the hundreds of seats that filled up the room before I climbed up onto the stage. On there I found a random piece of cloth and tied it around my bleed hand. The blood had been outlining my body. I also grabbed a pole turning it invisible as I backed up against a wall listening to the doors to the auditorium break down. Kamal walked in, grinning.

"So, your final attempt to slip away from me is hiding in the school's auditorium? For a girl who's trying to run away and hide, you're not doing a good job." He chuckled.

"Well my plans kind of got changed on account of someone trying to kill me."

"Do you consider Sam a friend? Maybe a loved one or should I say lover?" he asked. His voice getting closer.

My heart started to race.

"You know about mages and you know about Sam and me both being them. What I don't get is why he likes you so much. Did you know it wasn't an accident that you met him that day your friends moved away? Sam was never your friend to begin with. He was supposed to get close to you so that one day when you did become a dragon's whisperer he would bring you to me, along with that dragon, so I may take it's life and end the last dragon whisperer of the Whitsburg family."

"I don't believe you!" I said my hands shaking.

"The Whitsburg's were the first family to become dragon whisperers or should I say the first humans to create . . ." he sounded disgusted, " . . . the bonds between humans and dragons."

"You're lying," I said, gripping the pole tighter.

"You don't know anything about him. The Sam you know and love along with your family. Even if you tried to connect the dots, those old bonds, friendship and love never existed." He walked up the stairs onto the stage. "You've been played like toy, whisperer, and now the game's over and it's time to put you away. You're nothing but a toy that should be put away."

I swung around. Trying to hit Kamal with the pole, but he caught it with one hand. It was like he was expecting it.

"As I said before, why does Sam like you so much that he would betray his own kind?" He gripped the pole and pulled it out of my hands hitting me with it, cutting my brow.

The invisibility started to wear off as I dropped to the ground.

"You certainly have no fighting skills," he said kicking me over. "You say you know this place like the back of your hand but the thing is I know this school better than you. I've been watching this town ever since it came into to existence. There isn't one place that I don't know the full detail of."

My invisibility wouldn't work. It wouldn't matter if I turned invisible or not. Blood dripped into my right eye and I would still be visible even if I did disappear.

"You're not intelligent and you definitely don't have the desire or have the aspects to win," he grabbed the back of my neck and forced me to my feet and threw me into the podium back stage.

I gasped. The podium broke as I was thrown through it. My body hurt. I pulled myself back up on my feet, using the curtains to do so. When I knew I could walk again I stumbled to the exit, entering the first spring rain.

"Someone, help me," I yelled out, using the wall of the school to support me. "Please, anyone!"

I touched my head and looked down at my blood covered hand. My stomach turned, making me feel like vomiting again.

"No one is going to hear you whisperer. Not your family, not your Guardians, not even your dragon can help you now," Kamal said, leaving the building.

I looked back and saw his bracelet glow yellow and his body started to darken. I tried running but my body wouldn't move. I had pushed it to its limits. It needed to rest but I had no time. I had to move but where would I go? I couldn't go home and I sure couldn't go to Sam or the Guardians.

Kamal grabbed my arm. I couldn't pull away. He was too strong to fight against. When I did try to fight, I would see Kamal's wrist glow yellow then an electric shock would hit me. He did that several times until I was too weak to even balance myself out. I fell backwards, into his arms. I looked up at Kamal as he caught me and listened to his cold words.

"For a descendant from the Whitsburg family, you've turned out to be a pathetic excuse for a dragon's whisperer." He sent one last electrical shock through my body.

I started to close my eyes but not without seeing him in his cruel, murderous mage form. He swung me over his shoulder and carried me off. All I heard for the rest of that night was the rain falling.

A single voice woke me. My hands dangled over my head and made rattling noises. I forced my left eye open and saw a bright light shine through a single window sealed with bars. I reclosed that eye quickly feeling it tear up.

"Well look what's awake?" said Kamal.

I opened my eyes feeling the dry blood over my right eye crack as I opened it. He stood in front of me leaning against the cell bars that separated him from me. He shielded the sun's deadly rays from stinging my face. I couldn't move that far because my hands were chained to the wall above me.

"Where am I?" I asked.

"Doesn't matter, you're going to stay here until you tell me what I want to know. No food, no water until I get what I want."

"You're insane. I'll die," I stated.

"Then you better tell me fast," he said.

I was silent.

He sighed. "You're as stubborn as your old man and the rest of your family. Your whole damn family is the same even your frikin brother."

"Kyle?" I mumbled.

"Even he could tell."

"Tell what?"

"I'm surprised you don't recall. Ever since you and I first met you've always tried to avoid me. The way you always act awkwardly when I'm around. It seems my presence has the same effect on every Whitsburg family member."

"It's not that we're intimidated, we just know when we're around a wicked soul," I whispered.

Kamal banged his fist against the bars making it rattle, I jumped. "Don't you dare say any shit about a wicked soul! I've lived long enough to see them and I know who they belong to." He took in a breath and started to speak more calmly. "You know, it's amazing what kind of knowledge you can collect by going through someone's things," he pulled out the picture of my dad and Nix.

I struggled with chains. They were sharp and cut my wrists. I attempted to rise to my feet but I had no grip, the chains were too low for me to rise and the sight of my blood running down my arms made me curl up, and made my stomach turn. I refused to let my fear take hold of me at that very second. I straightened out the best I could and said, "That doesn't belong to you!"

"You're right," He moved away from the bars, letting the sunlight hit my face. "Do you know how many centuries mages have been looking for the nest? I knew the Whitsburg's had the location, but to have you just fall into my hands with the coordination's is simply . . . beneficial."

I struggled against the chains again.

"Right after I kill your dragon, these little guys are next."

I looked at the little stone unborn dragons in the picture. "You can't just kill off innocent lives."

"No, not yet at least. You'll have a few hours to behave or . . . well; you know what happened to your last Guardian. You'll end up the same way if I don't get your dragon." He left the room with a smile but I noticed that the odd tattoo on his arm was fading.

I waited for the door to close before I attempted to stand again, it didn't work. "Help, help, help me!" I screamed, "Someone! Can anyone hear me?!"

I watched the sun as it rose. It was the only thing that I could use to tell the time. For an hour I continued to scream trying to see if anyone would hear me, my voice cracked several times. No one came for me. I struggled against the chains continuously; they wouldn't break. It was like they were designed specifically for me. They were tight enough that I could just feel the circulation flow in my hand, but still loose enough that the sharp edges could cut me. The blood ran down my arms, staining my jacket and shirt. I lowered my head. The first thing that came to thought was Nightly, but I was not about to bring him here to get killed. He would be better off staying with the Guardians. The idea was not easy to ignore especially when my dragon started talking to me.

Connie, where are you? He would ask. *Why don't you answer me? Has something happened?*

Every time he asked me something, I knew I couldn't respond. It made my heart ache to do such a thing to him. The more questions he asked, the more silent I remained. The more his voice started to waver, the more tears would fall down my face. He even tried to find me through mind sequence but I kept my eyes tightly shut.

Hours passed, my stomach growled like a furious lion, my mouth was as dry as the desert sand.

As the sun set, keys rustled outside the door. I watched as the door knob turned and in walked the guy with the glass eye. He opened the door on the cell bars and then squatted down to my height.

"Now, look what we have here," he said. "A girl whisperer trapped in a cage like a little bird. The funny thing is there is no use for a bird to sing when it can't be heard."

I looked at him and straightened up. "You're the mage who impersonated Sam and got Nicole to fall in love with you. It looks like she didn't take the break up well."

"Ha, ha, very cute, but at the time, her name was Aqua. She was a dragon in her whisperer's body. It may have cost me an eye but at least she can never return to her dragon body. It's gone, along with the whisperer she was supposed to protect," he grabbed my shirt. "And I was supposed to confirm you as the darkness dragon's whisperer at the resort. Who knew you would know Sam well enough to know I was a fake?"

"It wasn't hard, after all, it wasn't how well I knew Sam it was how well he knew me."

"It doesn't matter; right now I'm going to enjoy paying you back for the way you treated me back at the resort."

He slammed his fist across my face making me spit out blood. One hit after another, it seemed this guy just wanted to have fun but I didn't. I straightened out my left leg, kicked him in the shin, bringing him down on one knee, that's when I delivered another kick to the side of his head. He fell on his back. I heard a growl, then he jumped back to his feet in his mage form and brought out a hunting knife from underneath his shirt. He walked towards me, grabbing my hair and pulling my head back, exposing my neck.

"I'm going to enjoy your screams of suffering as I slowly cut you to pieces," he said, placing the flat surface of the knife against my neck. "Before that can happen I still have to find that dragon mark."

He took the knife and started to cut through my clothes. The first thing that was ripped off was my jacket. Next thing that came off were my shoes and socks. He dragged his knife through the fabric of my jeans; ripping them open until my knees were revealed. I dared not to move. Blood covered my arms and a bit remained on my face. If any more was spilt I would have started to lash out violently with more fear then I already had. The glass eye of his glanced up at me as my stomach was exposed. It wasn't until I saw a malicious grin roll across his face that I knew he knew where to look. My head was forced down. I heard the fabric tear off the back of my shirt and I knew he had found the dragon wings on my shoulder blades.

"Found it, finally," he said, getting off me, "it was much easier to find it after taking away your dragon scale," he reached into his back pocket and held up my dragon scale anklet. With one tight squeeze he broke it in his hands. "Now I can start killing you nice and slowly. Scream loud bitch." He held the knife up high and attempted to bring it down on my chest.

Kamal appeared out of nowhere as if he were a ghost, he grabbed the mage with the glass eyes wrist before the knife's tip touched my skin.

"Enough, Edgar," he said. "You may leave now."

"Please let me kill her," he begged, "this whisperer has only brought torment and anguish. I want to hear her cry out in regret as her body is slowly peeled off."

"True, but that's what we all want. For the time being we still need her alive or we'll never get the darkness dragon," said Kamal, "dismissed."

Edgar dropped the knife and excited the room. Kamal closed the door behind him and walked towards me through the cell's door. He picked up the knife and stood in front of me.

"Your dragon's been trying to contact you," he said. "You're refusing to tell him you're in trouble."

"Shut up," I said.

"They found out that you're missing. They are trying to contact you in any way possible. Which is why I'm going to negotiate with them, you for your dragon."

"They would never do that," I said. "Guardians keep their whisperer's and their dragon's safe no matter what."

"Who said anything about the Guardians? I was talking about your family."

"What?" I said scared.

"*Yes,*" he hissed. "You know, families will do anything for each other. Even if it means giving something up valuable to them or committing murder that would make the family prosper." He bent down to my height. "Before that can happen I'm going to need something of yours to prove I actually have you." He grabbed my chin and forced my head down. The cold blade was placed at the back of my head and with one quick twist of Kamal's wrist a thin slice sound was heard and my ponytail fell off my head. I watched as my hair dropped to the ground still bound within the elastic. "This should do it."

I shook his hand off my face and head butted him. "Get off of me you creep," I yelled.

He smiled. A small line of blood ran down his lip. My stomach turned. I looked at the ground. Watching from the corner of my eye I waited to see when Kamal would wipe the blood away. He licked the blood clean off his lip and smiled. How could anyone enjoy the taste of blood? "You are an interesting whisperer, but also a doomed one." He grabbed my cut off ponytail then closed the cell door, locking me in.

Connie, what's happening?

Once I heard Nightly's voice I quickly shut my eyes and shook my head. "No, Nightly, stay out."

Kamal stopped in his tracks. He listened to me. Turned sharply and glared at me. "You're already talking with your dragon."

I opened my eyes and pushed myself against the wall. Fear overwhelmed me as I looked at Kamal.

He unlocked the door and sat down in front of me grabbing my throat and squeezing it slightly. *Listen here, dragon. If you want your whisperer back and alive you'll give yourself up. You will appear, during the day and make sure you're visible for every being to see.* He released my throat. "You better hope he shows or you'll be the one to die first."

He left the room. I panted and coughed, scared to the core of what he might do. The cell door squeaked as it swung open. The main door wasn't fully shut a small light came into the room, my only light. The sun had fully set. The only light that I saw disappeared when someone entered the room. The person closed the door, locked it and fled into the shadows. I held my breath. My heart began to race.

"Connie," said a weak voice out of the shadows.

"Who are you?!" I demanded, releasing my breath.

"It's me Connie, its Sam."

"Sam?" I could only see the outline of his body. Darkness filled the room and I didn't have my glasses to help me.

"Yeah," he said, "I had to see you."

"Sam what happened last night?"

He sighed. "I was packing to leave, after I told you to meet me at the baseball field. I found out someone else knew about our code."

"Kamal?"

"No, Jacqueline," he answered. "She made a copy of my sheet after we made the codes. She watched me signal you and when I was about to leave she trapped me in my room and told Kamal everything."

I gulped. "Sam, I'm scared."

"I did send you that warning, but I see it reached you late."

"No, I should have been more prepared. It's my fault."

"Some of it is partially mine. After Kamal returned with you he found out that I was going to run away with you." Sam stepped out from the shadows and into the moon light that shined through the single window.

"Oh Lord," I said devastated.

Sam had a black eye, multiple bruises and cuts all along the right side of his body.

"I never meant for this to happen to you, Sam. You're my friend I wish you didn't do this."

Sam walked forward and knelt down in front of me. A few tears fell from my face. Sam placed his warm hand against my cheek and cleaned them with his thumb. "Connie, listen to me. I wanted to; I wanted to do this for you. Your Guardian, James, right? He chose to be your Guardian, your protector. He knew the consequences of taking on the role. You, going night flying with your dragon was not your fault. It was a trap. Kamal set it up. Your Guardian just did what he was supposed to do."

I smiled a little. "Thank you."

"Is there anything I can do for you right now?" he asked.

"I'm going to assume you can't get me out of here."

He shook his head. "It's too risky especially if I go for help. When Kamal and I first moved here he made sure not a word would leave this place. This house is sound proof. No sound has ever left these walls. It's pointless if you continue to cry out for help. You'll only strain your voice." Sam went back to the main door, unlocked it, opened it and grabbed a grocery bag. Once he shut the door he pulled out a loaf of bread and a bottle of water. "I can give you this, though," Sam sat down beside me. "Eat and drink up. You're going to need all your strength."

Sam moved in front of me and started to feed me by hand. I was so grateful. Sam always knew what I needed and when I needed it. He first gave me some bread. I ate a quarter of the loaf, licking every single crumb out of the palm of his hand. The water was what I really was thankful for. Sam tipped the bottle up against my lips. It only took a few gulps until all the water in the bottle was completely drained. When I was done, Sam cleaned off the mess on my face, trying not leave any evidence that I had been regaining my strength. For fifteen hours I had been without food or water. Sam was my hero.

"Sam, I need you to grab something for me . . ." I took my time breathing " . . . from my bag . . . In the front pouch there should be a bag . . . in it are three different coloured pills . . . I need a blue and black one."

"You mean the whisperer pills?"

I began to speak normally. "Yeah, I need to block Nightly from my mind. If you can't get me out of here I at least need to forget everything that's going on. I can't afford to make any accidents. If I don't know what's going on nothing will slip out by mistake."

Sam got up and crossed the room. There in a corner, was my bag. Sam unzipped the pouch and took out the whisperer pills. I guess it didn't interest Kamal as much as coordination's to the nest did.

When Sam returned, he sat beside me leaning close to me. "Just pop them in my mouth and I'll do the rest," I said.

"You know, I heard about the history of these pills. I never expected to see them up close." He touched the black sear pill, grunting and groaning as he pulled it out of the bag. His skin started to change into a bluish purple colour. It looked like acid was eating away at his skin. Quickly, he placed the pill in my mouth and then retreated back to sitting up against the wall.

I swallowed it. At first nothing happened, then at the back of my head I felt as if someone hit me with a baseball bat. It was painless after a second. When I turned my attention back over to Sam his hand was bleeding and it looked like the veins started to spread. "What happened?"

"Sear, it burns mages like it does dragons. It hurts so much."

"Give me your hand," I said. He lifted it up. I pressed my lips against his skin, drawing the sear to the surface and into my mouth. I wanted to help relieve the pain but I couldn't draw all of it out. The bluish purple colour faded a bit but at least the veins were gone. "You helped me so I'll help you."

"Thank you," he said grabbing the blue 4-get pill.

"Will I see you tomorrow, after the pill wears off?"

"Yeah, goodnight," Sam popped the blue pill in his mouth, moved closer to me, reached for the back of my head and kissed me. His other hand was placed on my hip and turned me slightly. It took a few tries but eventually the pill was transferred into my mouth. I swallowed it and started to feel the effects of the pill immediately. I felt drowsy. Sam leaned back, stood back up and rubbed my head. "I love you, and I'm sorry."

"What, who are you?" I asked. I didn't know where I was anymore or who stood before me. The pill worked; in less than five seconds, I had forgotten everything.

The person who stood before me gave a weak smile and said, "I'll see you in twenty four hours." Then he walked out of the room closing the cell door behind him.

Night after night Sam would find a way to sneak in and help me. Every time the 4-get pill wore off Sam would be sitting in the room with me waiting to see when I would remember everything. He would feed me and give me water, just like on the first night. Then he would cover his hand with cloth so that the sear pill wouldn't affect him when he placed it in my mouth. The only other thing I would remember from those night's was when Sam would give me the 4-get pill. He always gave it to me through a kiss and only through a kiss. My only wish was to remember his warm touch during the times I was being tortured.

In the mornings Kamal and Edgar would come in and start there interrogation. I had no idea what they were talking about. When my memory would come back I would find more bruises and cuts on my body than before. The one thing I had noticed about the 4-get pill was that when my memory returned I didn't and couldn't remember the torturous events I had been through the following day. All that would come to me was unspeakable pain and the thought of why I was doing this. To protect Nightly. There was another problem though. The more night's I spent being held hostage the lower my supply of 4-get and sear pills became. It only gave me a limited amount of time before I would experience everything and remember it all.

Things were getting harder and harder but the fifth night I was there was the worst of all.

"Sam . . ." I called out, waking from a sound slumber the 4-get pill always put me through before I remembered everything, " . . . it's wearing off again, Sam."

Sam arrived when the sun had fully set. He walked in, locked the door behind him and looked at me through the cell bars. "Don't worry, I'm here now," he said slowly walking across the room. "Just let me grab your bag—oh no!"

"What, what is it?!" I asked, awake.

Sam backed up, his whole body shook. Out of the shadows a figure began to stir. It took his time walking out but the nearly soundless footsteps, I knew them. Those footsteps belonged to Kamal. "How dare you Samson! You go behind my back, betray me by helping a whisperer." Kamal was infuriated. The moon light showed his true emotions as he stepped out. My heart began to race. Sam and I were both afraid of him. "I knew something was wrong from the moment she asked who I was. The cries she made every day knowing full well that no one could hear her and let's not forget that she hasn't passed out from the lack of food or water. No, I should say she hasn't *died* yet. Then I find you sneaking in to help *it* and using the whisperer pills." Kamal pulled out the bag and dropped it onto the ground. He stomped on them, breaking each and every one of the pills.

"She has a name," Sam said, leaning up against the bars.

Kamal took him by the shirt. "Samson, you know more than what you're telling me. What is it about this whisperer that you find attractive and appealing to you?" Kamal threw Sam across the room and when he landed Kamal walked over to him and started to beat on him. After a few hits he began to throw him around again.

It was unbearable to watch him. I heard Sam's bones crack against the walls, cell bars and the door. The blood, the grunts was too much to take. I wondered if Sam went through this constantly.

Kamal lifted Sam off the ground by his shirt. He gripped his fist, ready to deliver another blow.

"STOP IT!" I screamed.

Kamal turned his attention to me. "If you care so much for the bastard, tell me where your dragon hides to end his suffering!"

"Connie, don't!" Sam pleaded. "I can handle it."

"You son of a bitch," Kamal hissed. He kicked Sam in the side and watched him crash into the bars and roll over, coughing. "I can't believe a bastard like you was ever born as a pure blood mage. Be lucky that this is your punishment."

"You're a monster," I spat, trying to look past the blood.

He scowled at me. "You actually believe the shit she's telling you?" He grabbed Sam by the shirt and lifted him up. "It's one thing to make a whisperer fall for you but for you to fall for the bitch, is a disgrace. Do you think that you'll be accepted just because of it?"

I couldn't bear to look at Sam, he was almost all covered in bruises and blood. I could tell he was having hard time breathing. He panted heavily and even clutched his chest.

"It's time we get something straight, Samson. We'll speak mage to mage." Kamal dragged Sam out the door. "Jacqueline, put her to sleep. I can't have her hearing what I'm about to tell the traitor here."

I watched as the school's nurse, Jacqueline, strolled in holding a needle firmly in one hand and in the other a set of keys. She took her time entering the cell, slowly turning into her mage form as she knelt down beside me. It was then I saw a mark in the middle of her shoulder. A mark of a single circle and two shaded ones over lapping it.

"Jacqueline, you don't have to do this. Lives are at stake here." I begged.

"Come on, whisperer," she said, grabbing hold of my arm forcing it to turn over. I fought with her but her strength was too much for me handle in my state, "it would be easier for all of us if you just gave in and told us where the dragon is," she said.

I heard a noise beyond the room, and it didn't sound good. She took the needle and quickly stuck it into my arm. The serum was slowly pushed into my body. Soon I began to feel drowsy. I shook Jacqueline off me. The needle fell out her hands and out of my skin breaking against the floor. I fought against the chains, screaming Sam's name over and over again until sleep had finally overtaken me.

When I began to stir I heard nothing, not a sound was made outside the room and no sound was made in the room. My eyes were slowly forced opened. An image of Sam appeared in front of me, he was sitting on the other side of the bars. My head ached from the drug, it spun and it seemed I couldn't keep my head up without it falling down and rolling from shoulder to shoulder. It took me a while to get my focus back. For the time being I was seeing about four Sam's.

"Sam?" I mumbled.

"So, now you're awake," he said, refusing to lift his head which was faced towards the ground. Shadows covered his face completely, the only way I could tell how he was feeling was from the tone in his voice.

"What happened?" I asked. "I was drugged before I could hear anything."

"Connie, it was nothing."

I didn't like the sound of his voice, he sounded confused, harsh and sad.

"Connie, what do you know of your family's history?"

"What has that have to do with anything?" I asked, confused. I leaned my head against the wall behind me still finding not enough strength to support it on my own.

"Answer me whisperer!" he yelled.

"You're calling me whisperer? Fine, I don't know much. Only that my great-grandfather and my grandfather were dragon whisperers before me . . . but my dad wasn't. He did make friends with mages though. My dad became best friends to two mages named Drake and Shelley Slayer." I had to stay calm. Sam was unsure of himself and I needed him to know I cared about him. "Sam, they were your parents."

"Yeah, *were* my parents?"

"What's that supposed to mean?"

"They didn't just *die*, Connie, they were *killed, murdered* in a fire started by a dragon. Evidence showed that the building wasn't burnt down by a regular fire. It was burnt down by an unknown source, a mystic fire. The only people close to them was your family."

"No, I saw my dad twelve years ago after that incident. He was severely burned and had to be hospitalized for a month and a half. You know you're being told lies and you know who is telling them."

"I don't know anything anymore!" Sam yelled, grabbing his head. His mage form was released. His ears stretched out, his skin darkened to grey and out of the shadows I could see his yellow slit pupil eyes.

"Sam," I said calmly, watching as grief took hold of him.

"I don't know if I love you or hate you. I don't know whether to trust you or my family. I don't even know what's backwards or forwards anymore. I can't be here, I can't go anywhere. I'm trapped in pool of lies!"

"*Sam*, you're having a nervous breakdown. Kamal wants you to do this that way you'll be out of his way while he tries to get me to talk. *Sam*, listen to me, I'm your friend."

Sam looked up at me and grabbed the bars in front of him. My body jumped and my eyes widened as I watched Sam react. "*Are you* or are you just trying to use me while I'm in this state? I've got to get out of here." Sam used the bars to pull himself up to his feet. He looked at me one last time with disappointing eyes then took off out the door.

"Sam! Sam! *Sam*, come back here!" I yelled trying to get through to him. I attempted to get up to my feet once again but like all the other times before I kept falling back to the ground.

"It really is a pity to see two good friends fight," Kamal said, casually entering the room. He looked over at me with his green eyes. A grin rolled across his face.

"What did you do to him?!" I said infuriated.

"Nothing, I just talked with him . . . the rest happened on its own. Ever since you came into the picture; he's been emotionally unstable and can't concentrate on anything around him."

"You killed his parents. You kidnapped Sam and you nearly killed my dad!"

"Not only that, but I killed your grandfather and your great-grandfather, too." He was full of pride, happy with what he did. His dark brown hair started to turn black.

"Why? You had no right to kill them. They never harmed a mage except for self-defence," I argued.

"It's because it was your family who started the human whisperers in the first place. Because of your family's existence, mages lost their original forms and powers. Do you know what kind of powers we used to hold?" He opened the cell door and looked down at me, his skin darkening to grey. "Magic, spells, incantations, potions. The Great Dragon appeared that day and took it all away exposing us to you evil gluttonous humans."

"How would you know that?" I asked. "No one could have known that, it was too long ago for anyone to remember . . . unless you were there at the time it all happened."

He smiled, Kamal closed his eyes for a moment and when he opened them again they weren't his green eyes but instead the yellow slit pupil eyes. His ears stretched out and became the black cat ears.

"518 AD was when I was born. I lived for twenty-nine years until we were cursed. It was all because of your ancestor in 546 AD. He found the nest and with that the Great Dragon and his accomplices. They gave him the mission to deliver eggs to 'worthy humans'. We mages knew what was rightfully ours so we took them back, but he wouldn't give up, just like all of you god damn Whitsburg's, you just don't know how to give up! Your ancestor approached the Great Dragon again and had him take our magic and our appearance away. Ever since then I've been slowly developing my magic skills ready for the day that I would change back into the perfect being I was always meant to be."

"How'd you survive so long?" I asked, regaining control over my emotions.

"By using this," He said raising his bracelet. After showing me the bracelet Kamal pulled up his shirt showing me multiple scars near his heart. "I transferred a dragon's heart into myself, my life span increased unbelievably. I've never aged a day since then. Every century I would have to tear out a new heart though, just because I don't get old doesn't mean the heart doesn't. Each new heart keeps my body young and strong as long as dragons live I can live while looking for the nest." He let his shirt drop down and showed me the bracelet again, "you see these gems? Each one I have possesses a dragon's ability."

"That's how you started the fire. It wasn't caused by a dragon it was the gem, but Malcolm didn't know his dragon then so you must have taken another fire dragon's life before."

"You're not as dumb as you look, yes, I did, but during my expanded life I've been running into your ancestors constantly. They got hold of my spirit bracelet and broke all the gems. I had to keep restarting but this time, I'm almost finished."

I looked at the bracelet. "Think again. You're still missing two."

"That's what you think," he said, lowering himself down to my eye level. "What you don't know is that I already have a light gem." Kamal pulled it out from his back pocket and clicked it into the bracelet. "Believe it or not, this gem came from your grandfather's dragon. I went to India to get the water dragon, when I heard there was a light dragon; I knew she would be the one to give me a new heart. Unfortunately she got away just like that damn dad of yours."

I glared at him.

"You shouldn't exist. I took your dad, held him hostage and used him as bait. Gabriel had to intervene. He was supposed to be dying by the hands of the centagon along with his wife. You damn Whitsburg's are a hell of a lot of trouble to kill. It's easy to kill one of you, like your grandfather," Kamal reached and grabbed my hair. He held it tightly and pulled me up a little bit. "He was easy to kill, obtaining his dragons ability was easy, but killing the next generation is a pain in my ass. Especially Gabriel Whitsburg, he ruined it. The line of Whitsburg's was supposed to end that day, but he had to show up and ruin everything. Your dad was saved but his father wasn't. Lucas Whitsburg and his light dragon died by my hand, and there is nothing more enjoyable then destroying a stone dragon."

"It wasn't his fault!" I spat. "You killed my grandfather before my great-grandfather could save him," I guessed. I looked at the bracelet again and saw no black gem. "You didn't take Gabriel Whitsburg dragon's ability."

Kamal gritted his teeth, dropped me back to the floor and grabbed what was left of my shirt. "He took the blow instead of the dragon. I was on my way to kill his grandson and his children when he intercepted me. He fought for his family to live even though his grandson had cut him out of his life." Kamal released a breath then grinned. "It doesn't matter now, because I have you and you have a darkness dragon, the last thing I need." He brought his face up to my ear, "and I will get him one way or another."

"Never," I said.

"Then suffer!" He grabbed both my arms and sent electrical shocks through my body.

I screamed, trying to get his grip off me. I thrashed around. Kamal placed one of his legs on mine, crushing them slightly. More cries left my mouth as the pain continued. I could tell he had no mercy planned for me like he had for James.

"Where's you dragon, whisperer?"

"Somewhere, go look," I yelled.

His bracelet glowed red. He released heat into my body. It burned me from the inside out. After he was done burning half my body he began to use his brute strength. His power was incredible. I could barely breathe after each blow.

"Don't make me ask again, whisperer," he yelled.

"Screw you!"

No matter how hard I squirmed or fought, he wouldn't stop. His body was too heavy for me throw off and his grip on me was tight enough that with one yank he would be able to pull off every limb I had. I screamed and fought for what felt like hours upon hours of torture. He then released me and walked to the end of the room. From the way he was holding his face I could tell he was exhausted.

"I'll be back," he panted. "When I return you better be ready to tell me everything you know."

He locked the cell door and the main door. I laid back and breathed heavily as I felt pain coursing through my body. There was no way I could go through another attack like that. I prayed to God that a miracle would happen before Kamal returned.

CHAPTER 31

Someone Rescues Me

The sun rose slowly, the stinging light didn't enter the room because storm clouds gathered and blocked the warm light.

"Help, please anyone?" I continued to ask. For the whole night fear had consumed me. Hope felt like it would never come. I could feel death draw close. I don't know why but I started to sing my song. My life was in jeopardy and I just wanted to do one last thing that had meaning to me before Kamal returned.

"Many things can happen, something horrible, something great. The past can carry burdens, dark secrets and lies. The future may hold promise, mystery and a thrill, but the mind should be more opened to what's happening now.

Today is the day to learn and grow. A gift is shown to those who hold promise and gratitude. For they look to today and carry with them a spark. The spark of determination and courage to brighten the day.

Tell me a story from the past, tell me a story about the day that has yet to come, but the one story you can never tell me about is what is happening now. Today is the present and that is all that matters, now."

I don't know how many times I sang it; all I knew was that it comforted me in that cell. That is, until I heard a commotion going on down stairs. I heard footsteps approaching. I struggled against the chains until my wrists started to bleed. I was scared who was going to enter through that door. The footsteps came to a halt. My heart began to race. I watched the door knob, it didn't move. It was quiet. The door broke down, frame, hinges everything.

"Sam?" I asked watching him enter the room in his human form.

"Connie, oh, thank God you're alright," he said relieved. Sam carried a sword in his grasp. It was an antique sword. One that you would find in a museum's medieval section.

"Why are you here? Kamal will hear you," I warned him.

"It's alright, Kamal, Jacqueline and Edgar can't move at the moment," he said. "Cover yourself."

Sam took up the antique sword. I curled up against the wall and covered my head. I heard the sword collide against the bars. The bars were sliced in half. I looked up at him and watched as he did the same thing with the chains that pinned me against the wall. My arms shook intensely as they dropped to the ground. Sam bent down and rubbed his hand against my face. I looked up at him and threw my arms around his body. Tears came pouring down my face. Sam dropped the sword, pulled me in close and whispered in my ear 'I'm sorry'. I continued to cry, soaking Sam's neck. When I finally got a hold of myself Sam took out a single key and unlocked the cuffs around my wrist. My body shook as the cuffs dropped to the ground. The room became dead silent, the only noise were the cuffs, crashing against the hard wood floor.

"Come on," Sam said, helping up off the ground, "let's get you out of here."

My body continued to shake. For the first few seconds, I kept stumbling until I regained my footing. "Sam, it was Kamal, everything was Kamal, he did it all," I said.

"I know," he said, wrapping my arm around his shoulders. "When I ran out of here I actually ran into someone who gave me a good pep talk. I'm sorry, Connie, for leaving you, can you forgive me?"

I gave him a small smile. Leaned in close and kissed him lightly on the lips. "That should answer your question. You did come back, after all."

His ears and eyes changed again and his skin darkened to grey. I looked down and noticed the mark on his chest. The same mark I saw when we were falling off the cliff at the ski resort. It resembled that same tattoo that Kamal had on his arm. The only difference was that Sam had it on his chest.

"What is that?" I asked, tugging on his shirt.

"My birth mark," he replied pulling his shirt down far enough that I could see the image clearly. It was exact same mark Kamal had on his arm. "It tells me what family I belong too and how strong I am. There are three different families for mages. Edgar and Jacqueline each belong to a different family. When we start to die the mark starts to fade as we originate into our original form."

"Wait, Kamal's mark is fading. If that means he's going to need a new heart," I looked at Sam. I remembered what Kamal had told me earlier, the real reason why he went to India, "he's going to go after Pearl."

"I need to get you out of here, quick," said Sam grabbing my bag and guiding me through the house. I leaned on his shoulder, limping alongside him. Every step brought pain.

"Sam," someone groaned, as we walked through the hall.

"Sammy," someone else groaned, as we walked down a flight of stairs.

"Samson!" someone yelled, as we trudged to the front door.

I stopped though. Before we could leave the house I forced the remaining strength in my body to go into my legs. I pushed away from Sam and started to walk on my own.

"Connie, we have to get out of here," said Sam.

"Kamal has the coordination's to the dragons nest. I'm not going to let him kill them." I grunted as I made my way to the dining room. There I found the three mages sitting in chairs, frozen. They each had wine spilt on them. The wine glasses were on the floor, broken. I saw the picture of my dad and the dragon eggs on the mantle. I limped towards it, grabbed the picture frame and dropped it. The frame broke in half and the glass scattered across the floor. I bent down, groaning in pain and snatched the picture up. "I got it."

I began to walk out of the room, panting, but Kamal caught my wrist. His grip tightened instantly. "I'm not going to let you escape just because I'm drugged."

"Let go," I demanded.

Sam came into the room. He had his hand covered in the same cloth he would use to put the sear in my mouth. In the cloth were left over pieces from the pills. He dumped the pieces on Kamal's arm. He yelled and released his grip on me.

"Connie, we have to go." Sam pulled me into his arms and picked me up off the ground. He broke the front door down and ran out of Small Valley, with me in his arms. His speed was still amazing like when I first witnessed it in the centagon's lair. He stopped for a breather out of Small Valley. "We got to get you some where safe."

"No, I need to tell my family that I'm safe and alive." I struggled in Sam's arms until he put me down on the ground. He knelt down beside me.

"We don't have time."

"Time for what exactly?" I asked.

Sam felt my face. "I met up with an oracle after I got the pep talk. He warned me about the death of this whole town," he said. "I was shown a vision. I saw your body hanging from the cliff. Your locket broke off around your neck and fell into rushing water. Everyone dies except us mages."

I held Sam's hands and looked into his yellow slit pupil eyes. "You were told that because the oracle knew you could change it. I know I sound crazy right now, maybe it's because I've been held in captivity too long, but I believe what you say is true. I want you to believe me when I say this. I'm not going to leave, not until Small Valley is evacuated. If another flood if going to happen I want everyone safe, friend or foe."

"Take this then," Sam reached into his pocket and pulled out a small bottle of silver dust. "It's called silver mist. It's a remedy. It works on mages and dragons, but I've never seen it work on humans."

I took the bottle. Twisted the cork off and downed the dust. It had no taste but once I gulped it down I could feel the immediate results. My cuts and burns healed, bruises faded and whatever bones were cracked became repaired. Sam took back the bottle. He didn't use it. He was still injured; I didn't understand why he didn't take for himself.

"Why?" I asked.

"I've dealt with these wounds before. Physically and mentally, but never emotionally, if I lost you . . . I honestly don't know what I would do." He turned back into his human form. "You should go. Now that you're healed you'll be able to notify your family. I'll sound the alarm."

"Sam . . ." I didn't know what to say. He had saved me and healed me. " . . . Promise me that we'll all live through this?"

"Of course," he replied with a smile. "You're strong; I know you can do this." Sam gave me my bag and helped me up to my feet.

"Get Judy, though. Even the strongest of people need help. Meet me at my house when you're done, alright?" I pecked him on the cheek before running back into Small Valley.

Nightly, can you hear me? I asked.

Where have you been for the last five days? He demanded.

Captured by mages, but Sam got me out. Listen, I don't care if my parents see you I want you to meet me at my place and tell the Guardians to prepare for a fight. I want to end this once and for all.

Are you sure you want to do this?

Yes, no one is going to get hurt or suffer because of me. Are you up for a fight, Nightly?

You know it.

Good, but can you work with a mage? Sam's going to join the fight same with Judy.

Are you insane? It's like you want them to die.

Maybe I am insane, but I do know that the three of us have been through a lot. It's like you and me. If one of us does something then we do it together.

Are you sure you want to get them involved?

Whether you like it or not Nightly, they're already involved in one way or another. I won't be able to stop them if they want to help.

You bring up a good point, but I still say it's too dangerous for them.

Well it's not up to you. It's up for them to decide. I just hope we can get everyone out in time.

Is something going to happen Connie?

I stopped running. I was at the park. Being there made me remember meeting Devonburg at the swing set. An old man without shoes sitting alone at a park. I thought I saw an image of him appear and he looked over at me. He smiled and gave me a wink.

Nightly, do oracles exist?

Uh, not that I know of. Why?

One approached Sam and warned him about my death and the town's. I think the dam's going to give when this storm hits.

Why would an oracle approach a mage?

I don't know, Nightly. I'm just going to take caution just encase. I'll see you at my house. I need to talk to my parents.

Good luck.

Devonburg vanished. I tried to reach out to him, wanting to ask him questions and receive answers. I didn't know how to react in a fight or a battle, but I guess I had to find that out on my own.

I got hold of myself and continued to run. When I reached my house I went around to the back door. I'd been locked away for five days. I wondered how they dealt with it. I took in a breath and unlocked the door. When I opened it I found Mom and Dad staring at me with awe.

"Connie?" Mom asked, dropping dishes onto the kitchen floor. She ran up to me and hugged me. She began to cry, soaking my neck in her tears. "I'm so glad you're alive . . . and safe."

Dad wiped his face, tears of joy leaked from his eyes. He pulled out my ponytail he had received from Kamal. "I thought you would be dead," he said, wiping more tears from his face. "I'm relieved you're alive."

"Please, Dad, it's an insult for a Whitsburg to be killed off that easily," I joked.

My dad joined my mom in the hug. He rubbed the back of my head, feeling my short hair. I wish we could have stayed like this forever but I had to get them out of the ravine. I broke up our little family reunion, by pushing them away.

"We got a problem," I said, "this whole place is going to be washed away along with the rest of Small Valley. We need to get the two of you and everyone else out of here."

The siren went off. My dad ran to the window and glanced out of it. Mom held her belly and waited for Dad to return. I lowered my head. I wished we didn't have to do it but we had no other choice. Sam did his job and it time that I did mine.

"Oh, dear," said Mom.

Connie, I'm here.

"Mom, Dad, I want you to meet someone," I said, "and please don't freak out."

I led the way back outside. Mom and Dad followed, anxious to see what was going on. I felt Nightly's presence stand before me. I stopped and held out my hand, resting it gently on his snout.

"Nightly, show yourself please," I said.

"If you're sure," he said turning visible.

329

"A dragon," Mom said surprised. "I haven't seen one since we were in college. Rick, it's like the old days with Devonburg, Drake and Shelley."

I turned around and looked at Dad. He couldn't take his eyes off me. He glanced up at Nightly once.

"Dad, I'm sorry for lying, but I became a dragon's whisperer before you came back," I said. "This is my dragon, Nightly. I love him and I will not give him up for you or anyone."

Dad sighed. "I was afraid of this. Do you really feel that way?"

"Yes, and I'll do anything to keep him," I said, stroking the scales on Nightly's face.

Nightly blew out smoke and growled.

"No, Nightly," I said.

He stopped and laid his head down on the ground.

"You really are a true Whitsburg, Connie. I should have expected you would become a whisperer," said Dad.

"Mom, Dad, I need you to do something for me," I said, walking up to them. "I'm going to sound desperate but that's because I am. You guys are the only ones I can trust with this. You have to make sure that everyone's evacuated from here while I go and do something."

"Connie," said Mom. She wrapped me in her arms again. "I don't want to lose you."

"Don't worry about me, Mom. Please, I need you to do this. I can't do this alone and I don't know who to trust if not my family."

Mom released me, turned and hugged herself. Dad wrapped his arm around her and held her close. From the way they were acting I couldn't tell if they were going to do it. I lowered my head, Nightly hummed trying to give me faith.

"Connie," said Dad, "do what you need to do. We'll handle the evacuation," Dad choked a bit, "just come back alive, my daughter."

Dad guided Mom out of the back yard and out into the public area of the town. I gave a sigh of relief. They didn't shun me like most people would. They trusted me more than ever now that I told them the truth.

"Your family really does love you."

"And I love them. That's why I am doing this for them," I said. "Will you help me, Nightly?"

"Of course I will. You are my whisperer and I'll do anything for you."

"We will win, Nightly. I need a few minutes to get ready though."

"Alright, but you better hurry."

I ran back into the house and prepared for the biggest battle in my life so far.

PART 4

CHAPTER 32

Time of Battle

When I entered my room I dumped everything out of my backpack. From the junk that I had in it I grabbed a fresh pair of clothes and changed into them. The only thing new about the outfit I put on was the jacket Judy gave me for gymnastics training and the dragon scale gloves James had made. My identity was already revealed there was no point hiding it any longer. I was itching for a fight. As I got ready I noticed that the picture of the nest was gone. I searched my entire room until I located it under my bed, next to the journal. I grabbed both, crawled out from underneath my bed and noticed that there was a loose piece of paper sticking out of the journal.

"What's this?" I asked myself, pulling the piece of paper out of the journal I found with my name on it.

"What's what?" Nightly wondered, sitting outside my window.

"I found a letter addressed to me," I said, turning the letter over in my hand, looking at the messy handwriting of a boy. "I think it's from my great-grandfather."

"Read it," Nightly insisted.

I opened the letter and began to read it out loud.

"Dear, great-granddaughter;

I'm sorry if I can't give this to you in person, but I'm afraid time is not on my side. For years, our family has taken the liberty of helping dragons by either becoming whisperers, a partner to a dragon bound to them as if we are a part them, or a knower, a person who knows the existence of the Mystic Realm but keeps it a secret from the Human World.

My son and I became dragon whisperers whereas your father became a knower. Witnessing the death of his father was truly something horrible. I tried to save him but sometimes there is not much you can do even if it's for someone you love.

It doesn't matter if you're a whisperer or a knower. The similar thing about them is that they both have consequences. Anything and everything has consequences, no matter what you do or say. I want you to remember something though. Always remember to move forward into the future. Don't fall behind, stuck in the past, because the decisions you have made are history to tell to the next generation. If you fall behind, grief, regret and revenge take over, corrupting the mind, body and soul. All you can do is learn from your mistakes and use it to make you stronger and brighter. Don't idle and lose sight of life. Live it, love it and go for it because you only have one. Use it to your fullest and make yourself proud to be yourself.

Love your great-grandfather;

Gabriel Whitsburg."

"Wow, those are strong words to keep in mind," said Nightly.

"They're not just to keep in mind but also in the heart," I said hugging the letter. "He knew I would become a whisperer all along."

"I'm going to assume that you're going to bring that journal with you."

"I'm going to have to if we plan on winning this fight. I still haven't read the whole thing and I bet you there are still some battle strategies we can use that we haven't read yet. The more we know about our enemies, the better."

I heard a knock at the door and it opened. Before I left my room I hid the journal under my shirt and tucked it into my pants. I ran up to the front door and to my relief I found Sam and Judy enter.

"Connie!" Judy cried, giving me a hug that nearly squeezed the life out of me. "You were missing for five days and people have been searching for you non-stop."

She released her grip on me, allowing me to take in air. "Well I would have been dead if Sam didn't save me."

Judy nudged Sam in the side and winked. "Oh, so you're the hero of the story."

Sam blushed while Judy laughed. I listened to them before feeling light headed. Something wasn't right. I knocked over a picture before dropping to the ground. That's when my ears started to ring. Nightly did the same thing. I heard him tearing up the backyard and roar out in pain. The ringing wouldn't stop and soon I could feel my ears start to bleed as a melody formed out of the ringing. It was horrible.

"Judy," I yelled, "Get the journal from my coat and find a way to block out this noise."

"What sound?!" she asked, looking around to see if she could hear where it was coming from.

"Don't bother," said Sam running into the bathroom. He returned with a bottle of peroxide and started to dab some on a cloth he had. "This should do it. If the noise is being caused by the flute then it will need to be erased by disinfecting it." Sam put the cloth in my ears and to my relief the melody vanished. I then looked up at Sam. "She's targeting you. Peroxide will only clean your ears of the noise for a short time. I suggest you clean your dragon's ears and head out here."

I nodded. He helped me stand and gave me the peroxide. I took it and ran out to the back yard. Nightly had nearly destroyed the entire back yard and was heading to the neighbours.

"Nightly," I said, grabbing his attention. He growled fiercely. "Nightly, calm down."

"I can't," he said covering his ears. *"The sound is too horrible to ignore."*

"Nightly, I know how to block it. You just have to trust me."

Nightly looked at me. His eyes were watering up. I knew for a dragon, a creature who could breathe fire, water would be a bad thing. I approached him cautiously, watching as he kept jerking his head and claws around. I had to wrestle with his head to get the peroxide in his ears when I did he laid on the ground humming.

"Now, how do you feel?" I asked him.

"Relaxed," he said as he continued to hum.

"That's great because we got to go," Sam said running out of the house with Judy. "If the flutes been played that means Kamal's on his way and he is not going to be happy with either of us."

"Wait," Judy said suddenly, "why's Kamal coming here anyways? Shouldn't he be evacuating along with everyone else?"

"Uh, well . . ." I didn't know how to explain myself. I would have figured she would already know about Sam after I told her a family under the name 'Slayer' was murdered. I've been trying to cover up the trail that would lead to Sam, but I wasn't sure what he wanted now.

"Kamal's a fifteen hundred year old mage who is after Connie and her dragon," said Sam.

"Kamal's a mage? Does that mean you're a mage too?"

Sam looked at me. I didn't really care if he admitted if he was a mage or not but he did with a nod. Judy flipped out at him. Yelling at him why he didn't tell her and then she yelled at me for knowing the whole entire time. She even went up to Nightly and freaked out at him for knowing as well. It wasn't until he snapped at her that she calmed down.

"Alright, now that all the secrets are out of the way we better get out of here and fast," I suggested.

All three of us climbed onto Nightly. Sam held onto me and Judy held onto him. My heart began to race again. We were all about to engage ourselves in a battle that has gone for centuries. We were kids. What could we do? One thing was for certain, I wasn't going to stick around to wait and be killed. I gripped the saddle and let out a breath, feeling my short hair blow back in the wind.

Nightly fly us to the Guardians.

We'll be there in a matter of seconds, Nightly flew faster than ever. He was right. When he turned invisible he flew and reached the secret area in a matter of seconds.

I looked over at the Guardians as each one of them held a weapon in their hand. Nicole held in her hand a circular blade. In the middle was the handle. Malcolm's only weapon was his small lighter and Teddy was armed with a four foot tall lightning rod. Pearl wore thin armour that covered her chest and head. The only person who wasn't armed was Baboline.

Nightly landed and became visible. The three of us hopped off his back. Once Baboline saw us she brought over the same kind of armour Pearl had on and began to place it on Nightly.

"Uh, Nicole, what are children doing here?" Teddy asked.

"Why else would we be here? We want to fight," I said.

Pearl looked over at Sam and sniffed him. She growled and pinned him under her claws. *"He's a mage!"*

"Whoa, whoa, Connie, a little help here, please!" he begged, his face turning a darker red than it ever had been before.

Nicole kneeled down and placed her blade against Sam's neck. "Alright mage, you got sixty seconds to tell us why you're here and what connections you have with the young dragon whisperer."

"Alright, I'll tell you if you get the light dragon off me!" he yelled.

Nicole removed her blade and stood up. Pearl continued to growl, she snapped at Sam once before she removed her claws off him and backed away allowing him to stand.

"I'm a friend of hers. It's true. I'm a mage, but I have never done anything to harm her and if I was with the other mages, do you really think she would be here right now along with her dragon? I want to fight. I want to fight alongside her."

"I agree with him," I said holding Sam's hand. "We can create something better if we work together not against each other."

"I don't really have a clue what's going on but I agree as well," said Judy.

"This is all new to me too but they are right." Nightly wore black smooth armour. He stood behind us proudly.

The Guardians looked worriedly at each other. We were kids, I get that. It didn't mean they had to fight on their own. Out of the four of us Sam was the only trained and was ready for battle. The rest of us were inexperienced and weak. Something wouldn't let me back down and I was sure Nightly felt the same way as well. For Judy I watched her and I knew she was terrified but like me there was just something that wouldn't let her back down. When Guardians finally got serious and showed their game faces on I felt a lot better.

Baboline grabbed me by the arm, I looked at her. She pulled me away from my friends and began shaking me by my shoulders. "This is no game, child. You have a prosperous family who have dedicated their lives to helping dragons and these people are ready to sacrifice their own lives for your protection. Devonburg gave up his life for you to become a whisperer. Don't make him regret his decision."

"Baboline, all I want is to live life and enjoy it with my friends and family. Even if these guys fight for me to live, I'll never forgive myself if any more of them die." I shrugged her arms off, "just in case any of us die I suggest you tell Pearl that you're her whisperer."

Baboline lowered her head. I thought I should give some space but it wasn't until I turned around that I finally heard her speak up. "I did. The five days you were missing was when I told her. Nicole was furious, of course. She had never met me before but she knew I had a connection with Pearl. Nevertheless, when Pearl found out I was her original whisperer . . . well, it didn't go well. For the first time, I actually did mind sequence with Pearl and told her. Knowing how I would react was the exact same way Pearl reacted. Outraged and infuriated. Nicole took it the worst. She was already a teenaged dragon at the time I abandoned Pearl. I took away her promising years and that's what drove her to constantly hide in her whisperer's body. Because of me she can never go back to original body.

The reason why I told Pearl everything was because of you and Nightly. Those five days you were gone tortured Nightly. He couldn't contact you and he couldn't find you. It made me rethink my decision on giving up Pearl. That was exactly how Pearl felt when I wasn't with her. Nicole is still mad at me but at least Pearl knows now. Keep that connection between you and Nightly strong. I'm willing to give you my life so you don't end up like me."

I widened my eyes. "Wow, if you really did that . . . well I don't know what it means. I'm just glad that you stood up and told Pearl the truth. Don't give me your life though. I don't want it."

"It's my choice and I will protect you. An old lady can still learn a few new tricks from you young kids, but like you, you can't tell me what I can or can't do. You and Nightly need to live on together because a dragon can feel every pain the whisperer endures even if they are separated by sear or death."

I turned my head slightly and said, "I'll keep that in mind." My attention then turned to my dragon as I approached him. *You ready for this, my dragon?*

As long as you are, he replied.

"Alright people, here's the plan," Malcolm said drawing everyone's attention. "We're going to lure the mages here. The dragons will light up the sky with fire which will alert the mages. They'll know we'll want a fight. Connie, I want you and Nightly to hide within the trees with your friends. Do not come out unless we look like we're in deathly trouble."

I gritted my teeth. I hated the idea. I wanted to help in a bigger way but I nodded in agreement anyways.

"Great, now Nicole will provide a mist field with multiple illusions. Keep in mind what's real and what's fake. During that time period Pear,

Teddy and I are going to attack. Baboline you are in charge of the medical aid, make sure your homemade pills are ready and I'm going to throw in Connie's human friend to help you."

"Hey, I have a name and it's Judy!" She yelled.

"If all else fails I want you, Connie and the mage to distract them until Teddy is all charged up and brings down the final blow. If that doesn't happen our key goal is to make sure the kids and the young dragon get out alive." Malcolm eyed Baboline. She pulled out an old cloth bag and handed each of us an En-gain pill. I looked at everyone as they ate there's. You could see the energy go through their bodies by just looking at them. It was almost as if you could see a pink colour outline their eyes for a quick second. I ate mine and released a breath. "Now that we are all energized, all pill access will be in the hands of Baboline and Judy."

Baboline went up to Judy and gave her another cloth bag. Judy took the bag and looked inside. She pulled out a small bottle of alcohol then placed it back, closed the bag and tied it to her belt.

"Now, for us Guardians, we will fight to the end of our lives, for you kids you will fight until we say 'get out of here'. Now, let's get out there and kick some mage ass."

"Agreed," said everyone.

Thunder began to rumble in the distance. I looked over and watched the lightning slowly making its way towards us. The storm was coming. It was the exact same storm that came through the night when Nightly hatched. Nightly had to nudge me to bring me back to my senses. When I got a hold of myself I went with Sam and Judy into the forest. From there we all watched as my Guardians split into three groups. Nicole was with Pearl, Malcolm stood by Teddy and Baboline was the only one alone.

I leaned against a tree and watched as Pearl and Nightly raised their heads, opened their mouths and released a colourful, bright, enormous flame into the sky. Sam, Judy and I could feel the heat from the forest. I had to look away because the flame was so intimidating. When the flame died down I looked over to see Nightly coming towards us. Pearl and Nicole flew up into the sky and raised the mist field.

"Why aren't you and your friends invisible?" Nightly asked, standing behind me.

"I don't have your dragon scale. The mages destroyed it when they held me captive," I explained.

"Connie, it was never the scale that turned you invisible, it was just used as a training tool. You've always turned yourself invisible, not the scale."

"That's a sweet pep talk dragon," Sam said, walking around my dragon with Judy, "but we really need to turn invisible right now, Connie."

"Connie, please, you can do it," Judy begged.

I took a breath. "Alright, hold onto me and don't let go."

They took my hands and squeezed them. I had to close my eyes to actually feel a connection to the power. The power Nightly had always shared with me but was never used properly till now. The power flowed through my body and turned my friends and I invisible. To my surprise, it didn't take as much effort as I thought it would. For a moment I was happy but that all disappeared as the mist field thickened. The only way I could tell where anything was if I touched it or when the lightning would flash the outline of a figure would appear.

What's happening? I asked.

Don't know, we're just going to have to wait and watch, Nightly responded wrapping himself around the three of us, turning himself invisible.

Lightning flashed revealing three people at the edge on the cliff side. When lightning flashed again they were gone. In the sky I heard Pearl roar, and that's when the battle started. Fire and lightning attacks came out of nowhere; the blows of weapons against each other were heard and the wind began to pick up. Dust blew in my face; I had to close my eyes for a few seconds before it died down. When I opened them again I saw someone approaching us. I don't know how, but as the figure walked towards us I knew one thing was for certain—it wasn't a Guardian.

"Where are you dragon, where are you whisperer?" Kamal asked in his cruel voice. "I don't appreciate playing hide and seek with you all the time."

My heart started to race. Kamal was getting closer. There was no way I would be his prisoner again. I tensed up. Sam and Judy held onto my hand tight relieving me of stress.

I could almost make out Kamal's image. He was right at the forest's border. His wrist began to glow red but he never had the chance to use it. Pearl had dove down and took Kamal back into the sky with her.

"Pearl," said Nightly.

She roared again but it wasn't a battle roar like before. Something dropped out of the sky and I watched as the dust flew off in every direction. Nightly growled as he heard his dragon friend cry out in pain. I took a small step forward to see what had happened to Pearl, but when I did I felt an arm wrap around my leg. My hands slipped out of Judy's and Sam's as I was dragged underground. The feeling was suffocating. It was like being buried alive. I would have died under there if I wasn't brought back into the open, at the top of the ravine.

I was trapped in a headlock. Edgar stood above me, slowly squeezing the air out of me. Invisibility didn't work when I was being attacked.

"Yeah, I got the whisperer," he boasted. "Thank you Boulder Dash," he said kissing a brown gem.

"That's James's dragon." I maneuvered my body around enough that I could deliver a foot to Edgar's face.

Edgar released me, stumbling backwards. I fell forward, reclaiming my breath. On the ground something sparkled. I crawled towards it and noticed it was the brown gem. I grabbed it and stood up. Edgar was still groveling. I had to move fast. I ran back over to ledge that led into the secret area and threw the gem into the forest.

"Sam, Judy, catch it," I yelled out.

Edgar pulled me back by the collar of my jacket and threw me to the ground. I looked up at him, noticing a tooth was missing from his mouth and a dagger was in his hands.

"I did not lose my eye to a water dragon girl just to lose the opportunity to kill you," he said raising the dagger up in the air.

I rolled to the side before the dagger could pierce me. The blade sank into the ground as I moved. By the time Edgar pulled it back out of the ground I had already regained the ground I had lost and held up my fists. The dragon scales pricked the palms of my hand. They were ready to be used in an actual fight and I wasn't afraid to use them.

"So, you want to fight? I've been waiting for this moment," Edgar charged at me with a firm grip on his dagger. In his eye I saw nothing but a killer's ambition.

His movements were sketchy. When he first attacked I nearly fell to the ground again. Edgar just missed my face, but he did manage to slice strands of my hair off. The gloves came in handy when he attempted to slice and dice me. When I hit the sides of the blade it bounced off the gloves like they were nothing. The only problem was when he started stabbing was when it got harder for me. Edgar managed to get around me and cut the side of my hip. I grunted. Before he could do another attack like that I spun around, did a back flip, landing another kick to his face. Before he could regain his footing I delivered a blow the Edgar's face. Three scratches were made on his cheek and one of them tore at his glass eye.

"Damn you," he cried out holding his face. "You'll pay for that."

Edgar's movements began to speed up. He started to run faster and move quicker than before. It took everything I learned to predict where he would strike. I managed to maneuver my body quick enough that no real damage could be done, but cuts were still left all over my body. Edgar swung his dagger like a mad man, laughing at me as I backed towards the ravines edge where Small Valley stood beneath. Thunder rumbled and lightning flashed. They were trying to cover up the sound of rushing water approaching. The dam broke, allowing gallons and gallons of water to come speeding down the ravine, violently. I looked over and saw the water stampede through, consuming everything under it's wet blanket.

I turned my head for a brief second that gave Edgar an opportunity. An opportunity that nearly cost me an ear. I just managed to block the dagger with my gloves, but not without getting another cut on my cheek. I jumped back away from the ravines edge and touched my face. The blood outlined the palm of my hand. There was so much blood. It was hard to stand up against my fear, but it didn't bother me as much if it was my own blood, it was when I saw others bleed that I couldn't stand anymore.

"Aren't you worried about your town washing away?" Edgar asked, examining my blood trickle down the blade. "No one will survive."

I kept my mouth shut. Anything I could say would be used against me.

"Wow, who knew you could be so heartless," he said. "I thought you were the nice and carrying one."

He made me mad. Without thinking I attacked him, missing every time making me more frustrated. I spun around him and aimed for the back of his head, but he saw it coming. He caught my hand and attempted to strike me with his dagger. I took in a breath and caught the dagger in my other hand, but not without letting out a cry of pain. The dagger twisted in the palm of my hand.

"Oh, now you're a risk taker," he said trying to twist the blade all the way around. "Well, let me tell you something. I'm not the same as the weak mage you know as Sam."

I don't know why, but I lost it when he said Sam was weak. I kicked him in the gut separating the two of us. "I've seen Sam jump off a cliff to save me," I said, delivering a blow to the chest. "I've seen him take on a centagon and survive while also teaming up with a dragon." I took another swing and hit his face. "How can you say he's weak?!"

Edgar caught my next blow and twisted my arm around my back. "He's weak because he fell for you," Edgar kicked me in the back, "and you fell for him, a mistake you made." He pushed me towards the cliffs edge where the rushing water was getting more and more violent by the minute. He pushed me off the edge but caught me by my necklace.

Edgar leaned forward and began to whisper into my ear. "I want you to know that the mage you love will never save you. I'll take back what he gave you. He'll never love again." He ripped the locket off my neck letting me fall off the edge.

Whatever the oracle told Sam was coming true. So far I had been beaten, my locket was torn off my neck and I'd been pushed off a cliff. I screamed as I fell close to a few branches dangling on the side.

"*CONNIE!*" Nightly called out as he appeared out of the cliff's wall. He grabbed me by the pants and pushed himself out of the rock wall and tossed me onto the saddle along with Sam and Judy.

Sam held onto the brown gem which allowed Nightly to borrow Boulder Dash's ability. We flew back up into the sky and as we passed Edgar I grabbed my locket from him.

"Later," I said

"NO!" He yelled outraged.

Nightly flew back into the mist close to the house where Baboline was. That's when we heard the horrible voice that belonged to Kamal.

"ENOUGH!" he hollered as the mist dispersed revealing everyone's location. "Jacqueline, Edgar, line up we're ending this now."

All three mage stood by each other as did the Guardians as they had a face-off with the mages.

"Jacqueline," said Malcolm.

"Malcolm," she replied with a smirk.

"Lead Mage," said Teddy.

"Theodor," Kamal said.

"Edgar," said Nicole.

"Aqua or should I call you Nicole now?" Edgar asked with a sly smile on his face.

"Murderer's," Pearl growled.

"Traitors," all three mages hissed.

"This is your last chance to negotiate with us," Kamal said. "Give us the dragon's and I might let you live."

"Never!" they all said sternly.

"Wrong answer, you just made today your down fall." Kamal raised his gun up to the sky. The gun went off. The bullet flew up into the sky as rain started to pore down. "You die, now."

CHAPTER 33

Mind, Body, Soul Fusion

The rain started to come down hard as if it were hail. The thunder's rumble turned in a roar and the flashes of lightning turned into strikes. Edgar and Jacqueline stood by their leader. All three of them released their mage forms when lightning struck the trees creating a fire in the forest.

"Sam, what are they doing?" I asked.

"Looks like they're getting serious," he said.

"What do you mean? They weren't serious before?" Judy asked. "But the odds are against them. It's nine against three."

"You haven't seen the extent of their powers. What you just saw was a warm up. It's not until they revert back into their mage form that their full power is released." Sam shuddered.

I leaned over Nightly and watched as Jacqueline held up her flute, smiled and began to play. Her melody was different from before. It wasn't hypnotic or had a painful ring to it either. It wasn't effecting me or Nightly. Sam fell off the saddle, grovelling as he held his ears. His mage form took over his body. He turned onto his back and thrashed around. I didn't know what was going on. Nightly sniffed Sam and gave him a little nudge. Once Nightly touched Sam he jumped off the ground, ripped off his shirt revealing his mage mark. Nightly backed away from him. The melody changed. Sam's body moved weird to the melody. He attacked Judy. He pinned her up against the ravine's wall, squeezing her neck. Judy grabbed his wrist and kicked him, but he wouldn't budge.

"Sam, let go! You're going to kill Judy," I yelled.

Baboline approached him. It only took one touch for Sam to react to what was going on. He threw a punch back and spun around, delivering a series of kicks to her. Then his attention turned back to Judy, who he continued to choke.

"Nightly, the flute! We have to destroy it. Sam's under a spell," I said.

"Connie . . . help!" Judy begged, loosening her grasp on Sam's wrists.

"Hang in there," I said latching myself onto Nightly. "We're going to break the spell." Baboline stumbled to her feet, wiped her face and caught her breath. She looked at Nightly and me, coughing. "Help Judy as much as you can. Just try not to hurt Sam."

"I can't hurt him but he can hurt me?!" she whined.

"You're old but wise. You'll come up with something." A cold chill ran down my back. The storm lightened a bit. Nightly dug his claws into the ground and took off.

Nightly sprinted towards Jacqueline. It didn't take long for Nightly to find her. She stood out in the storm. Standing in the middle of the area, refusing to move, unprotected, what was she planning? It wasn't until Nightly was a few feet away that we knew why. Kamal appeared and used the green wind gem to separate me from my dragon.

"Malcolm, cover me," ordered Nicole raising her blade up towards the sky.

Malcolm opened up his lighter. The flame stretched out and expanded. When the fire came in contact with the rain, steam was created.

"Connie, what are you doing out in the open. You'll die if you stay out here," Nicole said throwing her blade at Kamal.

"I had to come out! Sam's under some sort of a spell and he has no control over himself. The source of the music is coming from that flute. If we destroy it the spell will be undone." I stood and watched Nicole catch her blade. "I can't get close to her without her bodyguard blowing me away."

"I have an idea," she said, "and Nightly going to be a part of it. Call him and then I'll show you."

Nightly, where are you? We need you.

Coming. he grumbled. Nightly snuck over to us. *"What's the plan?"*

Nicole pulled in the mist and had it surround her and me changing our images. I looked like Nicole except for the gloves on my hand and she looked like me except for her blade she still held within her grasp.

"The Lead Mage is only after you. We're just something that's in his way. If I disguise myself as you he'll go after me and then you'll have a better chance to get to the mage and destroy that annoying flute. Go, and don't worry I always take good care of my kind."

I watched Nicole saddle herself onto Nightly and ride off into the mist. When they were gone I began to run. Illusions of my Guardians kept appearing before me, making me second guess myself, but all I needed wasn't my vision but my hearing. I darted through the battle field, escaping lightning, fire and wind attacks. Listening to the flutes music gradually getting louder as I approached. The mist began to fade as did my disguise as Nicole. Before the water dragon's ability wore off I spotted Jacqueline. For the first few seconds my instincts told me to stop and turn back. I didn't listen. She was so close and with one powerful punch her bewitchment would end. The scales of my gloves pricked against my palms. She turned to face me as I leapt into the air with a raised hand. She smiled. By the time I noticed, Sam had appeared. He took the blow instead of the schools nurse. I heard something crack as my fist came into contact with his chest. He spat blood on my face. I lost my footing and fell back on the ground, frightened. The flutes melody changed. I sat up and watched in fear as Sam's body moved to the sound of the flute's song. He had to be in a trance. When he looked down at me I could see no colour within his eyes. The blood from his chest dripped down to the grass. My stomach turned. I was the one who gave him that wound. Jacqueline's melody forced Sam to pin me down. He wrapped his fingers around my neck and began to squeeze.

"Sam," I mumbled, grabbing hold of his wrists. "Sam, let go of me!"

His grip tightened. My vision started to blur and no air was entering my lungs. I heard Nightly roar. He appeared behind Sam and whipped him off me with his tail. Jacqueline stopped playing. I cried out Nightly's name as Jacqueline leapt into the air, bringing her flute down against his head. A small line of blood ran down his face. He blew fire at Jacqueline. She retreated instantly. I coughed a few times, before standing. Nightly ran by me. I grabbed hold of the saddle and pulled myself up onto it. Nightly flew up into the sky. He turned invisible and dove back down. I held on tightly as Nightly took Jacqueline off her feet and head-butted Sam into Edgar. Nightly then landed. We both looked around to see most of the mist field gone. We saw three mages, including Sam. Where was Kamal?

"That trick won't work on me," he said. Nightly and I didn't even notice him appear beside us. That grin appeared. He cocked the gun and pointed it at us. Nightly began to run again. "You two aren't escaping me again!"

The gun was fired. The bullet was silent as it sored through the storm. It pierced me through the shoulder. I screamed. The bullet ripped through my flesh like it was nothing. Nightly retreated back to the house. When he finally stopped I fell off the saddle, grabbing my shoulder, panting, groveling in pain. I had never felt anything like it before.

"Connie, are you alright?" I didn't answer him at first. *"Speak to me!"* he demanded, becoming visible.

"I'm fine," I lied, crawling to my feet. The pain was unbearable. It felt worse than when I was poisoned by the centagon. A burning sensation, almost like it was a dragon's fire consistently burning through me. Baboline rushed to my aid. She removed my jacket and looked into the hole that the bullet had left behind. She shook her head and started to treat it. "Judy?" I asked. "Where is she?"

"Sit down." Baboline ordered pushing me down in a sitting position. "She's fine. Before any real damage was done the young mage left. She's just out of air. She'll wake soon." I winced as alcohol came into contact with my flesh. "That bullet went right through you. You shouldn't be so reckless."

I looked up at Baboline and noticed the blood and bruises covering her body. "What happened to you?"

"Your boyfriend is what happened," she said, aggravated. "Before he vanished he gave me a beating."

Nightly rubbed his face against mine. He was scared for both our well beings. Baboline finished applying the bandages then gave me an E.N. gain pill. I swallowed it and felt energy but the pain was still there. My dragon supported my weight as I stood back up.

"You won't be able to move that arm for the rest of the battle unless you want permanent damage. Try not to fight."

She offered me my coat but I refused. I looked over at Nightly. The blood on his head was still there. I lifted my right arm up and wiped it clean. I grunted a little as I attempted to move my left arm but the pain worsened with every movement.

The two of us looked over at Judy. She was sleeping, leaned up against the wall. Nightly stretched out his neck and sniffed her. *"I don't like this Connie. They're starting to hurt the people we care about."*

"I know, but what else can we do?" I asked, holding my left arm.

"Connie!" cried Baboline. She watched as Sam's arms wrap around my head and neck.

Nightly backed away. He knew that in my position I could not move or do anything nor could he.

"Sam, this isn't you," I whispered feeling his arm press against my neck. I held onto him with my only good arm. His body was shaking. He was trying to fight off the flutes magic. He even started to cry, soaking the back of my neck. "Please, let me go."

"Don't you dare Samson," Kamal yelled approaching us. "Keep her there until her dragon surrenders. If he doesn't, snap her neck clean off."

"Get away from her," bellowed Baboline.

Kamal casually walked up and pushed her aside. Like before his strength was unbelievable. Baboline flew into the wall next to Judy. I heard her shoulder pop out of place.

Nightly growled. He dug his claws into the ground. *"You leave her out of this. I'm the one you're really after."*

"Not till you submit to my will." Kamal walked up to me and touched my cheek. "Would be a shame to kill her, do you want that?"

"No," Nightly released his grip and lowered his head. *"You can do as you wish. Just let her go!"*

Kamal grinned. Out of his back pocket he pulled out a hand sized scorpion with a needle as a tail.

"No!" I yelled. I slammed the back of my head into Sam's face. "No one is going to die because of me."

Sam released me and toppled back into Teddy. Teddy grabbed Sam by the arms and sent an electric shock through him. Sam fell unconscious.

"Nightly, grab Connie and get the heck out of here," he ordered.

"Already on it," Nightly moved swiftly grabbing me by the back of my shirt. Kamal reached out and grabbed my left arm. I screamed. Teddy had to intervene. He electrified Kamal's arm. Kamal released me, but I couldn't help staring at the scorpion in his hand. Nightly pulled me away, turning the both of us invisible. He refused to stop until we reached the forest.

Nightly we have to go back! We can't let them face off against Kamal alone. We have to fight.

We can't, we're not ready Connie. You're hurt, I'm exhausted. Face it, we don't stand a chance. Nightly put me down.

I turned and faced him. *I will not leave them behind. I said it once before and I'm not going to have people die for me. If they give up their life for my sake . . . their life matters to and I won't take something as important as life away from them.*

What do you suggest then?

I lifted my shirt and took out the journal. *We have no choice but to use the mind, body, soul fusion.* I turned visible and began to read the book. *Are you with me?*

I have no choice now. How do we do it?

A few pages into the book explained everything. Gabriel Whitsburg drew pictures and wrote down specific instructions. *The journal says we have to drown out everything around us, put our heads together and concentrate hard until our body's, mind's and soul's fuse together to create one being.*

Nightly turned visible, placing his head against mine. We waited, listening to weapons clash, lightning crack and thunder roar. We both grunted as the noise was slowly drowned out by our hearts racing. I closed my eyes and felt my body go numb and move. Something didn't feel right. Our bodies were ripping apart not fusing. Nightly and I both cried out in pain. We were supposed to become one instead our physical forms were being torn apart.

Nightly! I yelled out opening my eyes.

Connie! He cried in return.

"Don't give up, you're almost there," said a voice.

"Concentrate," said another.

"We'll help, you just have to trust us," whispered a third voice.

At this point we had no choice but to trust them. Nightly and I both screamed then all the pain vanished. Our bodies collided. There was no more tarring, but instead relief. Two halves had become whole. We took a step together, sharing one body, one mind, one soul.

"*Mind, body, soul, fusion complete,*" we said, in unison.

Together, we stepped out of the trees and let out a powerful and magnificent roar. The fighting stopped. Everyone's eyes were on us. For the first time I looked down at our body. It was human shaped, covered in black scales. The gloves remained on the hands but the tips were ripped, the finger nails had grown out into claws. The hair was black, left eye was gold, right eye was hazel. Nightly's dragon features stood out the most. His wings stretched out from our upper back and his long spiked tail placed lower a few inches below. The only down side of being one being with Nightly were the wounds we had endured. Every single one was there and accounted for, even the tiniest scratch.

"I don't believe it," Nicole said amazed.

"They actually did it," commented Teddy, picking himself off the ground.

"Incredible, I've never seen something like this before," Malcolm said astonished.

Kamal looked around. He seemed disgusted. "Another mind, body, soul fusion," he spoke, "once you've seen one you've seen them all."

"*You've seen this form before?*" we asked.

"A few times before and they were all done by your ancestors. Mortals shouldn't tamper with things that they can't handle," Kamal scoffed.

"*You make it sound like you're not,*" we said.

"Not anymore," he held out the same scorpion from before and threw it at us. It wasn't a threat. All it took was a small flame to melt the scorpion away to nothing. "As I expected, a human figure that holds dragon abilities."

"*You're not the one we're after,*" we looked over at Jacqueline. Her eyes widened in fear.

We didn't even give her the chance to raise her flute. In one blink we had already flown up to her. Jacqueline raised her other hand, attempting to hit us. We caught it. With our other hand we grabbed the flute. We winced at the pain in our left arm surge through our body.

"*You hurt Sam hoping he would fight your fight,*" we tore the flute out of her hand and melted it with our fire breath. "*Fight your own battles you coward because no one's going to fight them for you any longer.*"

It was time for a little pay back. With one mighty swipe of our dragon tail, Jacqueline tumbled across the ground and fell unconscious.

"Hey, Dragon Girl, don't you dare forget me!" Edgar thought that he was powerful. The only thing that was powerful about him was his cocky attitude.

Edgar ran forward. Slashing his knife around in the air with the same killer's ambition in his eye like before. It didn't take much effort to read where he was about to strike. Edgar was so predictable when he was cocky. Any attack he made, we countered. A few times we had the dragon wings cover our body, having it act as a shield. For our final move against Edgar we glided up into the sky, did a front flip in the air before we dove back down and landed a punch to Edgar's face.

"*No more bloodshed, no more lies,*" we both said. Edgar's glass eye shattered when our fist connected with his face. We watched as Edgar flew into the house, destroying it. He came back out and collided against the solid rock wall. The force overwhelmed him, it cracked his spinal cord.

The pain in our shoulder hurt; it began to burn. When the pain passed we flew over to Sam, Judy and Baboline. My two best friends still laid unconscious. Sorrow came over us, but the pain in our shoulder was the thing we couldn't bear. As long as the two of them were breathing, there was nothing for us to worry about. Baboline looked at our shoulder. She began to treat it, re-bandaging it. We panted. Baboline was slower with her bandaging. Her right arm was in a sling, made from ripped clothing. If we could have done anything to help, we would of, but there was still one more mage to take care of.

The Guardians surrounded Kamal. Each one of them was badly beaten, but they kept pushing; refusing to stop fighting. Pearl's armour was dented and some of her scales were scattered across the area. It was odd, Kamal wasn't doing anything. He had his arms crossed with a smile on his face he failed to hide.

Sam and Judy stirred and awoke. Sam held his head while Judy's jaw dropped and pointed her finger at us. Sam looked at where she was pointing and his eyes widened when he looked up at us.

"Connie?!" they both asked.

"*And* Nightly," we said.

"Wow," Sam rose to his feet and looked at us in awe. "Connie, I'm sorry . . . for dragging you into this."

"*It's fine,*" we said.

"No it's not! I hurt you and Judy."

"You had no control over yourself. We don't blame you."

Kamal began to chuckle. Everyone looked at him as he burst out into laughter. He laughed so hard that he had to cover his face.

"*What's so funny?!*" we demanded, stepping forward.

"You," he replied calming himself down. He looked directly at us. "Connie Whitsburg and a darkness dragon took out two of my top ranked mages and changed ones personality . . . let me tell you something though. You're never going to win. You don't even know how."

"*No, we don't need to know how to win. All we need to know is that we can try.*"

"Then try to stop me." Kamal's wrist glowed green. The surrounding wind bend to his will. All he did with it was blow the Guardians away from him. Then his wrist glowed white. He stood before us in an instant. It was no surprise; we were the ones he was after.

Kamal hit our wounded arm forcing us to change locations. We grabbed him by the shoulders and took him with us to the middle of the secret area. Kamal kicked us off him and watched as we regained our footing and held our shoulder panting as the gunshot wound began to bleed again. Kamal smiled. He used the light gem again to appear before us. He then struck the gun against our face. We stumbled back and felt another blow hit us on the other side of the face. Our panting grew worse. When Kamal raised the gun again we grabbed his hand. We gripped so hard that our claws went into his skin. We raised a fist ourselves but Kamal caught it. He didn't care that there were claws in him or not. All he wanted was to kill us.

"Give up?" he asked.

Our tail swished back and forth. "*Never!*" We wrapped our tail around Kamal's ankle and threw him up in the air. We flew up and slammed our fist against his stomach. He crashed into the ground, creating a crater below him.

We knocked the gun out of his hand and held it in our own. We pointed it at Kamal with a trigger standing in between us and the death of a cruel, heartless mage.

"Go ahead," he coughed. Blood outlined a side of his face. "Prove that you're stronger than your family members before you."

We eyed him. The pressure was intense with everyone watching us, waiting to see what we would do. We were about to the unspeakable, and yet we couldn't do it.

CHAPTER 34

The End

We lowered the gun and shook our head. "*No.*"

Our bodies separated. What was one became two. A human and a dragon stood by each other proud to be who they were.

"It's not our life to take." I looked at Sam, his chest had been bandaged as well as his left arm. He walked up to me. "Sam, you have had to put up with him for most of your life." I handed the gun over to him. "You should choose if he should live or die."

Baboline and Judy were already out on the battlefield, treating the Guardians wounds. Judy looked at me as she treated Malcolm. She showed me a face of fear. Judy feared Sam as he took the gun out of my hand. All eyes were on Sam now. He cocked the gun and aimed it at his wounded, defenceless cousin. He shot a bullet, however it didn't pierce Kamal at all. Instead it lay by his head only a few inches away.

Sam took in a breath. "If I killed you, I'd be no better than the murderous mage you've let yourself become. Keep your pathetic life knowing you were defeated by what you hated most of all." Sam tossed the gun on the ground and wrapped an arm around me.

I flinched a little as he moved my left arm. I leaned my head on Sam's shoulder and walked with him.

"Let's go find you parents," he said, feeling my short hair.

I nodded and hugged him tightly, closing my eyes as I embraced him.

I felt Sam tense up. Looking up I saw his ears twitching and then his eyes widened. "He's not giving up."

Sam pushed me to the ground and then quickly turned around. Kamal had risen and slashed Sam's chest with the gun. Sam slowly fell to the ground, his bandages were cut open and more blood raced down his chest.

"That was supposed to be for the whisperer, idiot," Kamal kicked Sam to the side. He then raised the gun to my face. "Now, I'm not dying till I have your dragon and you are dead." I watched Sam's blood drip off the gun making me feel nauseous.

"I'll never let you," growled Nightly, appearing behind Kamal.

"Perfect," he said pulling out another scorpion and shoving it into a crack of Nightly's armour.

"NIGHTLY!" I cried out.

I stumbled to my feet and shoved Kamal aside. Nightly was dying right in front of me. I watched the colour of my dragon fade back to the stone grey his egg was once. He collapsed to the ground, unable to move and he could barely speak.

In between the pinchers of the scorpion a darkness gem started to develop.

"No, Nightly, stay with me!" I begged trying to remove the scorpion.

"That won't work," Kamal chuckled.

"Shut up! SHUT up! SHUT UP!" I yelled as I continued to pry the scorpion out of Nightly. It wasn't until the gem was complete that the scorpion came out. I threw it aside and hugged my dragon's head.

Nightly eyes were frozen open. He was stone cold, he had died. I began to cry. Kamal grinned as he grabbed the scorpion and took the gem out of its pinchers.

Nightly had turned to stone. He left me; I didn't want him to go. I trained to protect him, I trained hard to build our bond, and yet I let him die.

"Nightly, please don't die," I sobbed. "You can't die!"

I heard Kamal chuckle again as he placed the darkness gem in his bracelet. "Finally, now, no one can stop me as I take on the perfect form."

"What?" I whispered looking up at him.

Once Kamal pressed the darkness gem into the bracelet a huge gust of wind blew up and a blinding grey light hid Kamal from view. Sam, Judy, my Guardians, Baboline and I were pinned against the wall.

"Connie, what's happening?" Malcolm yelled.

"Kamal killed Nightly, he took his ability, and now he's completed his collection of the seven regions," I replied.

The gust of wind stopped and all of us fell to the ground. When I raised my head and focussed my eyes on Kamal, he was in the same form that Nightly and I were in when we fused ourselves together. Instead of black scales, his were grey. His eyes remained yellow with slit pupils. The bracelet was fused into his skin; it became a part of him with all seven gems visible for everyone to see including the earth gem. Sam must have given it to him while he was under Jacqueline's spell. There was no other explanation.

The sight of him made me remember of those grey eyes when Nightly first hatched. I felt them stare at me. The creature who owned the eyes laughed.

"Finally, gaze upon the perfect form, you pathetic mortals," he boasted. "I've become the Great Dragon himself."

"What's he talking about?" I asked.

Sam crawled towards me and tilted his head up. "It has been written that if a mage collects all seven regions in this case the dragon's abilities they will become one of the most powerful dragons themselves . . . with unlimited power."

"Is there any way to stop him and revive Nightly?" I asked.

"Your dragon is only encased in stone; he's not dead yet. A dragon can be revived as long as their soul can return to its original body. We'll have to move fast because I can guarantee if the stone body is destroyed; he's dead."

"I have to save Nightly!" I forced myself to stand.

"Connie, you're no match for him," Sam said, sitting up.

"Neither are you in your condition," I said, examining him along with my Guardians.

"We're your Guardians," said Nicole, rising off the ground panting. "We'll never forgive ourselves if we let you or Nightly die. If there is a chance to save him we'll do all we can to help." Her forehead and right arm was bleeding.

"He's the first dragon I've seen in years," said Pearl.

"You two . . . gave us a reason to be Guardians," said Malcolm leaning on the ravines wall. "I wouldn't have my life any other way."

Nicole lifted her shirt up a bit revealing her whisperer's dragon mark: a dragons claw. Teddy had a different shaped claw on his ankle and so did Malcolm. Malcolm pulled the shirt covering his shoulder down. Baboline lifted up her hair and revealed the light dragon mark: the head of the dragon. Then all marks began to glow and so did Pearl.

"Full power release," they all said as their dragon marks took on the colours of their region.

I did the same thing. I wobbled as I moved my shirt sleeves down revealing the dragon wings on my back that began to glow black. "Full power release." Any power that Nightly still had was transferred to me.

Baboline and Judy stayed back, treating Sam and watched Nightly's progress. Judy gave each of us an en-gain pill but handed me a black sear pill.

"What's this for?" I asked.

"It's just a hunch, but I think you're going to need it, so hold onto it," she said.

"Thank you," I said, placing the black pill in my pocket, "please take care of Sam."

"He'll be fine. Go already," said Baboline.

I stood with my Guardians our marks glow vanished. Everyone was charged and weapons were ready to strike.

"You want to take me on," Kamal grinned. "Then it will be a pleasure to try my new powers on you, especially you," Kamal lifted his arm and pointed a freakishly long finger specifically at me, "*new ex-whisperer.*"

I grinded my teeth, feeling the anger build up inside me but then it went away when Malcolm laid his hand on my shoulder. He didn't have to say anything for me to know the exact words that would leave his mouth. Keep yourself calm; don't let him get to you and focus."

"Come on; show me what you've got!" Kamal said, trying to antagonize us.

I turned invisible instantly. Nicole recreated the mist field and had Malcolm back it up. Malcolm took out his lighter, stretched out the little flame and created steam as the rain came in contact with the fire. Teddy spun his lightning rod in his hand and slammed it on the ground, creating a large electric wave that was aimed for Kamal. We all waited to hear if Kamal would cry out in pain or make some kind of sound. I went into the steam where Kamal was supposed to be, but he wasn't. My heart raced and slow, harsh breaths escaped my mouth. Not a sound was heard from anywhere.

"Where are you Whitsburg?" I heard Kamal hiss, breaking the silence. "I'm going to end your family's bloodline. You're not even going to have the chance to meet the new family member."

I saw a figure. It had wings and tail. It had to be Kamal. I started to run towards him and take a few swings but it was only an illusion. I turned around only to have my throat grabbed by Kamal. He lifted me up and somehow shut off my invisibility.

He grinned and pulled me in close to his face. "You have to be the most annoying whisperer I had ever hunted, but you are nothing without people around you. Whereas I have the strength of a billion humans and need no one."

I spat on his face. "Go die in a hole!"

Pearl appeared and took me by the shirt tossing me over to Nicole. Nicole caught me placed me back on my feet.

She grabbed my good arm and said, "Stay invisible, don't you dare show yourself with him around."

I did as she told me, but Pearl drew my attention. She cried out. When I looked at her, patches of scales were missing and blood poured out of the surface of her body. My stomach turned, but I couldn't look away. Kamal avoided Pearls jaws of death and grabbed her by the tail. Pearl's special ability couldn't help her. Kamal used the power of the light gem to hold his grip on her so she couldn't get away. What came next was unbearable; he threw Pearl into the ravine's wall. He went up to her and took an ear. Pearl roared out in pain, Kamal laughed and to end his fight with the dragon he hit the wall with unspeakable strength, making the wall collapse on her.

"NO!" screamed Nicole.

Teddy lost his temper; he started to swing his lightning rod letting loose random blasts of lightning. Kamal stood still. He collected the power; it didn't even damage him, when Teddy was done attacking he should have moved. I stood there and watched as Kamal flew up to Teddy and throttled him with his own attack. Teddy dropped. His neck was burnt to a crisp. I would have thought he was dead if I didn't see him move his hands to cover up his neck.

I walked around, watching as everyone's location was slowly revealed. The mist field was fading and it was only a certain amount of time before Kamal got to each and every one of us.

Malcolm and Nicole teamed up. They realized that attacking Kamal one on one had no effect. Nicole created a new mist field so dense you couldn't even see your hand in front of your face. The rain lightened up, making it easier for Malcolm to use his fire. I lost Kamal. The last thing I saw him do was sink into the ground.

"Nicole, he's below you!" I yelled, trying to find my way to her.

By the time Nicole heard me, she had already sunk down into the ground. Her head was the only thing that stayed above the dirt.

"Malcolm, burn the ground," she yelled.

The mist began to fade. Malcolm lit his lighter and set most of the ground on fire, but Kamal wasn't underground anymore. When the mist began to fade I scanned the ground, waiting to see when he would emerge. He did, but like me he was invisible. As I avoided the flames of the fire I watched as they outlined the body of Kamal, he was casually walking through it. I backed up into Malcolm; he quickly shoved me aside before he was thrown off his feet by a powerful wind.

"Connie, get out of here!" he ordered, holding his rib cage.

Kamal stood before him grinning with delight. Malcolm quickly lit another flame and shot it directly at him. That did nothing. Kamal threw the attack back along with a tornado. The tornado consumed him and then lit on fire. I heard gasps coming from it. The wind died down but the fire didn't. Malcolm was left on the ground gasping, his clothes on fire. He had third degree burns all over him. I felt so helpless. Kamal turned his head slightly and looked in my direction like he knew where I was.

"Now, there's only one left," he said.

I took in breath and with that a chance. My footsteps varied. I was trying to confuse him by sprinting, maneuvering in a way that would have him second guess himself. I lifted my right arm up, tightened my grip and ran up to him. After raising my fist I threw it, but he caught it. Kamal grinned as he cut off the circulation in my right hand.

"There you are," he gloated, grabbing my wounded shoulder, squeezing it.

I screamed, as he cancelled out my invisibility. He squeezed harder; it seemed my cries of pain was what he enjoyed most of all. I knelt down on one knee as if I was bowing to him.

"Your abilities won't work, I have the original power source, as long as I can touch you, you'll never be invisible again." I looked up at him panting. "I'll kill you first, then I'll finish off your Guardians, once they're dead I'm going after the light dragon. After I obtain my new heart I'm going after the townspeople you saved then a new era will start, the era of the mages. No one will rise against me once you fall."

I looked up at his eyes; there was nothing in them except for greed and his lust for power. "I'll never let that happen," I whispered barley loud enough for him to hear me.

He grinned and grabbed me by the throat tossing me up in the air. He flew up after me and slammed his fist on stomach. Blood escaped from my mouth as I crashed back into the earth. Dirt filled my lungs as I took in deep breathes and blood dripped out from my stomach. I pushed myself up and coughed out more blood. I couldn't take much more of this. Kamal wrapped me in his tail, lifting me up to his face. He grabbed my throat and laid his tail back on the ground.

"No one can stop me," he cocked his gun and aimed it in the space between my eyes. "You're as good as dead."

I closed my eyes feeling my body being overtaken by fear, but I regretted nothing. I didn't want to die but if I did, the decisions I made during my life were well worth it. My family and friends were the best. My body relaxed and I felt all my fear leave me.

"No, you can't give up." That voice belonged to Sam. Kamal cried out in pain. I opened my eyes immediately to see Sam holding Edgar's dagger. He had stabbed Kamal in his tail. "CONNIE!" Sam yelled, drawing me to my senses.

"You're a nuisance now," Kamal said, whacking Sam with his tail.

"SAM!" I yelled forcing my body to move. Kamal turned his attention back towards me. Determination was what he saw in my eyes. He was stunned as I slammed my fist into his face. He released me and stumbled back. While he did that I took the gun and ran.

"WHITSBURG!" Kamal roared.

I ran back into the trees and held onto the gun with dear life. This thing was important to Kamal, but why? It was a special gun, I could even see that. The design, the workmanship, everything about it told me it was designed in the Mystic Realm but made for both worlds.

"Come out, Whitsburg!" Kamal ordered. "Bring me that gun or I'll kill Samson and your dragon for good."

The hairs at the back of my neck stood up. I glanced behind the tree and watched Kamal walk up to Nightly's stone body with Sam wrapped in his tail, being dragged behind him.

I looked down at the gun and watched as a letter slowly carved itself into it.

"What the-" the letter 'W' appeared.

"I want that gun now!" Kamal roared.

I stepped back out into the open. Baboline and Judy were nowhere to be seen the same was with the Guardians. I focused my attention on Kamal and walked up to him.

He took Sam by the arm, forcing him to stand up and then grabbed him from the back of his neck.

"I'll only give you the gun when I know Sam and Nightly are safe," I said.

"You're a little late with your demands, Whitsburg," Kamal replied.

"How important is this gun to you?" I asked, grasping it with two hands. My left arm ached, but it had to be done. "I can break it easily with these gloves and I can do it quicker than you can kill both Sam and Nightly."

"Alright," he let go of Sam. He stepped forward, his wrist glowing white. He used the light gem to get behind me and grab the gun out of my hand.

I turned around and looked at him, astonished.

"I win, Whitsburg," he cocked the gun, but realized something was wrong. The gun started to burn him. He dropped it and looked at the letter engraved on it then back at me. A small smile crept across his face. "Well, I guess there is more to you then I knew. He'll be pleased."

Words didn't exit my mouth only a cry as I stomped down on the gun breaking it in two.

Kamal stared at me. "You just sealed your fate, girl, can't you see that no one can stop me."

"No, I'll stop you." I stomped down on that gun again and again. This gun was nothing like what we humans carried. It was fragile and it didn't take much effort to break it.

Kamal dropped his grin and back handed me towards Sam. When I landed he helped me back up. For a brief second the two of us smiled at each other. "The reason why I fight is to live on with my friends and family," I said to him.

"I'll kill you with my bare hands," Kamal roared, flying towards us. He wrapped his tail around me. "You want to be a whisperer? Then die as a whisperer."

He took me up high into the sky. The rain stung as it hit my bare face. When we were out of the storm clouds Kamal loosened his tail's grip from around me and grabbed me by the throat with his hands again. He tightened his grip as I grabbed his wrist with my one good arm.

"You'll die by my hands and my hands alone, Whitsburg. You see how high we are. You'll never survive, even if you get away from me. Do you have any last words, ex-whisperer?"

"Yeah," I coughed, reaching into my pocket. "Have a sear pill." I shoved the black pill into his mouth and watched as he lost power, loosening his grip on me. I grabbed the black gem from his wrist and yanked it out of his skin.

Even if he was a dragon, he would still be affected by sear.

"Nightly, I'm coming," I yelled, kicking Kamal off me. I fell back into the storm cloud.

Kamal started to revert back to his mage form and fell after me.

I exited the storm cloud and watched as the ground was gradually getting closer. "Pearl, wake up, I need you!" I called out, watching as Kamal tried to catch up to me.

It wasn't until Kamal got a hold of my shoe that Pearl came and rescued me. I took hold of her armour and slipped my shoe off before Kamal could grab hold of my ankle.

"You're late," I said.

"Better late than never," she replied as we landed. She was exhausted from fighting. Blood ran down the side of her head and that's when I actually threw up. Pearl shook me off her and growled at me. I wiped my mouth and looked up at Pearl. She wasn't going to last much longer in this battle.

I leaned against Pearl, regaining my footing. From there I walked up to Nightly. I refused to lose him. I threw the gem on the ground, it broke and it released a black dragon. He hummed and returned back into the stone body, reviving Nightly.

Welcome back partner, I said hugging his head.

Good to be back. His eyes returned to their original starry gold colour and his body a night black. He hummed as I hugged his head.

Baboline and Judy walked over to us. They were carrying Nicole, who they had to dig out, and laid her by a conscious Teddy and Malcolm. None of them could move and neither could Sam. Sam sat and held his ribs, panting.

"He's back," I said, tears of joy falling down my face.

"NO!" Kamal yelled, standing. "I will not lose! I refuse to lose!" His body was crushed in multiple parts and yet he was standing and living. Blood covered half his body but he just wouldn't die even after a sear pill was shoved down his throat.

"This is crazy!" I stated.

"Might I suggest a soul blast like the one we did against the centagon?"

"Do you think it will work?"

"It has to, we have no other choice."

Nightly stood up alongside me and faced Kamal. He was furious with us. The bluish purple colour that was left behind by the sear pill was clearly visible upon his neck and face.

Nightly stood behind me and touched my back releasing a huge amount of our energy. We stood there and felt our power drain; we dropped to the ground. I went up on my knees and watched to see if anything would happen. Nothing did.

I was shocked. "It didn't work."

"How's that possible?" panted Nightly.

"Because it was weak," Kamal boasted. "Just like each and every one of you. Where I have mastered six regions and have become immune to all dragons and their whisperer's attacks as well as sear . . . and it only took fifteen hundred years to learn," he laughed.

I stumbled to my feet, feeling the sweat and blood mix on my face. I leaned against Nightly before toppling back to the ground. Then, Sam grabbed my bare foot.

"Take my remaining energy and finish this," he said.

"Same here," said Judy, placing her hand on my shoulder.

The Guardians and Baboline placed their hands on Nightly.

"One last try," I suggested.

He nodded.

Kamal's eyes widened when he saw what we were going to do. "Jacqueline, Edgar, give me your remaining energy." A purple glow rose from the two remaining mages and was transferred into Kamal.

Nightly touched my back again and we both said, "*Soul Blast!*"

Kamal put his hands out, stopping the Soul Blast, but he was struggling. He dug his feet into the ground but still managed to hold himself together. "Ha, it's going to take more than this to stop me. I am immortal. I am God!"

"I'm almost out of energy," I told Nightly. "If we take any more energy from ourselves or anyone else, people are going to start dying."

"Take some of our energy then," said a familiar voice.

"Keep going. You'll beat him," said a second voice

"We'll help you all the way through," said the last voice.

I rolled my head back over my shoulder and watched three figures form behind us.

"I trust you." With that said an over whelming power overflowed our bodies and strengthened our soul blast.

Once again I stepped forward. I yelled as well as Kamal as he took hold of another Soul Blast. Energy ran through my body, it had not limit unlike Kamal. One final battle cry left my lips before Kamal collapsed and took on the full effects of an Unlimited Soul Blast. He let out a cry of defeat as our attack consumed him, incinerating him. All that was left of the Lead Mage was his brass bracelet along with the gems that it held.

I dropped to the ground and turned over onto my back. I saw the three figures that helped us. One was a huge dragon, the other a griffin, and the third was a phoenix.

"Incredible," said Nicole.

"It's the Great Dragon," said Pearl.

The Guardians went onto their hands and knees and bowed before the Great Dragon.

He was a gold colour, with white eyes filled with life. The griffin had a white eagle head, golden lion body and giant white eagle wings. His brown eyes filled with courage. The phoenix was a twelve foot tall bird on fire. Her orange eyes were full of love.

"Who are you?" asked Sam, sitting up.

"*I am known as the Watcher. I watch from the heavens and send either my Protector or Helper to save the ones in need,*" said the huge dragon.

"I am known as the Protector," said the griffin. "I take on the pain and suffering of those who hurt in the world and treat it as my own."

"And I am known as the Helper. I lend my power to anything or anyone who would use it for a good cause," said the phoenix.

"Why did you help us?" asked Judy.

I looked at Judy, surprised. "You can understand them?"

"Yes I can," she said. "I can hear them, but only them."

"*So she still can't hear me,*" said Nightly, lying beside me.

Baboline took in slow shallow breaths. "I don't believe it. Devonburg said there were three great beings watching over the Mystic Realm but I never expected him to be right." Baboline held her side, feeling pain overwhelm her body.

"*You have endured much,*" said the Great Dragon. "*You deserve a long rest.*"

"What about Pearl? If I go she'll die as well," said Baboline.

"*I'm also tired so I'm fine with it. At least in death we can be together and not apart. I've experienced much and found out a lot of things in this world, but now that I can pass on my will to the young dragon, I'm ready to go.*" Pearl stood by Baboline and helped her up onto her feet.

"Pearl," said Nicole walking up to her. "I'll miss you. You helped me get used to my whisperer's body."

"*I love you Aqua. You've helped me through a lot too.*"

Nicole and Pearl hugged each other saying their last good byes.

"*Nightly you stay strong and work hard. Human, whisperer, Connie, I was wrong about you. You are worthy to be a dragon's whisperer after all. But if you screw up, I'll come back and personally tear you limb from limb.*"

"Thanks Pearl, I appreciate it," I said. She never changed, not even for a brief second.

"*Rest in peace you two. You deserve a long-awaited rest,*" said the Great Dragon releasing them from their mortal form and allowing their bodies to turn into a light. The light rose up and scattered the clouds up in the sky, allowing sun light to pass through.

"Goodbye," said Teddy and Malcolm.

"Take care," said Nicole.

"Wow!" said Judy amazed, "that's incredible."

"Now we must release the trapped spirits within the gems." The griffin went over to Kamal's remains, grabbed the bracelet and dropped it before the Guardians. "Each of the Guardians will release their own dragon's soul, the mage will release the earth gem, the human the wind gem and you, young whisperer the light gem."

Each of the Guardians grabbed their dragon's region coloured gems and broke them, releasing their dragon spirits. Inferno, Hercules and the original human Nicole broke out and faced their once partners. They all smiled at each other before the spirits vanished into the sky.

"Goodbye," they all said in a happy voice.

Sam broke the earth gem and watched Boulder Dash come out. I pulled Teddy down and whispered into his ear. Not long after, Teddy went into the remains of the house and brought out James's cowboy hat and gave it to Boulder Dash. Boulder Dash smiled, flew around, grabbed the hat and vanished.

Judy broke the wind gem and freed a wind green dragon named Cloud. She looked like Skier, Devonburg's dragon. She smiled then vanished as the wind blew by.

I, on the other hand, didn't break mine.

"What's wrong Connie?" Malcolm asked, standing over me.

"I'm not the one who should destroy this gem. My dad should. It was his dad's dragon after all," I said sitting up. "He'll be happy to see it anyways."

"A wise decision, young whisperer," said the Helper. "You were able to accept your calling as a dragon's whisperer and you also accepted the ones around you whom you love. Not many whisperers can do that."

For you bravery, determination and love for others your town will be restored and shall be protected through many year to come and go. The Great Dragon leaned his head down and touched me. My wounds healed instantly as did everyone else's. *I'm looking forward to seeing you again, Connie Helen Whitsburg. Your life isn't going to be easy though.*

"Chances will be opened to you and your friends," explained the Protector.

"Risks will be taken," added the Helper.

But when the time comes, whenever you or any of your friends are in dire need, we'll be there to help you. The Great Dragon stretched out his neck and

369

looked up to the sky. *"All of you are blessed with loved ones. To change a world takes many people. Luckily you will meet them as the years pass."*

"As we take our leave, I bestow sleep on you, Connie Helen Whitsburg. Sleep well, and when you awake a brighter new day will appear before you to live in." The Protector touched my head and I slowly lied back down and slept.

CHAPTER 35

As Time Passes

I awoke in Sam's arms. I smiled at his human face as he looked down at me. He was carrying me through the ravine. The water was gone; everything looked beautiful. The Watcher, Protector and Helper did as they had promised. In the distance I could see Small Valley. It was revived; standing; there appeared to be no damage at all. It was the same as I left it. The one thing I was really happy about was that the bullet shot in my shoulder was gone.

"Shouldn't I be dead right now?" I joked, leaning my head on Sam's chest.

"No, you should be alive like the rest of us," he said.

I smiled. "Where is everybody?"

"Those who have remained as your Guardians are escorting the townspeople back into the ravine. Judy's with them, she wanted to see how her family was doing and your dragon is watching us as we speak from above."

"So, Pearl and Baboline are really gone?" That part I wished was a dream.

Sam said, "Baboline was old and worn. Her last request in life was to find the dragon she once abandoned. Now she has, thanks to you."

I sighed in relief. "Anything else I should know?"

"Yes. You should know that the three most powerful beings known to the Mystic Realm, allowed Jacqueline and Edgar to live and escape."

"Why would they do that?"

"They said that in the future, we would find out. Each of us has a role to play so let them live theirs so lessons can be learned."

"Can't argue with that," I said, outlining Sam's mage mark with my finger. "We'll just have to wait and find out for ourselves as time passes."

"Connie, you are truly wise," he said kissing my forehead.

"You know, I am all healed. I can walk on my own."

"I know, but for once I want to carry your weight instead of you carrying mine. I also wanted to give you this," Sam pulled out the light gem from his pants pocket and handed it to me. "This is your dad's right?"

I nodded as I took the gem out of his hand.

"Look, Connie. It seems I'll be handing you over to your family."

We were still quit a distance from Small Valley, but I saw them. My mom, my dad and even Kyle was awake, standing and moving on his own. I looked up to where I thought heaven would be and mouthed 'thank you'.

"Connie," Dad said, relieved, running up to us. He took me out of Sam's arms and into his own. He hugged me. His eyes were closed; he was trying to stop the tears from falling down his face.

"I'm fine, Dad," I said. "I have something for you, though. Let me down." Dad placed me on my feet. I held out the light gem and placed it into his hands. "This belongs to you."

Dad opened his eyes, astonished with what was in my hands. "You . . . you retrieved this?"

I nodded.

"What is it?" asked Kyle looking over my shoulder.

"My father's dragon's spirit," Dad took a good look around. Seeing no one in sight, Dad raised his hand high and threw the gem down on the ground. It shattered and the white light dragon was released. She looked down at my dad and hummed. "Angela, you're free. Go join your partner up beyond our world and rest peacefully."

She hummed again and then vanished.

"Wasn't Angela the name of your mother?" asked Mom.

"Yeah, but after she died, my father had a hell of a time taking care of me. He wanted help. He couldn't look at another woman the same way he saw my mom. The way he filled the void was by becoming a dragon's whisperer and gave his dragon took the name of my mother."

Dad messed up my hair and smiled at me. "I was raised by a dragon and a human. When I saw them die, I felt all alone. I didn't want to become a dragon's whisperer because of what I might put my family through. I didn't want them to be a dragon's whisperer either but that was your choice, not mine."

"Dad, I have a question." He removed his hand off my head. "How long did you know?"

Dad and Mom looked at each other and smiled. "Ever since you entered high school, your mom kept updating me on your behavior and soon enough I put the puzzle together. Devonburg's death, followed by my daughter running off to other places unknown and then having dreams controlled by mages, all the signs of being a dragon's whisperer."

"That was you! You were there the night I stood up to them," I realized.

"You had to do it on your own. It's easy to tell when a mage and human meet. The human will talk out loud when a mage invades there dream."

"Whoa, hold it right there," yelled Kyle. "What's this talk about dragons, mages and what was that white thing?"

Dad shook his head in disappointment. "You still haven't figured it out?"

Sam leaned over to my ear. "Maybe this would be a good time to call your dragon."

"I agree." *You heard him, Nightly. Get yourself down here.*

I'm already on it.

I saw him circle around in the sky. He dove down, but glided over us for before landing beside me. He stretched out his long black neck and lowered it down to my height.

"D . . . d . . . d . . . d . . . dragon?" Kyle stuttered.

I burst into laughter. Kyle's face went white as a ghost and then fell over. Soon everyone was laughing including Nightly.

Small Valley lives, my family and friends live and we're all together again. What was not to be happy about? Now as time passes it will be much easier to live my life.

* * *

Morning arrived and my alarm clock went off. I didn't want to get up. I was already comfortable and I didn't want to move. However, that noise was getting on my nerves. I stuck my hand out and felt around for the clock. I found it but it wouldn't turn off. I tried slamming my fists on it but that didn't do anything. Finally I pocked my head out from under my covers and turned it off with both of my hands.

"Stupid annoying thing," I commented as I stood up and stretched.

I walked across my bedroom towards the mirror and looked at my new long flowing hair. It had been two years since I became Nightly's whisperer. Today was my graduation and my last day in Small Valley. My plan for the day was simple. First I would go to graduation, second, I would finish up packing and the third and final thing I would do was say my goodbyes and leave the ravine with Sam, Judy and Nightly.

I pulled my hair back up into a pony tail and put on my everyday clothes then pulled my grad gown over top of it.

Hearing my little sister laugh in the kitchen reminded me of breakfast. Off I walked into the kitchen to find my two year old baby sister in her high chair and our mom cooking up breakfast.

"Good morning, Mom, Adri," I said sitting down.

"Connie," Adri yelled, flinging her arms up in the air.

"How are you this morning Adri?" I asked.

She smiled and gave me two thumbs up.

"Cute," Mom said, placing a plate of bacon and eggs in front of me. "Good morning, Connie." She gave me kiss on the head and then started to clean Adri's messy face.

"Hey, Mom, do you know if Kyle's going to be able to make to my graduation?"

"Yes, he will. Your dad left early this morning to go and pick him and Kristen up.

Oh yeah, Kyle got the courage to ask Kristen to marry him. To my amazement she said yes. Now they're each other's betrothed. I had to deal with Kristen a lot when I was younger I wonder what Adri will think of her as she grows. So far Adri likes her but I can't say the same thing for Kristen. After all, every time Kristen is here Adri clings to her like a monkey and she hates it. It at least makes me happy.

"You look beautiful today, Connie," Mom commented as she sat down across from me. "Adri is excited to see you walk across the stage today"

"Thanks, Adri." I patted her small little head which was as big as my hand.

Her full name was Adrianne Grace Whitsburg. She didn't have the same eyes as Kyle and me. Instead she took after Mom and had her pale blue eyes which were always open wide, excited to see new things in every new day that comes and goes. Her blond hair just covered her head and she wore a bright yellow dress.

I ate my food and ran out the door taking the keys to the repaired orange Chevy. It took us year to find a garage that would fix the vehicle up for a cheap price and so far it had been running well, and with Kyle living in another city the car's all mine.

"Bye, Mom, I'll see you after the ceremony. Bye, Adri," I called out.

"Bye, Connie," Mom said holding Adri in her arm's as she saw me off.

"Bye-bye," Adri giggled, waving her hand at me.

I started the car up and drove off to Judy's house. After I pulled up I didn't even have to honk. She came running out of that front door in her grad gown the very second I pulled up.

She opened the door and hopped into the back quickly. "GO! GO!" she said, in a panicked voice.

I drove off instantly before Judy's family came out of the house.

"Do I want to know?" I asked her.

Judy sighed in relief. "My mom refused to let me go until you arrived. My two step brother kept trying to hide whoopee cushions in my bag and my step sister wouldn't stop messing with my hair and clothes." She leaned back and sighed again. "I'll tell you, being the oldest out of a family of four makes the adults think that they're never going to see you again."

"I know what you mean. When Kyle was graduating my mom did the same thing. He almost had to drag her across the stage just to get his diploma. She didn't want her first born child to leave."

"It's not just that. We're also leaving tonight, so they're being more up tight than usual."

"Yeah, Nightly's really excited."

"How is the dragon anyways? He lives up in that secret area all the time, alone now. Doesn't he get lonely?"

"No, he likes the chance to hunt and I always visit him every night. After all, I can sleep over there now. I'm glad Malcolm and Teddy fixed the house before leaving. It makes it easier on me. I'm surprised Nightly hasn't burnt it down though."

"You and me both," Judy said.

I pulled up to Sam's house and honked the horn a couple of times. He came out, in his grad gown and he had a huge smile on his face.

For the past two years Sam's been living on his own. I don't know how he did it but he got emancipated, now he's legal to live on his own without parents or guardians. What bothered me was why he didn't move out of that house. Bad memories remained in that place for him and me.

Sam stuck a 'SOLD' sticker on the 'FOR SALE' sign in his front lawn. I sighed in relief. That house freaked me out.

"Morning," Sam said, as he entered the vehicle.

"Morning," I said, giving him a kiss. "I see you finally sold that house."

"Yeah, last night a family of eight bought it. I tried my best to fix it up for them but there is only so much a man can do."

"But you're not a man, you're a mage," Judy pointed out. There was an awkward silence. "So . . . Sam, are you ready for tonight?" Judy asked changing the subject.

"As long as the dragon is," he answered.

"He's ready," I assured him. "He's been waiting for this day for over a year."

"Can't blame him," said Judy, "after all, when we're out of here he won't have to hide as much."

I nodded and drove off to the school. We went straight to the auditorium and sat on one side of the room while the adults took their seats on the other side. As the room settled down Mrs. Blue went up on stage, stood up at the podium and began to give a speech.

During her speech Judy, Sam and I decided to give each other 'end of high school gifts'. We thought that since no one really cared for the speeches they wouldn't mind if we exchanged gifts at this point.

I went first and gave Judy a dragon shaped silver bracelet and to Sam I gave him a silver watch with Roman Numerals as numbers. Engraved on the back was his full name and a little message on the back. 'Samson Drake Slayer, I love you just the way you are'. I strapped it on his wrist and gave him a smile. He gave me a kiss.

Judy went next. She gave me a new pair of glasses. They were black with a silver dragon on the sides. Then she gave Sam a new earring. It was a black cross with one diamond in the center.

Sam went and he gave Judy a silver cross necklace. It was strung around a beautiful black thick ribbon and shimmered in the light.

Sam told me to close my eyes. As I did he strapped something around my neck. When I opened them I saw the locket he gave me for my fifteenth birthday hanging around my neck.

After our battle the locket was badly damaged. Sam asked for it back so he could try and fix it and he did.

It was a bit different from before. The heart was fixed but it had a dragon curled around it like a guard protecting treasure. It reminded me of my lamp Nightly broke. A dragon was curled around the locket, his eyes were open and if need be, it would come to life and protect me. When I opened the locket I found a new picture in it. It was a picture of my Guardians, Judy, Sam, my family and me when Adri was first born. We stood at the top of the ravine. We were proud, happy and grateful to be together.

By the time we were done exchanging gifts the principle was up at the podium and started to call out names of the graduating students.

All the students lined up in alphabetical order and one by one they went onto the stage and received their diploma. I didn't pay attention to the names he was calling out unless it were the names of people I knew well.

"Judith Bachor."

Judy is girl I can always rely with secrets when it comes to the Mystic Realm or the Human World. Whenever Martin Miles got close to finding Nightly or pressured me to tell him what was really going on she would step in and be the road block on his discovery path.

"Britney Shine."

Britney always hung around Martin Miles, even after he graduated. He uses her. Britney tries to get close to me, act as my friend so I can confide in her. Truth be told, she wasn't as good as Martin. For the most part, I had nothing to worry about. There were also plenty of opportunities for us to get rid of Miles but Britney would always get in the way and defend him. I don't know what she sees in him, but I don't like it.

"Samson Slayer."

Sam's been my boyfriend ever since we got rid of Kamal. He's always protected me, my family and Nightly for better and for worse. Even if he's a mage we weren't afraid of him. He wanted to help us and he loved us like we were family. That's why we accept him and love him.

"Connie Whitsburg."

As for me, I hadn't done much over the past two years. I kept Nightly hidden and my mind opened to any new chance I got. Never would I resist a calling, especially after what the Watcher, Protector and Helper said.

After all our names were called, all the graduated students gathered together and threw our grad hats up in the air celebrating our finishing of high school.

When the ceremony was finished most of the students left for the after party. As for Sam, Judy and me, we met up with my family and drove back to my house. The three of us still had to prepare ourselves for tonight. When we arrived at my house I saw Nightly, in my front yard, visible. There was something in his mouth; my grad cap from the ceremony.

"Nightly," I ran out of the car and up to him.

"I told you I would be there," he hummed.

"Turn back invisible, dummy. No one's supposed to see you," I said.

"Hi, Nightly," Judy said, coming out of the car.

"You don't have to worry. It's summer, and if people aren't at the graduation party they're already on holidays," he said.

"He's right you know," Sam said, "it's not a big deal."

Mom had just pulled into the driveway. She got out and unstrapped Adri from her car seat. "Connie," Adri called out, as she waddled over to me.

"Hi, Adri," I said picking her up, "did you like the ceremony?'

Adri shook her head.

"What was wrong with it?" I asked.

Adri open and closed her hand, "talking."

We laughed, agreeing with her.

"Hey, one of my little sisters has finally graduated," Kyle announced, stepping out of dad's car along with Kristen.

I was upset with Kyle. He told Kristen about Nightly right after I told him that he couldn't tell anyone. I should have made him take the dragon oath. Kyle claims that secrets kept hidden from a loved one cause's pain and suffering. I kind of had to agree with him on that but I would still prefer if Kristen didn't know. Nightly's scared of her. She tries to dress him up like a human. Whenever she comes around he hides. The only thing that we can still do to her is disappear and scare her.

"Well, the little dragon girl is all grown up with a diploma," Kristen commented holding onto Kyle's arm. "You look so cute."

Nightly and I both rolled our eyes.

"I'm sorry we arrived late," said Kyle, "but we did get to see you toss your hats up in the air."

"Kyle, mean," Adri hugged me, "Connie, better."

I smiled and patted her on the head.

"You told her to say that," Kyle said, pointing at Adri.

"It's not my fault if Adri knows the truth. I'm just an honest and kind older sister," I said.

"You two will never change," Kyle shook his head.

"That's a sister's bond for you," said Judy.

"Dragon," Adri said reaching out to Nightly.

Nightly lowered his head allowing Adri to touch him. He hummed, she giggled and the rest of us smiled. He placed my grad cap on my head and straightened up. Adri grabbed my grad cap and placed it on her own head.

"I have to go," he said. *"Nicole, Malcolm and Teddy are waiting for me. I just came to say hi."*

"They're already back?" I asked, straightening out my cap.

"Yeah, they found a home for three eggs. Soon three new dragons and whisperers will be born."

"Does that mean Nicole, Malcolm and Teddy are going to see us off tonight as well?" I asked, excited.

He nodded.

I spun in glee. That was some of the best news I had heard all day. "That's great, but you should get going. You never know if there is a weasel lurking around like Martin Miles."

"*Ha,*" Nightly scoffed, "*I eat animals like him for breakfast, lunch and dessert. Dinner is what I save the bigger animals for.*"

"I love you," I replied hugging his head, "be careful."

"*Hey, it's my job to worry about you, not the other way around. See ya.*"

My dragon slipped out of my arms and disappeared into his surroundings. A huge smile appeared on my face as I used my senses to follow Nightly before he had the chance to take off. Our bond had grown extraordinary through the past two years. There wasn't a second that I didn't know where Nightly was. Other than that, there wasn't really anything different about us either than Nightly growing to be fifteen feet tall.

Once I placed Adri back down on the ground Kyle attacked me, putting me in a headlock and started to give me a noogie.

"Hey, let go," I complained.

Kyle let go and patted me on the back. "Come on, it's something we'll always do. It's a sibling thing."

I smiled at him before elbowing him in the stomach. "Yeah, it's a sibling thing."

"If you two are done," interrupted Dad, "I think we need to get the three graduates packed before they leave tonight."

"Where are the three graduates going again?" asked Kristen.

"We're all going to Chicago," answered Judy.

"Any idea what you three want to major in?" asked Mom picking Adri back up.

"Well, I know I want to major in the medical department of things, and I know Connie wants to become a history teacher, but Sam's having a hard time finding a major," Judy explained, pointing back at Sam.

"Actually, I think I found something. I want to major in crime investigating."

"Really," I said, "what made you decide to major in that?"

"It's actually been on my mind for a while now. I was just wondering how I could help both societies with my powers. The first thing that came in mind was law enforcement. So that's what I want my future career to be, I hope."

I kissed him. "You will achieve your goal."

"Lucky," Kyle whined, "Kristen only let me major in sales and business."

"It was a mutual decision," Kristen stated.

"No it wasn't," Kyle argued.

"Adri, be singer," she said pretending to sing into an imaginary mike.

"Cute," Mom said.

"Connie, I have to go and meet up with my family but I'll meet you back here at six tonight." Judy watched her mom pull up and honk the horn, "see you later."

"I'm going to catch a ride with her," Sam gave me a kiss. "I'll see you tonight."

I watched my best friend and my boyfriend leave. I turned around and faced my family and followed them inside. Kyle and Kristen brought in their luggage and started to set up in the living room. Mom and Adri went into the kitchen and Dad followed me into my room.

I took off my grad gown and hung it up in my closet.

"I can't believe you're all grown up." Dad sat down on my bed. "It seems like it was only yesterday I was teaching you how to walk without Kyle pushing you down."

I pulled out a suitcase from my closet and set it beside my dad. "Now I'm eighteen and I've grown to be a strong, courageous young woman thanks to you."

"You can ride a bike, walk, talk, drive a car and take care of a dragon all on your own."

I stopped packing and looked up at my dad. "Hey, Dad, can I ask you something? Why did Devonburg give me the dragon egg instead of Kyle or after a few years, Adri?"

Dad was silent. He rubbed his head and looked at me. "Well," Dad lifted his sleeve and looked at his tattoo. "Your great-grandfather wanted everyone who was a part of the Whitsburg bloodline to be a dragon's whisperer. When I got this writing tattooed onto my arm my grandfather thought it was a joke. He gave me a dragon egg anyways. I carried a grudge with me. I kept thinking about the past and never moved into the future. I gave the dragon egg to a complete stranger. A stranger who grew fond of the Mystic Realm and became my best friend because of it. The thing about being a dragon's whisperer, you have to be willing to sacrifice to gain. Even though any human can become a dragon whisperer, doesn't mean they're fit for the role.

I've noticed that Devonburg only picked dragon whisperers that were self-confident and carried something that I couldn't see until you showed your mom and me your own dragon." There was a pause. "You carried acceptance with you. You didn't care who it was you were protecting or what they were you just accepted them. At first it would seem you were over protective but when you started to rely on others and not just yourself and trust them . . . well, let's just say it was something I could never do as a kid. I always pushed it away and ignored it. Maybe one day Adri will become a whisperer and she'll learn acceptance from you but as for Kyle . . . for him he's already past the point of no return."

I laughed and Dad hugged me.

"Kyle had a good life. He didn't need to gain anything from the Mystic Realm. As for you, all you wanted was to get out of here and you were willing to sacrifice your normal life because of it."

I pulled away from the hug. "What's so important about this ravine anyways? You're the only one how has left it and on the rare occasion Mom would leave too."

Dad sighed. "This ravine . . . this town . . . the mystery you had always been trying to unlock. For as long as the Whitsburg's have become whisperers we have guarded the nest from those who would destroy it. Devonburg helped. When I was gone on my business trips he would watch over my family as well as the nest.

To accept different things in our life is a big challenge for people of all ages. If you can accept something like dragon in your life then you are a risk taker but at least you move forward to a better future."

"That's what great-grandfather said in his letter."

"Ah, so you did read it. Your great-grandfather died on the day you were born. He gave me that letter a few hours before you arrived into the world. I didn't want you to become a whisperer but look at you. I could never have kept you from your fate."

I stood up and began to pack some of my belongings, but stopped. "Dad, did Kamal really kill great-grandfather?"

"That I do not know. Your great-grandfather had a heart condition and he was old. It could have been Kamal or it could be his age that took his life. What I do know is that Kamal was a fifteen hundred year old mage that refused to move forward. Instead, he stayed where he was, hoping that with his new power he could return life to what it used to be." Dad stood and helped me put clothes into the suitcase. "Ever since you defeated Kamal no one's going to have to worry anymore."

"I'm not sure about that. After all, what fun is living life if there aren't a few challenges in the way? I didn't defeat Kamal, not alone at least." I zipped up the case and looked at my aging Dad. "Thanks for believing in me."

Adri waddled into my room and looked at the two of us. "Time to go."

Dad smiled, he got up and snatched up his youngest child. "Come, Connie, it's time for you to leave your own nest."

Time passed quickly and there wasn't enough time to say goodbye to everyone. I hate short goodbyes, but when Judy and Sam arrived I knew it was time to leave. Before we left the house I looked at my friends. Sam and Judy, both out of there grad gowns and were ready; they were ready to grow up and leave. I wasn't going alone on my journey through life. Sam, Judy and Nightly all supported me and my family believed in me. That's all needed to help me move forward.

My family, my friends and I all took a long walk to the hidden passageway and led them into the secret area. I led everyone to the area where Nicole, Malcolm, Teddy and Nightly were waiting.

"Nice of you to join us," Nightly said.

"It was hard saying goodbye," I replied.

"Or just had trouble packing," Sam added dragging his suitcase and sheathed sword with him.

"Uh, Kyle, come help me load this luggage onto Nightly," Dad called, taking Judy's, Sam's and my luggage.

"Alright," he said in a drowsy voice.

Adri followed them attempting to be a big girl and help out her dad and older brother.

"Congrats on graduating," said Malcolm. "It's nice to see that you can take care of a dragon and get by school too, impressive. The ceremony could have been shorter though."

"We managed to pass the time," said Judy, touching her cross necklace.

"In more ways than one," said Sam, tightening the watch on his wrist.

"I'll sure miss you kid," Teddy said, pretending to give me a little punch on the chin.

"Don't worry about the nest, we'll take care of it or at least Malcolm and I will," said Nicole.

"Hey," yelled Teddy.

The three of us laughed.

I gave my remaining Guardians the coordinates to the nest. Ever since we defeated Kamal and his mage followers there was no need for them to stay in Small Valley. For the past two years they had been traveling the world, handing out dragon eggs to worthy people who holds the abilities to become a dragon's whisperer. They've also been looking for Jacqueline and Edgar. Those two knew what had exactly happened. They were given a chance to change. I hope they did. Heaven help us if they didn't.

"You guys are constantly are on the move. I'll bet you we'll run into each other soon," I said.

Judy straightened out her new purple dress and let her bracelet shine in the setting sun light. "I'm glad you guys came to see us off."

"Yeah, it has to be a short goodbye though. We have to go check on some of our new whisperers. We've already spent a lot of time just attending your graduation ceremony," said Malcolm. "I'm sorry we couldn't stay longer."

Teddy walked up to Sam, holding out his hand. "You did well, mage. Thanks to you I have a whole new perspective on mages now. Not all of them are bad, they can still change all they need is good friends."

Sam shook his hand grateful. He had no reason to fear my Guardians or hide who he really is anymore. I watched as a smile made its way across Sam's face. Malcolm patted him on the back and Nicole just smiled. Mom, Kristen, Judy and I all thought that it was magical.

I went up to Sam and linked my arm around his, joining the happy party.

Dad and Kyle came back carrying Adri, while looking over at us, the happy graduates.

"Everything's ready to go," said Dad.

"Nightly's excited, but he almost stepped on Adri," said Kyle.

"Hey, I said I was sorry! Besides it was her fault for tickling me," Nightly pouted.

"Poor Adri," Kristen said in a sad voice, but refused to go near her.

The three of us gave everyone one last hug then strapped ourselves onto a wider saddle courtesy of the Guardians. Nightly was happy when we all got onto the saddle. He hummed, delighted. All of us were together and we weren't going to let anything separate us.

"Call us if you ever need anything," said Mom.

"Use your mark to signal us," said Malcolm.

"Feel free to drop by our place anytime," said Kyle, wrapping his arm around Kristen.

"Thanks," all three of us said. We were so happy to be together.

"Bye-bye," waved Adri.

Let's go Nightly.

Tell your friends to hold on tight because I'm going to have the time of my life as we fly.

Nightly flew up out of the ravine and towards the sun set. I took one glance back at my family as the wind blew through my hair. I smiled at them one last time. As we left I looked over at Judy. She looked terrified to be up so high, but I could tell she was having the time of her life. Nightly remained excited, for the first time in both of our lives we were going to leave the ravine and not have to return for once. I felt like, for the first time, I could stretch my wings without being trapped. Then there was Sam, who was the happiest out of all of us. He was free from the Lead Mage and free to live his life the way he wanted to.

My name is Connie Helen Whitsburg and I am a dragon's whisperer.

CPSIA information can be obtained at www.ICGtesting.com
Printed in the USA
LVOW041328081212

310641LV00001B/15/P